THE BOTTOM OF AUGUST LAKE

Chris Kassel

Paperback Edition

First Printing: August, 2019

Copyright © 2019 by Christian Kassel

Published by Black Tongue Press

To Ekaterina Divina

ISBN-13: 978-1727590265

ISBN-10: 1727590260

THE BOTTOM OF AUGUST LAKE

In eastern Michigan, in Fuller County, less than fifteen minutes from the interstate, twenty square miles of hill-strewn, state-owned wilderness surround a shallow lake that formed in 1837 when Indian Creek was dammed.

Today, collectively and somewhat optimistically, that rugged spread of swamp and forest is called August Lake State Park.

For budgetary reasons, camping is prohibited there and overnight stays are limited to a single rustic cabin in the area's North Unit. Even so, the miles of rugged trails, trout streams, wild game and thirteen thousand acres of non-developed land should have made it a natural draw for the hundred thousand winter-water-wonderland zealots who lived up and down the nearby interstate corridor.

Yet, August Lake is one of the most rarely visited recreation areas in the system.

And since the Department of Natural Resources is set up so that funding is allocated to these areas proportionately, with the most popular parks receiving the lion's share of the money, August Lake is so poorly funded that the entire thirteen thousand acres is maintained by three rangers, a handful of seasonal, minimum wage flunkies and such volunteers as can be attracted through local fraternal organizations and court-ordered community service mandates.

In the face of a stagnant economy, August Lake is the last stop in DNR careers, and for residents of Fuller County, it is the cold hole at the end of the road.

Part One: *Never and Forever*

1.

I've always been vaguely and persistently spooked by birds, especially when they fly overhead. Maybe 'annoyed' is a better word, because I'm not necessarily petrified of them like people were in that freaky Hitchcock flick, but birds in flight do bother me because they always seem so confident, so determined, so filled with a sense of direction and purpose. They're always heading somewhere, always quickly, and they never seem to have the slightest doubt as to where they're going.

In all honesty, bird paranoia ranks low on my list of peeves, but even so—*what's going on in those little bird brains that makes them so fucking self-assured?* I mean, it's sort of awesome; I get that. I'd love to feel that way. In fact, I wish I was as confident about anything as birds are about everything.

Blow can do that for you, but only up to a point, and that point lasts about twenty minutes. My brief if significant dabbling in cocaine made me feel like a new woman, but unfortunately, the first thing this new woman wanted was more cocaine. Blow is confidence without identity: You like the new you, but you have no idea who she is or where to find her after she's disappeared.

Corky—the man-boy with whom I simultaneously shared and wasted four years of my life—preferred members of Clan Opiate, especially the supremely dangerous synthesized one he called Grey Ice. Heroin was never my poison: Grey scares the shit out of me and I never saw value in abusing substances that scare you shitless. It was dodging fear that impelled me, not embracing it.

In the end, I abandoned coke and went with alcohol. I built up the requisite understanding with booze and settled in with it; it let me forget about my ragged search for confidence and pull the quilt up around my ears.

I started career drinking fairly young. When I was fourteen, in fact. That was in Cadence, a stark, sun-bleached, dissonant town like every other stark, dissonant town in central Ohio. Maybe Cadence had once sported a storybook, Norman

Rockwell prettiness, perhaps as an archetypal turn-of-the-century oasis with porticos and parades. The Cadence Library features occasional monochrome exhibits with old photos from various attics and steamer trunks. But by the time I came along, it had disintegrated into Dollar Stores and CVS corners, where an imploded manufacturing base stripped away the final vestige of Main Street charm. When I was born, the only cohesive glue remaining was the Purina factory that made the entire south part of town from Franklin Street to Pickaway smell like kibbles, although it employed most of the fathers in my nondescript, middle-class neighborhood, including my own.

I lost my virginity at fourteen too, although that landmark occasion was only tangentially related to the drinking. That was the same year that, in the ultimate love-betrayal, my beautiful Daddy died, forcing me (as I saw it) to grow up instantly and prematurely, like a baby born at 36 weeks. For the most part, from my rudimentary teenage perspective, drinking liquor and fucking people were the high floodmarks of adulthood, so after Daddy's death, those were the pinnacles I sought to reach as soon as my private world had re-aligned itself into some semblance of sanity.

I was angry then, and as a matter of fact—since my Daddy and I had an implied covenant stating that neither one of us would do something as unaccountable as die—I still am.

Let me state here for the record that I despise it when grown women call their fathers 'Daddy'. The creep factor is in overdrive. But I request a pass in relating this because my Daddy died when I was young enough to have still been calling him Daddy, so I've never really thought of him in any other way—certainly not as Byron Mason Pickett, which is what it says on his headstone.

At the time of his death I had begun to identify heavily with classical poetry and read it rather compulsively, but when I tried to write credible poetry myself, all I could string together was saccharine, adolescent doggerel. It was only later that I discovered that my greater talent lay in painting, but at fourteen, pre-Daddy death, my escape from stark-town drudgery was into the fantasyscapes of Gwendolyn Bennett and Walter de la Mare and a few other dreamers whose anthologies and collections I found at the Cadence Public Library.

Don't get me wrong—it's not like my childhood was all emotional blight. I'm filled with memories of King's Island, Skyline chili, summers on Lake Erie—our ocean— and trips to Hills Department Store where the cashews roasting in honey always smelled savagely yummy. I remember picking happily through the huge pile of gravel on Hall Road, aged eight, convinced that if I stuck to it and was diligent, sooner or later I'd find a diamond. Those magical images pile up in my mind like gentle drifts against a snow fence. I remember Friday nights, when my occasionally distant mom would retire early for some 'me time' and Daddy took over the dinner duties. Since he only knew one recipe, it was always the same thing: Pancakes he made by putting all the ingredients in a quart Mason jar and shaking it. Those pristine instants hover nearby always and cradle me still.

But then my Daddy died, and my memory bank bisects into what came before and what came after; a fault line that remains keen and desperate to this day.

To me, Daddy exists on a purity plateau that doesn't really exist. I know that, obviously. Far from being perfect, he was overly religious and sweetly, if unrelentingly naïve. He never read novels or plays, and certainly not classical poetry, but likewise, he never smoked or gambled. He never swore or lost his temper and he never drank more than a bottle of Stroh's beer on a Sunday afternoon. His foundational attitude was one of control and patience; he spoke in measured phrases and carried himself as the town's most elegant and handsome Purina dog food salesman. He always dressed with an impeccable sense of purpose and direction, and it was only much, much later that I noticed that there was also something impeccably tragic behind his eyes, at least in the photographs of him that I most cherish. He was fifty when I was born and sixty-four when heart disease took him out, years before I noticed the melancholy in the pictures and years too late to ask him what it was.

For a long time after he died, I tried to find things about myself that were impeccable too; some genetic claim on impeccability, but nothing quite measured up. Everything I did seemed to have overtones of the peccable. Thinking back, I suppose I learned to drink with certain impeccability, but I'm pretty sure that doesn't count.

Daddy died in January, and the first time I got drunk was in the autumn that followed, when Mom took me to the Durhamville Oktoberfest along with Toby Murphy, a big, soft-spoken foreman at the Purina factory. It was not a date, Mom promised, because what still-grieving widow would go on a date, let alone take along her teenage daughter? It was, she maintained (protesting too much, methought) nothing more than a chance to get us out of the house for an afternoon.

At the festival, amid smells of tent plastic and musky cigar smoke, the non-dating couple allowed me a single sip of beer, and the face I made amused them to no end. I insisted that the beer made me need to pee immediately and Mom and Toby thought that was even funnier than my scrunchy-faced revulsion over the taste. They didn't laugh when, on the way to the Porto-John, beneath the pounding thuds of the stupid oompah band, I snatched remnants of other beers that people had left at picnic tables so that by the time I got back to the platonic posers, I was blotto.

Two months later I relinquished my maidenhead, checking off the second item on my short, indignant bucket list. There was a geeky clerk at Cadence Video who'd turned me on to films like *Gummo* and *Cat Soup*, which we'd watch at his smelly, moldy bungalow on Dunkle because I could never watch those sorts of videos at home. His name was Kyle Andrus; he was twenty and had a shithole rental house on the low end of town which he filled with saltwater aquariums so that it always stank like a fish market. He was tall, but not in a good way, and insanely devoid of ambition. Physically, I wasn't the least bit attracted to him. Then again, I don't care for beer either, but like the leftover Oktoberfest lagers, he was the available outlet, and as my Daddy used to say, *'We make do with the tools God gives us for the job.'*

In early December I went over to Kyle's fish house to watch *Nekromantik*, and midway through, I attempted to initiate sexual intercourse as blowback punishment for Daddy's abandonment and as a sort of reward for Kyle for having taken me under his aesthetic wing. Turned out that he wasn't particularly interested in me like that, and who could blame him? At fourteen, I was knob-kneed and flat chested, and that night I was hyperkinetically aggressive. My agenda overrode anything resembling romance and it must have showed. I think it turned him off, but we drank our jug of Gallo anyway and watched the rest of film in awkward silence, and when it ended, he went to bed alone. I still had two hours to kill since

I was supposed to be babysitting, and fifteen minutes later, I crawled in after him, more from exhaustion than arousal, and promptly nodded out. Sometime later he woke up and decided he was now willing to fuck me, no doubt while pretending I was someone else, so I reached my symbolic milestone through a fog of Hearty Burgundy, algae smell and my partner's thrusting, slobbering indifference.

And—just as I discovered that I really liked to drink—I sort of discovered the opposite about sexual intimacy: I could take it or leave it.

Still, I missed my next two periods and blew up into the sort of panic that can only steamroll teenagers when they realize they have screwed the pooch—no pun—beyond all recognition. It got so bad so that Ms. Magdy, my school therapist, noticed. She was a wonderful, understanding woman who had been counseling me regularly since my Daddy died, and she first won my confidence, then helped me through a pregnancy test (negative), followed by a clandestine visit to her gynecologist who prodded me and speculumed me, checked me for STDs and gave me a blood test, and in the summation announced that I had an endocrine disorder called PCOS that might account for both my low weight, my breastlessness, and especially, my non-pregnancy, since PCOS compromises ovulation. The doctor prescribed birth control pills, whose side effect was to regulate my periods and she suggested that when the time came that I actually wanted to be pregnant, science may have made the condition treatable.

I never even picked up the prescription—the chance of birth control pills being discovered by my mother was somewhere between pre-ordained and inevitable, and anyway, by then I had developed a little PTSD to go along with my PCOS. I had no more interest in sex, at least not in the immediate future, and the idea of having children did not appeal to me even in the distant future. In all, the diagnosis was pretty much a godsend.

So back to Toby Murphy, my mother's non-suitor, who continued to infiltrate my life. Toby was bigger than my Daddy, bald and bland with giant arms like Smithfield hams. He was not fastidious and not the least bit impeccable and there was something boorish about him I just couldn't warm up to. In the long run, I didn't care, because by then I had a secret life: I was using babysitting money to buy Southern Comfort from Mark Haddad, whose parents owned Bottle & Basket on

Township Road 180. I hid it in a defunct Caloric barbecue grill in the alley behind our neighbor's house, so that if my stash was tripped over by anyone, it would have been unlinkable to me. It never was. In those days, a fifth would last me a month as opposed to a single Netflix marathon; I mixed it with orange juice and it bolstered my fragility like a frame around a thin sheet of glass.

By the following June, Mr. Not-a-Date had become my genuine stepfather. I went along with the charade and even scattered petals at the wedding as the non-sober and hymen-free flower girl, but when I saw them at the altar I came to the disconcerting conclusion that the burly plough horse with field hands might have been much more Mom's speed than the formal, graceful, picturesque Southern gentleman who had been my father. Even worse, I realized that having a husband who was not only on her limited intellectual plateau but was her own age (Daddy had been twenty years her senior) probably fulfilled Mom's fondest adulthood fantasy. And worst of all, when I heard her warble 'I do' with jittery, white-hot exuberance, it occurred to me that she might have been lusting after Toby from afar even before my Daddy died.

Still, making waves is not my style, so I settled into it as best I could, drinking on the sly, calling Toby Murphy 'Paw-Pop' like he expected and essentially, counting the seconds until I could vamoose.

In the end, for a multitude of reasons, vamoosing took longer than I expected.

In my junior year at Cadence High School I began to seriously date Jason Alton, who was tall in a good way and had ambitions beyond Purina: He wanted to be a commissioned officer in the U.S. Navy. Jason insisted that he loved me, but he never pressured me for sex because we were both members of *True Love Waits*, an abstinence program at whose functional core was the purity pledge we signed, vowing to wait until we were married to have intercourse. At the time it seemed like a feasible goal since we intended to get married as soon as we banked our high school diplomas.

Jason didn't know about me and Kyle Andrus, of course, but apparently, he also didn't know that the Ohio State Naval Reserve Officer Training Program frowned upon married Midshipmen, so we wound up having to postpone nuptials until after college, when he'd be assigned a post, and as a result—at least to him—celibacy began to seem like an open-ended sentence. Throughout his freshman year, I drove my third-hand Plymouth Breeze an hour and a half to visit him on weekends, and during one of these visits we got carried away with our petting regimen and actually wound up doing a sloppy, hurried version of the deed itself, which was no biggie to me since I had signed the purity pledge under false pretenses, but apparently, with all his nascent military commitment to personal integrity, honor and individual responsibility, it was a major biggie to him. And, predictably, he totally blamed me. Over the next few weeks, he pouted and cooled and finally called off our engagement, stating that he couldn't marry a girl who lacked firm resolve. His pet name for me had been 'Bitty Bit' and in retrospect, it was a name so dismissive and diminutive that it should have been a flag the color of a Class IV hemorrhage.

For a while, I was crushed and angry and rejected and snooty, and then I slipped into what I think of now as 'my long quiet'. I took a day job at Family Dollar and a night job at Love's Travel Stop, rented a bland apartment in Breckenridge Square on Township Road 180, and, like Paw-Pop Toby Murphy and his new bitty bit bride, I slid headlong into a nothing life, a pointless life, a life echoing with Cadence's cadence, where dullness is not only a birthright, it's a cause—though unlike Mom and Toby, I was neither content with it nor righteous about it.

I generally drank alone and detached myself from further thoughts about marriage or dates or boys or orgasms, but my body continued to fill out anyway. My breasts may have only topped out at B-cups but as late as they bloomed, they were ripe and early-apple hard, the perfect size for the gym when I managed to juggle jobs and hangovers well enough to work out. I was blonde and late-teen lissome and men regarded me with increasing interest, and if it was pretty much unrequited, I became vain and imperious about my looks, which I reckon curtailed a really comprehensive descent into physically-annihilating alcoholism.

Besides, along the way I had discovered my twin guardian angels: Canvas and color. I'd always had a talent for drawing—far more than for poetry—and I found that I was able to parlay this childish knack into a series of vibrant, adult paintings, and they became a barrier against the weight of resentment that was pressing me into the earth.

As I view it now, from across the great chasm, those years were portentous; water building up against the dam. I presented an apathetic exterior, but within me, storms boiled and twisted and tore. I worked my stultifying jobs in a persistent slog, and on my days off, I put Natalie Merchant on my resale-shop sound system and painted furious landscapes and intensely private portraits. I read many great books over that frame of time, which of itself is a patently isolating habit. I read about the history of art and I absorbed what I thought were key lessons—I read Russian novels and was haughty in my belief that I alone among Cadence's nine thousand residents could pronounce, let alone discuss, Ludmilla Petrusheyvskaya.

Not sure how long I could have gone on like that—never and forever, I suppose. But somewhere along the way, I heard about an art school in Detroit that I believed (at least, according to the online reviews I found) attracted the sort of bohemian, lost, insecure but scrappy and talented individual that I imagined myself to be.

In fact, when I weighed the evidence in the aggregate, I concluded that I was much closer to being a sincere, if troubled Detroit art person than a foundering Cadence Jesus hypocrite.

For those of us in rural central Ohio, the massive, frightening thunderdome called Detroit looms ever overhead, an unfathomable set of dimensions far removed from our lives—a place where the plot is so dense that it defies boredom, because in Detroit—we imagine—survival instinct precludes boredom.

And I *was* bored; as deeply into my tissues as that emotion goes. I was—as I then thought—madly talented and overdue for a dream quest. For sure, I needed some friends. Even *one* friend, boy or girl, it made no difference. Perhaps it was a combination of factors, but in Cadence I didn't seem capable of making enduring friendships, and that should be one of the few advantages of living in a small town, along with the unshakeable feeling of having something solid underfoot. So far, both had eluded me. I saw Detroit as a place with greater imperatives and significant possibilities, far more than I could understand, let alone reach, from a Cadence vantage. I saw Detroit as a place with panoramic potential, and it was only two hours away.

My Daddy had left me a modest college fund, as yet untapped. I was 23 years old when I enrolled in the Detroit Institute for Creative Studies and migrated north one sweltering summer afternoon like a rabid thing with wings.

My name is Dixie Pickett and the story that follows is my life's defining insignia—my consummate and convoluted nightmare, my ultimate fail and fuck-up, and in all its desperate detail, it's the reason why I ended up scraping mud at the bottom of August Lake.

2.

I didn't last long in art school—a year in total—but among the life-changing lessons I picked up during that year is that 'good-bad art' is a thing.

Yes, Norman Rockwell and his impossible small town wet dream was good-bad art, even when it was intended as irony. Dali was a good-bad artist; also Maxfield Parish and Magritte. Even Michelangelo's frescoes, with their hyperbolically 'roided, glued-on-boobs women, were good-bad.

I learned this from my Conceptual Art professor, Jory Malone. Malone was a bedraggled, wet-dog-looking ex-hippie and he presented us with a whole list of good-bad painters, and during one abstract lecture he gleefully and savagely digressed into poets as well. Apparently some of my favorites, including Tennyson and Shelley, are good-bad poets. Keats, he insisted, is 'indubitably preferable'.

Sadly, it turned out that at that point, I wasn't even a good-bad painter. It took me about six months of rubber-necking artwork produced by my classmates to reach that humiliating conclusion, along with a few pointed asides from my instructors. Far from the land of struggling me-types I'd been anticipating, I found that the Institute for Creative Studies was largely populated by aggressive preppy kids from wealthy Detroit suburbs; clean cut, snob-nosed jerk-offs in acid washed jeans and Italian shoes who wore cologne to class and saw me for exactly what I was: An out-of-her-element hayseed who knew she liked art but had no sincere end goal worth pursuing. They were all headed to lucrative careers in automotive and industrial design, a skill at which many of them already excelled.

There were some misfit cliques, to be sure—aimless pockets of young people as insecure as me—but emotionally, most were toast and in far worse shape than I was. These were the suicide-prone kids with life-holes like bottomless pits, and far from finding the enduring friendships I was after, I found myself further alienated on a level so profound that it almost defied belief.

Compounding that, of course, was the nearly universal talent I encountered among them: As shipmates, we couldn't even communicate on that level, since as far as I could tell, they'd all been born with inner visions that were as foreign to me as perfect pitch. There was something innate about the way they translated their world into canvas and concrete and cold-pressed Bienfang paper. I loved color. They *understood* it. I loved portraiture; they imbued character in their caricatures that I could never quite coordinate in mine.

In time, I suppose I could have developed the technical chops to hide most of my creative flaws, which may have been the point of the school accepting me on the strength of a weak portfolio (that and my ability to pay the tuition), but for a number of reasons, mostly related to ego and alcohol, I decided not to pursue it.

I arrived in Detroit on a stupid whim, but even so, on perhaps a stupider whim, I decided to stay.

For the next few years, I eked out a small, personal slice of Cadence nothingness in a crumbling neighborhood on the northeast side of the city, working several shifts a week at a dumpy 24-hour Coney Island restaurant and sharing a pathologically unhealthy relationship with a boy called Corky Geshke.

During my first week in town I'd rented a room from Corky in a small brick house on Robinwood in an area known locally and colloquially as Woltown. It was about two miles from the art school, and I signed the lease because it was in a decaying Polish enclave where a handful of stubborn old ethnic types still hung on, although they were being gradually supplanted by dopers and thugs. Corky's house had previously belonged to his grandmother, now a denizen of nearby Transfiguration Cemetery, and it still had an extensive wooden ramp leading to the front door. To me, at the time, the environment seemed edgy, but safe.

I describe Corky as a 'boy' because he was, in a literal sense, exactly that when I first moved in with him. He still had a haze of whiteheads on his nose and not long after I unpacked my stuff, he invited me to his Senior Homecoming dance. It turned out that he was some kind of math whiz-kid genius who had graduated from Detroit Jesuit High School at sixteen, and two years later, he wanted to make his grand, look-at-me-now reappearance with a twenty-three-year-old date.

He loved epic fantasy novels and major league baseball, and had a prized Louisville Slugger bat signed by every member the 2009 Yankees. He was insanely smart in a fluky, fractal way, and he was also an apotheosis of the entitlement attitude. His parents were in equal measures terrified of him and indulgent to the point of spookiness. They'd ceded him the grandmother's house shortly after she died because he'd threatened to move to New York City otherwise.

His birth name was Emil, but everybody had been calling him Corky since he was a toddler. He looked like a Corky, too—soft, physically pliant, pale as a lily and prone to acne eruptions. He was mentally rigid and utterly self-absorbed, and I slept with him whenever he wanted me to (which wasn't very often) and as a result, I lived rent free and allowed him to tell our crotchety old über-Catholic neighbors that I was his wife.

For a while, this gave me a tingle of stability, and I began sliding down massive a denial funnel that would have been fascinating if it hadn't, in retrospect, been so pathetic. It was almost as sad as the disgust with which Corky's parents regarded me: They were moderately wealthy people trying to do their best by their prick of a son, and he mocked them to their faces, mocked their possessions, mocked their indulgences, mocked their pain and their useless hope that he'd grow up when he wouldn't, and yet, it was me they chose to despise, even though I was totally on their side.

Anyway, I wouldn't have actually married him, but I did agree to be his date for the homecoming dance. That's the night I discovered he had a drug habit; something about which I was still Cadence naïve. On the big night, he got so fucked up on Grey Ice heroin that he zoned out on the couch in his ridiculous tuxedo, as I, in my ridiculous sequin tulle dress, put a quilt over him, got wasted on Southern Comfort and watched HBO alone.

3.

Like there are good-bad artists and good-bad poets, there are good-bad days. I stopped drinking on one of them, four years after I moved in with Corky Geshke. That was a day that blasted me from my doldrums like a squall from Xibalba.

It began, like most of my vapid days, with a single Southern Comfort and orange juice. That was my limit, price-wise, before I switched to two buck well vodka at Wolski's Tavern.

One remarkable phenomenon of chronic alcoholism is that you no longer get hangovers. Instead, you get exhaustion in bottomless doses, water-retention where you used to have cheekbones, cellulite on your thighs and ass and weird pains in unexpected places. But, since you take a drink shortly after you get out of bed, any rebellion from the recovery system is quickly neutralized. You have, apparently, confused your hangover into thinking it should wait until you actually finish drinking. *'Hair of the dog'* becomes a joke once you've morphed into the dog, fleas and mange and everything. This is about the time when the concept of binge drinking loses its relevancy.

Another odd thing about long-haul imbibing is that time passes and you barely notice. Things happen and you barely care. That's probably one of the reasons why Wolski's was a draw to the stagnant neighborhood boozers (that and the two dollar slammers, except for call brands like Southern Comfort, which were three). Most of Wolski's regulars were decades drunker than I was and had been coming to the featureless bar on the corner of Jameson and Six Mile throughout their lives, and in all that time, nothing much about it had changed beyond toilet paper rolls and lightbulbs. There was a velvet painting of John Wayne over the pool table, a menagerie of stuffed deer heads wearing generations of sunglasses: At one time, each disembodied buck had been dispatched by Thaddeus Wolski, the pub's original owner and the man after whom the Woltown district was named. There was still a phone booth at Wolski's Tavern and a cigarette machine with knobs you pulled, and in the corner by the restrooms, a jukebox which hadn't worked since the Nineties and had records in it from the Seventies.

Wolski's Happy Hour began at eight in the morning, when well-worn, middle-aged

Bibi Lisiewicz unlocked the front door. At that point, on an average day, a small knot of cocktail-desperate diehards, including me, tumbled inside. Some had just finished shifts at nearby Detroit Axle, some were about to begin shifts, and for others, drinking at Wolski's *was* their shift. These were my mentors, only on Opposite Day—people I could study perversely and analyze didactically in order to not end up becoming them, although it must have been obvious that I was, by then, already them.

One thing is for sure: We were all soon in our groove. A Pavlov drool began at the sound of the deadbolt and the first whiff of wet beer-carton cardboard and dry rot. Bibi locked the door behind us, and from then on, if you wanted entrance to Wolski's, you had to ring a buzzer like it was some after-hours joint or an exclusive club and Bibi had to approve you on the closed-circuit monitor. The truth was, nobody but regulars ever drank at Wolski's except on Pub Crawl Fridays, when the place was invaded for half an hour by suburban people with a 'local icon' list. Wolski's was known, at least on Pub Crawl Friday, as one of Detroit's oldest dives.

Shortly after arriving one morning in early October, and once the shakes subsided, I entered into a meaningless conversation with a retired lathe operator called John Kowalczyk. I knew he'd buy me a couple rounds if I listened again to his convoluted memories of Sea World, with which he always assumed I had a sort of proprietary fascination because it was in Ohio. The tiny grandchildren who had accompanied him on that trip were now in their twenties and the park had been closed for a decade, and I'd heard the story so many times I could fine-tune any detail he missed. Bibi knew I was milking him for rounds, but she didn't care. John was loaded, she assured me, collecting both social security *and* a pension. Bibi liked me, and why not? I was sort of a sweet drunk, and since I was usually drunk, I was usually sweet.

The highlight of a typical day at Wolski's was when a news anchor called Anna Lerner read the winning Powerball numbers on *Fox 2 Detroit*. The lottery was the only cash outlay anybody at Wolski's sprang for beside drinks. Everybody played and everybody, for some reason, expected to win. The funny thing is, not one of them had the time or the faith to become rich. They were all exactly where they wanted to be and where they needed to be—within their place of sustenance—and at this stage, if any windfall had affected their lifestyle, they'd all have wound up miserable.

Shortly after the numbers were announced and nobody won, the buzzer sounded and Bibi, who still used the 'n' word, used the 'n' word. Rather than open the door, she stumped across the old, stained wooden floor, around the pool table, around the Formica booths, and opened the door in person.

After a minute, she came back and said to me, "Dixie, you should go talk to this lady. I can't understand her. It's something about your house."

The woman at the tavern door was LaDonna Grimes. She lived on the corner of Robinwood and Trexel and sometimes, on my walk home from Danny's Coney Island, I nodded to her as she trudged to the Woltown Food Center with her little blue grocery carrier. She had an only child, an unruly fourteen-year-old wannabe thug named Tivon to whom, like Corky's folks, she catered with typhlotic giddiness. Now, in thick, vaguely worried vernacular, pronouncing 'police' like it had the word 'poe' in it, she frowned: "They's a police at you place."

Finding me had been easy; your neighbors know your habits better than your friends. "Thought you'd wanna know," LaDonna nodded before moving along into the clean blue afternoon.

I leaned against the tavern's old clapboard siding, above the row of cinderblocks that lined Wolski's at street level. In the spring, Bibi had filled the holes with dirt and planted impatiens and now they competed for space with cigarette butts. I was square with the bar—Wolski's was not the kind of place that let you run tabs, nor were the regulars the kind of people who would pay them if it did—but to this day I'm not sure why I hesitated so long above the concrete flower pots before heading home.

I followed the familiar route down Jameson at as steady a pace as I could manage under the fatalistic constraint of being shit-faced. I wended through the defunct video store parking lot where you could still buy videos from a guy in a van, alongside Transfiguration Cemetery with long, elegant Polish names on every stone and past the Detroit Savings bank branch which had failed and become a gay bar which had failed and become a chop suey joint which had failed and become a Hindu temple which had failed and was now the domain of weeds and graffiti, which were succeeding. By the time I got home there were three police cars and an EMS truck wedged in front of our little brick house on Robinwood with its weathering, useless wheelchair ramp.

I suppose I had assumed that sooner or later Corky would be busted for drugs; that he'd wind up in the emergency room because of drugs, that he'd suffer some sort of psychic break from drugs or alienate his long-suffering parents due to drugs, but even in my most twisted iteration I didn't figure he'd be murdered for drugs. The cop standing by the police-tape perimeter was an inch shorter than me, and irrationally, I wondered if the police force had height requirements. Education is one thing, but how do you lie about your height? The next-door neighbor Mrs. Nazwisko was among a growing clot of gawkers and she pointed me out as 'the wife'. The miniature man in the blue uniform asked for my identification, and in a growing panic, I began fumbling through my purse, but all I could come up with was my old Ohio driver's license.

LaDonna Grimes' son Tivon was among the crowd, and he knew me by name from Danny's Coney Island where he and his fellow jitterbugs loaded up on two dollar chili dogs after school. He likewise vouched for my identity. The little cop finally radioed his supervisor, and by then I was in full-blown hysteria, imagining it somehow relevant to point out the difference between being a common-law wife and being an actual wife.

In time, a sandy-haired, middle-aged detective named Berrios came out of the house and down the wheelchair ramp. He hustled me over to the bumper of a patrol car, beyond the earshot of the crowd, and in a tone at once cursory and crude, explained to me that somebody inside the house—they were trying to determine who, but they had reason to believe it was Emil Geshke—had been bludgeoned to death with a baseball bat while duct-taped to a recliner.

"The blue one?" I asked stupidly, as if it mattered, having immediately conjured up an image of the chair in which I had last seen Corky sprawled that morning, high as a cloud and nodding into a volume of *The Icewind Dale Trilogy*.

My comment raised Berrios' eyebrow. I wasn't asked to do the body identification, but I was asked a lot of other cop-type shit: My whereabouts all day, details of my relationship with Corky Geshke, my explanation (if any) for the gruesome scene inside the living room, discovered by a UPS driver who'd pushed the unlocked front door the rest of the way open.

Teetering on the silver bumper of the prowler in the late October sunlight, I tried to clear the vodka fog from my brain and answer the detective's questions sincerely: Yes, I was willing to cooperate. Yes, my common-law husband was alive when I saw him last—he was reading his elf book in a blue easy chair, sans duct tape. No, I never once left Wolski's Tavern from eight that morning until LaDonna Grimes came to tell me about the police cars—Bibi Lisiewicz and John Kowalczyk and half a dozen other resident sad sacks can confirm it. No, I had no idea who did this or why. I swore I didn't know who he might have pissed off or who he owed money to. I didn't know his friends, didn't know his enemies, and frankly, I wasn't even sure what his middle name was.

But I dealt myself the coup de grâce with the next question, the last one the detective asked before he read me my Miranda rights and put me in handcuffs. I was hyperventilating, emotionally lost and totally terrified, and I wasn't thinking about lawyers when I should have been. I was thinking that a two dollar shot would have served me better in that moment than in any previous moment I'd slammed one. Detective Berrios mentioned that his team had searched the bathroom looking for other victims, and instead found some stuff that 'we weren't supposed to have'. I guessed he was talking about Corky's works and I answered quickly, "Okay, look, I know he's an addict, but that has nothing to do with me or *my* life. We're common-law married, not even officially husband and wife. Check the records. The junk in the bathroom is his, not mine. I don't do hard drugs..." and I held out my pasty, trembling arms as if to demonstrate that they were free of track marks.

I suppose I had come a distance from the little girl in the straw-colored Ramona Quimby bob sneaking beers in Durhamville, but not far enough to realize that the detective had trapped me into admitting I knew there were Schedule I drugs inside the house where I lived, and since he didn't believe I was being entirely forthcoming about who might have murdered my common-law junkie husband (even though I was), I became, for the moment, his primary suspect.

Needing a reason to hold me, at least until I saw the light and gave up some information, Berrios arrested me for possession of a controlled substance and physically removed me from the bumper and put me into the back seat of the patrol car.

There I sat for an hour, claustrophobic, screaming until my ears hurt because all the windows were rolled up. I began to shiver, but not from the booze, since withdrawal shakes were still several hours away.

People peered in at me, but I scarcely noticed them. For some reason, though, I did notice a dead rabbit in the middle of Robinwood Street that had been run over so many times that it looked like a cut-out cardboard bunny. It was right in front of my house, and not only had I not seen it earlier, I had never even seen a rabbit in my neighborhood before. I didn't realize it then, but that rabbit—pathetically ignored and ludicrously flat—was the first step in a heightened process of awareness that hasn't ended to this day: In every nanosecond, countless things happen all around us, in front of us and behind us, and like neutrinos, they pass directly through us without knocking anything loose. And sometimes, they should: For all I knew, I ran that rabbit over myself.

Corky's corpse was identified by Mrs. Nazwisko, who'd known him since he was a boy. Whether it was an ordeal for her or a ghoulish delight, I wasn't to learn; by then, I had been transported to the Detroit Detention Center on Mound Road and dumped into a stark holding cell to await the pleasure of Detective Berrios, who—as the sadistic intake sergeant informed me—had lost a daughter to smack and was unrelentingly cynical about people who lived 'that life', devoid of mercy or compassion. The clerk's recommendation was a quick flip and a plea bargain, and he offered it as he escorted me to a stark concrete cell to stew on my predicament. But I was still too pickled to stew and had yet to figure out that the whole thing was nothing but a bizarre, byzantine scam to get me to turn over information that I really didn't have.

Drink is the greatest resource ever invented for the useless, and without it, the light of reality turns cold pretty quickly. Soon enough, the twitter of adrenaline and the physical crackle of my system's dying buzz completed the spiral. By the time Detective Berrios dropped by to see if I'd had a change of heart about narking anybody out, I was annihilated— steamrolled without my dog hair—and I had come to understand that with me and alcohol, the only thing that had changed was the venue: This place was no Oktoberfest tent, but I wanted that drink no less now than I had then, and this time, I was willing to debase myself to get one.

To no avail, of course: Berrios wanted bad guys, not blowjobs from diaphoretic drunks. He tried and succeeded to shock the living hell out of me by showing me splatter shots of Corky curled in a fetal position on the floor of the house, his brains beside his elf book and his autographed Louisville Slugger with blood and hair on it. I puked, and afterward, the closest I came to redeeming myself was asking for an attorney before I'd speak to anybody else. In disgust, Berrios left me to sprawl on cold plastic, pee into stainless steel and obsess over where I'd ended up.

And that I did: For the past four years, Corky had been living mostly on money provided from his parents, wired regularly from Jupiter, Florida. Otherwise, they might as well have been living on Planet Jupiter for all Corky cared. I still had money remaining in Daddy's college fund since I hadn't been relying on it, but instead, had been existing on handouts from Corky, Five O'Clock vodka and free, greasy food from the restaurant where I worked. Still, at that point, four years after coming to Detroit—in fact, for the entire 27 years of my life—I had little to show beyond bloat and bleariness and a dirty little yellow cell on Mound Street that reeked of knock-off Pinesol.

I wound up being arraigned the following day before a bored judge who agreed with the prosecutor that I was a flight risk because of my Ohio driver's license and the fact that Michigan didn't even recognize common-law marriages, and—since I was a suspect in a murder case—refused me bail. At least I wound up with an court-ordered attorney, a frumpy, frazzled, painfully dedicated woman called Andrea Crouch. She was around fifty and she came across as a stubborn old-woman-in-a-shoe who was standing up for one of her kids. Unfortunately, at the time of my arraignment, she had around a hundred kids in her shoe.

She did inform me privately that the whole case was bullshit and urged me to do my best to survive the two weeks of barbarism looming before me in Building 500, where I'd have to spend my time prior to my next hearing, when she was confident she'd get the charges reduced or dropped, especially if I agreed in advance to attend AA meetings and perform some requisite community service.

"Take it," she urged. "Otherwise, Berrios will just get on the stand and lie his *tuchus* off. If these fucks weren't willing to perjure themselves at the drop of a hat they wouldn't get more than three cases a week in front of the judge."

I did agree, and in fact, I survived my two weeks in Building 500 rather swimmingly, probably because within that hierarchy of psychopathology, the other rock-hard inmates thought I was too insignificant to bother with. The women of Building 500 simultaneously guarded their own horror stories while retching out some version of them, and in honesty, I was merely their pale-skinned counterpart minus the sexual abuse many of them had dealt with since they were children. I was, however, one of the few in *'how did I get here?'* mode, since most of them were pretty confident of how they got there and in general, had no major issues with it. In many ways they were in their happy place, confident of meals and comradery and high quality dope that was even easier to get in jail than it was on the street.

I was drink-sick a lot of the time anyway and barely engaged anyone. What I remember most about those weeks were my lucid withdrawal dreams. Of those, I had multiple version of the same one, full of rich detail and freakishly vivid color, crazier than my wildest paintings. These dreams were identical in theme: I was always at some massive party filled with hundreds of people, many of whom I recognized. There were tables loaded with savory food and gorgeous desserts precariously balanced on skull-white tablecloths. The bizarre thing was, although I was by necessity cold sober in reality, I was totally drunk in my dreams. I kept knocking over tables and colliding with partygoers and asking them where I could find the bar.

Over those days, I suppose I did grieve for poor little Corky in my inimical, self-contained way. I was certainly conscious of the desperate waste of a person he'd been, both in life and death. In retrospect, the whole affair was monumentally pitiful through all its complicated layers, more for his parents than for me, of course. But he had taken me in, like Stanley Kowalski did for Blanche in *Streetcar,* and in the end, though we were both enablers, Corky was pretty harmless. He even produced art; intricate, spaced-out, geometric drawings he worked out from mathematical formulas, and he thought they had a purpose.

Thinking of his strange, cryptic creations makes me even sadder than his death:

Now, I keenly regret having done nothing but roll my eyes at them, since that's exactly what the hipsters in their Levi plaid shirts and Acqua Di Gio had done to mine.

I guess that was my near-term concession to mourning, although for me, the five stages of grief contained an all-encompassing sixth: Detox grief, the stage during which everything you ever did in your life, even the noblest acts, you somehow, on some level, feel awful about.

Beyond that, the scant jail time I remember tiptoed by in excruciatingly slow increments and then, at the close of every day, they were all dumped out like a factory part, each one identical to last. Due to my charges, I was facing decades in prison, and masochistically, I imaged what that might be like. I concluded that it would be exactly like this, only the days would be years.

The chance that it might actually come to long-term incarceration? I was at least rational enough to doubt it. I had no record and no connection to the drugs in my bathroom and nobody could prove otherwise. Besides, my attorney maintained that the search that uncovered them may not have been entirely legal. In fact, midway through my second week, she paid me a massively encouraging visit. She had spoken to the district attorney, who was even more overworked than she was, and he had agreed to reduce my charge to—ready for this?—public intoxication.

And from there, the news got even better: Although Corky's imploding parents wouldn't let me back inside the Robinwood house and had hired movers to take my few possessions to a nearby storage facility on Six Mile, Crouch knew of some apartments on the outskirts of Auburn Hills that were spacious, nice, and affordable. She'd provide me with a referral letter, and thus, I'd have a start-over option many miles from the cesspool of northeast Detroit.

Best of all, she had spoken to the owner of an upscale café in the trendy part of Pontiac, and based on my years of schlepping food at the Coney joint, she was willing to interview me for a server position. Naturally, I was humbled by such unnecessary bursts of regard from a relative stranger. Perhaps I really did have something of Blanche Dubois about me; maybe it was in my aristocratic Deep South DNA. In retrospect, I can see why Andrea Crouch might have seen more potential in me than in the usual parade of wasted losers she represented, and among my rather sizeable list of regrets about that slice of my life's story is that I did not sufficiently thank her before she died.

Ultimately, the judge accepted my plea and, pending successful completion of six months of bi-weekly Alcoholics Anonymous meetings and forty hours of community service, he was willing to expunge my record altogether.

And that was it.

My paper trail was one thing, but in the meantime, I had private sins to expunge, and to my great surprise, I discovered that sobriety suited me. Within a couple of months, I felt inordinately, almost embarrassingly healthy. In a pure sense, I was a kid again, delighted beyond expression at a world where waking up in the morning was not offensive. I was used to leaving for work feeling like you should feel when you're coming home from work, and now, my energy levels were off the charts. Tentatively, I even tried a painting redux, remembering to tone down my colors and with my newly-found dead rabbit sensitivities, intent on emphasizing life's subtleties.

If there was a fly in the recovery ointment, I suppose it was Corky's unsolved murder. Despite the pathos of his parents, pestering anyone who would listen and occasionally mentioning my name, the case ultimately grew cold.

Meanwhile, on Andrea Crouch's recommendation, and for under six hundred dollars a month, I moved into a nice apartment on Perry and Fredrick Douglass. I took available shifts at the Alchemy Bistro on South Ottawa Street, and began attending AA sessions in the basement of St. Bede Catholic Church, filling my name and new address dutifully into the roster, standing up before strangers and winning praise and applause for my first public statement about sobriety:

"Taking it one day at a time is easier when you realize that the days keep getting better and better."

Like every first-timer in any cathartic group session, I was painfully guarded at the outset, but I gradually loosened up and shared my story: I told them about Corky, about mocking his mandala-like artwork, about trading my body parts for a roof and incidentals since all my tip money went to booze, and there were many nods of earnest been-there, done-that assent. I told them that I never worried about getting knocked up because I had polycystic ovary syndrome, and I told them about brainy Corky's brain matter batted out of his skull and looking like a peeled plum on our living room floor.

In the course of these sessions, I even found someone with whom, on a cautious, if intuitive level, I warmed up to: A bustling, self-confident black woman named Takosha DeYoung.

Takosha was streetwise beyond anyone I'd ever known. She'd been raised in the un-trendy part of Pontiac and freely admitted that she turned tricks to survive. She was also candid enough to point out that accepting rent-free living from Corky in exchange for sex was not demonstrably different than hooking, and it was a point I quickly conceded. Like me, she had started drinking in her early teens, and like me, she was attending AA meetings under court order and had to breathe into a county-issued Smart Start in-home breathalyzer at random times during the week. I noticed her initially—as most people did—because of her breasts, which were titanic and unconstrained in the loose sequined blouses she was fond of wearing. But I also noticed that she routinely wore a gold-chained crystal pendant that dangled into her Marianas Trench cleavage, and she was pleased when I mentioned it, since it had been a gift from her late father, whom she lionized. The Daddy connection sealed the deal for me.

At the insistence of the group moderators, our AA table contained only members *forced* to attend meetings, because it was assumed that we had a less driving motivation to succeed than the other sad, sincere alcoholics. "We'll call our table Apathetics Anonymous," Takosha announced and I almost peed myself laughing, answering, "Oh my god; you're my new best friend."

In time, I learned that Takosha also owed the state a week's worth of community service, and although she initially told me that she intended to blow it off and was confident she'd fall through the same cracks she'd been falling through her entire life, she was the first person I called when I Googled my options and found out that a lot of people had done their community time at a nearby chunk of wilderness called August Lake State Park.

25

"Come on, Takosha," I urged her over the phone. "Let's do it together. A state park? Sun, trees, water, little squirrels and happy bunnies? How wholesome does *that* sound?"

And to my delight, after some lobbying, she agreed.

4.

Takosha lived with her sister Danita in a row of fairly new townhouses off Wide Track Drive; I had dropped her off there a few times after our AA meetings. The complex was called Carriage Circle and was in an otherwise no-go zone in Pontiac, meaning that white folks took extra care when passing through it.

The whole Carriage Circle set-up struck me as unrelentingly bizarre, although I was not yet close enough to Takosha to mention why: There were three massive green dumpsters in the middle of the parking lot, in front of the townhouses instead of behind them, and they loomed and stank and uglified the common area where the resident children played. Circling the dumpsters, cookie-cutter doorways still smelled like new paint and the shared walls had the spit-shine of new siding, but some of the windows were already boarded up. There were battered toys scattered around concrete sidewalks, plastic cars and baby playpens, but there were also ominous, shady-looking people hanging around in the spaces between the buildings, like the Woltown jitterbugs killing time outside Danny's Coney Island.

Carriage Circle looked like a newborn ghetto, still pink and plump from recent birth but already showing signs of inevitable decay. Carriage Circle was like a fresh corpse in the midday sun, rotting precociously, and I suppose that even if Takosha had been a closer friend to me I still wouldn't have said anything. If we're totally and brutally honest, there are some things that white people just won't say to black friends, not for fear of being misinterpreted, but from fear of being interpreted correctly.

The city of Pontiac itself was like that: An incongruous blight that had no business being where it was, on the periphery of some of the wealthiest communities in the country. Pontiac was a monument to its own failed potential. You can even vaguely

26

understand Detroit as a one-trick-pony town that couldn't reinvent itself after people stopped buying its only product. Add to that a succession of shit mayors and a school system so bad that half the adults in the city were functionally illiterate, and you have an explanation for Detroit that you can wrap your head around.

But Pontiac had no reason to mirror that. Despite having an entire car division named after it, it really wasn't a motor city. And it wasn't in broke Wayne County; it was in incredibly affluent Oakland County, which should have shored it up. It could have been—and without much trouble—the sort of safe, vibrant urban environment that sterile edge-city folks in undulating places like Auburn Hills, Bloomfield Hills and Rochester Hills seem to crave, and it was directly next door to them, sharing common borders. And yet, Pontiac was Detroit without so much as a vestige of Detroit's hardscrabble, punked-out charm. It was the ugliest city I'd ever seen, even in pictures.

I pulled my rust-riddled Focus into the Carriage Circle common on Monday morning at seven o' clock. A couple of weeks before, I had contacted the headquarters at August Lake State Park and spoken to a forest ranger called Alan Loya who my radar told me was already a couple of cocktails into it. I rolled my eyes, holding my phone a foot away from my ear when he got too happily loud. Whether a disease or a predilection, it's everywhere, infiltrating all strata, snaking through every profession. He told me that they had a community service project beginning in May, consisting of basic springtime maintenance chores like litter sweeping and leaf clearing. It wasn't particularly grueling work he promised, and five eight hour days would fulfil my weeklong requirement. He said that a carpool vehicle generally waited in the parking lot of Pontiac Family Services to shuttle volunteers back and forth.

It sounded perfect, and it might have been, except that by the time Monday morning rolled around, I had the flu. On the preceding Saturday night I'd slammed through a busy dinner shift at Alchemy Bistro, juggling a full house with multiple table turns as my face became increasingly flushed and my throat started to seriously hurt. I got through the night woozily, and once home, I ate a handful of Vitamin C tablets with a Melatonin Ultra chaser, hoping I could beat the virus with sleep. Half a bottle of Nyquil would have done the number in style, but because I had to take random checks on my in-home breathalyzer, Nyquil was off the play list. As the stern sentencing judge had promised me: "The law does not recognize excuses for alcohol readings that may come from other sources."

I managed to sleep, but whatever it was that I'd picked up managed to hide in my squishy places all the following day and only reemerged late on Sunday, waking me at around midnight. I would have begged off the August Lake deal, of course; I would have rescheduled, retreated and recuperated. But it had been such a coup for me to get Takosha to agree to do the week with me (which I saw as vital to her whole-body recovery) that for her sake, I decided to gut it out. I didn't want her to risk falling through bureaucratic cracks, because I assumed that that the place she fell to would be even worse.

Meanwhile, *my* world got even worse. A weather front began moving through the lower part of the state, and by the time I got to Carriage Circle on Monday morning, the sky was thick and threatening and fat drops of rain had begun to slap the windshield. Daddy's work ethic—*'The hardest part of any job is walking through the front door'*—would have to apply even when there was no front door to walk though. We'd be outside, in the rain, in the cold, picking up garbage.

Takosha was twenty-five minutes late in coming out of the shiny, newly-painted townhouse door. I called her cell phone twice while I sat in the idling Focus, gunning the engine to keep the heat circulating to forestall the shivers. By then, my fever must have been approaching a hundred. She finally ambled out with her usual combination of pique and pissiness, unhappy about rising before three in the afternoon, looking crazily buxomy in a leopard print V-neck blouse with her inevitable crystal necklace bobbing around on the sea of sepia flesh. I was wearing jeans to her Aerie Chill leggings and second-hand, Salvation Army work boots to her Neon Coral Graviota sneakers, but since she was keeping up her end of the bargain, I wasn't going to offer fashion advice. She slid in the car beside me, reading my mind, rolling her eyes and saying, "Boo, my body shape come with specifications," and promptly lit a Kool, which, to my sore throat, was like gargling Drano.

I said nothing. I let her smoke her Kool. I cracked open my window and reasoned that the Family Center was only five minutes away. That was me—no waves. That's who I was then, and, categorically, who I probably still am today.

Waiting for us in the lot was an old green Ford 150 with *State of Michigan DNR* in a circle emblem on the side. The driver was a thin, taciturn, grey-skinned, shaved-head teenager wearing shades despite the clouds. I knew instinctively it was not the dude I'd spoken to on the phone, and it wasn't—at least that's what the skinny white women in the passenger's seat told us. She was the only other volunteer who had shown up that morning, and after we wedged into the truck's back seat among cheap park brochures and greasy rags, she introduced herself as Naomi, and told us the driver's name was Gabriel.

She added, "Other than that, he doesn't say much."

Naomi did though, and in a voice like a fingernail on a chalkboard. She was obviously one of those high-strung people sufficiently numbed by medication to make them functional, but who can't mask their mental illnesses entirely.

Naomi's face had so many wrinkles that it looked like a piece of paper that had been crumpled up and then uncrumpled several times in succession. She began to chatter haphazardly, claiming that she was doing her service for a trumped-up charge of assaulting her adult son, who, she said, would not work, would not mow the lawn, would not move out of her house, and she was on the same topic as about it as ashen, silent Gabriel pulled onto 1-75, where a thread of commuters had slowed because of the wet weather. Whereupon, she switched to complaining about the commuters and the weather and she was still complaining when the traffic eased and we picked up speed.

Takosha was trying to sleep and finally barked, "Bitch, can you shut the fuck up for ten seconds?"

So Naomi harrumphed and ticked off ten seconds, then called her son/victim on her cell phone and carried on complaining to him.

Fifteen minutes passed like this. We pulled off onto a two lane interstate highway beneath a mountainous landfill, and further down, after several miles, we took a dirt road and bounced on ruined shocks into increasingly forested land, where the trees had leafed out and the branches formed a pendulous arch overhead. At the end of the road, a squat brown building stood beneath a thick stand of trees.

Moss grew on the shingles and the cheap, rough-hewn siding was bowing. It looked greenish and gloomy, like places do that never entirely dry out.

We piled out of the truck, and without saying a word or removing his sunglasses, Gabriel ushered us into a musty room with a long central cafeteria-style table. There were maps of the park on the wall and big pieces of random farm-type equipment scattered about in various states of disrepair, and the room smelled like what it probably was, a combination kitchen, break area and garage.

In the center of the table was a stack of papers with *'Verification of Service'* at the top and spaces for times and dates and emergency contacts and a box where some verifier would do the verifying. It was the same businesslike bullshit as we were obligated to fill out at our AA meetings, where the end game was paperwork, not the value derived from our attending. There were pens, so I shrugged and began to fill in boxes. Half-heartedly, if begrudgingly, Takosha lit another cigarette and did too.

And into the room stepped Julian Vaz.

At the time, of course, I didn't know his name, and I'm not entirely sure I do today. But he was one of those people whose appearance is startling; someone who commands presence without making the slightest effort. In fact, as I think back on those first moments, I immediately picked up on a sort of abstract shyness around him, a radiant remoteness. I remember finding him attractive; middle-tall, like my Daddy—and that's in a good way—wire-muscled beneath his rolled-up sleeves. His fair hair was bound in a ponytail and his eyes were of a shade that, set into an olive complexion, I'd call harmonizing; the color of foliage reflected in water.

It meant little enough then as he stood at the doorway of a hall that led to darker places in the little building and said, "Alan is running late, but don't worry. Your patience counts as community service."

There was something behind his expression that I couldn't quite pin down, though something that I found vaguely intriguing. It stuck with me and I thought about it, and determined that the impression he gave off was one of primordial serenity. I thought that his was the most peaceful smile I had ever seen, both cool and incandescent, like something in the distant sky.

Naomi jerked her thumb at Takosha and snapped, "Is she allowed to smoke in here?"

Julian's expression remained intact. He said, "I'm not much of a rule enforcer. Sorry."

Naomi harrumphed, "If you work for the state, you should have rules."

He offered his warm-cold smile and replied, "I do. Only, they tend to be a bit more abstract."

A band of young people filtered into the room and formed a knot around him. I assumed by their caps and logoed t-shirts that they were park employees. The first one was an effeminate, Hispanic-looking kid with delicate Indian features. The next was an older teenager with a cocky pout and arms threaded with tattoos, and finally, the alabaster-colored boy whose sunglasses were still on inside the murky building. Gabriel. A moment later, Alan Loya stumped down the hall and swept into the room, bombastic, unsteady, unshaven, crazily happy, inappropriately loud and clearly boiled to the gills.

To my mind, Alan was as strange a specimen of the male gender as exists outside of animatronics. He was squat and Hobbit-like, with bushy eyebrows and blunt features capped by a bulbous, beet-red nose stippled with pock marks. He looked to be about forty, but in gnome years, who knows? He launched into an irrelevant, unnecessary explanation for his tardiness: "Oh, I had no hot water in my shower this morning so I went down to check the pilot, right? Who wouldn't? No hot water? Sure as Jesus, the light is out, and I'm thinking it's gotta be the thermocouple, probably a dirty thermo, so I pulled it and cleaned it good with sandpaper, but the pilot still wouldn't stay lit, so I'm thinking pilot tube—maybe the tube is clogged, so I get a safety pin and open it up and clean the bugger, but the pilot still won't stay lit and..."

As he spoke, his face became redder and his eyes grew glassier and I tossed a look at Takosha who made a quick private gesture with her hand like upending a bottle, and then, for some reason, I glanced at Julian. He winked at me, and the moment sticks because it was our first personal exchange.

31

Perhaps he'd seen Takosha's gesture, and maybe Alan saw it too because he suddenly pointed at her and said, "Oh, ma'am, this is a smoke free environment."

I doubted that Takosha would snub out the Kool, and she didn't. I'm not sure she even heard him. She was looking at Julian, and her brows were arced above a puzzled grin. That moment clings to me as well, because—embarrassingly, in retrospect—I felt a primal sting of jealousy. Maybe he'd been winking at her, not me. My head hurt; my throat felt like Alan's thermocouple after the sandpaper and I wished I could pick up a six-pack of Nyquil and sleep for the rest of the week in my childhood bed on Scioto Street.

An old sense of futility began seeping in around my edges as Alan went on: "So, here's our game plan, ladies. You can lock your purses and phones in the safe if you want and then you'll go out on litter patrol in the park's North Unit, and know who you'll be making really happy? That crew right over there. They'll love you to death. Why? You'll be doing their work for them today, courtesy of the court system! Let me introduce them. Little guy with the long eyelashes, that's Serafin Tercerio. Big name for a little fella, huh? Ink man is Potter—his bark's worse than his bite, promise. Gabriel's the strong, silent type—he wears his sunglasses at night, like in that song. And they all report to Park Ranger Julian Vaz. Julian's my right hand man. He's the fellow who really runs the show here at August Lake. I owe him a lot."

Julian's face remained perfectly still. From the perspective of an artist, I thought it was an intensely compelling visage; basal beauty underscored with deeper lines of tranquility.

"Julian does my heavy lifting," Alan went on. "Not that you'll be doing any heavy lifting. It'll be nothing but old beer cans and McDonald's wrappers prob'ly. We want the place in ship shape for Memorial Day coming up so maybe we'll actually get a few visitors this year! Not the greatest weather for outside work, I admit, but we'll provide you with rain gear and stuff and Doppler says it will clear up by..."

And so on. Serafin Tercerio pulled some fluorescent green ponchos from a locker and handed them out along with some clippy pincers for picking up garbage and the bags to put it in. I put my poncho on—little more than a glorified trash bags itself—and Naomi put hers on, but naturally, Takosha snorted and said, "Not my specs" and began typing into her cell phone instead.

I assumed that Takosha's profession required some outdoor work in inclement weather, and okay, so I was being catty, but I was a little ticked off at how casually she was taking all this. I didn't want to be here any more than she did. But by now I was resigned to it and willing to struggle through today and let tomorrow bring what it might.

Meanwhile, Alan appeared to be losing steam: "Tomorrow, we'll find something else for you guys to do. For now finish up your paperwork." His bombast went through its final sputters as he turned back to the dark hallway. "Julian will sign you out at the end of your shift. Me, I have some errands to run."

"I bet you do," snorted Takosha.

Outside, misty drizzle filtered down. We piled into the green Ford pickup again. This time, Potter drove, with Serafin and Gabriel in the bed, perched precariously on the side panel. Takosha snagged the front seat , leaving Naomi and me wedged into the cramped rear. Where Julian Vaz disappeared to during that first hour I have no idea, but he was not in the truck with us.

Quickly, I began to fade. I leaned into the cold glass, my head ricocheting off the window as we bounced over washboard roads, zoning until we rumbled past the park's namesake attraction, the spread of water called August Lake.

That perked me up, primarily because I was impressed by the lake's sheer chromatic weirdness. Since then, August Lake has figured so prominently in my conscience that it's important to me to recall and record precisely my first glimpse of her. I still think of the lake as gender specific, despite having learned that it was named for Levi August, a man. Seeing the lake was even more disconcerting that my first glimpse of Julian; she was a color I couldn't identify despite my years of squeezing paint tubes, although I'm reasonably certain it was nothing that Winsor & Newton ever manufactured. At the time, as a place holder, I decided that it was some variation on bleak opaque; lead flecked with other, deeper, more unpleasant tones; Aquadull and Payne's Noxious, if I was going to make a painter's inside joke out of it.

Can I phrase what I actually thought without corniness? Maybe I can't. At least during that initial viewing under the steely overcast sky, August Lake appeared as something vital without any vitality. If the lake was a woman, she was an ugly woman. Still, those were fever impressions, and that made strange worlds possible.

In the front seat, Takosha suddenly said to Potter, "You know who I am, right?"

Potter glanced over. "Some nigger?"

"Oh my God," gasped Naomi and I thought that Takosha was going to strike out with her fist, but instead she offered an easy, mordant laugh, lit another Kool and said, "That's right, boo. Some wise old motherfucking nigger."

And there was nothing more said to clarify the exchange. Potter had his tattooed arm extended rigidly against the steering while Takosha sucked aggressively on her smoke and finally Naomi snorted and said "Fine," and pulled out her own a pack of cigarettes and lit one too.

A noxious cloud formed inside the truck and it was too much for my system. I fell into a serious coughing fit until finally, Takosha turned her head and locked eyes with me as if I was intentionally circumventing her rule rebellion. "This ain't just white folk drama is it, honey?" she asked.

"No," I said, embarrassed. "I swear I have like a bug or something. It's been coming on since Saturday—I've been eating Tylenols like M&Ms. I'm… sorry."

"Don't be sorry, boo," she said, opening her window and flicking the cigarette into the wet morning. "You should have said something earlier. We coulda both slept in."

Naomi flicked out her smoke too, snipping, "Oh, honestly. Nobody can make up their minds anymore."

I quickly owned it: The whole day—the fresh-air-blue-sky community service option—had been a shitty idea. My bad. At the far edge of the state forest, about three miles down a vacant country road, Potter turned the truck around. We clambered out and at his terse direction and began to patrol the gravel shoulders looking for trash. It was easy enough to find since it was everywhere; fast food cups, Coke bottles, gum wrappers, old plastic toys covered in mosaics of mold—the random crap people toss out of car windows without the slightest shit given as to whether or not somebody comes behind them to pick it up. But somebody was coming along behind, and that was our obligation to the state for the next eight hour on that cold May afternoon.

I took the left side while Naomi, sighing and complaining, took the right side. Takosha took neither side, but went clipping on ahead of the truck, directly down the center of the road. I felt wisps of rain on my hot hands and it felt prickly, like electricity. It revived in me a memory of Arnie Tencer, a kid in my fourth grade class who once tricked me into putting a nine volt battery against my tongue. Arnie probably experienced some prepubescent, horny thrill watching me stick something gross in my mouth and flinch, but the same fizzy and decidedly non-sexual sensation now jittered across my exposed flesh.

Thinking of the fourth grade made a squall of unexpected loneliness wash over me. Fevers do that sometimes, but it nearly bowled me down. I missed being a little kid, with all the pomp and circumstance that accompanied catching the flu: My mom, for all her self-indulgent wackiness, certainly knew how to mollycoddle a sick kid.

But that was long ago and light years away, so I steered though the sweet memories as best I could and steeled into Daddy's transplanted ethic, soldiering on for as long as I could, kicking at clumps of weeds, exposing muddy beer bottles, CVS bags, junk of unknown origin; an old pair of gym shoes, laces knotted...

Occasionally, behind the trees, you could see ponds and swamps appear like spectral apparitions. Diligently, mechanically, I filled my trash bag as Potter drove the truck at two miles an hour behind us: On the far side of the road was Naomi, hoodie up, haggard, scraggy as a hen and walking like a penguin, trying to get the hang of her pincers. Takosha walked in stupendous arrogance, snickering, refusing to do anything, picking up nothing but adding her occasional Kool filters to our litter stash.

After an hour of this, I was physically spent. I had abused my body for so many years that I had pretty much compromised my reservoirs of youthful strength and I hadn't been sober long enough to entirely top up the engine. I felt sapless, like I was going to lose it.

At a country crossroad, where another ungraded artery trickled off into the forest, I stopped and stood unsteadily with my eyes closed until a pair of hands found my drizzle-damp face. Julian's hands. I had no idea where he'd come from, if he'd been tracking us, or what, and the others didn't seem to have noticed. The truck had moved on and nobody glanced back.

Julian looked at me briefly, but fully in the face and with intense concentration. As strange as the sudden and unexpected encounter was, it didn't strike me as the least bit off-base. I believe that most of us have evolved a sixth sense about malignant people, and if this was a danger zone, I think I would have noticed something. Cadence naïve or not, by then I'd been in jail and had lived for four years with a junkie. Here, I felt no need to have my guard up. In fact, I felt nothing but relief in seeing him.

He had a pleasant, earthy smell that I could not entirely account for. He held out a leather bota from which a warm scent was rising said, "I have something that will make you feel better."

Naturally, I hesitated: "Thanks, but what's in it? I have to do random screens as part of my probation."

His fleeting smile came again and when he spoke, it sounded oddly distracted, like he was communicating from a long distance away: "No worry; it's called *Jivarrão*. It's a native tea recipe. Everything in it is grown right here in the park. Mostly peppermint, marshmallow root, evergreen leaves and wild ginseng. Everything is legal and I promise, more effective than anything you can buy at CVS."

"You're a regular Daniel Boone, huh?" I answered, laughing lightly.

The tea aromas were enticing; exotic, heady and sweet. He said, "Full disclosure: It won't cure you, but it will make you think less about what you've got. An infection like yours is bigger than tea. In fact, it took out the natives who invented the tea."

"It does smell awesome," I admitted. "Smells like something from when I was a little girl, like the honey lemon tea my mom made when I was sick."

36

"It's pretty close. Lemon balm and honey from my hives. Drink it, lie down in the back of the truck for a while and see how it goes. I'll take your spot in the litter sweep and I'm sure the others won't mind."

So I did, and he did, the tea was sensational, and truth told, I was beyond caring whether lazy Takosha and whiny Naomi minded or not. Julian was right, I needed to get off my feet. He trotted forward and a moment later, I was curled up in the rear seat of the truck, shivering under my poncho and the fleece jacket that Julian had left for me.

From his precarious perch in the bed of the truck, I could hear Serafin Tercerio clapping his hands in glee as Julian stooped to pry a mossy, deflated football from the mud: "I'm the lookout, Julio! There's a trash over there too! Go pick 'er up!"

Framed by the oval truck window, I also saw Gabriel's elevated figure; aloof, dignified, alone, and utterly cool. Behind him, the spring leaves had unfolded into a beryl screen. From my vantage, it was the image of a carved and passionless statue—an alabaster god—and suddenly, for some reason, that was a painting I wanted to make. The notion came as a surprise: Artistic inspiration was not what I was expecting during that shivery, wasted morning.

The truck itself was a relic and the shock absorbers were shot, and at high speeds it would have been a nightmare. But at this pace, a couple miles per hour, it was a gentle, rocking cradle. I was mesmerized by Gabriel's wordless dignity, and I wondered If this is how his namesake archangel might have appeared to the Virgin Mary. The Ford wallowed rhythmically through puddles; I was lulled and feverish and finally, I nodded off to sleep.

And then I started to vomit.

It came on quickly; waves of stomach cramps followed by eruptions of throat bile. I did it with a certain élan because puking is a core competency among binge drinkers and I hadn't lost the touch. But, as in most pickup trucks, you needed to open the front door before you could get to the back one, so by the time Potter realized what was going on, my chuck was well on its way up. Gratefully, I got most of it outside, into the gummy dirt and only a little on the battered panel. I rolled out the door and into the mud.

Julian was quickly beside me, trying to help me up, but my knees were spaghetti. As I heaved out the last few sputters of my digestive tract, I began apologizing profusely to everyone, and to Julian in particular. I was woozy and obviously, I felt like a total goober. Naomi wanted to call an EMS and Takosha looked on with a quizzical frown.

I said, "For Christ's sake, I don't need an ambulance. I have the stomach flu. I just need to lie down for a little, maybe back at that headquarters thingy place. Dock me an hour off my community service. At this point, I couldn't care less."

Julian said, "There's a ranger's cottage even closer. Half a mile from here. There's a cot, there's blankets, there's heat. Why don't you let Potter drive you over there? Serafin Tercerio will stay with you. If the rain keeps up, the whole crew can call it a day at noon. I'll sign you all out for a full eight and we'll see what happens tomorrow."

"That's fine; whatever," I said numbly. "But just for an hour, then come back. Fair's fair; this whole clusterfuck was sort of like my idea in the first place."

I slithered back into the truck and Potter slewed down the soggy dirt road, turning onto another soggy dirt road, and that one wound into a small dell where a stone cottage sat amid a bower of spring flowers. To my delirious perspective, it looked like it had been beamed down from a book of fairy tales, even in the rain.

Had the hut been a painting by Bob Ross it would have been bad-bad art, but in the here and now, in front of me, with its fieldstone porch, chimney leaking a trickle of translucent smoke, garden filled with plots of the herbs I assumed I'd ingested then spewed back up again, it was amazingly quaint and unrelentingly inviting.

Serafin Tercerio tumbled out of the back of the truck singing, "Let me show you my *guitarra!*" as Potter drove off with Gabriel, the immobile archangel, roosting in back.

We went inside, and despite my state of mind and body—or maybe because of it—I quickly decided that the pine-paneled interior was even cooler than the outside. It leapfrogged quaint and settled into just plain fucking kick-ass. For starters, everything looked hand-made or home-grown. The rustic furniture was hewn from logs; there were carved bows on hooks in the wall, fish spears, lures, a shelf filled with delicately preserved animal skulls and another that contained gourds and acorns. The ceiling was festooned with drying roots and herbs and seed pods and strings of wild potatoes. An elaborate wooden kayak hung from a peg and there was a two-sided axe leaning in a corner. Scattered here and there, hand-thrown crockery pots contained leafy houseplants. A bowl held shiny duck eggs which, I later learned, were then in season. There was a cast iron stove and a butcher block beside it with a loaf of brown, crusty bread.

The guitar Serafin Tercerio had mentioned was remarkable, especially for someone like me who proudly retained an artistic eye. It was delicately carved with sylvan scenes—deer and leaves—and expertly assembled. He beamed as he pointed it out and I strummed it as it hung on its peg. I'm no musician, but to me, the tones were ethereal.

Serafin's voice was softly accented. "He show me how to find blackberries in the woods and to steam food underground. He teach me to weave yarn belts and he built me that *guitarra*! He make me to understand things that even afterward I don't understand!"

I washed my face and arms in a sink basin. In a corner, there was pine bed with a lovely quilt spread across it, and that looked even better the *guitarra*. I wondered if Julian had built the bed himself, and was willing to bet next month's rent that he had.

I asked, "I can lie down there?"

"Oh, sure!" Serafin answered, his delicate face frozen in a broad, toothy smile and his eyes like big marbles. "We all lie still when we get low. Especially Gabriel with the cancer in his blood."

It took me a moment to process. "My God," I gasped, taken by a private horror moment because I'd missed something in my alabaster angel that suddenly became obvious: The sunglasses, the pallor, the bare skull, even the aloofness. I'd played the angel angle up in my aesthetic imagination, but in fact, it might have been the effects of chemotherapy.

My shock was evident, because Serafin tried to soothe me: "It's okay. You can die, but you can't perish. We will see Gabriel again wherever God is."

Serafin began to tinker around the room, stirring up the fire, adding wood to the stove, as noisy as Gabriel had been mute. "We save Gabriel when he needed work. Julio save me too! *El Guero!* I was special needs, I couldn't go to school, I was bullied on the street. I had no work either, and now I do. I was a stupid boy and he make me smart."

"Julian made you smart?" I asked, settling into the bed's soft textures. "I could use some of that. How?"

"He teach me that I'm not alone. That I am connected. That I'm part of a beautiful storm."

"Julian sounds like a kind man," I said, growing spacy and spreading myself across the feather mattress. " I felt that in the way he treated me, too."

"Yes, he is; he keeps all things in the balance. He gives, I give. We like to keep the balance in our world."

"Your world?"

"Not my world. *Our* world. Me and *El Guero.* "

The cottage was filled with fierce but delicate aromas of smoke and herbs, the smell of harvested thyme and maple logs passing into new matter, back to the source, life and death at the same time. There was a cornucopia of memory scents surrounding me and I loved them all. Sights and sounds tell you where you're going, but smells remind you of where you've been. Smell is the most tangible sense. It is alive inside you. Light can't lodge in your clothes; sound can't cling to you. But smells can.

These were the enigmatic, esoteric, otherworldly thoughts that eddied through my mind as I pulled up the quilt comforter. It hadn't yet dawned on me that they were a byproduct of Julian's native tea.

It soon did, but in the meantime, I felt snug and secure inside the house. I felt a protective, paternal presence in the aromas and the attitude. Still, I had no reason

40

to think about Julian beyond the situation's immediacy. At the time, I wasn't conscious of any insuppressible physical attraction to him. Although I understand the psychology behind girls falling for father figures, there could not have been a male archetype more opposite to my Daddy, who was an urbane and delightfully simplistic businessman. Julian appeared to be an oddly intellectual outdoorsman. I wonder if Freud recognized a summer-camp-counselor complex.

A tapping sound came from outside a window and Serafin opened it. A massive, ink-black crow sat on the ledge, Poe made manifest. Serafin laughed heartily and began to feed it crumbs from his pocket.

'Vaguely and persistently spooked by birds'. That's how I've described myself. And yet, the crow did not intimidate me in the least. In fact, a veil of silk had begun to slide over me, gently and persistently, swallowing me in increments like a tide. It was so profound that I knew it had been induced by Julian's tea, and whatever it contained had likely made me puke, too. Spiritual purging. Peyote does that, at least according to Carlos Castaneda, one of my teenage standbys. But nothing in the moment made drugs in my system seem worrisome, nor did anything spook me about the crow on the window ledge either, who cocked his head and made soft croaks of interest, looking at me like the anomaly I was.

For an instant we commiserated, and the moment was pure and perfect. I felt interconnected and, like Serafin Tercerio, part of a vast and wonderful cyclone.

"Does the bird have a name?" I asked, smiling.

"His name is Serafin Tercerio," said Serafin Tercerio, saying his own name, and his accent sounded lilting and charming.

I fell asleep and dreamed I was a bird. Not a crow, but one of those tiny nursery rhyme blackbirds that they baked inside a pie. But there were no pies in the dream. I was flying above a broad, grey-brown lake, confident of my direction, and when I awoke, I found that it was time that had actually done the flying: The shadows had pooled and it was late afternoon.

I startled upright. The bird was gone, Serafin was gone and the psychotropics were tempered. I still felt sick, and yet I remained in an emotionally peaceful place, and it clung to me even after I realized I was not alone.

Julian was sitting quietly in a corner on a homemade chair, whittling a piece of hickory.

5.

I was content, but clearly, I had self-orchestrated obligations.

"Oh, for fuck's sake," I gasped. "What time is it?"

"Four o'clock," said Julian. "It's fine. You needed to sleep."

"It's actually not fine," I whined. "You said you'd come back at noon. Or sooner. I'm supposed to be Takosha's ride home. Takosha, the black chick..."

His voice was delicate and ineffably patient. "We did come at noon—all of us. It was raining. You said you wanted to sleep. The others agreed that we should just let you be."

I didn't remember that, but I also didn't doubt it. I've always been a hard sell about getting up when I was solidly under, and I'd been every bit of that. "But my car is in the lot at the Pontiac Family Services place," I said. "I was supposed to be Takosha's ride home. Takosha, the black..."

"It's all fine, Dixie. Gabriel drove Takosha back to her sister's apartment, the one she listed as an emergency contact. Now, if you're up to it, he can take you home, too."

I leaned back on the pillow with my hands behind my head and let out a sigh of resignation. It *was*, in part, white folk drama, and actually, I was glad to be where I was. I liked hearing Julian say my name. It made me blush and it made me feel as if I'd been of some minor but memorable import that day even if I hadn't schlepped much roadside garbage.

Neither did I feel any menace being alone in a cabin in the woods with a near-stranger. I ran with the adage that a face reveals a soul, and this face, I believed, was trustworthy. And in the half-light, strikingly appealing.

I admitted sheepishly, "Know who I wrote down for my emergency contact? Andrea Crouch, my court attorney."

"That would make sense."

"Not really, considering she died two months ago. Her best friend owns the place where I work and we catered the wake. She was in a car crash on Joy Road. Can you imagine dying on a road called Joy? Writing down her name was silly, but I had nobody else. How pathetic is that?"

I tried to gauge his reaction, but there wasn't much to gauge. Still, I felt settled. Quiet and comfortable. I knew I would have to shortly marshal the energy to motivate myself off the warm fluff, but in the meantime I was jockeying for a little more conversation, some essential interactions between myself and a strange man who didn't appear like his major motivation was jumping my bones. Truthfully, it had been a while.

I wanted Julian to say my name again. So instead of collecting myself, I kept the small talk alive: "What was in that Indian tea? Tell me straight, and don't tell me it was herbs and pumpkin pie spice—I feel like I mainlined a week's worth of Xanax."

"I did tell you," he smiled, picking a leaf from the plant growing in the crock beside him and rubbing it between his long fingers, slipping it into his mouth and chewing it. "Jivarrão. Perfectly natural and entirely legal. It's in the coffee family."

"Is that what made me puke?" I asked, blushing again and wondering if the reek of gack still clung to me. "I'll never live that one down."

"Could be," he said absently. "Or maybe it was your virus. Whenever we try to be the alpha predators, some virus is waiting to take the bragging rights."

"And what do we conclude from that?" I answered, smiling.

"That a virus has nothing to prove. It only needs to demonstrate."

"A pretty deep interpretation of stomach flu. You should write it down."

He answered with a shrug. "I don't have anything to prove either."

There was certainly something in Julian's calm charm that I found persuasive. Primarily, I thought, in its lack of impetus to persuade. So I followed with something I felt I must say, because we were talking about truths and I meant it: "You should have told me about the tea, though. I'm not supposed to be getting fucked up on anything. I'm in recovery, in case you didn't pick up on it."

"I did," he answered easily. "And as a matter of fact, Jivarrão is used to treat addiction."

"Your boss could use a shot, then. Am I right? Takes one to know one. His breath could have lit his broken frigging pilot light."

"Alan's useless as a ranger, obviously, but he knows his place. In the park, in the world. He's comfortable. For most people, that's a remarkable achievement."

I suppose I could see that. A lot of drunks are settled and content; they're the ones who seem to live forever. I was never settled, then or now, but by then, I was quite confident that my place in the world was not sucking well vodka in Wolski's Tavern nor wrestling garbage from some random gutter in August Lake State Park.

I lay in the communal low-people bed, feeling less low with my hands cocked behind my neck. But it was time to get up and I became self-conscious about how mussed my hair was and how flushed my fever face must look. Outside, the light had changed and I delayed rising another minute.

"What are you carving?" I asked, and to this day, I don't know if his response was intended as wit, or irony, or some obscure allusion that went over my head.

"Something for the Philistines," he said and held up a wooden slingshot.

Gabriel's shift ended, and shortly, he pulled the truck around to the front of the stone house. I could hear the wheels squishing in the mud. I hauled myself to my feet, thanked Julian for his kindness to a stranger in her hour of need. I thanked him for his gentle words and, without further implication, for his bed. I thanked him for his Indian tea. It had been a number of years since somebody who I wasn't paying, or who the court system wasn't paying, had shown me that kind of regard and I

44

told him so. I shook his hand and wanted to hug him, but for some reason, I didn't. Instead, I joined Gabriel in the Ford.

The day ended with me collapsing in my own bed, awash in my own smells, smothered by my own pillow, soaked in my own sweat, and subsequently, weltering in deep oblivion.

But the ride back with Gabriel had ended on a stranger note:

The first half had passed in silence. I felt awkward with him now and rather ashamed. I could no longer see him as a symbol, a votive or a god; I saw instead a sick kid who had, like me, found succor among strangers. Ultimately, though, I found that image no less compelling and no less picturesque.

Rain began to fall heavily again. I tried Takosha's cell phone and left a message apologizing for the day, apologizing for having dragged her out to the park and saying that I was far too sick to do it again the next day. Maybe that would appease her and maybe she'd save room for me in her bureaucratic crack in case I also needed to fall through it.

Ten minutes later I tried Takosha's phone again. "She won't pick up," said Gabriel.

"How do you know?"

"Instinct," he answered.

6.

The rest of that week is critical to this tale's trajectory, so I am trying as best I can to reconstruct my mood when I dragged myself up the following morning. The arc of my thought process during those early days is—for me, perhaps more than for anyone else—key to understanding what happened to me.

I know my fever picked up during the night and my system took its final physiological dump at around four. I drank my final two fingers of DayQuil with an Aquafina chaser and went back to sleep.

At six forty, I came around again. Outside my window , the rain was soft and steady, tapping like a crow. It had reached the soothing stage and I lay there collecting myself and rallying my strength. Returning to August Lake that morning was out of the question, obviously, and—whether necessary or not—I called the desk and left a message. At seven, I tried Takosha's cell again to let her know, but it was full and had stopped taking messages. Just as well, I thought, since I doubted she had the slightest intention of going back to the park and I was out of reasons to convince her that she should.

I lay in bed and looked around my apartment. After six months, it was scarcely furnished, flecked half-hazardly with some things I had picked up at Goodwill and the few sticks of furniture that Corky's parents had stuffed inside the storage unit. I was only doing the busy shifts at Alchemy, mostly Friday and Saturday nights and filling in otherwise whenever asked, and I hadn't yet banked a lot of cash with which to warm up the place. I had hung some original artwork, but not much, since I hadn't been satisfied enough with anything I had painted since I'd surfaced from my vodka sewer. I had one of Corky's bizarre, precise drawings displayed in the bedroom, the one that he'd once called his favorite, or at least the painting he'd believed best represented his worldview, where everything was an angle and defined by numbers so acute they were virtually visible. I hated the painting, but it was a guilt tribute to him and my singular lack of missing him. It was intended to be a commemoration of a real person, but actually, it augmented the loneliness of the place.

I'm sure to an outsider, the apartment would have looked like the lair of a cold mind. Even to me it still felt like a temporary shelter; the house of a transient. So far, there had been no second opinions. Other than me, the only person who had crossed my threshold had been a crazy neighbor woman who once thought my gas might be leaking. True to my newfound rhythms, I had not yet invited anyone over. My desire to socialize sort of evaporated with the booze and I either had little need or little competence in the art of sober friendships. With Takosha, I had sort of laid groundwork for one, or so I had thought, but she wasn't returning my texts and I was about ready to toss in that particular towel.

That's one of the reasons I think that Julian's do-it-yourself cottage had left such an impression on me. In my own deflected hunt for stability, his skill at building

46

his own backbone seemed like a superpower. It was like photosynthesis, where an organism is born with a knack for creating a self-sustaining source of nourishment.

Not that I wasn't capable of surviving as an independent. After all, I lived alone, and only children have autonomy drummed into their personalities. For what it's worth, sobriety had made me more productive, more sardonic, more aloof and, ironically, more lonely.

But being alone while sick? That's a different emotional nut entirely.

When I was a child, my yearly bouts with the flu were accompanied by a personalized set of rituals. I had developed them, like MacGyver, out of a minimum of available resources. It was my comfort protocol. For instance, I always like to wear the same pair of pink, footed pajamas with kangaroo pockets, and when I outgrew those, I found a cozy flannel nightgown dotted with prancing lambs that worked as well. Since our television set was in the living room and I generally remained confined to my bedroom when sick, I had a roster of books I liked to read, volumes that promised a universe of discovery amid my solitude. I generally began with a tattered book of jokes so excruciatingly awful that they were deliriously funny, but I soon graduated to a pair of Childcraft volumes; one with nursery rhymes and marvelous, emotive pictures and another one filled with folk tales which, though illustrated less copiously, had more literary substance.

There were stories I liked to read over and over again, and through my childhood years, doing so became a sacrament as soul-defining as anything my parents could have ferreted out of church.

As for them, I'd have to admit that through my sporadic childhood infirmities, my mom had a firmer handle on the situation than my Daddy. She became solicitousness on overdrive, coddling me and making me slimy three-minute eggs, which I didn't particularly like, but which she claimed were somehow curative, and—when dipped in whole wheat toast—became borderline edible. Tangerines contained Vitamin C, so there were lots of tangerines, and she dosed me hourly with honey and lemon juice, a standby trick she'd learned from her Irish grandmother. When I was sick, my Daddy tended to keep his distance, though it never struck me as being from a lack of compassion. He was awkward with contingencies that did not fit inside his business ledger, and his dread of sickness later became understandable at his funeral when I overheard a distant relative confide he'd had a baby sister who'd died from the measles.

Anyway, if such a day exists, Tuesday was the right kind of day in which to be sick. The cloud shroud remained low and ominous and by ten in the morning, the rain became scudding and monotonous. I had no pink pajamas, but my go-to slumming outfit was a pair of old sweats from Cadence High and a faded blue hoodie from Detroit Institute for Creative Studies. I saw no reason to change out of it; I didn't have the strength to go out for more DayQuil had I wanted to.

I didn't have my good-bad joke book handy, but I did have *The Woodland Fairy Book* with impossibly cool, good-great India ink sketches by Arthur Rackham, accentuated with watercolor on the more elaborate plates. The book was filled with stories of magic and seduction, and the weirdest, most intriguing one was 'The Wild Swallows'—a rare fairy tale that finished on a tragic note:

"So, though the princess committed herself to being eternally faithful to her beloved, he married someone else. One night, her former beloved appeared on a white horse and took her away to the place of their first kiss, and it was there that she was found dead in the morning. And this, readers, is one of those stories that has a happy ending not."

The story may have been a buzz-kill, but the accompanying Rackham drawing was not; it was steeped in sensuous lines and textured shadows and his brilliant, translucent tints. On that sick Tuesday in May, it became an unexpected and commanding inspiration: I still had images from the previous day swimming around inside my fevered brain.

In the afternoon my fever broke, and feeling marginally better, I began a pair of paintings, spreading my acrylic tubes on the counter and setting up brush camp on a stool, flip-flopping between two canvases as my mood shifted. The first was my attempt to capture the spooky visage of August Lake. I stole the composition from Rackham, but that didn't matter to me; it was the lake's unique, maudlin color I was after. I wanted to capture the tone of dull dam water reflecting soot-grey clouds overhead, but I couldn't quite pin it down. It was as if something lurked in that mire that defied replication, and gradually, I began to focus on the second painting. Using the canvas as a frame to mimic the rear window, I painted Gabriel in the position I saw him while I lay in the back of the Ford truck.

Gradually, remarkably, ebulliently, Gabriel's portrait did what any decent likeness does: It came alive. Somehow, where the color of the lake had eluded me, the pallor of Gabriel's thin, silvery chemo skin was something that I found I could effectively blend. Where I'd originally seen the obstinacy of marble, I now tried to capture the delicacy of ceramic. When I had outlined the counters of his face and had built the exact hue in his various highlights and shadows, I settled into a painting that became, in my humble estimation, the best work of my truncated career. I felt that I was within striking distance of the stratosphere I'd gaped at in college. Somehow, on that feverish day, I had made a living man out of resin and fabric.

I worked on it until past midnight, then collapsed into my sick bed and slept soundly for a number of hours.

I remember waking with a eureka moment. No doubt, as I think back on it, in that furious microsecond I matured to the level that I had recognized in my most precocious classmates at art school. I got up and returned to my original painting of August Lake. Re-mixing the bloodless, cancer colors I had created for Gabriel's profile, I splashed surface detail across the water on the lake, shrouded sparkles from a sky lit with suffused and struggling sunlight. I mirrored those colors in the overcast sky—I licked at the clouds with chemo dullness and added a spark of light beneath.

And it worked.

I could scarcely believe what I had accomplished. The color was right, and the more I examined it, the more right it seemed. I knew who I wanted to show it to, too. The reasons for that may have grown complex with time, but in the moment, it wasn't complex in the least. I didn't want Julian Vaz to think I was nothing but a dry-drunk with a court order and a virus.

Meeting him had been propitious happenstance, for sure, like encountering a transient on a dark stair in a house you didn't recognize. At that point, I wasn't after his heart. I didn't want his devotion and I didn't want his erection. I simply wanted the guitar-maker to consider me his creative kindred.

Thus, the impetuous success of that painting was foremost among the reasons why, on Thursday morning, with a slap of cold blue air on my warm red face, I left my apartment, drove my Focus to the lot at Pontiac Family Services and waited for the truck to come and shuttle me back toward the cerebral right-hand-man at August Lake.

7.

And yet, it was not to be! It was a simple thing, too: Thursday was Julian's day off.

It wasn't Gabriel at the wheel of the truck, either. It was a black man in a DNR uniform and a ranger's badge that read *'Stony'*.

It can be hard to tell about age with African Americans, but based on his wiry, wooly, white-tufted hair, I'd have placed Stony anywhere from fifty years old to his mid-sixties. In fact, I was outnumbered: The only other community service candidate that morning was a shriveled, shuffling black fellow who had to be in his seventies. He was the color of road tar and had yellow-red eye sclera that I am used to associating with liver damage, but he was polite enough and introduced himself as Odell Bridges. I couldn't imagine what sort of crime had landed him here, but it occurred to me that he might have already spent decades in prison. The system tends to be harder on black men than on pretty young white chicks.

"All aboard," cried Stony, and in deference, I allowed Odell Bridges the shotgun position in the front seat while I hunched in the back again alongside the fire extinguishers and old work gloves.

"Four months to retirement," Stony announced a moment later by way of random small talk, and I assumed it was aimed primarily at Odell Bridges, so I listened half-heartedly for a minute, and in a conversation lull, I asked him what wort of work Julian had assigned us that day.

"Not like on Monday, missy. I hear you spent your whole time sleeping in the ranger's house. Forty thousand winks. Julian off today, back tomorrow if you all want to wait till then. Not too late to take you all back to the parking lot."

Actually, I considered it. But it seemed too obvious and we were already on the I-75 onramp, so I said, "I was sick on Monday. I feel better now, thanks."

"No problem, missy. Young folk always take to Julian, boys and girls alike. He's a poet. Pretty good one, too. I read some of his stuff online."

I replied, "Hey, all I know is that he treated me right and I appreciated it. I was sick. It's over now, I feel fine. I'm here to fulfill my obligation to the great state of Michigan, that's all, then get on with my life."

"I hear that," Stony nodded. "Four months to retirement."

For the rest of the ride, the two coots drawled and rattled at one another. I wasn't sure if they were old friends or if it was merely hood talk, but in either case, they shared life experiences that I did not, so I withdrew.

In the rearview mirror, Stony had me in a sharp, grandfatherly eye. "You remember those pretty young things, don't you, Odell? Back in the school days?"

"Damn sure do," answered Odell. "They all old ladies now. All we done is blink."

Twenty minutes later, we arrived at the park headquarters and as soon as we stepped from the truck, Alan roared from an equipment shed riding a John Deere tractor with some sort of toothy farm implement on the back. He was so tiny he looked like a wart on the back of a triceratops.

"Dixie Chicks!" he sputtered through a florid grin as soon as he saw me, like I hadn't heard some variation on a 'Dixie Chicks' reference several trillion times already in my life.

I nodded wanly and politely.

"Off to rake the beach, boss?" Stony asked.

"Yup! Love you guys, you know that, but I don't trust nobody but me to rake that beach!"

51

"You know best, boss," said Stony, deadpan.

"Whatcha got planned for your chain gang?" Alan chortled.

"We cleaning vaults today, top to bottom. Got to get 'em all spic and span for Memorial Day."

"Yes, indeed we do!" cried Alan. "That's gonna be a big day at August Lake! I can feel it!"

Alan's nose was the color of Odell Bridges' sclera and his own eyes, set deeply behind skin pouches, sparkled like little beads. Before he rumbled away down a two-track he tossed me another waxy grin that made my skin crawled as badly as it had in jail during detox. When he was gone, I said to Stony, "I could smell drink on his breath all the way from here. Hope he doesn't drive that thing into the lake."

Now a semblance of a smile crossed Stony's lips and he showed his white teeth. "If he did, we ain't never gonna hear from old Alan Loya again. Deepest point in that lake there's a drop off over a hundred feet."

I huffed, as righteous as the newly-dry tend to be: "Well, if he's going to run heavy equipment like that, somebody should step in and stage an intervention or something."

"Not for me to say, missy. I'm just trying to keep my head down. Four months to go."

Even without Julian, the day did not seem like it would turn out too horribly. Stony came across as a practical and relatively good-natured fellow and Odell Bridges was frail and polite. The sky was hazy, but it was warm for the middle of May and there was no rain in the forecast. Anyway, 'vault cleaning' sounded like an indoor operation.

We loaded some brushes and bottles of bulk cleaner in the pickup bed. I clambered back in and we drove into the interior of the park. As before, we passed August Lake, where on the far end I saw a moving blip—the tractor with Alan Shanda as a blippier blip straddling it. I thought about the hundred foot hole and Alan driving into it, gleefully, obliviously, but pointedly. Drunks do that with their lives, so why not with their tractors?

Even beneath a brighter sky, August Lake looked murky and corrupt, just as I'd portrayed her with my acrylics. I felt a rush of satisfaction: For a painter, that's the consummation devoutly to be wished.

But the rush quickly faded. Vaults, it turned out, were outhouses. I learned that shortly when we paused before the first of many small, stinking wooden structures scattered throughout the thirteen thousand acre park and Stony sent me inside with a cheap brush, a raggedy broom and a bottle of industrial-strength chemicals. I set to work scrubbing away a lot of caked-on, namelessly repulsive drek clinging to the plastic toilet bowl, the particleboard walls and the stained concrete floors, sweeping down a haunted house's worth of cobwebs. The crapper did not appear to have been cleaned in months, if ever. But I did it diligently, because that was the catechism into which I'd been drilled.

It took me nearly half an hour to finish cleaning the first one, and when I trailed back to the truck, damp, disgusted and sour-bellied, the two black men were still in the front seat, still chatting easily, neither having lifted a finger in the meantime.

If this was Stony's way of punishing me for having overslept in Julian's cottage, I felt suitably punished, and after having repeated the operation at three more outhouses, all the more so. We wound deeper into the empty park and found many of these crude little wooden buildings at the outskirts of trail heads, shadowed by gaunt oaks and maple giants.

Given that it was shaping up to be a solo endeavor, I was able to develop an effective system: I basically hosed down each place with the floral-scented solution and while I waited for the various messes to loosen up, I took the broom to the cobwebs that hung from the rafters and dodged the fat spiders that dropped to my feet like acorns in the fall. As I came to grips with my demeaning purpose that Thursday, among the ammonia fumes blasting from grotesque pits of composting feces and toilet paper, I could hear birds flitting among the branches overhead.

As I've said, I don't like to make waves, and for all I knew, Odell Bridges had some pre-existing condition that preventing him from squatting down and scrubbing crusted excrement off surfaces. Maybe he was arthritic. Who knows? But in the afternoon, returning to the truck for the ninth or tenth time to find the men leaning against the door and talking lazily about the transmission that one might be willing to swap to the other, I spoke up. "This really isn't fair, is it?"

Stony looked at me quizzically and Odell looked away. I shrugged, by then willing to stand my ground. "We're both here on a work program and I'm the only one working," I said.

Stony waited a long time before he responded I know he was searching for the right words and I gave him space to do that. At last he said, "You been in prison, miss?"

I didn't think the two weeks I spend writhing with delirium tremens in county jail counted, so I didn't bring it up. I was here primarily to *avoid* prison I asserted, shaking my head.

"Let me tell you something then. First word of advice they give you inside is to serve your own time, not somebody else's time."

Odell stumped slowly to the edge of the forest, took his hands from his floppy blue jeans and ran fingers through his wiry white hair. Before him, the dappled foliage grew thick and tangled. Leaves trembled and the opaque light filtered through the chuffing clouds and illuminated hidden places.

Stony said, "Odell Bridges cleaned enough white folk toilets for one lifetime."

Well, when a black dude plays that card, you're toast, right? There is no conceivable response. And so the day went. I was petulant, terse, but I troupered on sheepishly. I did my time, not Odell Bridge's time. To his credit, Odell didn't gloat; he talked about how his neighborhood had no street lights and his corner store stopped carrying Swisher Sweets in blueberry. Ultimately I concluded that he had dementia, something Stony may have recognized from the beginning.

It turned out that there were only three more vaults anyway. We had reached the end of the dirt road that marked the periphery of the park, and after that, the shift was done. Stony signed us out and as he drove us back to the Family Center, he continued the ghetto drawl with Odell Bridges while I sat in the rear and pouted, feeling like the lily-white Ohio cracker he rightly supposed I was.

At home I stripped and flung everything into the washer on the two-rinse cycle, and when they were done, I washed them again. In the meantime, I took a shower as hot as I could stand. There is no act of purification more liberating that a hot shower, although I imagine that might be what divorce feels like. I stood under the steaming stream until the entire twenty gallon tank was empty, divorcing myself from stranger shit and the sickly-sweet odor of toilet cleaner. I scrubbed my skin with Aveeno exfoliator and smelled my hands a dozen times to make sure that they smelled like me again. The scrub was advertised as 'Skin Brightener' and randomly, I wondered if black girls strove for 'bright' skin, and this made me think of Takosha again, so when I was dry and inside my terrycloth robe, I sent her another text:

'Why the big ignore, boo? Spent 8 hours cleaning shitters at August Lake. U missed nothing, but I miss U.' - Dix

I didn't call people 'boo', she did, but it made no difference. It was the final volley of warmth I intended to toss over her bow. If I received no response, I wouldn't try again. Sooner or later, pride has to supplant loneliness, right? Maybe I'd catch up with her at a future AA meeting and maybe I wouldn't, but I felt like some bond of intimacy—which may have originated in my own head anyway—had been forever compromised.

I slipped into a long linen night shirt and snuggled into bed. I was not alone; I brought my two paintings with me.

I itched to putter; to doodle with a ripple here and a broken reflection there. But if I learned anything practical in art school beside good-bad art, it was that there comes a time when you need to step back and resist all impulses to dick around with work after you've finished it. We even had a saying: *'Drop the brush and step back from the easel.'* It's like those statistics proving that when you change an answer on an exam you are more likely than not to change it from right to wrong.

I opted to marvel instead. First at the living art, and then, at myself, which was perhaps overdue.

As for tomorrow, short of an overnight diarrhea convention, there were no more outhouses to clean at the park. I'd done them all, and done them well, and I'd done them alone. Tomorrow, Julian would be back on shift. The weather forecast was sensational. I wasn't sick anymore and I had a painting—a portrait, really—of August Lake that I still needed to show off.

I felt as free as a bird overhead and so self-assured it was almost supernatural. When morning came , I knew exactly where I intended to be.

8.

I fell asleep around nine and set my phone alarm to go off at five. I was out of bed, coffeed-up and in the process of retrieving my clothes from the drier when something that Stony had said popped back into my head like a flash of heat lightning. Something about Julian being a published poet.

I fired up my laptop, Google-searched *'julian vaz poetry'* and it came up blank. But I did find a reference for *'julio vaz poetry'* on a site called *poetica.org* and I remembered that little Serafin Tercerio had, in fact, called Julian 'Julio'.

There was no author photograph and the biographical blurb was no help either—it said only, *'Julio Vaz was born in Taiambé, Brazil'.*

Since I hadn't noticed the slightest trace of an accent in Julian's voice, I might have relegated the match to the post-modern internet inconvenience known as 'coincidence'. But then I started to read the poems, and there was something so familiar in Julio Vaz's disembodied words in that lonesome pre-dawn hour that I became instantly and irrevocably intrigued. I first heard it first distinctly in a poem that ran:

I cast your destiny on a suffering day,

In suffering scapes built of suffering clay.

Could I paint your eyes, though sweetly blind?

If so, I would deftly, delicately unbind

The colors in the rippled wake

On a lucent, rising, nameless lake.

The lake—the *color* of the lake? How odd was that? I was hooked, and even more so when I read further: Julian's compassion toward those in need seemed to seethe joyously inside Julio Vaz:

Unblinded and unbound you'd see

Escape unleashed eternally.

Your tears as dew gems, gently dried

Your sobs as soughs are cast aside

Just as we were cast away.

Our lives re-cast this suffering day.

I repeated the next one out loud and found I could easily commit it to memory:

Meadow, grove and healing field,

Soaring spires and sparrow.

You are a circle of events;

You are not an arrow.

Be here now, but cyclically

Around the curving firmaments

And there you'll find your mortal Grail:

Temporary permanence.

I wanted to be at the Pontiac Family Services parking lot early so I could have some justifiable claim to a shotgun post in the truck, intending to pump whoever was driving for a little more information. I became so engrossed by the poetry that I nearly—but not quite—lost track of the time.

For now, sipping coffee, my emotions churned, and I had to check them, because basically and pragmatically, they were total nonsense. I had once fallen in love with Percy Shelley and Lord Byron based on their word imagery alone. I still melted over phrases like *'So when thy shadow falls on me, then am I mute and still, by thee...'* and *'To strongly, wrongly, vainly love thee still...'*

I nurtured and cherished a fantasy image of each of these men as ideal partners in the roiling dreamscapes of Rackham, but in truth, for all I knew, they were men who lived their genuine lives as misogynistic hucksters. But that's what art people do. I understood that: We consider reality little more than raw material from which to build our preferred World Order.

And yet, can you seriously maintain that this line from 'Endymion': *'Of noble natures, of the gloomy days, Of all the unhealthy and o'er-darkened ways..."* echoes with immortality more profound or shivers with emotion more explosive than these words from Julio Vaz's poem 'Formas Naturais'?

Because I can't:

> *The difference of indifference*
>
> *In this evening calm?*
>
> *Yours to me is agony—*
>
> *Out here it's perfect balm.*

> *It rains, it dries, it rains again,*
>
> *The season grows and dies.*
>
> *A circle of rebirth , unlike*

The death within your eyes.

And to me, more provocative still were the dates at the bottom of these poems. They were more than a decade old. If Julio Vaz was Julian Vaz—who looked to be around thirty—he had written them as a teenager.

9.

'The bittersweet tang of reality is more poignant and painful that the isolated tragedies.'

A little heavy for six in the morning? No doubt. But although I had long since given up on composing serious poetry, I remained an avid aspirant, and I had, over the years, jotted down random, non-cohesive thoughts in a journal, a lot of them after my third beer but before my fifth or sixth.

That line was one of them. It was about the death of my Daddy. I pulled out the old journal and it made me cry.

The poems of Julio Vaz inspired another emotional cataclysm, though: A crisis of confidence regarding my painting. At least, about bringing it with me to the park that morning. My plan had been that the piece would establish my identity with Julian, but suddenly, it became more important for me to identify *him*. If Julian was Julio Vaz, spinning such cogent words from a child's mind, it meant that he had talents that were, in my opinion, more prodigious than any I'd dared imagine. That sapped some of my vanity, for sure. In any case, if my feet were not exactly cold, they were chillier than they'd been the night before and I decided that I wasn't eager to show off anything quite yet. Self-doubt began to tiptoe back inside my secret little cubbies, and I felt let down and ridiculous, like a bird afraid of heights.

In the end, caution seemed the prudent course. The painting wasn't going to vanish. It would exist for another time, another encounter, and potentially, for another person.

At least, that's what I told myself.

One thing I knew for certain was that, two wash cycles or not, I didn't want to put on yesterday's clothes in case some rank outhouse residue found a cosmic wormhole. I put on fresh jeans, a cotton hoodie with the fairly neutral *Made in Detroit* slogan on it and did a final mirror check. I thought I looked acceptably humble, clean-cut and forest-pumped and certainly, more than passably pretty.

I stepped out my front door into a sensational morning and the first thing I saw was a cream-colored butterfly flitting around a stray daffodil. It was delicate and translucent, and I took it as a good omen because, ever since he died, my Daddy has existed in my imagination as that particular symbol. When I see a butterfly, I think of his beauty, his lightness, his simplicity and his airy exit.

I was early to the parking lot, but it was overkill: When the green DNR truck showed up, I was the only one waiting. Potter, the grungy tattooed punk, was at the wheel. His skin was sallow and had an un-washed tone. "Looks like it's just me today," I said, climbing into the passenger seat.

"Who else?" he snickered. "That old chick sure couldn't hack it and the colored whore will probably be found in a ditch somewhere."

"Takosha? She's my friend. Why would you say something like that?"

"Because it's true," he said, scratching at a scab on his tattooed forearm. "You didn't hear what happened to her?"

Uh oh. We were pulling onto the freeway; I braced myself like you do when you sense the other shoe is dropping. "What?" I asked.

"Monday? When I was dumping you at the ranger house, the skank found an old half-full bottle of Crown Royal in the weeds and ended up drinking the whole fuckin' thing. By herself. How repulsive is that? Though, considering where her lips have been, maybe not so much."

I experienced the same download of horror and shame I had when I found out about Gabriel's cancer. Potter may have had an air hovering around him so filthy that you couldn't wash it out—not even with the full twenty gallons in an apartment water heater—but this wasn't his fault. If anything, it was my fault. I had convinced Takosha to go pick through the underbrush in the first place.

But the more I thought about it, the more I realized that my guilt had perimeters. As Stony had wisely suggested, Takosha had to serve her own time. I couldn't serve it for her. We're all one long hot swig away from relapse, and metaphorically, there are half-empty Crown Royal bottles everywhere. I was here, trying to improve myself and my lot in life and Takosha was probably working through the bender that would inevitably follow a wagon fall: She'd been candid about her history. At least it explained why she wouldn't return my texts; relapsing alcoholics are like the girl who returns to an abusive lover again and again. Tell me it's pathological and I won't disagree but the fact is, the girl is convinced that she loves him and that this time, it will be different, and becomes obsessed again. Likewise, Takosha no longer had any use for me.

I admit that in ways I was becoming my old Navy ex-fiancé, with no real patience with people lacking resolve to become better people or to keep their word. So maybe I needed to forget about Apathetics Anonymous and become Assholes Anonymous. I had begun to think of drink as immoral, and in my case it pretty much was. What might I have achieved without it? How many August Lake paintings had I aborted, choosing drink over skill? I understood that Takosha was only humoring me anyway. I was a curiosity—a mayonnaise Midwesterner who had briefly inhaled the rarefied atmosphere of total degradation. I wasn't born to it like she was. I was an alcoholic, but I wasn't alcohol itself, and she was. It sounds trite, but there's a difference. You only become the substance you abuse when you are prepared to accept all the consequences that accompany it, and I was not.

Still, I felt that Takosha needed some minor defense, especially against the ditch comment, so I answered: "Julian told me that she made it home safely. That she was dropped off at her own apartment."

"Ah, you'd have to ask Leukemia Boy about that. He drove on Monday, not me."

"'Leukemia Boy,' seriously? What the actual fuck?"

A condescending snicker: "I only do loser delivery on Fridays."

"Fuck you," I replied. It was all I could think to say since his description of us—of me—was essentially accurate.

The rest of the ride passed in grumpy silence. Certainly, I was wondering why Julian hadn't told me about any of this, but I figured I wouldn't have to wonder long. I'd ask him directly.

And I did. But as it turned out, not right away.

When we arrived, Julian was bent over the rear of the tractor with a socket wrench. I came from behind and stood over him and watched graceful sinews contract in his neck. His hair was tan against tan. I said, "Beach comber?"

Julian looked up and seemed genuinely surprised to see me. "It's a landscape rake," he said. "But yeah, we use it at the lake."

"Not to sound like a total 'doesn't-know-about-landscaping' nerd, but why would anyone rake a beach?"

"Geese love that beach more than park visitors. They flock there."

"You mean they crap there?" I laughed. "Oh, well, now I get it. You should have me do it, then. Cleaning up visitor shit has become my core competency." I pronounced it 'shite' to sound funny rather than pissed off.

"I heard," Julian said, shaking his head. "Well, sorry. I'd have spared you that. Anyway, it's great you're on your feet and feeling better. I didn't think we'd see you again."

"Really?" I sniffed. I'd have preferred he said 'I' rather than 'we', but I went on: "Well, for all my minuses, I'm loyal. I committed to forty hours community service at the park and I'll do them come hell or high fever. *'You can't always work with enjoyment, but you can always work with perseverance'.* That's what my Daddy used to say."

Julian stood up, wiping his hand. "I don't put stock in doing things you hate. Most of them don't need to be done anyway. Woods are a haven—they shouldn't atrophy anybody's soul."

"If I hinted that my soul had atrophied, I may have exaggerated slightly."

His bright green eyes were cryptic; his voice was soft, almost a caress. He said, "We can take a trip up to the recycling center today. That will make for an easy shift, I promise."

"Whatever, easy or hard, I am beholden, sir. I'm yours. Where's the recycling center?"

"On a hill that overlooks the lake. It's about a mile from here, but if you don't mind an uphill hike, it's pretty."

"I'm game for a pretty hike."

"Good," he said, laying the wrench on the landscape rake. "Then we'll go."

And so, the conversation about Takosha was temporarily derailed. We started down a trail that snaked from behind the equipment shed and rambled immediately into thick woods where the trees were fifty feet tall and made a stately ceiling. There were chirrups and rustles from darting birds; the air grew moist and so concentrated it felt like I was breathing from a machine.

We came to a low spot near a huge pile of logs that someone had once cut and then abandoned to the ferns that now nearly enveloped them. We had to slow down and pass single file. Tentatively, I said , "Hey, Julian? Can I say something honestly?"

He continued to pick a way forward and paused before he answered, "Of course."

"Potter, that dude who picked me up? He seems to have a problem with black people. Thought I'd mention it, because it's uncool. He drops the 'n' bomb a lot."

He replied, "Potter is pretty rough. He aged out of foster care last year and he's learning. He's basically a street kid trapped in the identity he thinks was defined for him. I suppose he still believes it. I'll talk to him."

"Guess I can identify with identity issues. I don't think you need to say much; just about that word. Bet he doesn't say it around Stony."

"Stony understands forest therapy as much as anyone. It gives street kids perspectives that even their worst memories can't ruin. He's living proof."

"Little Serafin told me something similar. Admirable, I must say."

"Serafin Tercerio is wise despite what schools tell him. He knows truths more valuable than state capitals and multiplication tables."

"He also said that Gabriel has cancer. Is that true? My God, that's some awful shit for a kid his age.

This time I didn't pronounce it 'shite', but I said, "You don't have to say more about Gabriel. It's none of my business. Just tell me if I'm talking too much."

"Everyone should talk less in the woods," he said. "You experience more."

I didn't get the impression that the response was an admonition so much as a statement of fundamentals. So I shut up: I stood beside him in total stillness for a long time; ten minutes or more. I cleared my mental calendar. I forgot about Gabriel, Potter and Takosha. I listened and sought out whiffs of scents. All around us were patters, clicks, chirps and hums among the leaves. The air was silvery and spiked with forest incense. I've never been inside a genuine Renaissance cathedral, but I imagine the experience must be like this.

When Julian finally spoke again, his voice was sonorous and soft. It glided over me: "Now you have your head where it belongs."

"Wow," I said, genuinely impressed. "Is it too late to change my mind? Working for the DNR is kind of kickass after all."

"Don't let the logo throw you," he said, pointing to his left, his right, then over his head. "We work for the seasons. Every time we're outside, we're answering to nobody but nature."

"How's it feel to have a female boss?"

He smile was placid and sincere: "Like there's order in the cosmos."

I sensed no sarcasm, but only reverence, though clearly a reverence he knew more intimately than me. As a trait, I would come to associate such gentle eddies of humor as one of his most charming traits. In fact, the expression he wore at that moment was the one in which the lay of his features seemed most at ease. Like the poems of Julio Vaz, his words burrowed deep inside me, and I was quickly conceding that he had things to teach that I saw value in learning.

We veered upward into gloom and we climbed through trailing vines and heaving roots, across little trickling creeks and steadily thicker underbrush. Huge, moss-slicked boulders appeared on either side, looking like they'd been hurled there by giants. Julian picked his way through them and I followed as best I could. He was obviously used to this walk, and with his sleeves rolled up, the muscles in his arm looks like knots in a rope. Gratefully, he didn't look back too often, and when he did, I gave him a thumb's up to indicate that my head was still where it was supposed to be.

In time we emerged onto an open hilltop that stood in the stark, beautiful sunshine like an eye in a storm of trees. It was a meadow spangled with yellow wildflowers and ringed with half a dozen weathered limestone grave markers.

At their center was a marble angel reaching plaintively toward heaven; the real deal, not an image from a truck window. The inscription read *'Levi August, Departed this life November 12, 1845, Aged 37 years, 4 months and 12 days'* and the epitaph was a couplet: *'With a greater thing to do; Deep peace of the quiet earth to you.'*

I was thoroughly charmed. "Where are we?" I asked. "I thought we were going to the recycling center."

"And here we are, standing in the dust of our patron capitalist."

I was delighted and began to skirt around, brushing grass from the faded stones and reading out the names. Beside Levi, there was his wife Lillie and their four children.

"This is totally cool," I cried. "And yeah, I get it. They've all been recycled. So, what am I gonna do up here? Weed?"

"Why would you weed?"

"Because there's no outhouses to clean. Weeding is maintenance and I'm here to maintain."

He shrugged. "Everything seems to be maintaining itself fine."

The cemetery was about fifty feet across and the ground was still damp with dew. Ancient rings showed where trees had been felled to make the clearing, and from the proximity of Levi's angel, you could see the broad vista of the park, a sea of lime and emerald beneath a seamless sky with only the anemic lake as a blight on the beauty.

The temperature hovered in the mid-sixties. The breeze was neither warm nor cool. As a kid, this was the kind of weather I'd always hoped for on my birthday, the one day in the year when kids are programmed to feel unique, like the entire goddamn universe should pause to acknowledge their remarkable existence. And what better a demonstration of one's remarkableness than the universe tossing you perfect weather?

Birthdays, of course, over-promise and under-deliver, but on this particular Friday morning in May, squatting on a hilltop, a breath of new life suffused my body. I felt fluttery, and in shameless hyperbole, I said, "Is this the most beautiful day in history, or what?"

I think it was the first time I heard Julian laugh out loud, and the sound struck me as light and unaffected. I added, "Except for that that silly lake. No offense, but it's the only thing I can see from here that's unrelentingly ghastly."

"Do you want to know why?"

"Absolutely. I'm a little OCD about it—it's been bugging me for days."

"It's the only thing you can see from here that's man-made."

Julian sat down on the warm grass and I sprawled kitty corner. With his head slightly tilted, I saw him in profile. Thomas Hood might have described his nose as 'delicately aquiline'. His cheek was smooth and vital, and in this light, at this moment, he was my idealized version of the gender—crisply masculine and serenely, almost sadly, contemplative, the kind of profile that ends up on a coin. I thought he had a sun-like quality that made staring unwise and I turned back to the panorama.

"Stony said there's a place in the lake that's like a hundred feet deep. What's up with that?"

"It's dam water, mostly under ten feet and a lot of it under four. But yeah, near the center there's a sinkhole. There's a limestone deposit underneath that keeps dissolving. It's a hundred feet deep now and it gets deeper all the time. The interchange of currents is what keeps the silt churned up, cold water from the bottom of the hole and warm water from the surface. It never clears up, so anglers don't like to fish in it and swimmers don't like to swim in it."

"What about you, Julian? Do you like it?"

"I see a body struggling against an imposed order and I find that intense. Is that 'like'?"

"Why not? Anyway, I was struck by the awful color from the moment I saw it; how out of synch it looked with everything around it. It's the same shade of yuck under a blue sky as under a storm. I've never seen anything like that before. In fact, I ended up doing a painting of it and it took me two days to get the color values right."

"A painting, really?" Julian asked. "I'd like to see it."

The idea sounded heartfelt and I answered, "Actually, I'd like to show it to you, too—to see if I caught what you see. The color especially. I mean, if you had to name the color of the lake right now, to describe it in language instead of paint, what would you say it is?"

"I don't see a single color. I see an infinite regression of colors."

"Humor me then? Try a description anyway. When you speak, you're very eloquent. Words are your talent, but I think you know that. Channel one of the great bards if you want to. How would a famous poet describe the color of that lake?"

He stood up and faced the expanse and was so long in responding that I wondered what imposed order he might be struggling against. In a moment, I began to regret having asked at all, but finally, he said, "If you illuminated a shadow and there was nothing substantial underneath? That's the color you'd see."

My breath quickened. "Wow," I said. "Incredibly beautiful—that's it exactly."

In art school, one of my professors said that the concept of shadow color belonged originally to Renoir. I ran with the thought, saying, "Illuminating shadows is what morning does, right? Morning vanquishes darkness and goes looking for the substance again. I felt that sort of energy the minute I stepped out of the darkness of the woods and into the sunshine here. Dawn is something you just want to be a part of it, if for no other reason than to try absorb some of that strength."

"The might of morning," he replied.

I'm a sucker for alliteration, then as now, and figured I'd wriggle through the wormhole: "By any chance, were you just channeling a poet named Julio Vaz?"

He gave me a curious look; placid, but vaguely puzzled. I added, "I don't want you to think I stalked you or anything. I hate that kind of thing. It's nothing like that. Stony told me you were a published poet, so I Googled your name. Julio Vaz came up and I wondered if it was you, like in a former life. I'm sorry if that sounds creepy."

"It's fine," he said. "It's the same life, but it was a long time ago."

"If you don't mind me saying so, what I read sounded completely fresh. Immediate: *Something in the veiled creation, when the world first came to be: One was you and one was me.* See, I even memorized one of the poems. Are you flattered? I would be."

He didn't seem flattered so much as privately amused. "Those were lyrics," he said. "When I was a kid, I built a guitar and afterward, it seemed silly not to play it, so I wound up writing some songs. *Veiled Creation* was one of them."

I nodded earnestly. "I can see them as lyrics, definitely. The words are musical. Isn't that what poetry is supposed to be? Life turned into rhythm?"

He shrugged; wind took a strand of his hair. "I don't see the world like that anymore."

"Why not? It's a wonderful way to see the world."

"But it's not the correct way. The world doesn't rhyme. Nature doesn't think like a poet. There's nothing good or bad; things are merely adapted to an end. Once that occurs to you, you adjust your output accordingly."

"No more poems from Julio since then? Debbie downer. Anyway, what I read was amazingly fluent, and I should know; I've been reading poetry compulsively since I was a kid."

"Reading poetry clears your pathways, Dixie. That's fine—they're yours to clear and yours to follow."

"Well, you must have thought so too at one time or you wouldn't have had them published."

"Oh, well, I didn't."

"Well, somebody did. Who, then?"

"Madrinha."

Insanely, I felt the same quick stab in my soft parts as I did when I thought he was winking at Takosha instead of me; a peculiar, silly, totally-out-of-line heart thud: "I assume Madrinha is the person you wrote *Veiled Creation* for? Your lover?"

"*Madrinha* means 'godmother'. That's an important title for a woman to have where I was raised, especially if you believe in symbols. Madrinha shared a lot of things with me. Does that make her a lover?"

Unless he was having sex with his own godmother, I was pretty sure that it didn't. He didn't seem eager to say more, and I respected that. Anyway, if he was writing to his godmother and not to his paramour, it quelled my brief, breathless, idiotic pangs.

I sat up. Far off on the chlorotic lake, I saw another man-made thing: Alan, looking

69

like a canker with his tractor and his landscape rake. Even from this distance his head looked too big for his body.

"Raking the beach looks pretty basic." I pointed out. "Why doesn't your boss trust anyone else but him to do it?

"Is that what he said?" Julian answered, shaking his head. " Well, he's paranoid, that's true. Did you notice the cameras installed in the park? He sits in his cage and watches loops of tape. He doesn't trust anybody."

"He seems to trust you," I said.

"He doesn't have much choice if he wants to maintain his lifestyle."

"Still, it must be sort of nice to have your boss be so dependent on you. I mean, as long as you're doing something you really want to do. Are you? Working here in the park?"

"Being outside all day, tracking cycles, seed to deadfall? I've never wanted to do anything else."

I lay back in the spongy turf. Around us, birds rose from the sumptuous forest and chased each other across a sky dappled with soft white puffs.

"I don't know why people bitch about this community service thing," I said suddenly. "It's pretty sweet. Even that silly lake restored my belief in what I could do."

He said, "See? That's the right way to view the world. It's accurate. There are only two revelations worth anything at all. Your relationship with nature and your relationship with yourself.

"Now, I really wish I had brought the painting with me."

"So why didn't you?"

"I don't know. At the last minute, I got cold feet. Lukewarm feet anyway. Stage fright."

"Why?"

Why? Well, maybe I couldn't say it out loud just yet because it got thick too quickly. Because I've had a strange few years? Because I went to art school with some ungodly talents who were becoming tradesmen and craftswomen while I was sitting in Wolski's waiting for some drunk to buy me a round? Because, viruses aside, I was suffering from the real alpha predator, the one truly at the top of the food chain—personal doubt?

But it was a sunny day in May and I answered simply, "My ego chi wasn't up to it, Julian. I really wish I had, though. I have to work tomorrow and Sunday at my real-fake job, so I can't be back to the park until Monday. If I want to be a show off, it will have to wait."

"Not if you go home and get it," he replied simply. "Bring it to the cottage. I'd be happy to have you back again."

I tried to couch my response with less excitement than I felt. "I'm sorely tempted, believe me; your charm precedes you. I hear you're the Pied Piper of August Lake. But, I imposed enough on Monday—I took some crap about that from Stony. Even a tender heart like yours must have limits."

"Test them as much as you want. You know where I am. I have trout from the stream and ramps and morels from the forest and if you come, there's a spot at the table for you tonight, painting and all. "

A breeze took another errant lock of hair. His face was a perfect outline. I couldn't name the color of the lake, but in my sappy version of poetry I might have said his hair was a blend of toffee and tarnished gold. Good-bad imagery ? I suppose it is, which is why I stick to graphics.

But I was nosy and I said, "Can I ask you one more question about Gabriel? Not to be morbid, but is he going to pull through? Recover?"

"Another round of chemotherapy starts next week," Julian replied.

"Again, it's none of my business, but who *pays* for all that? Didn't you say he was a street kid?"

Julian's lips pursed slightly, but the words seemed offhand. "I pay for it."

That stopped me, and I felt some limestone dissolve beneath me. "Wow, isn't that, like, a fortune? Silly question. It must be."

The lag time came, the wink between the flash of lightning and the crash of thunder. He answered and I sensed slight but profound tension: "My father was wealthy and when he died, I inherited a lot of things I didn't want and certainly don't need. It turns out that Gabriel does."

Now, obviously, I had to wonder if Gabriel was his lover. I *had* to wonder that, naturally. And I considered it very seriously. I was a lot less Cadence naïve than I'd been, but even so, there wasn't the slightest vibe to indicate it, and anyway, I wasn't entirely sure it mattered. At that point, my groundswell of infatuation did not require hanky panky.

But unless I had lost all my instincts about men, I felt physical chemistry between us, and certainly, sparks of attraction directed at me. They were the same ones I'd been fielding since high school. Although I was not necessarily in pursuit of a sexual fling, if I was honest, I wasn't keen on a godparent-type relationship either, though I was quite certain I wanted someone to write a *Veiled Creation* about me.

Ultimately I concluded that something much more intimate was at the root of the relationship between Julio/Julian and his mysterious gang of street urchins. The whole thing began to spiral a bit in my mind, so I pushed a final question that now occurred to me: "How old were you when your father died?"

"Fourteen," he said, and the bond which may as yet have been imperceptible to him grew mightily in me.

I sighed, and really was done with the prying. He seemed complacent again. I had broached delicate stuff and had not been shut down completely, and I saw no reason to spoil it further. We didn't speak again for a long time, and in that hush, I thought that something profound was moving. I don't know how to better craft that sentiment; I'm no Julio Vaz.

In time I rose and explored the family plot. I stroked the cool, moss-mottled flesh of the stone angel and imagined the sculptor, a century before, finishing up, daubing sweat and surveying his work with pride. To the left, an old tombstone lay lightly above Hannah August, who had died at the age of three. The inscription was disintegrating and barely legible. The epitaph read, *'Daughter of Levi & Lillie August: A little bud of love to bloom with God above.'*

The other children had survived their father by more than fifty years and they, no doubt, had lived with their own bittersweet tangs of reality, their own missed opportunities and their own tragedies. I wanted to tell Julian about my sweet Daddy who also died when I was fourteen. I wanted to tell him about the friendship I shared with my father and how my love for him grows more precious as the years go by. I wanted to ask him if he felt the same way about his father. I even wanted him to know about my shoe-gazer common-law husband who'd traded his life for his lifestyle, getting his brains beaten out while I sat in Wolski's trying to flirt my way into free vodka.

As for the tides that were shifting within me, as much as I hated to make the analogy, I knew I was becoming intoxicated. And I wanted another round. I wanted an emotional infusion of Julian's street kid altruism and I wanted it directed at me. My hungers were not chemo-level, but they were keen nonetheless.

But as Serafin Tercerio had maintained, there was politesse. I didn't want something for nothing. I wanted the equilibrium upheld. Suddenly, I didn't just want him to see the painting, I wanted to present it to him as a gift.

So later, as the day began to wear away, trying not to sound too pathetic, I said, "That portrait of August Lake is really sort of a feather in my vanity cap, I admit it. Were you serious about me bringing it around tonight to show it to you?"

His tone was soft and gentle, without a trace of condescension: "I think you know I was serious."

I tried to temper my pleasure by sounding lighthearted and casual: "Who knows what in the fuck I know, Julio. It seems like I only make friends by accident."

10.

That evening, I returned again to the small stone house in the forest. It was set snugly into the fold of a hill and there was a soft glow from the windows and a snake of smoke corkscrewing from the chimney.

As I pulled my rusting Focus into a bare spot beneath a stand of pine trees, I had a flashback to a conversation I'd once had with Corky while scrolling through some good-bad art by Thomas Kinkade. There was a painting of a cabin in the forest where the sun was low and there was soft ochre leaking from the windows and chimney smoke skewed toward a beetling mountain rage in the background.

Minus the mountains, the scene I now faced was identical. The conversation with Corky had been memorable because I had been bothered by a single element in the otherwise moving, if totally cheesecake artwork: I didn't know if it represented dawn or dusk. To me, that was massively important. I was trying to place myself inside Kinkade's mind to gauge why he'd made certain choices related to composition, the variety and intensity of pigment and the placement of landscape elements. Certainly, the might of morning and the drive of dusk required different approaches, and since I could not figure out which one was portrayed, it represented an aesthetic fail.

Yet glancing at it, Corky remarked instantly, "It's evening."

Although he was oblivious to the macrocosm, Corky had been a whiz at minutia. He said, "Prevailing wind comes from the west. Look at the shadows to see where the sun is supposed to be, then look at the direction the smoke is moving. It's evening."

Outside, the shadows and the smoke from Julian's chimney confirmed the physics, and the lesson was the opposite of the standard one; it was the same one I had learned with the flat rabbit on Robinwood: There were times when you should indeed sweat the small stuff. I stepped out of the car and I inhaled deeply, as you do before you spring from a diving board. The air was pine perfume and my own exhaust.

Julian met me at the door. He was wearing a light muslin shirt covered in intricate, embroidered patterns; his flaxen hair was also loose. He made a different picture than he had at the park a few hours before. At that point, we had parted company and I'd shaken his hand in a perfunctory, business-like gesture, but now that I was off the clock, I set the painting down just inside the door and greeted him with a warm hug. He did not draw back and I embraced with all the nuanced instinct that many eons of evolution have engineered; the subtle language that expresses in nanoseconds what poets—even the best ones—struggle to do in volumes.

From this proximity, the smells of him were his signature. If I had to guess, it was woodruff or something else savory from the herb patch. I'm sure if I'd asked, he'd have told me. He'd probably have told me made his own soap out of it, and that would account for his scent.

The electricity in a battery travels irresistibly along a set path, and that question would have been the opening salvo of an interesting evening, except that at that moment a bright but weak voice cried out, *"La Guera!"*

It was an interesting evening all the same.

It turned out that Serafin Tercerio had come down with my flu and was now resting in the pine sick bed, hands behind his head, eyes somewhat glassy, with a goofy simper on his face. Julian said, "He calls you *La Guera* because of your hair. I'm *El Guero* because of mine."

"I read a lot of Pablo Neruda between cocktails," I said. "I thought *'guera'* meant 'war'."

"That's *'Guerra'*," Julian replied, trilling his 'r's, smiling lightly. "Show me your painting."

He stooped to pick it up, unwrapped it and held it at arm's length, and seemed instantly absorbed. Since there is nothing on earth more awkward for either side than watching someone appraise something you care deeply about, I turned to Serafin Tercerio.

"Don't come close to me or you'll catch it again," he warned in a lilting chirp.

"Aw, honey, if you caught it from me, I'm immune for a while." I bent nearer and put my hand against his hot forehead. "That's how it works—otherwise we'd all be passing these bugs back and forth like a volleyball..."

His eyes were large and lucent: "You can't catch it anymore?"

I shrugged and smiled. "Not for a while and I'm not even sure why. You'll have to ask Father Nature over there. Julian?"

It was an excuse to shoot Julian a sideways glance. He was still studying the painting. He said, "Even alpha predators have their underbellies," he answered.

"Let me see the picture!" cried Serafin.

Julian carried the painting over to Serafin, and, standing very close to me, held it up for Serafin to see. "What do you think?"

"That picture will be alive after the lake is dead," Serafin pronounced with solemn exuberance.

"See that?" Julian said. "I told you he was wise."

"Do you think he's right? Truthfully? I mean, you can be brutal with me, Julian. I went to school with some of the biggest art assholes on the planet, so trust me— criticism, I can take."

"But I have no criticism," Julian answered easily. "It's a spectacular painting. It's correct on every level."

"Oh my God," I blushed. "I am beyond flattered. I was so worried..."

"But why? You don't recognize your own authority?"

"Oh, I do. I just didn't think anybody else did. I'm used to that. For me personally the painting works, but other than the color and my own head trip, I'm not really sure why. Frankly, I wish I did."

Julian answered as if it was the most obvious thing in the world: "Because with most art, a painter begins with an exterior and works a path inward. In this one, it looks like you started from the inside and worked your way out."

"I did!" I gushed in giddy amazement. "Exactly! I was so obsessed with that silly lake, but I couldn't put my finger on it until I got ahold of a brush. The ugliness is so unique it tormented me. I was desperate to reproduce it."

"But there's no ugliness in your painting. There's only truth."

"Well," I said, not entirely willing to unravel the skein of compliments by contradicting him, but curious anyway: "Can't something be ugly and true at the same time?"

"I've never seen it. I don't now. Ugliness is superficial and there's nothing superficial here. You painted what you saw, and you saw what goes deeper than eyesight. You saw what's invisible because your eye was fixed on metaphysics. That's what you were looking for. There's not a trace of ugliness here, just another strata of beauty—the one that exists beneath the water, beneath the sinkhole, beneath everything. It's a composite and it's much better than words, mine or anybody's. Actually, I'd love to hang it up, if you'd allow me to."

"Allow you? I'd be forever honored, Julian. You appreciate truth? Here's some: When I was finished with it, I sort of understood that I wanted you to have it, but we were basically strangers and I just didn't have the nerve to say so."

He nodded, but seemed neither appreciative nor dismissive, as if his ownership of the painting—my presenting it to him here and now—was the correct order of the universe. He removed a dark wooden plaque that had hung above the hearth and replaced it with my painting. He stood back and looked at again.

"Now the trillion dollar question," I said nervously. "You like the piece, okay, but does it fit here? Inside your home?"

"As if it lived here all along," he answered instantly.

Thus, I was delivered into that special heavenly cozy reserved for five or six instants in our lifetimes, and I really didn't want to risk milking it further. So I settled into my glory and examined the carved board he'd removed to make room for the painting. It was dark and exotic, with strange words formed in it: *'Naa tüpüla taashi süma sülu'u nakua'ipa.'*

"What in the world does *that* mean?" I asked. "And in what language?"

"It's tribal—Luanhão people from the Mato Grosso. It means, *'Forests Without White Men'*.

I thought about that for a second, and, having no suitable response, resorted to my default attitude— facetiousness: "What about white women?"

The shadow of a smile crossed his lips. "You'd have to ask Madrinha. She carved it.

The heart darts that had afflicted me earlier were gone: Above the mantle, in Julian's home, where he slept, my artwork now supplanted Madrinha's.

In awe of myself and this magic moment, I turned back to Serafin. His bright eyes were striking; if I was a poet, I'd say that somehow, they held pain without melancholy. He exuded an overwhelming innocence and a trace of an otherworldly stupor.

"Serafin looks like he's had some Indian tea."

"Indeed," Julian answered. "Would you like some?"

"I'm really not supposed to be getting high."

"It doesn't work like that," he said. "Jivarrão doesn't make you high, it makes you transcendentally wide."

"Oh, it's fattening? Then I *really* don't want any."

Julian nodded and when I said, "That was my attempt at a joke," he answered, "I know."

Above his head there was a garland of dried garlic bulbs. He removed a papery head and began to peel it. His fingers moved quickly, as deft as any chef's. On the butcher block by the cast iron stove were some fat, pinkish fish fillets and a jumble of wrinkled brown mushrooms. The workspace was constricted, and rather than be a further distraction, I said, "Hey, Serafin Tercerio. Want me to tell you a sick-kid story while *El Guero* cooks?"

"Yes!" he cried in glee.

"Okay then!" I answered, and I began to tell him 'The Wild Swallows' and by the time I got to the part where the gorgeous prince asks for the princess's hand in marriage, Serafin was asleep.

I held the boy's fevered warm hands and before I rose, I kissed his rosy brow. Then I moved to a stool by the hearth, by my painting, and watched Julian cook.

He was facile with a pan. More so than I was, for sure. He sautéed the wrinkled mushroom buds in garlic and leek, and stirred in a reddish sauce from a jar that looked to be home-canned.

"I love this cottage." I said at last. "It's something out of *The Woodland Fairy Book*, all incense and forest smells. How come you've got it instead of your boss? Nothing personal, but it seems like a place like this would be an executive perk. Do you have secret photos of him or something?"

My scattershot sense of humor seemed to miss more marks than it hit. Julian answered, "It would be his, but Alan has teenage children he sees on weekends. This place isn't really set up for those kind of kids—there's no Wi-Fi."

"Serafin seems comfortable enough. Does he live here too?"

"Whenever he needs to. The park crew knows they're welcome here when they need a place to go. A lot of them come from broken homes."

"That's really magnificent of you, Julian," I said, and I meant it.

On the shelf above his head were Mason jars filled with sauces of various shades, with labels that read things like *'Molho'* and *'Churrasco'*.

"Guero, Guerra... Are you fluent in Spanish?"

"It's Portuguese," he said as he placed the rose-colored filets in a sizzling pan.

"I saw in the bio that Julio Vaz was born in Brazil. I thought I might have heard a little Latin cadence way deep inside your voice. Where do you come from, originally?"

It was tentative territory and I didn't want to push into too aggressively, but, with the room warm and food scents wafting, he seemed comfortable and within his element. In fact, his response was soft and no longer seemed strained. He said, "I come from a river town on the Tocantins. Taiambé. Very rural and remote."

"Not to bring it up again, but I know what happened when you were fourteen. Did you come here before that or after that? "

"Just after. We had a cousin here who helped set us up."

"Can I ask you about your parents? Is that fair game? Like, how they met or something?"

"My father had a big medical practice in São Paulo, but he spent time in the field. He was in Taiambé with a group dealing with a local outbreak of Rycanosoma—a disease spread by bugs that live in straw roofs. My mother had it and they met her when he treated her."

"Wow, that's weirdly romantic. Bronte sisters stuff. Were you close to your father?"

"I wouldn't say so."

"Then I won't talk about him again unless you want me to. Is your mother still here? Are you—were you—close to her?"

"She's a little eccentric. She's still in the same house in Bloomfield Hills we bought when we moved here..."

"If you can afford to live in Bloomfield Hills, you're allowed a bit of eccentricity. How is she eccentric? In what way?"

"In most ways. At least, when she's judged by people not from Taiambé. It's a river village, on the edge of the forest, and people from the forest have unique attitudes to say the least. They have primordial faith, and that's something you can't wipe away."

"If you don't want to say more about her, I'm fine with it."

I gave him space, and in a moment, he said, "Well, we grew up around animals. In Taiambé, she rescued hurt ones from the jungle. When she took in strays here, it struck people in her neighborhood as strange."

"Strange? It's actually beautiful that she still does it."

"Ah, well, she's debilitated now. Her disease could be treated, not cured. It progressed. My sister cares for her. "

"Oh, geez—I'm sorry to hear that. Again, don't talk about it if you don't want to. But a sister? Talk about her, then. I'm an only child. I wish I had a sister. What's yours like?"

"Pious," he said. "She's a *curandeira,* a spiritual healer. Very skilled in that way."

I was thinking of my own family story now, and I wanted to share it, of course, but before I got to it, I had a question. It was insolent, but fair, I thought, in the 'all's fair' sense:

"I shouldn't pry," I said as I continued to pry: "I've heard about your sister, your mother and your godmother and I'm compelled to ask you, *El Guero.* Don't think too awfully of me. Are there other women in your life right now?"

"The cosmos. You said so yourself."

"That's all?"

"That's all," he answered.

I felt inordinately and disproportionately appeased.

Julian served the meal on crockery plates and it was marvelous. The trout was buttery, sweet and perfectly cooked. We had a three-star chef at Alchemy, but this blew away Catch of the Day by a country mile. "I take it these fish didn't come from August Lake."

"There's no trout in that lake," he said. "But there's a stream in the North Unit that's not part of that system at all. That's where the wild ramps grow. The morels are from the underneath the pines out front; they'll only be in season another week

81

or so."

Serafin murmured in his sleep. Maybe I was still percolating with the exhilaration of Julian's praise, but I was washed in genuine emotion, a feeling of being part of some offbeat family unit. I'm not sure I've felt that rush of belonging since I was five years old. I felt cushioned by my surroundings and strangely maternal.

And maybe that's why I went and stroked Serafin's hot cheek. I never thought my passions ran toward motherhood, although I guess I had tended to Corky's needs more like a mom than a wife. He'd been such a human mess that he needed that level of cosseting and he'd been such an entitled twat that he thought he deserved it. In retrospect, I wondered if that was why the sex was so sporadic. Moms make better servants than fuckmates, and so, the tangled web is woven.

I said, "Should we wake him up while the food is hot?

Julian said, "His stomach is probably still off. This will be too rich."

"Know what my mother used to do? She could never remember whether to feed a fever or feed a cold, so she just fed them both. I could boil him some of those eggs. My mom said boiled eggs were curative."

He looked at me closely. "I think you'd make a very tender mother, Dixie."

That stopped me. I don't entirely know why. I had wanted to share my entire story, of course, bliss to blisters, but the opportunity had eluded me. Now it presented itself on a zephyr. "No I wouldn't," I whispered. "I won't. I can't have children."

I did a series of slow yoga exhales and inhales, but without warning, the bubble that had welled in my throat burst the levee and I started to cry. I was mortified, even when Julian came up behind me and laid his hands on my shoulders, holding them there with firm, incessant gentleness.

I was touched to the core, but too embarrassed to appreciate the physical intimacy for long. I choked and tried desperately to get it together. Wiping my eyes with one hand and stroking Julian's hand with the other, I said. "Well, having children was nothing I ever really planned on anyway."

Softly, he replied, "Madrinha can't have children either."

"Well, then; there's something else I share with her. That and wall space."

I rose and gradually took charge of my emotions, and after that, we washed dishes together in a pair of enameled basins. On the subject itself, I wanted to reciprocate, to ask him if he had children, or if he wanted children, but I still felt too raw to risk it.

Instead, I asked him his age, first volunteering my own. "I'm 27," I said. "28 this summer. You?"

"I think of age more as insight, not years."

"I respect that," I answered. "I can come close to working it out anyway if you wrote *Veiled Creation* as a teenager."

"Oh, I don't mind telling you," he said. "According to the legal papers, I'm 30."

"Well, legal papers are good enough for me. And if it's any consolation to you for my nosiness, you have the insight of someone who's 130."

The last of the yellow light had faded from the sky; candles were lit throughout the room—they were made of beeswax and bayberry. I know because I asked. Serafin awakened and his nostrils dilated against the scents; the bed creaked as he shifted positions and sat up.

Julian had called it: He wouldn't touch the trout, but I boiled him duck eggs and he ate them with gusto. Afterward, he said in his softly broken English, "Tell me the rest of the princess story, *Guera*."

I thought about it for a moment and said, "Maybe not that one, Serafin Tercerio. Let me tell you another one, right from the beginning. This time, I'll tell you one with a happy ending."

11.

To me, that Friday remains suspended in a sort of holiness; a day where it remained sunny until long after dark and briefly, Julian became my Apollo, my golden morning.

I stayed past eleven and when I left, I kissed Julian with ardor, if not necessarily passion. Not yet, not with Serafin there, and he kissed me back with identical intent, or so I thought. I once read a poet—whose name, regrettably, I can't call to mind—describe such a kiss as *'a kiss of essence'*.

In the time after Serafin drifted off to sleep again, I asked Julian if he could explain Madrinha's cryptic carving, which was—I was forced to concede after viewing it more closely—a marvelous piece of folk art, quite skillfully done.

He said: "Before white men, before white women too, before borders, before countries, people were obligated only to what surrounded them. There was no hierarchy, no bureaucracy, no possessions. Survival meant cooperation. Competition was fatal. Look around August Lake. You have to pay the state to enter the park and it's empty. In the meantime, it could be sustaining an entire tribe."

"I know we really raked American Indians over the coals, if that's what you mean. That was pretty uncool."

"Things are adapted to an end," he reminded me, his voice turning briefly hollow. "But you can still see the paradox. It was a chance of a lifetime, but meeting natives didn't make white people more philosophical or complex. They annihilated the native mindset. They didn't care about metaphysics . To them, it was economics."

"A meditative, metaphysical mindset. I'm sick of being faithless, so alliteration is now my new faith! I may have dumped the one I grew up with, but I think I could learn to embrace that one."

"You genuinely believe that you're faithless?" he asked with gentle skepticism.

"I'm an atheist, I guess. I tried that church-every-Sunday things when I was a kid under penalty of eternal damnation. Guess I never saw the return on the investment."

He was quiet for a long time, but then he said, "Church doesn't represent faith, Dixie. When you die, you either come face to face with your soul or you come face to face with your nothingness. Either way, whether or not you accepted any of it makes no difference."

That made sense and I agreed.

"But you aren't an atheist," he said, casting his arm in the direction of the hearth. "Look at your painting, overflowing with perception and insight. As keen and perceptive as it is, it's still only a mirage of a lake. How can you maintain that the copy is the work of an artist but not the original?"

He had philosophies I was interested in learning, and this was one of them. I told him so. In any case, I had two more days of community service owed, and although it was now a gentle joke, It remained a non-awkward link between us. I asked him about it and we agreed to meet again, Monday morning. No more truck shuttle—our business relationship had ended, and it was realistic to both of us if I just drove out to his cottage.

"We'll go subsistence hunting, then," he said. "I'll show you how to do it. The park is overflowing with wild turkeys this time of year."

"I've never shot a gun in my life," I confessed.

"I haven't either," he answered, and took a wooden slingshot from a hook near the mantel. It was the one he'd been carving when I'd awoken from my fever in the cottage, the one he'd said was for the Philistines.

I was flushed, and I remained blissful and comfortable on the ride back to my apartment. I thought about what he had said about the lake, about my painting, and I conceded his point about ugliness. The lake was strange, for sure. But 'ugly' is a judgment. Strange is merely an admission that you have gaps in your ability to appreciate.

When I got back to my apartment, I resurrected my old poetry journal and on a single page wrote *'Virile domesticity'*.

Among the random, pretty thoughts I'd written there, it was one of the few snippets not even remotely related to my father.

12.

The next day I worked the dinner shift at Alchemy. I arrived at four twenty and was getting a jump on the side-work, folding linen napkins, polishing wine glasses and organizing silverware, when the owner approached me.

Jennifer Kannenburg was a gym-thin woman in her forties who had opened Alchemy Bistro with her husband five years before, then won it in the divorce settlement. I had no idea how her personal finances stood—the place was always busy, but restaurant margins are thin—and I know she had some investors.

One of them was Dr. Simon Mackie, the board chairman of St. Luke Midwest of Pontiac. He was a cloying, mealy old dude with stained teeth and a rictus grin, the kind of guy who, should he accidentally brush against you, makes you want to take a shower in scalding bleach. In addition—in street parlance—Dr. Mackie was a flaming queen and he always showed up at the restaurant with an entourage of young male interns; whereupon, he made a pretentious show of ordering pricey wine and talking about obscure vintages. The kitchen disliked him even more than the front of the house because, although he didn't tip them, he still expected perfection, even if it meant sending a lamb rack back two or even three times. Granted, for us servers he was fabulously generous—rarely less than a couple hundred on a five hundred dollar tab. But he was so demanding that whoever wound up with his table took it exclusively, with no other customers the entire evening, because he insisted on dominating the whole of your attention.

That Saturday afternoon, Jennifer informed me that Dr. Mackie's seven-thirty reservation was mine, adding, "If you don't mind?"

The question was rhetorical, of course. I was low chick on the totem pole, and Blake—the only male server working that shift—was even more creeped out by Mackie than I was. So I cooled my heels in the coffee area, turning over the strange turn of events of the previous week in my head until Mackie's party showed up.

In tow that evening he had a malt-brown Indian and a blue-eyed blond, both in their mid-twenties, though Mackie had to be fifty. As usual, they were given the restaurant's best banquette, and I proceeded to go through my standard opening ceremony, delivering drinks and, after an orchestrated length of time, reciting the evening's specials.

I suppose I didn't really crank up the Dixie charm that night, but I was certainly efficient. The Indian stopped me as I described a caramelized root vegetables appetizer and wanted to know if it contained any animal by-products.

"Dev is a vegan," Dr. Mackie explained. His cheeks had a gin-and-tonic sheen and his teeth were filmy. "I'm sure Chef can accommodate."

"Of course," I replied. "But the puree of root vegetables is meat-free. Scout's honor."

For some reason, that childhood expression convulsed the table. The blond clapped his hands. "Free scout meat? Dev's a vegan, not a celibate."

Seriously, I thought. Pedophilia jokes? They were making fun of me. If Blondie was a doctor wannabe, I hoped I never came down with whatever he was specializing in. I rolled my eyes, and perhaps it was too obvious.

"Oh my," said Dr. Mackie with treacly sarcasm. "Someone is on her period tonight."

Two particularly grueling hours followed, although in all I thought I handled the table—replete with three flamboyant, incorrigible assholes—quite admirably. But after the shift was over, Jennifer called me into the little office annexed to the bathroom hallway and closed the door, and that's never a good sign.

"Dixie, Dr. Mackie had some complaints about your service this evening. I can't remind you in more emphatic terms how important he is to this operation."

"I know," I sighed, trying not to sound exasperated. "I guess my head wasn't where it's supposed to be tonight."

"It happens," she said, and I think had she been closer she would have delivered a patronizing pat to my hand. "Look, I hired you because I'm a huge believer in second chances, and up 'til now, you've been an exemplary employee. Really, I'm lucky to have you. I admit I had some hesitation initially—people in recovery sometimes have a hard time working around alcohol and social drinking. So—and I think I have the right to ask—your lack of focus tonight… It isn't the result of any backsliding?"

"Oh no, not at all. I'm stone cold sober and loving it. Scout's honor."

"In which case, I will choose to believe you."

That was, of course, a qualified version of actually believing me, but rather than let it piss me off, I said, "I'll be honest. I met a guy last week, and I think I like him, and maybe I was a little mentally foggy tonight. It's not professional of me, I know. No, I'm not goo-goo eyed. I'm a little old for that."

"We're never too old for that, Dixie," she smirked, but gently. "Okay; we all have off days, and we'll chalk this one up to one of yours. I seriously hope the new relationship works out for you."

I wanted to tell her to pound sand, but instead I said, "It won't happen again, Jennifer."

She answered: "I'm going to have to hold you to that, Dixie. Okay?"

The following morning I did the Sunday brunch shift and managed to pull it off without a complaint. I was home by two, and after I did the usual chores, I sat before the canvas of Gabriel and re-evaluated it using the highlight of Julian's critique—the most flattering part where he claimed I could see with an eye to the invisible. Had my painterly sleight of hand managed to bring the disease that prowled through Gabriel's veins to the surface, just as I'd somehow brought the swirling, mysterious silt to the surface of the lake? Was I really supernaturally perceptive? Cézanne essentially painted in an extra dimension, so they say. Could I be pulling that off on some freshman level?

Well, why not? I'd certainly worked hard enough at it over the years, at least when I was caroming down the highway straight. The ego is a bizarre residual organ, sort of like an appendix or a baby toe: It may have had a use at one time, but now exists only to become infected or stubbed. If I was going to judge my output based on the opinions of the haters, why not occasionally allow those who appreciate me have their say?

In the end, couldn't I could learn from both and become a better artist?

Even so, I concede that compliments have the same effect on my creativity as vodka did to my social ineptitude. They prod me, for good or ill, out of self-conscious inertia. Full steam ahead: At first, I wanted to trifle with the paint on Gabriel's neck, to lighten a shadow here and darken a glow there. I wanted to touch up with the hollow of a cheek and the place where the skin of his scalp once had hair, wondering what color it had been, or, if he lived, if it would grow back.

But I didn't touch a thing. I heeded my own rule against correcting test answers from right to wrong and I started another painting entirely. This one was to be a portrait of Serafin Tercerio as he lolled languidly and wisely on Julian's hand-hewn bed, a special needs kid with special insights. I quickly sketched out a composition that worked, effectively capturing the boy's nervous confidence, his eager smile and his luminous, watery eyes.

But when I began to apply color, it went haywire from the git, and I knew from the first few brush strokes that I'd taken a wrong turn. The blues were off, the wash was tarnished and his flesh tones proved to be, in their way, even more elusive than Gabriel's ghastly pallor. Sometimes, such unexpected pathways take you into realms more awesome than the one you've mapped out, but the problems I encountered here were more fundamental than that: Despite his fever, the real Serafin Tercerio almost shimmered with health. His patina had been alight with a peculiar splendor I couldn't quite recreate. It was getting late, and after a few halfhearted attempts to right the good ship Serafin, I rinsed the brushes and switched my attention to a more pressing concerns: My own body.

For me, sexual encounters have never been casual. They are an interplay far too complicated to be treated simply as biology. They'd been so relatively few for a woman my age (I assumed) that I still approached them, and the potential for them, with the utmost circumspection. Not in the hypocritical zealot way, the philosophy I'd been forced to embrace as a member of *True Love Waits*. I didn't think of sex as something sacred, but it was certainly monumental enough to be worth boning up for—pun intended—like the test where I wanted my first answer indisputably correct, with no impulse later to go back and scribble something out, right to wrong or otherwise. Although, now that I think about it, wanting to scribble out certain sexual encounters is probably among life's table stakes.

One of comments Julian had made on Friday night, pre-kiss, was about August Lake's only rental unit, a rustic cabin built of logs that sat in a secluded corner of the park's North Unit. It was a favorite lay-over for Scout troops, but that Monday night it was unrented, and he offered it to me delicately as a place we might go to later in the day. My girly instincts took that as a reference to the fact that Serafin Tercerio might still be safe-havening it at his stone cottage.

And I realized without question that if Julian made physical overtures, I'd acquiesce. Even if it went no farther than a single night in a cabin in the woods, I wanted to take his spirit inside me and carry it away with me. If it was a one-nighter, so be it. Maybe I'd get a tattoo on my forehead that said *'Will Fuck for Compliments.'*

At the very least, I wanted to make sure I had all contingencies covered, so I showered and scoured and defoliated, and afterward, I took off my terrycloth robe and took a methodical inventory of myself before a full length mirror.

I would be twenty-eight in a few months. My hair, limp with shower water, had stayed pretty blonde even without the high lift. The coconut-white fringes of childhood were now buttery, but I thought they complimented my hazel eyes even more. Six months sober, those eyes glittered with fires I still found astonishing. My breasts were firm and my ass was rationally toned. Thanks in part to orthodontics, my teeth were even pearls. My lips were full, but, as I noted, so were my thighs, though just a bit. Naked, I figured I was an eight, with another six months at the gym nudging me to a nine. My waist was trim and reasonably taut, but my skin, which had always been yogurt pale, had an undeniable bluish tint under the fluorescent light. I wondered if it might be a turn-off to Julian, since it was clearly the complexion of someone who has lived indoors too long.

It was honest, real-time introspection, but my ulterior motive was unabashed vanity. Why deny it? I appraised myself critically because I could and still come up consistently in the plus column. At forty, having sloughed off points as I tacked on years, such an appendage-by-appendage reckoning would be desperate and sad, although I had little doubt I'd still be doing it.

I slept soundly after that. Besides caffeine, Melatonin is the only drug I'm allowed to take. Initially, my dreams were jumbled and oozing, filled with horrific shapes, but in time, they morphed into wild birds rising in a frightened bluster as I—suddenly empowered—began to kill them with clarity, strength, and even, nonchalance.

13.

It was five in the morning and still dark when I wheeled onto the expressway. I was still haunted by my final string of graphically violent hunting dreams; they'd been of an emotional sort that requires the bleaching effect of sunlight before they can fully evaporate.

The distorted lights of early commuters were in my eyes, and I coughed up another disturbing memory, one that I hadn't thought about in twenty years, though it had gnawed at me relentlessly at the time.

It happened on a Sunday night at the tail end of a long Thanksgiving holiday. We were driving home from my grandparents' house outside Columbus and I was curled up, asleep, in the rear seat of our Town & Country, sated, safe and settled. Saturday had been the opening day of rifle season, and a lot of Ohioans had spent the weekend in the woods shooting deer. The I-270 corridor was clotted with returning hunters, many with dead animals strapped to hoods and car roofs. I sputtered awake and looked out the car window into a sea of gore: All around our minivan, through every window, dead deer faces lolled, swollen tongues mushrooming from mouths, blood dribbling down quarter panels, racks bouncing on sheet metal and skulls smacking against fenders. For most animal-loving children—little girls especially—the blood lust inherent in hunting provides an immediate and nascent moral dilemma. Now, suddenly, hunter vehicles were everywhere, zipping by or pulling beside us at an even pace, so that the dead heads hung just outside the window, three feet from my face. I began to bawl hysterically and even the patient, embarrassed explanation from my Daddy couldn't quell my terrors and I rode the rest of the way home with my head underneath his overcoat.

Bouncing down dirt roads now, headlights illuminating the minefield of pot holes, I kept a lookout for deer, and the feeling dogged me all the way to the cottage, standing dark and desolate against the totemic glade of trees.

Inside, there were no lights visible. I parked beneath the pines and stepped outside. Bleak winds blew high overhead, rattling branches, but at ground level, there was an ominous stillness. Suddenly, I was apprehensive. There was something uneasy about the cottage and I didn't want to approach it.

A voice behind me whispered, "Dixie."

I yipped. Julian was crouching beneath the pines, three feet from me, the same distance away as the deer heads had been.

"God, you scared the eff out of me. I didn't see you there."

"That's the point."

His response bore no trace of menace, and I hoped my reaction did not indicate fear. In fact, I was relieved to find him there. The stone house looked cold and formidable and I didn't want to approach it. Even so, my voice trembled. "Guess I'm lucky I'm not a turkey."

His response was cast gently: "If you were a turkey, you'd have known I was here. The secret would have been making sure you didn't know why."

Somewhere, dawn may have been breaking. It may have been visible from the recycling center on top of Cemetery Hill. But here, darkness gathered in low spots and the clearing before the cottage was—as Bibi Lisiewicz might have phrased it—blacker than Sambo's ass. I felt Julian's breath on my neck as a soft sensual snuffle, though there was nothing overtly sexual about it.

"How do I smell?" I whispered.

"Clean."

Well, I was every bit that. Super clean. Squeaky clean. I suppose there was soap smell that lingered. "That's not a problem, is it?"

"It won't be," he answered and pressed a bundle in my hands. It felt like soft, heavy cotton cloth , like the shirt he'd been wearing on Friday. It was hunting gear. In full novice mode, I asked, "Do these go on over my clothes?"

"They won't fit over your clothes," he answered.

I had, of course, anticipated the chance that I'd be taking off my clothes in front of Julian, though admittedly, not quite this early in the day. But I had no problem with doing it now. It was too dark for modesty anyway. I was wearing Victoria's Secret under my jeans, nothing too boudoir, because it made me feel feminine, but Julian had moved away, and now, from a small distance, he said, "You should leave your things in the car. There are some new hires staying over in the cottage, and I don't want to disturb them by going inside. They had nowhere else to sleep."

So I left my clothes in the car, including my Memory Fit bra, despite the rather wide oval of my new shirt. With the light from the open car door, I saw that I had donned a set of supple muslin garments dyed in swirling, muted patterns of brown and green. Julian was beside me again, and in the same light I saw that he was wearing a smock made of animal hide with the fur on the inside. We looked ready for a Renaissance Festival and I told him so as he pressed something else into my hand: The slingshot he'd been carving on Monday afternoon.

"When it gets lighter, I'll show you how to use it. For now, put your hand on my shoulder and keep close to me."

So I did, and we moved off into the forest, *La Guero* and *La Guera*, the blond leading the blonde.

Slowly, in flat, drab tones, morning came on. "The monochrome of morning," I whispered, hoping he caught the allusion, and with some reluctance when dawn made it no longer necessary, I relinquished the intimacy of my hand on his shoulder.

We were on a footpath beneath a vaulted green glade, enveloped by fog and surrounded by dangling creepers. Industrious squirrels had begun to patter through the underbrush and a silvery creek tricked through the bracken, growing wider until water lapped over stones. This was the creek, Julian said, where the trout had come from, and in fact, I could see them swimming lazily about as he knelt down and drank from it.

"Are you sure it's safe?" I said. "I sort of remember reading that you always have to boil river water before you drink it."

"Totally safe. It's a separate system from anywhere else in the park." He offered a leather pouch around his neck. "I also brought along Jivarrão, from the forests before white men. You should drink some, absorb it. It sharpens the perceptions."

Truth told, I had Googled 'Jivarrão' and there wasn't much to be found. But there was something:

"Jivarrão is an Amazonian shrub whose leaves are capable of inducing altered states of consciousness. Ranging from mildly stimulating to extremely visionary, Jivarrão is typically ingested as tea, and is used primarily as a medicine and as a shamanic means of communication with spirits."

The article also said, quite graphically, *"The psychoactive compound in Jivarrão is not included in a typical drug screen, nor is it included in any known extensive drug screens. It is also not chemically similar to substances that are typically tested for, so the likelihood of triggering a false positive for other drugs is zero."*

But, I was still taking my sobriety seriously, and although I had ingested the tea a week before, it had been an inadvertent high, like second-hand weed smoke. Now, in the crisp springtime air, I wasn't sure I wanted to test my limits by drinking it intentionally, so instead, I went through the motions of sipping river water, but I was grossed out by it and let most of it dribble back.

After another hour of snaking through pillared shade, miles away from where we'd begun, we emerged at a trail head. There was a corrugated steel guardrail overgrown with weeds and some posts and a sign containing weasel words from the DNR about hiking rules.

It was at this point, while catching my breath in the sudden patch of sunlight, facing an ungraded road that may or may not have been the one we'd litter-swept my first day inside the park, that Julian offered me slingshot lessons.

In the darkness, I hadn't looked at the weapon closely, but I did now. It was a beautifully shaped Y with the same sort of carving I'd seen on his guitar. It felt warm and comfortable in my hand, and I fondled it as Julian set up a small, delicate clay figurine as a target. When I asked what it was, he said that Serafin Tercerio had made it for me as a votive.

"I don't want to break anything Serafin made," I cried.

"You won't," he answered.

Indeed. I was hopeless from the start. I liked the feel of the lesson though, with Julian's firm arms adjusting my own and puffs of his breath on my neck again. I dug the contact with his animal smell, the hand-sewn deer pelts he was wearing. With all the hyperactive shit he did, it defied reason he had time for a full time occupation as well and when I said so, he replied with his customary shrug, "Remember when I said that most things people do don't need to be done? I don't do them."

He added: "Hunting is one of the things that does."

Still, slingshot school was an unmitigated disaster. I galled myself. The smooth, round stones he gave me, placed in the leather pocket and drawn back with all the strength my stringy waitress arms could manage, went everywhere except in the direction of the clay creature standing defiantly on the boulder. I hit the guardrail a couple times and once I hit Julian when I somehow managed to launch the stone behind me, a feat I didn't know was physically possible. Julian was more patient with me than I was with myself and fed me stones like you feed ice chips to a terminal patient in the hospital. He gave me an analogy: "You're David, that's Goliath."

I answered, "Aren't I supposed to win?"

We worked at it for an hour and Goliath kept getting execution stays. Any progress I made was nominal.

At one point, Julian stopped me as something outside the scope of my senses attracted his attention. He led me briefly into the thicket beside the trail head where, at his insistence, we stood without moving. He whispered, close to my ear: "Hunting teaches the value in stillness. People move too much—they miss the link between now and before. Everything around you flows through an eternal now except the past. The past is utterly still."

I heard poetry in his voice. I heard the play of poignancy and the lilt of precision. Shortly, a truck rumbled down the road, and apparently, that's what he had heard. It was the Ford from headquarters, with Potter driving. I didn't recognize anyone among the motley collection of kids in the bed—they were black, Hispanic, rangy and strange. Gabriel wasn't there and I remembered, suddenly, that this was his chemo week. How desperately sad, I thought and I wanted to mention it, but we were in the throes of our stillness. As the pickup rumbled by, steering around some potholes and careening into others, nobody in the truck noticed us, though we were standing three feet from the road.

After they passed I asked, "Are your boys off to do things that don't need to be done?"

Julian voice betrayed a trickle of disappointment, as if he'd hoped they'd suss us out. "They're sharp in the streets, but they haven't yet learned how to be sharp in the forest. But they will. So will you."

I nodded; somehow, he'd made that seem like a worthwhile goal.

"Look," he whispered, pointing at a darkish clump about twenty feet up a tree across the road.

I saw nothing but leaves. "Is it a turkey?" I asked, feeling like a dweeb. "Like, a nest?"

He said, "It's a camera."

"One of the ones Alan uses to spy on the bad guys?" I asked.

He nodded. I squinted at the tree, and I suppose I made out what might have been the glint of something shiny amid the leafy screen, but I wouldn't swear to it. Slipping the slingshot from my fingers and loading a stone in the pouch, he said, "One for the Philistines," and hit the camera squarely in the lens, shattering the glass.

"Show off," I sniffed, but I was indelibly impressed.

Julian had brought along some kind of color-flecked jerky and as the sun peeked out, we leaned against the guardrail and ate it. Because I asked, he described the process by which he dried venison in the sun, ground it with wild blackberries and deer fat. Basically, it tasted sensational. He drew tea from his pouch of Jivarrão and offered it again. I'm not entirely sure why, but amid the majestic monoliths of the forest, the clear and sibilant symphony of birds, the cold babble of running water and the rich redolence of nature in the spring, I wanted to be part of his mind as much as I did his body.

Besides, I hadn't taken anything substantial from the creek, and that was hours before. I was thirsty, and I drank. In the distance, the caw of crow came cutting in. Overhead, a dark bird ripped across the clearing sky. Close behind, zipping around him as in a game of tag, were two smaller birds.

"They look like they're playing," I said.

"Don't they?" he answered.

In a moment, he said, "But they're not. The crow just raided the orioles' nest. It's probably filled with babies this time of year and the parents are chasing him away."

"Righteously, too," I nodded as the strange, aggressive dance whizzed overhead. "Like my grandmother used to say, 'They're certainly giving that crow some *what-for.*'"

"They are," he answered. "Except that crows are smarter than that. They work in pairs. While the parents are chasing this one away, the second crow is back at the nest eating the young. Next nest they find, they'll switch places."

Wow. That animals were capable of such awesomely gruesome trickery would not have occurred to me. I shook my head in amazement and wondered about the Shakespearean melodrama unfolding around us every moment, completely within the scope of our senses and totally ignored by nearly everyone.

"Alienation from nature," he said. "I can't imagine a more severe form of dysfunction."

"But it's so diabolical and bloodthirsty. Most people like to think of the Great Outdoors as more... idyllic."

"Out here, everything is adapted to an end," he said. "Maybe they should think about it this way: Ideals are for those too weak to confront what's real."

We watched other birds in the sky, and heard them bickering and posturing in the undergrowth. Julian explained which songs were territorial and which ones were erotic come-ons. Vultures came in gangs and circled something dead they'd found somewhere off in the forest. As we watched these vital interactions, I felt a wash of warmth and the same waves of doughy relaxation slide through me as I had the week before, sick, on the rear seat of the pickup truck. It was, unaccountable, an entirely wonderful sensation of being enveloped in pristine sludge.

My vision sharpened as if someone had a hand on a toggle and cranked up the light. I saw layers of detail in the forest and heard harmonies in the bird songs. An awareness of the tactile beauty around me swelled up, and it went beyond simple admiration. The forest scents mingled, but retained individual identities. The broken camera glass among the pebbles on the far side of the road glittered like tiny beads of fire. Friday's sun had exaggerated the freckles on the back of my hand, and they were now small golden medallions. I wondered if the ones on my nose looked like that to Julian. I reached out and took his hand and placed it against the warm knit of my cheek. He did not recoil and I kissed his palm. I might have jumped his bones on the spot, but a cramp became a hiccup and I threw up instead.

There was nothing particularly embarrassing about it this time. To me, it was a whole different game. I rinsed my mouth with tea and spat it out. "An outpouring," I said, "of everything."

A crow fluttered down from the trees behind us and perched on the guardrail.

Julian fed it scraps of jerky, and the bird eyed me, then took off again.

"That's the same crow that came to the cottage," I announced. "The one Serafin Tercerio named after himself."

"Today, he's our liaison," Julian smiled.

"I thought I had imagined the whole thing. Or maybe I did and it's a hallucination now. Carlos Castaneda was always seeing weird visions on peyote. He even turned into a crow once, I think."

Julian closed his eyes and drifted for an instant, then opened them again. The sharp green of his irises was glorious. He quoted from *The Teachings of Don Juan*:

"It takes a very long time to learn to be a proper crow. But you did not change, nor did you stop being a man..."

"Amazing recall," I nodded.

No further die need be cast. I felt empowered, energized—relaxed, but not lethargic.

"You set your course by being here, Dixie," Julian returned. "It should be clearer now. You removed the obstacles without slowing down more than necessary. Try Goliath again, here in this moment. Or, if you don't like the source, *be* Goliath; David never expected a rematch. Become a predator. Whatever you do, *be here now.*"

Where I'd been skeptical, now, somehow, I wasn't. So I took up the slingshot again and—I do not make this up—I hit a bullseye on my first try, shattering Serafin's clay votive into a thousand dusty pieces.

14.

So, my stock began to trend upward. But a figurine is one thing; a moving animal, with a heartbeat, a sense of danger, a ticking, throbbing, squishing metabolic system and arguably, a personality, is another.

I expressed the thought and, as we circled the guardrail and found the trail again, Julian responded: "Why should it be? Guilt is human construct. There's no ascendency out here. Nothing exists in any sort of hierarchy."

"That sounds pretty Godless," I said.

He replied, "Actually, it's the very soul of Godness."

Indian tea coursed in my veins. Never before in my life had I felt more aligned to my surroundings. I could certainly understand why this concoction was used to treat withdrawal. In my scant decade as a grownup I'd concluded that adulthood was essentially a prolonged wait for the other shoe to drop, and although most alcoholics drink to squelch that dread, it was clear to me now that drinking merely jostled whatever shelf the shoe was on. Jivarrão, on the other hand, made me feel like I was in an exclusive shoe store trying on sexy new imports. Good and bad did not exist, except as we make it so. Shakespearean melodrama was everywhere. Everything is adapted to an end.

For now, the frontier drew back, and we followed it. This time, the silence was my own volition; I was vigorous, and suddenly, efficient. I found I could move with inordinate stealth, even when peppered with eagerness, just as Julian had suggested.

We emerged from the trees to face a sprawling field spangled with tiny blue wildflowers. I remember every event that followed in perfect detail, both as isolated incidents and as a collective phenomenon; each fiber of every cell on every leaf was resonating in essential euphony.

Perhaps I'm more aware of the significance now than I was at the time: Julian led me to a blind at the edge of the field he'd constructed from tall weeds and branches. He arranged me within it, and squatted beside me, facing the opposite direction. My senses remain keen as a scalpel. Shortly, the unmistakable gobble of a turkey arose from him. Had he transfigured?

"To become a crow is the simplest of matters..." Why not turkeys too? The thought occurred to me—was Julian my Don Juan? *"But you did not change, nor did you stop being a man."* The quote went on: *"There is something else..."*

In this case, something else turned out to be the shell of a box turtle that Julian carried in his pouch. To the back of it was affixed a thin piece of slate. He showed me how to rub the slate with a wooden striker that dangled from it by a rawhide strap, and when he did it, the loud, shrill, throaty call of a turkey emerged.

When I tried it—at least at first—it squeaked like chalk on a board.

It took time for me to get the hang of it, but less than I might have expected. I was primed for the experience, for any number of reasons. My Daddy had not been much a hunter, though hunting was such an ubiquitous mid-Ohio ritual that, as a salesman for a mid-Ohio corporation, he'd been required to host customers on any number of hunting trips. When maudlin Bambi references came up during one of my pre-adolescent piques, he confessed that he'd been carrying the same bullet with him on every hunting trip he'd ever been on, never having used it. At the time, it made me love him all the more.

But this was different. This was bonding; with wildlife, with my companion, with the sky and the clouds, with the dirt and the tree roots. I felt no sense of ascendency, no lording hierarchy, no drive to be the alpha-predator. I didn't even feel particularly human and I certainly didn't feel like myself. But then again, I hadn't felt much like myself when I was flirting with retired iron workers to gold-dig drinks or slobbering over Corky's junkie junk. I believed that whoever I had morphed into on that cool May afternoon was finally on the right side of Dixie Pickett.

In honesty, I felt what hunters of any species have probably felt throughout the eons: Immediacy.

"Maybe if you were not afraid of becoming mad or losing your body, you would understand this marvelous secret. But perhaps you must wait until you lose your fear to understand what I mean."

These were words I'd read so long ago that I couldn't recall the circumstance, but now, miles from the book, I finally understood what they meant: I stroked the slate and in doing so, I became—for all intents—a wild turkey.

In time, a large, fat, regal, purple-red bird stepped warily from a covey of sumac trees. He stumped on scaled reptilian legs, looking inquisitive, wary and supremely intelligent. Carefully, Julian reached over and raised my arm. He placed a blood-warm stone in my palm, and I put it in the leather pocket. The turkey took tentative, curious steps forward until it was nearer than Serafin's votive had been, ten feet away.

I remembered: "If you were a turkey, you'd have known I was here. The trick would have been making sure you didn't know why."

Our eyes met and mine, I determined, held the more universal understanding, but I may have been wrong: The stone I shot went wildly left and made a dust puff among distant weeds. The missed shot should have scared the turkey off, but it had the opposite effect: It drew him in. His head wobbled above a glowing red throat; he craned his neck to determine if the shock of undergrowth I hid behind was dangerous. His tail fanned, showing multiple deep and beautiful earth tones and a stripe of black sandwiched by white. His throat skin was brilliant, as bright a shade of crimson as exists. There is no truer primary color to be found in nature: Blood is red without condition. My second shot missed by a lesser margin; my tom's head darted the other way as I released it, but he stood his ground.

Julian said in a voice as soft as breeze, "There's no away, Dixie. Be here now."

For every dolphin that saves a drowning man, I suppose there is a rabbit somewhere eating her own babies. We interpret circumstances based on a somatic agenda. My third stone caromed off the turkey's skull and he dropped heavily among the weeds. But he didn't die. I'd hit him in eye socket and he lay flopping in the dirt and grass, raptor claws upright, clutching nothing. He made a low, pathetic squeal. I didn't panic, but although I knew what had to be done, I had no idea how.

There was a whisper puff from behind my neck. "I'll do it if you want."

"No," I answered, and I was honest: "I don't want. I have to do it myself. I have to be here now."

So he described what I had to do and I did it. The turkey was making a ghastly, ghostly plaint, like a child, and I, with a peculiar but overwhelming sense of compassion, wrung his neck, and then, with the bone-handled knife that Julian handed me, cut the creature's throat. Blood spurted, but somehow, it didn't offend me. It splattered my clothes, but it didn't disgust me. I had vomited earlier, but now, I had no urge to throw up, although later, thinking back on the ease and violence with which I killed that turkey, I did.

Throughout the grisly moment, I loved my connection to the universal storm. I felt respect for the bird as I did for our unison, and it occurred to me that such respect is precisely what was lacking in men who strap bucks to the hoods of their tough-dude trucks and let vacant heads bounce obscenely against their fenders. Respect, perhaps, was my Daddy's motivation for keeping the bullet in the pocket of his orange hunting vest, but I had chosen to adapt it to an end.

The turkey probably weighed fifteen pounds, but as he expired, I clutched him tightly and felt his jerking, quivering spasms resonate through my body. I felt the vibrations in my bones, straight through to my skull, and they became a part of me as surely as his flesh would be processed into my flesh when I ate him. Had I been on the scene, I believe I would have held Corky in the same way as he toppled over in his favorite recliner, strapped in place with duct tape, and died. And in some vanished cultures, under duress or desperation or ritual, in some forest without white men, I might have eaten Corky too.

When the bird was dead, Julian offered to carry it, but I wouldn't relinquish it. This was the level of life I'd sign up for when I showed up this morning, and I held our bird against my breast like a baby.

The image of dead Corky remained with me as the turkey blood cooled on my blouse. There was less need for silence now, and as we walked, steeped in a cocktail of empathy that was partially induced and partially innate, I poured out Corky's murder story. And for this first time, I wept. Like puking, it was physically cleansing. I finished by saying: "They never caught the dude that did it, but even if they had, the worst he'd have gotten is life in prison with three squares provided, courtesy of you and me. Michigan has no capital punishment. At least in Ohio, sooner or later, we fry the motherfuckers."

When Julian responded, I though his voice had taken a preternatural edge. By then, we had crossed through the field of bluebells, and had found a path that led down a dale, into a darker stand of trees with a meandering brook at the bottom.

103

He said, "That's another concept that white men brought to the forest. A kind of justice that sees murder as a crime against the state, and a killer's life is forfeit to government. Tribal people see murder as a crime against the victim's family. It goes no farther than that; relatives are permitted to retaliate without consequence. They have only once chance, though—there are no lingering blood feuds. It's the ultimate deterrent, because one way or the other, some form of retaliation is mandatory. *'If I kill you, your people will kill me, and my people will not answer back—they will accept that the incident is over, now and forever.'"*

"Wow," I said. "Does it work?"

"It does," he said. "In Luanhão villages, there are very, very few murders. To adapt that system in white society, the guilty party would be held in a jail cell, and the victim's family would be handed a gun with a single bullet. Blood for blood, without legal ramification. When it's over, the matter would be over too."

"See, that seems like justice to me."

"And to me," he said. "Because, there's a chance that the victim's kin will choose to let the killer live, and tradition still holds: That's still the end of the incident. There is no chance for changing their minds later. So there's room for compassion, and in either case, for the society and for the individual, there's a stabilization of the spirit that no other system can equal."

15.

We washed in the brook, first ourselves with wads of moss, and then the dead bird. Julian showed me how to remove the fat insides, still steaming in the cool of the fading afternoon, and he helped me skin it whole, leaving a bald carcass, pink as a newborn. With our hands touching, the gruesome chore knitted us.

Above us, pine trees towered, the tops bobbing like cattails on a pond, as majestic as any herd of elephants. Despite our fascination with wildlife specials and *National Geographic* centerfolds, I guess we're not programmed to recognize that. I know that I was floating in a lingering universe brought on by psychotropics, but so what?

It was not an artificiality brought on by vodka. This was real; this was the sweet breath of the genuine forest and it was monumental. I said, "It's really a privilege to be out here, Julian."

"Not so," he said, "It's a right. The forest upholds, and has an equal right to expect that we uphold in return."

"Too cosmic," I pressed, "I mean, it's a privilege to be here with you."

But he knew what I meant. Jivarrão had a shelf life, and mine began to fade. It seemed to expire as I climbed to the top of the rise above the creek. I say that, because any sense of awe and commiseration had vanished by the time I saw the cabin where, presumably, we would spend the night.

It was backed into a clearing among the damp pines, a blackish pile of old logs with an oblique and ponderous chimney. Something about it struck me as gut-level sinister, even more than August Lake had. Where the lake was impersonal, like a malignant tumor, it was not angry. The cabin radiated something vicious, something menacing, something made of flesh. Where Julian's cottage nestled, the cabin crouched. The sun had dropped behind the tree line and the scene was being swallowed by twilight.

"I can't go inside there," I said the instant I saw it.

"You don't have to," Julian answered, hanging the dressed turkey carcass from a tree branch. "I can build a fire here and we can stay outside. Or we can go back to the ranger's cottage."

"Well, I don't want to go all the way back. It's getting dark. But I'd rather sleep in a snowbank than inside that place. It's got mojo worse than the lake. The lake is morbid, but the cabin? I'd be afraid even to try and paint the thing."

He paused and considered the cabin, hushed behind the darkness and solitude. "I think you *should* paint it, Dixie. There's power in your brush and it might exorcise the history."

"God, there's history? See that? I sensed that, but I don't think I want to know what it is. Oh, fuck that—of course I do. What?"

105

"Have you heard of a doctor called Kevorkian?"

I remembered the name. In fact, I'd watched a documentary on him a couple of years before. "The assisted suicide guy?"

"Yeah. He used that cabin to dispatch some of his people. Alan Loya remembers—it was when he first started here."

"Oh, God, no. I won't go in there, no way, not even with a bunch of Girl Scouts. I'm sorry, but I'd rather be outside freezing my ass off."

"We won't freeze," he said and headed for the cabin, leaving left me in a small clearing where the charred of an old campfire remained, returning a minute later with a massive animal fur, big enough to be a wall tapestry

"What in the living fuck is that?" I cried.

"A bear skin. Kodiak. Alive, it weighed almost two thousand pounds."

"You took down a Kodiak bear with a slingshot?"

"No," he laughed. "I spent a couple seasons trapping up north and a furrier I sold skins to had it in his house. He knew I liked it and he wound up giving it to me."

It looked warm, that's for sure. And it was the size of a room. Julian spread it on the ground like a throw rug and built a fire before it, which in itself was a treat to behold—he used a small bow, a wooden spindle and a board and nothing more. In less than a minute he had a spark, and then, a flame, and in another few minutes, tongues of fire were licking at deadfall logs. I couldn't have lit a fire that quickly with a box of matches and a can of gasoline.

"You and your primal links," I said.

"Basic survival skill," he said "It's not hard. Next time, I'll show you how."

I also marveled at his deftness in butchering the turkey and cooking the meat over a spit he fashioned on the spot. He was madly efficient. I pressed him. "Tell me more about life as a trapper," I said. "It sounds so… Neolithic."

He sighed and said, "When I first moved here, I thought I was witnessing the last days of a system. I wanted a world where fish shoal and plants fruit and wild animals migrate. I wanted to be ahead of the game, to leave before the pitchforks came; I wanted cycles of wilderness, not cycles of culture. I wanted to live someplace where I could build a house wherever I wanted; somewhere there is no property to own and no jurisdiction even if there was. I saw culture as chaos and nature as order."

"What about now?" I asked.

"I see it now more than ever."

"Then why do you stay here, Julian?"

"Oh, I have obligations here. In the end, two years in the wild was I all I had before they caught up to me."

"Are you talking about your mother?" I asked, softly. "I'd like to meet her some time—eccentric disabilities and all. I never felt obligations like that to my mother, and I envy you, frankly."

"There's nothing to envy," he answered gently. "Our obligations are the same. We get up and confront nature and all the contingencies. Whether we do it on autopilot or not is up to us. Today, we chose not to. There was no complacency in you today, Dixie. That's how I try to live every hour, not just this one."

"But isn't that harder when you feel surrounded by a chaotic system you don't believe in?"

"Sometimes," he said. "Because when I'm here, I become the chaos."

I stood up slowly and said, "That happened in my life, Julian. I watched it happen in slow motion. First, it's a little over the line, then it's more over the line, and then one day, you understand that there is no way back from the chaos."

"Except that you found one."

At the time, I assumed that he was talking about my sobriety. A quick ember darted across the eastern sky like an electric spark. His inner light seemed to me to be a pagan portal. I was enthralled by him. I hoped it was reciprocated, because suddenly, as far as all my woman instincts told me, it was zero hour:

"If you want to share my body now, you can."

I was blunt, not because I thought there was something sexy in bluntness, but because, beneath the towering giants and the wheeling universe, there seemed no way more appropriate to approach what I now viewed as inevitable. My hunting get-up was crusted with gore and deliberately, I let it fall to the ground. "So, do you?"

"That was never a question. But you know that."

"I guess. But right now... Do you think I'm beautiful, Julian? Like this? Raw and open? I mean, in the poetry way?"

"Entirely," he answered. "In all ways. You are lovely in all ways."

'Lovely' was an old-fashioned compliment replete with nostalgic purity, and I believed it because as a man, he must have known that he could have me without having said anything at all. I felt bridal; I trusted him and I wanted to see him without the camouflage. And I did, as Eve saw Adam in the forest before the fall, shivering with anticipation in the olive shadows.

My first time, with Kyle Andrus, I'd been a newborn colt trying out wobbly legs. My second time, the lone encounter with Jason Alton—who I assumed had long since married a Christian brood mare—I'd been a filly itching for a starting pistol. With Corky, I had become something of a dull, unwitting, unresisting workhorse.

With Julian it was a different track altogether. We made a den beneath the fur and we took dark refuge. There were delicious thirsts and tameless hungers; our fingers interlocked, then our limbs. My hair fell across his face, and after a change, his hair fell across mine and we were gilded in sweet perspiration. We surfaced for air and above us were stuttering stars and an icy moon and the drone of high winds, far away, whirling through leaves.

He throbbed with an underlying delicacy and a ferocious tenderness; the finer points of desire. I felt like an animal. I wanted to *be* an animal. I trembled with animal purpose quite beyond the scope of anything I'd experienced or expected. I burrowed in him and took him in me like a girl beast. We enwrapped and when the thing was satisfied at last, we lay close and sticky, cocooned in closeness and guttering firelight.

I was exalted. In response, I felt magnetism in him, if perhaps less exaltation. And that was fine; I had taken him into me primarily because he was not like every other man who had ever wanted me and not only had I presumed that the indulgence would be unusual, I'd have been frustrated if it wasn't. The common denominator among the men I've allowed to enter me has been, on some level, their need to self-inflate, to square themselves. Here, there was none. Was that honesty? I suppose, and I suppose that's how he intended it. But there seemed to be a gap at the foot of it; an odd chromatic contrast to my glow. I was engorged and sensually confident. I wanted to feel for the hollows now, while I had him curled around me, humid and gluey with impulse. Every woman I've ever known—intimately or otherwise—wanted to fill gaps in their lovers. For me, I was not sure I had the stamina or the skills to fill any gaps, but within Julian, there was a shadow place and at least, I wanted to illuminate it.

I said softly, drowsily, nearly a chant, *"Now we shudder from the mold, to let our natural shapes unfold..."*

I thought he might have fallen asleep, but after a while, with cinders popping and crackling beyond our fur shroud, he said, "That voice is so distant it's lost its meaning."

"Whose voice? Yours or mine?"

"Julio Vaz's."

I answered, "I wrote something in my journal once a long time ago, and right now, I'm not sure who it's for: *'To love someone inextricably is the source of all ecstasy'*. I felt nerve tips I didn't know existed, Julian. Tonight, for the first time in my life, I felt ecstasy. Did you?"

He answered softly: "You can't let yourself take this the wrong way, Dixie, but to me, being happy or sad is of no consequence. The natural state is neither—it's to exist. Even at the end, your turkey had no fear that the system would collapse without him. He was comfortable and secure in his identity. Any emotion otherwise is an exception. Perhaps you are more a part of the exception than I am. Maybe to me, the ecstasy is simply to be."

The wind died; a hush fell over our world and I slept and dreamed about the forest to retrieving its due from the white men.

16.

When I woke up, the first beams of sunshine were piercing the woods. Julian was stirring up the fire and he had two pots of water heating over it. One was to wash. Inside the other a warm, nutty-smelling porridge was bubbling.

"No Indian tea?" I asked.

"As a remedy or a ritual?"

"Huh?"

"That's what Jivarrão is. It's deliberate. Yesterday we engaged the circle and the storm and you acquitted yourself beautifully."

"I did, didn't I?" I grinned, blushing. "I widened and walked off the weight. Quite an amazing experience, Julian. For a while, I became an effective little turkey and an effective turkey hunter. I gave him some *what-for*—some Dixie moxie."

"You took nature at its word," he said, then swept up my discarded, blood-caked garments from the day before and threw them into the fire.

I was warm, but still naked under the fur, and that was such an odd, unexpected move that I said, "Won't that make for an awkward walk back?"

"It shouldn't," he answered and handed me a bundle that had been sitting on an adjacent log. It was a clean and neatly folded white linen skirt and a tunic of same material. The tunic was embroidered with colorful images, and the whole ensemble had Julian's herbal scent about it.

I was delighted and flattered. I held up the blouse. "I saw this same needlework on the shirt you were wearing on Monday night. Did you do it?"

He smiled again: "No."

I took a closer look. The embroidery was arrestingly beautiful, three-dimensional in places, with rising loops of colored floss forming intricate patches. It was done in multiple sylvan colors, but as I tried to find recognizable images among the knots and stiches, I saw instead slithering forms. Unpleasant pressures blew up suddenly within me: The style was identical to the carving that had hung above Julian's hearth.

"Oh, God—do these clothes belong to your Madrinha?

"There's no Madrinha; not any more. She relinquished her role."

"How can someone relinquish being your godmother?" I asked, genuinely confused, and then something occurred to me and I whispered it: "By dying?"

His mint eyes fixed on me for a long time: "She wasn't *my* godmother, Dixie. She was *a* godmother. To many people. There would be a lot of cultural things I'd have to explain to you to make you understand how important it is to be called 'Madrinha'. I can do that. And I suppose I probably should."

"So, she *was* your lover? This is so crazy, Julian, It's not my business, but maybe it's more my business this morning than it was yesterday morning."

"Well, Madrinha shared things with me that people share, especially when they are bound together by circumstance."

I couldn't be proprietary about his body, obviously, but I could do my due diligence. And I could adopt a tone of petulance, so I did: "I'll take that as a yes and will avoid further reference."

In response, his attitude wasn't one of shame or remonstrance. Perhaps I was still in hunter mode, but something in his expression reminded me of my tom turkey as he inched toward my lair: Not fear, not second thoughts, but the purest distillation of curiosity.

But here, I wasn't a predator I was an ancient friend. In purest biology, I was his hen. I couldn't entirely let it go, and said, "Although, I know it's fair to ask if you're still sleeping with her."

Deftly, lightly, even wistfully, and I believed, truthfully, he said, "No."

And I guess that's all I needed to re-establish some feeling of ascendancy. I washed, put on the fresh clothes and threw my arms around his neck and held him, feeling pulses of warmth resonate through my new tunic, and it snaked through all the way to my bones.

I made a determined effort not to cling or clutch, but I suppose I did. A tiny crimson dragonfly darted into the shaft of light that was burrowing into our clearing and Julian said to me softly, *"Libélula;* the dragonfly. She doesn't ask if she's beautiful. The dragonfly may not even appreciate how beautiful she is. But none of that has the slightest effect on the reality of her beauty. You understand that, don't you?"

"I do—of course I do."

"Be *Libélula,* then," he said, and kissed me again like he had the first night, with essence.

Behind us, the Kevorkian cabin was glinting in the morning light. Dark fires shone on weathered black logs rising from the tall grass. With the rich greenery unfolding behind it, I supposed I might have been too harsh in my in my original assessment. By daylight, the cabin's aura seemed that of a victim, not of an enforcer: It looked forlorn, abandoned and pitiable.

I wanted to see inside. After all, if nothing else, there was historical significance. Something for the bucket list.

"Go inside then. I promise, it's harmless," Julian said. "There's not much to see beyond the view. I imagine that's why he chose this place and why they all agreed to it, don't you? It's beautiful and peaceful. Far nicer than any hospital, which is where these folks would have drifted off otherwise."

"Doesn't it freak you out a little, though? All those death vibrations concentrated in a single room? Those were human beings who died in there, not turkeys."

He prodded me gently: "Why would that make any difference? Aren't all life cycles equal?"

"I suppose. I get that interconnection stuff. I'm not a flag waver for the species, believe me. But still... To die inside a wet shack in a dark woods with nobody but creepy old Dr. Mengele breathing on you, pumping you full of poison?" I conjured up an image I remembered from the documentary seen about Kevorkian. "Imagine that mug being the last thing you ever saw."

"But those aren't the final visions, Dixie; not really—they can't be. There can be no away. Those lives were blinks, but the blinks will go on for eternity."

A moment later, as Julian put out our campfire, I approached the cabin and stepped inside. It smelled acrid and musty, like old smoke, but otherwise, as Julian had said, there wasn't much to see. The silence was pervasive and the soft sunlight, distilled by the surrounding trees, filled it with abstruse radiance. There were few furnishings; a steel-framed bed bolted to one wall, a large storage chest made of pine and a Gibraltar stove like a squat, black, miniature black rhino. But in the rear of the single room there was a large picture window that looked out over a tumble of trees, and if you squinted past them, there was a sloping green meadow, clean and pulsing with the vibrant spring morning. And a bit farther, you could see a tiny lake—a real one, nature-made, shimmering like a pool of liquid silver. As I watched, a pair of snowy swans lit upon the rippling surface.

I thought of Gabriel again and I imagined him—with all options having failed—seated at this window, rigid and exquisite as an ivory obelisk, a snowy swan himself, gazing at this very sight as his blinks dissolved into eternity. I wondered if such a scenario had been discussed with him, and I felt comfortable enough with Julian now to ask him, and I would have done that, but just then, a glint from the upper portion of the window caught my attention: Something was hanging from a nail sunk into the wooden frame.

It was Takosha's gold-chained pendant.

There was no question in my mind about what it was. I'd spent six months at AA meetings staring at the thing rising and falling with her gargantuan chest, and, of course, we'd talked about it several times. It wasn't an expensive piece of jewelry by any stretch, probably less than twenty dollars on eBay, but, to her, it was a Hope diamond.

I slipped it from the hook and was turning it over in my palm when Julian came in with the bear fur.

I stared at him, at a total loss. "This belongs to my friend Takosha, Julian. How do you think it could have gotten all the way out here? It was a gift from her father. She never took it off. If she lost it, I'm sure she'd have contacted the park or come looking for it."

Julian approached me, and touched the pendant in my hand, "Stony mentioned that he'd found a piece of costume jewelry on the trail. He assumed it belonged to one of the Girl Scouts who stayed here last month, so he left it here, hanging in the window, in case she came back for it. "

"Well, it doesn't belong to any Girl Scout. It's Takosha's. You heard what happened to her, right? She found a bottle of whisky in the woods and fell off the wagon so hard that AA had to change their software. I was being petty about it when she wouldn't return my texts, but now I'm worried. You said she got home all right?"

"Gabriel told me that he left her at the address on her emergency contact form. Her sister's address."

"God, I wish I could talk to Gabriel right now. But I can't, can I? I'm sort of surprised at you, Mr. Observant. You didn't recognize the pendant? I thought everybody noticed Takosha's boobs. I'll just have to assume you were too mesmerized by mine. But if she got home in one piece, I guess that's all you're obligated to do."

I held up the chain and watch light refract in the crystal. Scraps of color ricocheted around the log walls. "Can I take it, then? To return it?"

"Of course," he said. "May she be safe. There are people with a resolve to succumb, not to overcome. Alan heard the story about your friend and spent the rest of that afternoon cruising ditches looking for more bottles."

"You don't drink any alcohol at all, I take it?"

He shook his head, and it occurred to me then that this might be the disability that afflicted his eccentric mother. And, despite what else I wanted to say, I didn't. Not yet. For the moment, my exaltation was somewhat conflicted. I slipped the pendant around my own neck and remained weltered in worry and wonder during the long trek back to the pretty cottage nestling in the dell.

17.

I'd been hungry for Julian for as long as I could remember. For *a* Julian, I suppose; for the concept. I sensed, beyond a doubt, that a new epoch was beginning for me. I believed that my emotions and whatever they entailed were now beyond eluding. But, I didn't want to elude them. I didn't want to overcome; I wanted to succumb.

At my car, I offered to return the beautiful dress to him and he wouldn't take it. It was mine. Rather than prolong any awkwardness, I said, "So, is this everything? Goodbye for us?"

"I hope not," he answered.

There was no follow-up suggestion and I held him again, snugly. I was in too deeply to drop it. I said, "Okay, so by my math, I'm done with my community service. If this is your life, Julian, this forest, this cottage, this air, this park, I could always fuck something else up and get sent back again."

At the moment, I couldn't quite isolate where within that vast landscape between something and everything I wanted to alight, but beneath the perfumed pines, the feel of my breasts against embroidered linen and then, against his chest, was delicious beyond describing.

As odd, if innocuous as it sounded to me at the time, it turned out that for Julian Vaz, there *was* another life:

He began with this: "Actually, I have to disappear for a while now. The park system is holding an annual retreat through parks along the North Country Trail, from the U.P. to Minnesota. I have to represent August Lake. Alan can't do it, obviously. We'd all be out of work by the time it was over."

"Aw," I whined. "I was hoping for an instant replay. How long will you be gone?"

"A week. The thing is, I need someone to do me a favor on Friday, Dixie. I'm not sure I have anyone else I trust enough to ask. I'm trying to sell a bar in Pontiac and I need someone to pick up papers from my attorney."

"You own a bar in Pontiac?" I asked incredulously.

"Well, it's my mother's. She bought it a long time ago as an investment. She can't handle it anymore. As I said, she's disabled."

"I'm amazed, that's all. I cut my teeth in bars. What kind of bar is it?"

"It's a private club; an exclusive deal for members only. Not my kind of people, I promise. I'm not a member. Anyway, I'm trying to sell it for her, and the lawyer will have some paperwork ready for me on Friday afternoon and I need someone to pick it up. Normally, Gabriel would go, but this won't be a good week for him."

"God, I'm sure it won't. How awful. Of course I'll go. I'm not working Friday anyway. Where's the office?"

"Oh, it's a distance, but there's no need to drive all the way out there. Someone can meet you on this side of town. There's a Sunoco station at Woodward near the freeway onramp. Know where it is?'

"Sure, it's ten minutes from my apartment."

"I mean, it would be really be a load off me since I'll be out of touch all week. Can I tell the lawyer two o'clock in the afternoon? I couldn't thank you enough, Dixie."

I made a scrunched-up face to indicate that it was a no-brainer. "Of course, Julian. It means extra life points for me, right? What should I do with the papers when I have them? Bring them to the park?"

116

"It's probably easier if you leave them in the apartment over the club. It's closer to you, and I won't be back to the park until Tuesday. I rarely use the apartment. I'll give you the key and the address and you can leave the papers there on the black stone table by the door. You can't miss it."

"Whoa! Giving me a key to your apartment so soon? You know, in some cultures that officially means we're married."

I was kidding, but not so much when I added: "But it's a sad day when Luddites needs to deal with lawyers."

"I agree," he answered. "Again, it's a huge help. Friday, at two? He'll be driving a powder-blue Lexus."

"Tell him to look out for a rust-colored Focus."

I embraced him and hung on to him until there was stirring from the cottage, and a tall, tousle-haired, sleepy-looking teenager stepped outside.

Julian went and spoke to him quietly for a minute, went inside, and returned with a key and an address on Ottawa Street, only a block from Alchemy. I punched it into my cell phone, and before I drove off, I distinctly remember my final words to him on that cool Tuesday morning:

"You and a nightclub? I still can't wrap my cerebellum around that. You're a mystery for sure, Julian Julio. I guess that's the pitchforks coming. I guess that's part of the chaos."

18.

As I relate what happened over the course of the following days, I'm reminded one of the most overlooked, underappreciated sequels in the Bible:

After the fall, Adam and Eve went on to live long, productive lives.

Even so, regarding the men who have highlighted my life, I will say this about my sweet Daddy: Once you got to know him, nothing he did was unexpected. With

Julian, apparently, there were caverns delving beneath the caverns.

That Monday morning, after leaving the park provoked by confused energies, I stopped by Takosha's apartment and pounded relentlessly on her sister's freshly-painted townhouse door. In fact, I went back in an hour and did it again. There was no answer, but then I remembered that Takosha's sister, a nurse who worked odd shifts at St. Luke, owned a lime-colored Cadillac, and I didn't see it in the lot.

Tuesday night was one of our AA nights, and I wended through the folding chairs, altar banner and stacks of old hymnals in the basement of St. Bede Catholic Church hoping Takosha had sobered up and would appear, but she didn't and nobody had heard a word from her, not even the moderators.

Around noon on Wednesday, I cruised the lot of Carriage Circle again, finding a lot of folks clotting up the sidewalks but doing little; old coal-black men with snow white beards that made them look like Frosted Chocolate Pop-Tarts, kids on bicycles circling endlessly like turkey vultures, and one scene so peculiar that it might have come from a Bosch painting or a David Lynch movie: A pair of strapping black teenagers swaggering down the center of the complex flanking a white, bleached-blonde midget who was doing a pimp roll of her own. God, did I want to hear *that* backstory.

But, I was looking for a lime-colored Cadillac and it wasn't there, so I ran a handful of time-killing errands and went back to my own apartment. I was thinking about Julian, of course, and trying to stem those thoughts before they reached a tipping point. Inside my cheerless rooms I was increasingly restless. I picked up my brushes and paints and tried to breathe a little life into Serafin Tercerio sprawled on the hand-hewn bed in the cottage. I imagined him as he'd been: Crisply alive with a ruddy complexion and Jivarrão visions dancing in his saucer-shaped eyes. Alas, though my filberts and bristle brushes had minds of their own, my likeness did not, and, despite my diligent application of self, Serafin never materialized from the muddy smears of acrylic. Ultimately, I concluded the painting was worthless and threw it away.

I returned to the Carriage Circle complex at around five thirty, where the jitterbugs on their garish dirt bikes continued to make aimless, vaguely intimidating loops like they used to do in front of Danny's Coney Island back in Woltown. The metaphor was so inevitable I hoped it wasn't accidentally racist: Julian had taught me that crows are clever, diabolical birds that work in pairs and think things out while vultures simply circle and wait.

This time, I was successful. Ten minutes after I pulled into an open slot by the dumpster, Danita DeYoung arrived in her lime-colored Cadillac. She was a fleshy woman with one of those bodies that seem to settle on African American women in middle-age and hang around for the rest of their lives: Her topside was barrel huge, her upper arms slabs of black beef while her legs were bean-pole batons that dangled beneath. White women, especially in the Heartland, seem prone to the opposite kind of physique, with halved-grapefruit breasts on small upper torsos swelling prodigiously to encompass massive hips and thighs. My recurring nightmare is that, thanks to generations of stodgy proletarian lunch bucket-types from Central Ohio I have inherited this body type. *'Ever vigilant'* is my motto, my tagline and my dietary mantra.

Danita, who I'd met once before when dropping Takosha off after a meeting, had a lyrical, popping quality to her voice, and she had clearly made an effort lose the ghetto accent that still blossomed in her sister. Although Danita was a professional woman, Takosha had once confided that her big sister had been the one to instruct her in the finer points of hooking. Cash-and-dashing had put the elder DeYoung through Chamberlain College of Nursing and was, in her particular subset, a more viable option than overtime at Meijer's. Today, Danita looked haggard and resigned, but her mood blew up into something close to anger when I mentioned Takosha: "Haven't seen that girl since the morning you took her to work off some community time or some damn thing," she said.

When I asked if she'd filed a missing person report, she rolled her eyes like I'd just asked if she'd eaten the neighbor's patio furniture. But, she could not entirely camouflage her worry, and she wavered a minute before setting down her Burlington bag to fish her cell phone from her purse. "Maybe you know what this means, though. It was the last text I got from her. Week ago Monday, while I was working..."

She handed me the phone. On it was a message from Takosha that had come at

9:06 a.m., about the time she was tromping down the middle of the dirt road while Naomi and me were scrounging the shoulder for old tennis shoes and gum wrappers. It read, *'You never believe who they got me working for out here.'*

"You know who she was talking about?" Danita asked, glowering.

Technically, Takosha had been working for Julian that day, but I didn't bring his name up. The brief exchange in the cab of the pickup truck came back to me and I asked, "Have you ever heard her mention someone named Potter, a sort of grunge-punk trashy white dude with tattoos? Something happened between those two that morning. Nasty words were exchanged. Words I won't repeat."

Frazzled pique weighed Danita's face. She said, "Honestly, don't know who she goes with much these days. She's had a drink problem her whole life long. Never heard about anybody called Potter. Anyway, why are you here? When I saw you, I thought you might have heard something."

"I really haven't," I apologized, but I slipped the crystal pendant from my jacket pocket. "Except that one of the rangers found this on the trail at August Lake park. That's where we were working that day and I was hoping I could give it back to her in person."

Danita took the piece reverently, pressing it against her own massive bosom. Her eyes misted over. "Our daddy gave this to her. I think on her twelfth birthday. She wouldn't have just… lost it."

"That was my first thought too," I said. At this point, I didn't want to tell her about the whisky bottle by the roadside. "But, people do lose things. I know how much it meant to her; I just wanted to return it. If you hear from her, anything at all, please let me know. She was—she *is*—doing so well. We're all so proud of her in the group."

Danita softened perceptibly, and as the carrion birds began to fade back into their ghetto rookeries and a handful of gainfully employed townhouse residents returned from jobs, she shared a number of details of the hard knock life that the sisters had grown with; the racial stigmas, the fallout from drugs, the endless poverty and chains of abuse, making my own innocuous childhood alienation seem overwhelmingly pedestrian. She talked of street code and an opposition culture in which there was an expectation that people raised in such primeval wastelands would wind up in prison or dead. The segue into 'decent values', as Danita put it, was the exception, not the rule.

I had thought that Takosha was the most streetwise woman I had ever met, but as the daylight arced, with the hoodrats returned to their nests, I realized that the real wisdom lay in rising far enough above it far enough to view the street in bird's eye.

I left with a network of revelations about Takosha DeYoung and her motivations, and equally, with the conviction that I would never see her again.

I missed Julian. I was frustrated that I couldn't consult him; that he had no cell phone. On the other hand, he was likely somewhere up in Buttfuck Egypt without a signal if he'd had one. I wanted to file a missing person report for Takosha myself, but I sensed that a spotlight on the park was the very thing he was trying to avoid by taking drunken Alan's place on the retreat. I even called the park and spoke to Stony, and he was vague and dismissive. He only had nine months to go, he reminded me. But he confirmed that he'd found the crystal pendant on a trail near where we'd been litter-sweeping and left it on a cabin nail to glisten in the stubborn sunshine.

On Friday, just as I was leaving to retrieve Julian's legal papers, Blake from Alchemy called and begged me to switch shifts with him; his Friday night for my Saturday night so he could attend some fag-o-rama concert in Detroit. I agreed, though the timing would mean that I would have to wait until after my shift to take the documents to Julian's phantom apartment in downtown Pontiac.

But I was as good as my word: I pulled into the Sunoco station at five minutes before two, and the powder-blue Lexus was there already, parked between the air hose machine and an orange box for shoe donations. Nice car, too. A GS 350. The man driving looked the part; he was acerbically good-looking in a metrosexual way with airy, feathered hair and a Prada suit.

It looked like carefree affluence, but his attitude didn't match it. He unrolled his window just a crack and snapped, "Who are you?"

121

I answered as tersely, as though having slept with Julian once made me inextricably linked to his daily drama. "Well, I'm Dixie Pickett. Why, is it a problem?"

"Where's the other kid? The bald one?"

"He's sick," I said. "Julian sent *me* instead."

It was mad vanity on my part. Besides, the man had already closed his window and was briefly on his phone. Beyond, the squat gas station, on the cusp of Bloomfield Hills, one of those most prosperous communities in the country, had a huge sign that said *'We accept bridge cards.'*

A moment later, the Lexus man lowered the window slightly again and passed me a sealed bubble-wrap mailing envelope with nothing written on the outside, and promptly peeled out of the lot.

That was it. The whole encounter took less than five minutes, and a half an hour later, I was polishing silverware at Alchemy Bistro with the envelope locked in the trunk of my Focus.

My shift was slow, with a smattering of regulars and a cranky older couple who insisted that their Ahi tuna tasted fishy—a comical complaint, but I suppose these are the types who'd find my paintings too painty. They were my last table; Jennifer claimed that most of our demographics were, like Blake, at the concert downtown. It was okay by me and I was out the door fifteen minutes after the cranky couple left.

I walked out into a clean, crisp and wintery night. My breath came in short puffs, like white cotton-candy fog. The bars and nightclubs on that small strip of Pontiac were hopping, but any illusion of viability ended at the intersection with Huron Street, as if there was a power outage just beyond it. The address Julian had given me was in that next block, and there was enough vitality leaking over to make the building something slightly less than intimidating. I'd driven by the apartment already and assumed that I'd misheard him say that it was over a nightclub. The stairway leading to the upper floor was the rear of the building, only a couple of blocks from Alchemy, but the storefront below it was one of those elaborate nineteenth century façades with cast iron columns and sandstone cornices, but it was boarded up, with bars over the boards. The recessed doorway was overgrown on either side with weeds, already tall in May.

The fact that it looked abandoned didn't alarm me. There were plenty of empty storefronts in Pontiac along what had once been a prime commercial ribbon, and lots of the apartments over them were still occupied. In fact, opposite the address was the beetling, empty five-story Masonic Temple Lodge 25, built in the twenties and abandoned in the eighties. There was only a single business on the whole block that seemed to be solvent: Gail's African Hair Braiding.

Around back, I maneuvered beyond a trashed easy chair and mattress upended against the bricks, and I climbed the series of rickety wooden steps that led to a deck landing. A concussive thumping pulsed through the railing, coming from somewhere far away. I assumed that another apartment over one of the adjacent storefronts was playing music.

At the top of the stairs, I faced a very ordinary door; unmarked, weathered and once, a long time ago, painted brown. Normally, after dark, this sort of scenario would have scared the bejeebers out of me, but there was something unexplainable here that made me feel perfectly safe. Maybe it was my conviction that Julian wouldn't have sent me anywhere squirrely, or maybe the percussive vibrations gave me that visceral, prescient thrill that the jungle drums do in the old Tarzan movies. Certainly, I was insanely curious to see what sort of city dwelling my Henry David Thoreau kept, even if he didn't use it much. The key fit; I went inside and turned on the light.

I don't know what I was expecting, but not this.

The apartment was much larger than the outside suggested. It was loft-sized, minimalist, immaculately finished off and almost hysterically pristine. The first thing I noticed was the Victorian-looking table just beyond the vestibule, exquisitely polished and gilded with black onyx. It was such a striking piece that it must have been the stone table that Julian mentioned; someone entering for the first time could hardly have missed it.

Beyond, the room was furnished sparsely but elegantly. About midway through, a three-sided glassed-in fireplace sprouted from the floor to the ceiling, and before it were conversation-pit pieces of furniture upholstered in warm, tufted leather. To the left was an open kitchen fitted with state-of-the-art appliances and an open door leading to a wash of neutrals with a pop of green; a bathroom. The wall hangings were of a theme: Extremely well-executed drawings of young men, what a prude with an eye for art might have called 'tasteful nudes'. I swear, taken in aggregate, the apartment was something an aesthetically-driven gay couple would have swooned over.

But, no way. No... *way.* I'd interacted with gay boys for two years in art school, and I half-suspected Corky Geshke of harboring a little manhole curiosity. I was convinced I was keen to the clues. Besides, I'd felt Julian move within me and there'd been nothing in his response that was anything but red-blooded hetero.

And yet, there was an awful lot of *'and yet'* inside that apartment loft.

I might have pried. I might have gone through the drawers or the medicine cabinet, but there was such stylized sterility about the place that I doubt I would have found anything personal. It was all lines, geometry and mirrors that reflected everything back on itself.

I had thought Kevorkian cabin was the flip side of Julian's cozy cottage in the dale, but clearly, on a level that was much more mystifying, this apartment was.

Awestruck, baffled, fascinated and lethally snoopy, I moved inside deeper inside. A single master bedroom lay on the far end of the great central room. It was lined in rich coal-grey carpet with a massive black statement chandelier suspended from the center of the ten foot ceiling. A bed sprawled beneath it, framed in lacquered ebony and capped with zebra skin pillows. A large settee sat at the base; opposite was a gold cabinet that housed a sixty-inch television set and a PlayStation for games.

Gradually, a weird dreamlike fugue flooded me, far different from the sharpened acuity of Jivarrão—this was a feeling that I had stepped from the colorless door of my crashed Kansas farmhouse into a different world where the rationale was entirely beyond my grasp.

The rhythmic thumping that had resonated through the wooden railing outside was stronger and more ominous here, and I understood suddenly that it was coming from inside the building. And, inside the bedroom, I noticed that what I had taken for a walk-in closet was actually a sort of mini-vestibule that led to a personal, glass-enclosed elevator.

Julian must have known I would see all of this. He'd given me the key, hadn't he? Could he have known I'd take the elevator?

And how could I not?

Now, suddenly, I was no longer Dorothy. I wasn't even Alice pulling back the curtain to find the tiny door that matched her golden key. I was every girl in every horror flick looking at the cellar stairs while the audience screams *'Don't go in the basement'*, knowing, of course, that she will, that she must, that things have spiraled beyond choice and into mandate, and that what she'll find at the bottom is her own personalized and exquisite doom.

The elevator went down several floors and opened into a labyrinth of motile, heady, smoky activity, sumptuous and corrupt, intimate and expansive. Had the Mad Hatter tumbled through his own looking glass, this is what he might have seen: A world even madder than his Wonderland asylum. In the time since I stood in that sprawling basement, I've found a line from Beowulf that fits the scene I stepped into:

'He dwelt for a time among the banished monsters, who lurked and swooped in the long nights on the misty moors where reavers from hell roam on their errands'.

Lights of various colors, some garish, some subdued, flashed against walls painted in a number of motifs. Elaborate Egyptian hieroglyphs and cartouches ran up one while on another, a sinuous, sensual tapestry showed a Bacchanalian scene with naked boys playing lutes and pouring wine. A third was a mural-ized recreation of Caravaggio's ideal, *Love Conquers All*. Architectural cinderblocks were practical panache making Deco columns, and the roof appeared to be domed; a rare sight in a cellar, for sure.

A purebred blonde chick in waitress get-up must have also been a rare sight in that raging cellar. I stepped from the glass elevator into a crazy male melee. Men within turned to gape at me with such surprise that, thinking back, I might have sworn that even the music—the strange, modal beat I'd heard ringing through the railing and oscillating through the floor—stopped.

Nearest me, a freakishly tall dude with a shoulder-length platinum bob stood in orchestrated lethargy, with long fingernails sharpened to points and tattoos running up each finger. "Oh my," he said, affecting a stagecraft sashay, "Here comes trouble."

His partner, clinging to him in an exaggerated show of neediness, wearing a polyurethane jumpsuit and face paint that made him look like an anime minstrel, hissed, "What's urban decay come to?"

Beside him, a fat man wearing a Tank Girl beanie and a toga with a Kaiser Permanente logo cuddled a tiny poodle whose right paw he made wave to me: "Say hello to the nice lost *shiksa,* Barky."

It was a dress-up game inside vast playroom; a Satyricon confab of silk and spandex and floral jeggings. Men meandered about, many holding drinks or props, a Slush Puppy hand purse, a wand, a pet, while adolescent twinks wended between them dressed in checkered skirts and red pillbox hats. The boys were dispensing items from a tray held by a neck strap and I guessed that whatever they were distributing was not Lucky Strikes.

At first glance, it was a sideshow of purest overkill, next-level weird, a preposterous parody of a fifties theater lobby or a chic Hollywood cabaret. To me, honestly, it was more cool than horrifying.

So why did my legs go out from under me? It was an inner ear thing, I think. It was like motion sickness, where your brain tells your body one thing, and your body tells your brain another. In this case, I suppose, my brain told my body I was asleep and should be lying down.

Because, the most freakish part of the entire scene was that I knew many of the people that were suddenly staring at me, just as I had recognized familiar faces in my old detox dreams involving gigantic parties filled with hedonistic excesses. But— exactly as happened in those dreams—nobody I recognized was behaving quite as they did in waking life. Everyone appeared to be a nightmare version of themselves.

In a low conversation pit around an open hearth, Serafin Tercerio was dressed in one of the cigarette girl costume but with a wreath of roses around his head instead of a pillbox hat. He sat between two men in Dead Poet Society-style tweeds, with a nylon-clad leg on the lap of one of the men who was stroking the sole of his foot. The newest member of Julian's crew—the tall one I'd seen him talking to outside the cottage on the morning we went hunting—was there in a boating blouse, a captain's cap and blue loafers. The boys I'd seen in the back of the truck when Julian and I were hiding in the underbrush were there as well, circulating among the older men.

But, the strangest, most inexplicable and unshakably dreamlike sight of all stood off to one side, wearing an open, periwinkle robe and an insolent Jack-o-lantern smirk. It was Simon Mackie, the doctor who'd ratted me out to my boss at Alchemy. He stood spread-legged while the Prada-clad lawyer whose paperwork I had retrieved that afternoon whispered in his ear. In fact, I had just left those papers on the onyx table upstairs. The two interns who'd been with Mackie at Alchemy were there as well, preening and snickering.

Vertigo kicked in and down I went.

There was a swift swirl of strident voices around me. Briefly, I was caught in a vortex at the base of a waterfall:

"...narcolepsy is a bitch..."

"Squalay!"

"...give me a real; membership goalposts moved again...?"

"...I'm gonna have to rethink my whole aesthetic..."

"...she looks like my mother before five kids, menopause and a thousand gallons of Vat 69..."

And, to feather the cap of the lucid nightmare, I was shortly lifted to my feet by a grunge-punk trashy dude with tattoos: Potter, now bare-chested, with electric blue hair.

"C'mon, hon, we need to get you out of here now. Where's your car?"

"Out back," I said weakly, "Julian said..."

"Never mind what Julian said," he answered, tugging my arm, propelling me violently and quickly toward the rear where there was an arch and a shadowed hallway. Behind us, the thudding rhythms and cacophony of voices continued:

"...oh, leave her be, Potter; she's come to avenge the souls of the fallen..."

"... what *are* they going to send in next, mustard gas?"

...she found the prize at the bottom of the three thousand square foot Cracker Jack box, queens. It's the insanity of postmodern consciousness."

I didn't struggle and Potter was strong enough that it would have been futile if I had. We passed beneath the arch, down the hallway, through a dark doorway and up a series of concrete steps that were lined, I noted, with something textured made of hard rubber—safer than concrete, perhaps, for lifts—and into the alley with the cast-off arm chair and vertical mattress. Potter hustled me into my Focus, saying, "I don't know what you've got going on with Julian. The dude's life is one long, stoned *Survivor* episode. But this culture is no place for you, not ever. If you're okay to drive, I recommend you do it and don't come back."

I did drive and he watched me go. I went home to my hollow apartment, where I stayed awake the rest of the night, drinking organic kombucha and turning the sequence of events over and over in my head like a backyard compost pile. And, like the compost pile, no matter how many times I turned it over, it kept coming up shit. His mother's club? Could you take eccentric disability and raise it to the power of infinity? And, beamed down from a gay spaceship behind the meteor, Simon Mackie in nothing but a bathrobe? For a guy with a salary in seven figures, I had no wish to know what went on inside *that* head. And how in the living fuck did my new Earth Daddy fit into this pederastic, Gatsby-esque nocturnal emission?

No way to get there from here. Not to Julian Vaz, the man whose memory was tugging at my heart and body.

128

When the sun came up, I was no closer to working any of it out, but that point, I suppose, goes without saying.

19.

This brings me to the following day, and the pivotal occasion on which the rest of the story turns.

I spent Saturday in a sort of narcoleptic daze, unable to focus on much. I tried some therapeutic housecleaning and did some rudimentary, pointless shopping, buying things I really didn't need. I tried to jog, then I tried to nap, but my brain remained in overdrive and every time I closed my eyes, I saw an intricate latticework of images, none particularly pleasant.

I even drove down Ottawa again. Gail's African Hair Braiding was now open and in front of it, a woman sat on a folding chair. With her neon red dashiki and neon cornrowed buns, I concluded that she had everything she needed to be a member of the club across the street except her gender. That particular building looked as deserted and godforsaken as it had before, but around back, there was activity: Apparently, the vertical mattress was actually a lean-to, and now, a middle aged man squatted before it making little piles of found electronics; earbuds, computer cables, old telephone cords. I drove away.

By Sunday, I was ticking down the hours until Julian came back from his trip doing whatever it was that park rangers did in Minnesota. At nine, I left for my brunch shift at Alchemy, and as soon as I got there, Jennifer Kannenburg asked me to step into her annexed office in the bathroom hallway.

"This is awkward and difficult, Dixie" she said. "To be frank, I'm not even entirely sure that it's legal, but I'm really out of options. Sue me if you want, but something tells me you won't be hiring lawyers unless it's for... the other thing."

I sat there with my mouth open. I knew how I must look: I'd seen the same blank, slack-jawed expression I was wearing on the faces of schoolkids in Ohio in algebra class, like they'd eaten one too many PB&J sandwiches and had a permanent wedge had formed in their palates. I'd seen it on the faces of homeless junkies in Detroit, and I suppose I'd even seen it on my mother's face when I'd announced that I was abandoning Cadence for the heart of a city that she'd once referred to, under her breath and in her pea-brained perspective, as 'Niggertown'.

Jennifer went on: "Simon Mackie was in last night, and he took me aside and shared something that disturbed me deeply. I hope you understand; at this point, on his part, it's nothing but hearsay. But as you also know, he has a lot of influence over the direction Alchemy will take going forward."

"Spit it out," I snipped. "What's the problem?"

Obviously she was talking about my unexpected appearance at the creepy nightclub in the basement of the so-called abandoned building down the street. Well, that was perfectly innocent, but Mackie's mincing bathrobe prance through a sex rave that looked like it was even too far left field for NAMBLA might not be.

But that's not what she said. She said:

"Dr. Mackie says that he has it on authority that you are involved in an extortion scam targeting a friend of his, who also happens to be a lawyer, by the way. You ought to be aware of that and the legal liability. I don't know if this is tied to the new guy you've been talking about, but Dixie, I think I know you better than this, so I'm guessing it probably is. None of my business, none of it, but if the shit were to hit the fan—and sooner or later, I can't see how it won't—a scandal like that can't be allowed to touch Alchemy. That would be the end of us. So, sorry as I am, Dixie, I wish you the best in getting your life together before it's too late. But I gotta let you go…"

And off I went. There was nothing I could say. She wasn't open to alternative explanations, nor did I have a particularly credible one to offer. Sucks to be Dixie. And so my life, orchestrated with equal parts caution and carelessness, entered, on that warm morning in late May, another relentless collapse.

A final note here:

The intimate night I spent with Julian Vaz beneath wheeling constellations in far corner of August Lake State Park was only the fourth sexual relationship I'd ever had. My cherry-buster with Kyle Andrus had been a lonely sizzle, a bottle rocket dud. The second time, with a semi-tanked fiancé, was a quick revelation of the hypocrisy inherent in those who claim to love you. The dozen or so incidents of textbook intercourse I'd bestowed upon poor trust-fund Corky were essentially me accommodating a rutting season: His, not mine.

With Julian, of course, the lights had come on in some secret arcade within my psyche, but that's not even the point.

The point is, thanks to a diagnosis when I was fourteen years old by some hack doctor in Cadence, Ohio, I was led to believe that I had sterility built into my hardware. As a result, for me, using birth control was never even an afterthought.

So, to this day, one of the inscrutables that has underscored my addled, luckless life is how I managed to come up pregnant.

Part Two: *I went from God to God until they cried from within me: "O, Thou I"*

20.

Sexual communion without procreation may be trivial on a biological scale, and it may even be trivial on a social scale, but since we aren't organic machines and since it's the most intimate form of physical expression we can share, if it's trivial, we're trivial.

And I refuse to believe that.

Obviously, I didn't yet know I was pregnant when I parked my Focus beneath the pine stand in front of the stone cottage at five in the morning on the Tuesday that followed. My impetus was raw confusion and my goal was raw confrontation. The sandstone had dissolved under me and the sinkhole was engulfing me. Fuck the mildly cosmic Jivarrão jive: I had the unshakable fear that I had mainlined something so huge and nihilistic that it could chew me down to atoms. It was Grey Ice made flesh, and the juxtaposed players must have had some soluble connection, but none in any universe I could rationalize.

And my God, I'd tried. After three days, the gentle rocking, the serene consummation, the fierce but tranquil presence that had so kindled me still had no place in the scene at which he was the indisputable center. There was no way to connect the dots. All people have secret cellars, I knew that. But when there is toxicity flourishing down there, creeping like mold up the walls, only someone who had learned nothing over the past four tumultuous, private and painful years could miss it.

Whatever it was, I wanted the answer down and fixed, so I settled in with a collection of poems by Rumi and a couple of protein bars and waited for the sun to come up, intending to sit in my car for as long as it took for Julian to re-appear.

Over the past three days, I'd spend many hours ruminating and only few sleeping. On Sunday after I'd been fired, I'd bounced around my immediate world in a stupor of indignation. Drunk people do stupid things that land them in handcuffs, but sober people realize that falling down the throat of an impersonal but ravenous legal system is always on either side of our tight rope, so we are ever on the alert.

Had I been inadvertently scammed? The possibility was so horrific that it deconstructed me. It took me back down my life like a film in reverse until I felt like a hollow husk, the way I'd been at birth. And it occurred to me as a vague epiphany that I needed now what I needed then: Maternal omnipotence.

So I called home.

Home, where there was no identity but plenty of stability; where there was, at least, bland sanity. In my mood, the blander it was, the better. Without question, home represented at least an illusion of rootedness and the security of boredom, and the tone of the conversation with my mom went much better than I had any right to expect.

It helped that I was looking for neither validation nor penance, only base-level mommy comfort, like I had when I was six and had the flu.

So far, I had kept the juiciest bits of my personal life on the down low. Although Mom and Toby Paw-Pop knew that my landlord had been murdered, they didn't know we had been, In some nominal **sense**, a romantic couple. They knew I'd had legal issues related to my drinking, but they didn't know how deeply into the swamp of nihilistic alcoholism I'd crawled. They certainly didn't know about my jail time. The few conversations I'd had with my mom over the past four years had been deliberately heart-shaped and strained through emotional cheesecloth, and her reaction to Corky's death had simply been to breathe relief that I hadn't been home at the time. Now that I was on a firm path of sobriety, she expressed eternal eagerness to help. I spilled my tale of losing my Alchemy job through a series of unfortunate events and beyond that, I didn't elaborate. I told her that since I couldn't use Jennifer Kannenburg as a reference, my biggest worry was that I had nothing respectable to put on my resumé for what I'd been doing for work over the past six months.

I was not fishing for someone to bail me out, but somehow, she did.

Since around the time I'd left Cadence, Paw-Pop had been supplementing his Purina income with a small contracting business he'd started, mostly drywall work and light construction gigs. He operated out of an extended garage on Scioto Street and mom had set up a small office in my Daddy's old library.

She said, "Well, I answer phones and do featherweight bookkeeping for Paw-Pop's company. You know, if you wanted, I'm sure he'd be happy to say that it's *you* who have been working for him. I can email you details of what I do and how I do it, and if a recruiter called us, we'd just say it's you who's been doing it, like as your job. And you *could* do it, Dix—you were always good at math."

"That must have been some other daughter, Ma—I sucked at math."

"You didn't. You got Bs. And a B+ in geometry once. That's better than I did. Anyway, it's easy. There's an old Quicken program I use and Toby has more work around the corner. He's a genuine handyman—you should see what he did to the basement. At this rate, he'll do his thirty-and-out with Purina and it will be a full time operation for him."

"Well, that's awesome for the two of you, I guess."

"In fact, you know what *would* be awesome? If you actually did it. Came back home and took over the accounting end of Toby's business."

To be sure, I wasn't ready for that, but I was willing to bask in the glow of her love and trust for a little while. It was evident that she wanted us to be closer, and I chastised myself for not having made more of an effort over the past four years. I answered, "That's a sweet idea, Ma, but believe it or not, I'm still building some sort of life for myself up here. But I will take you up on your offer to use Paw-Pop as a reference."

And I did. I went online first thing Monday morning, after the snow blindness of Sunday had somewhat abated and my hearing no longer reverberated with the thunder-clap of Jennifer Kannenburg's voice, and I filled out an application for Matrix Temporary Services using Murphy Construction of Cadence, Ohio as my current job. I said that it was a family business, and that I worked out of my apartment, on the internet, and voilà, as far as my recent employment history went, the bullshit of Alchemy Bistro vanished like a wisp of fog over August Lake.

As soon as it got light, I went and peeked inside the windows of the stone cottage. The guitar hung on its peg, the kayak was suspended by ropes, the shelves were filled with jars and bowls and bundles of herbs, and, above the hearth, my painting oversaw it all. But today, apparently, there was nothing to oversee: The house was empty.

I returned to my car and a short time later, the green pickup truck rumbled up and pulled alongside me. Potter stuck a crooked elbow out the window. There was a tattoo of the crucified Christ on the arm, only each point of the cross was bent like a swastika.

"Seriously?" he snickered. "Obsess much? Julian isn't even here."

"I'm waiting for him. He'll explain what happened the other night. What I... stumbled into."

"No he won't," Potter laughed. "You can get into his pants but you can't get into his head. What do you care? That's not your world anyway. You didn't belong at Sophrosyne any more than you belonged in the Suicide Suites out there in the North Unit."

The smirk hung on his ugly lips like a smear. I eyed him lightly and intuitively and in that brief continuum, I understood as truth what I'd previously only suspected: "You know what happened to Takosha, don't you?"

"Queen Kong? She went missing, that's what I know. Read a newsfeed. It happens all the time to people who'd rather live on their knees than on their feet."

"You're completely sick," I replied.

"Damn, I am—I have a case of white superiority complex. Hey, come on—tang is tang, but if a dude's gonna fuck a nigger he should at least pick Venus Williams who's worth a hundred million dollars."

I ignored the ham-fisted stupidity and pressed on, because it seemed like now or never: "Is Takosha alive? Her sister deserves to know."

"Oh, the sister? She deserves a boat back to Zimbabwe. Look, nobody here gonna

135

magically produce anybody, so you'd better stop asking."

"My God," I said in disgust. "Do you talk like this around Stony?"

That really broke him up: "If Stony doesn't like how I speak, he can tell me himself. Tell you what, I'm easy to find."

The boys in the back of the truck were also cawing with laughter. There was the tall kid from the club and a couple others who I believe I might have also seen in the periphery that night dressed in outlandish gear.

Next to Potter sat Serafin Tercerio. I didn't notice him at first because he had his head turned away, buried in his jacket, obviously embarrassed. "Serafin Tercerio," I barked. "You have to know that degrading stuff you were up to on Friday night is illegal. You're way too young to be in bars anyway, let alone pervert bars. There's something going on there even more fucked up than pedo shit, I know that for a fact. What in the world were you…"

And then, my phone rang. I'd have ignored it simply to continue the sermon, but it was Kara from Matrix Temporary Services. I sighed in exasperation, rolled up my window, as, with the echo of chortles from the kids in back, the truck thundered off.

Kara introduced herself and said, "Everything on your application seems to be in order, Dixie, and I actually have something that might be a good fit for you. What sort of availability would you have to come in for an interview?"

"Any time, really," I answered quickly. "Tomorrow morning, first thing? I'm eager. Like I said in the cover letter, my step-father's business is in the doldrums right now."

"Great! I like eager. But, the position begins as soon as I can place someone; the sooner the better. How about coming in this afternoon, right after lunch? Around one? Possible?"

That caught in my throat. Today was my Julian confrontation day, and I'd been watching the hourglass since Sunday at noon. She went on: "It's a small manufacturing firm out in Sterling Heights. They're looking for a receptionist to fill in for the next two weeks due to a medical emergency. It sounds perfect for someone with your background, but I need to flip the position quickly, as you can probably appreciate..."

I could, so I re-evaluated my situation and re-set the hour glass. I could certainly pull off an interview at one and be back here at the park by late afternoon. And maybe that made more sense anyway: There was no telling what sort of emotional mess I might be in after speaking to Julian. Not only that, but for whatever mind-trick reason, when her name came up on my phone I thought it said 'Karma' instead of Kara. So, I agreed.

It was a wrench in the catharsis though, and predictably, I was batting so many conflicting thoughts around the backcourt that I got physically lost, tooling down several cookie-cutter country roads until I found something familiar: The sparkle of broken glass from the camera Julian had shot with the slingshot. I followed that road, and ultimately, I came upon the park headquarters.

It was still only ten in the morning, and there was plenty of time for me to leave a message for Julian here like the one I'd left on the door of the stone cottage. I pulled into the tiny lot and went in through the front entrance. Inside, there was an empty desk paneled in knotty pine, a darkened hallway—the one from which I'd first seen Julian emerge—and, on the far side of the desk, an office door, slightly ajar, from which bleary, bluish light escaped.

I pushed it open and said, "Hello?"

Alan wasn't even startled. He was too far gone for that. But this time, I guessed, it was not solely alcohol. He was staring at a computer with a look of emptiness so heartrending that the only place I'd ever seen it before was in photos of famine victims. Other than the backwash from the computer screen, the room was dark and the shades were drawn. Reflected in the pale blue, I could see photos of two fat teenagers on the desk and a plaque that read *'The Hurrier I Go, the Behinder I Get.'*

"Sorry to disturb you, but do you know when Julian will be back?"

The computer speakers leaked a jumble of frantic voices; he was watching *Smoky*

137

and the Bandit. "What day is it?" he asked without looking up.

"Tuesday."

He considered it for a moment and when he spoke, he sounded strained and hoarse: "He's not on until tomorrow. Tuesday is, ah... a Stony day."

"If you say so, Alan. I'm asking if you know when he's coming back from back-packing in Minnesota or wherever the fuck he is. He's been gone for a week. You're aware of that, right? Dude, come on. Get your shit together."

Now he turned his head and his eyes seem to constrict further behind his swollen nose. The profundity of sadness is one thing in a face, but this was an expression absolute, unyielding vacancy: "Ah, as long as him and the little Band of Brothers get the work done, he can make his own schedule. Unless I hear complaints from park visitors, I have to assume that—ah— the job is being done right."

"I've been through the park, dude. You have no fucking visitors that could complain."

The weight of addiction hauled him down and I was familiar with it. He gaped at his computer screen and I backtracked out of the room. As I did, I added, "By the way, one of your secret trail-head cameras is broken. There's glass all over the road."

At the front desk, on a pad of paper by the phone, I wrote a hasty note to Julian: *'Need to speak with you, obviously. Dix.'*

From the office behind me came Alan's hollow, hounded voice: "Why do you call them *my* cameras, Dixie Chicks? Pretty boy put them up, I didn't. I'd take 'em all down if I could find 'em."

Another head scratcher, but I did the right thing: I wrote a number down on another page from the notepad and slipped back into Alan's office, saying, "We meet in the basement of St. Bede's twice a week. You should do yourself a favor and come."

He gazed at me through his tiny red eyes and in that instant I recognized something almost majestic in his self-destruction. It was like watching a slow motion film of an atomic blast. From the speakers, ominous music seeped, followed by Jackie Gleason's voice: *"Hold up on that car, white gen'lemen."*

"You may feel like you're alone, but you aren't," I said in a tone that I intended to be perceptive, supportive, and encouraging, but it probably wasn't. In the end, I was spewing AA rhetoric, which even I no longer even bought into, and I dropped the number beside the cyanic photo of his fat kids and split.

On the way home I stopped at Target and bought a conservative, pale-peach blouse. I showered again, and assembled myself in what I guessed would be considered business casual at a small manufacturing firm in Sterling Heights: Coordinated separates, neutral slacks and an older pair of Franco Sorto loafers with two-inch heels that I spit-shined into looking new.

The interview was a total victory. Kara and I hit it off immediately. She was about my age and we appeared to share a little instantaneous, if subconscious understanding about the requisite level of bullshit involved in our charade, where she did her dopey job as I tried to score an even dopier one. I aced all her questions, and if she suspected any resumé finagling, she didn't let on. She was satisfied to the point where she told me to wait in the lobby while she made the call to Molnar Manufacturing. After fifteen minutes, she returned with a smile: "The job is yours if you want it and if you can start tomorrow morning at eight. It pays a little less than you're used to with your step-father, but on the plus side, you won't have to do any math."

Okay, so it was a temporary job, but that was fine. It was also a temporary ego boost and it allowed me to postpone financial meltdown for a while. I figured if I did as well at Molnar as I had done in the interview, there'd be a string of such positions available in the future. Kara had said as much. Not only that, but a lot of these jobs ended up being permanent.

That load was lifted, and it's amazing how liberating it was to my spirits. It allowed me a clearer head to consider every complicated snare that had snagged me over the past week, the past month, the past twenty-odd years. With Julian, there were esoteric, poetic grounds; the communion of the heart's-a-lonely hunter with the hunted and the mystery of repressed emotion. It was heady territory, and if I needed to, if I put my mind to it, if I was tugged by an addiction again and if addiction was an inexpungible demon, I was convinced that I'd be able to intellectualize my way out of the specifics. I concluded that since horniness had never been my boogeyman, I must have been blinded by a literary crush.

Even so, there was no intellectualizing the gonadal thrill I felt when I pulled into my apartment complex and saw Julian sitting on the concrete landing in front of my apartment, legs bent gracefully into the *padmasana*, honey hair loose, mint-green eyes alert, shimmering with his quiet light and—as I saw it then, but no longer do—a profound emotional contradiction: Intense indifference.

21.

It was him redoubled, wrapped in the moment. I knew I'd written my address down on my form, but my mind had to adjust to seeing him outside his park, just as I would have had to seeing a beautiful beast on the far side of a zoo wall. It was a fundamental modification and ultimately, it was ridiculous because I knew he'd just spent a week outside those walls. But my nerves tingled. Double vision threw me. It was intimidation seasoned with intrigue. The peculiar luster of his marigold skin and butterscotch hair reminded me of Monet's water lilies. He exuded even-keel confidence and his force of character was evident in every crook in his limbs.

And I found that desperately sexy. So, crucify me: At that point, there was no threat without concession, and my own sense of self-preservation overrode my libido, thank you.

I approached him tentatively, if eagerness can be so oxymoronic. "Do you have any idea what I've been dealing with for the past three days?" I asked, perhaps louder than the situation required.

His voice and eyes were perfectly clear; he was composed and not in the least defensive. "Probably not. I know some and I'll listen to the rest."

Observe and register, I told myself. I said, "You need to do more talking than listening, Julian. Unless you totally catfished me, unless you never wanted anything more than a bail-money kind of relationship with me in the first place, I need that.

Dude, I mean seriously. Something insane is going on inside a place where I thought I'd finally found some sanity."

Meanwhile, I was still trying to reconcile the strangeness of the current scenario: "How did you get here, anyway?"

He sounded forthright, genuine and half-amused: "I'm sure you have some doubts about me, Dixie, but not about my sense of what's practical."

"Well, maybe, but it's hard to know what I know. You get that, right? I've been waiting to talk to you since Friday night and suddenly, now, I don't want to say anything at all. I want *you* to talk to *me*. Forget the fucking macho minimalism for an hour. I want you to tell me what's going on."

"Alright," he answered easily.

"Maybe you should come inside?"

"Do you trust me enough to take me inside?"

"That's a point," I nodded quickly—my concession. "I trusted you inside my body, but right now, I don't think I trust you inside my home."

Actually, I didn't trust myself, but I didn't say that. He didn't need to know, although in honesty, he probably did. He replied, "A roof keeps snow off. It's sunny and we're better off outdoors. *That's* home."

In the rear of my apartment complex, near the transformers and a reasonable distance from the dumpsters, there was a small grassy area with a picnic table and a park bench beneath a flowering red buckeye tree. I loved this particular perk of the place; we had a tree like this in our yard on Scioto Street, and I liked to use the bench to snuggle beneath the spreading brown limbs and read, especially when oppressiveness of my half-finished apartment weighed on me too heavily. It was, in every sense, a safe spot, unlike the common area at Takosha's townhouses on the other side of town. Although my neighbors were mostly black people, they seemed to be less restless and more affluent here. As I led Julian around back, a young girl rode by on a pink Vespa while a pair of boys passed wearing clean red t-shirts from the Pontiac Technology Academy.

I scented Julian. I wanted to hold his hand; I wanted to touch the indentation below his cheekbones. I wanted to stroke the nape of his neck, I wanted to lay with him on the grass. His shirt was remarkable; it was the most beautiful batik work I'd ever seen, filled with serpentine shapes of many dimensions, many hues. It seemed organic, almost part of him.

We took spots on opposite sides of the picnic table and I didn't mention the shirt. Or the taut torso that steamed beneath it. I did my best to keep my own keel even and my voice on the good side of whiny. I said, "At least start with explaining why I got fired from my job. Who is the dude in the blue Lexus, and are you blackmailing him?"

His response was measured and immediate: "His name is Kevin Winters. He's a lawyer, and he's in the process of buying Sophrosyne, the club. He's paying it off in installments. You picked up one of the installments."

"Come on. I was fired over some supposed extortion plot. At least, that's what my boss told me. I could tell the lawyer dude was pissed off. He didn't want to hand the envelope over. Are you *forcing* him to buy the club, Julian?"

"There's complexity in that, for sure. Last month, Kevin Winters was involved in an incident with Serafin Tercerio at the park. It's on video. It's not cool. He's buying the club as a consequence and Serafin will be taken care of from the proceeds. My mother doesn't want or need the money."

"Oh, my god," I cried. "It *is* a fucking plot. For Christ sake, Julian—why didn't you just say so? Why me, though? I came to the park to stay out of jail, not go to jail. Why not go to the cops? If it's sex, Serafin is fifteen and it's statutory rape. You *have* to go to the cops."

"Can't. Serafin has no papers. He's here illegally. Besides, going to the police is not a solution I work with. I'm sorry, but that's the way it is. It's white man resolution. This was a crime against Serafin's family and we are his family and it happened in his forest. We don't make Kevin Winters forfeit to the police, we make him forfeit to us. My mother needed to sell the club, and now she has. It works."

It was wise, manipulative language, but behind it was something much more volatile: I recognized a total lack of artifice in the explanation. And perhaps as a result, I began to buy it. It was clever and, as far as I could tell, clarity amid the fog.

Why it had to involve me, though? Another story: I said, "Picking up a drop? Is that what you wanted me for, beside my cootch? I don't mean that as nasty, Julian, but, come on. After our night, did you ever hope for any sort of relationship with me? I mean, you didn't exactly take my cherry, but on Friday, when I thought I was doing you a solid, you took my frigging income."

"That shouldn't have happened, Dixie. That's why I'm here, to fix things. Potter messed up on Friday night. He thought you'd already been by earlier in the day, in the afternoon, and he accidentally left the door to the elevator open. He knows better than that. As for your job, I can put that right. I can: I know the right people to talk to. Mackie. And if you don't want your job back, you know you can come and be with us. You can live with us, and work with us in the park."

"Oh, please; that's not what I'm after, Julian. Anyway, I have another job already. I'm coming from the interview. And that's not why I came to see you at the park anyway. I *wanted* to see you again and I hoped you wanted to see me again too. We had a lovely set of hours, and if that's going to be the end of it, that's life. Let's say goodbye now. But if it's not, I need to know what's going on in the basement of that abandoned building. How fucked up was what I saw? Let me count the ways. Your lawyer was there with the boy he raped. How could a place like that belong to your mother? To *any* mother? It's a mother's worst nightmare, I'd think. It looked like a pedophilia theme park."

His voice remained insufferably patient: "Sophrosyne is a concept from Charmides. It means 'to act the trust,' to pay heed to the nature of things. The handiwork of Sophrons has been my mother's hobby since she was a girl."

I was flustered. "See, everything you say is tinged with *huh?* I thought you said your mother was from a fucking tribe in the fucking Amazon."

"She's from Taiambé. My father was an intellectual and he wanted an intellect for her as well. He gave her Plato to read. He tried to patch her into his world, and in some ways, it worked. In fact, it worked better for her than it did for me."

"That's even more screwed up, then. Look, Julian, we can save ourselves some heavy grief. A simple question. Do you want to see me after today?"

"I do," he answered.

"Then seriously, you have to help me work this out. I need an emotional baseline. How does anyone get from a fishing village in Brazil to kiddy-diddler paradise in an abandoned building on Ottawa?"

This time, and for the first time, he frowned. "There's a lot of my past in the answer."

"Well, sure. Why not?"

"Because those are memories I don't summon."

"But why, Julian? Was it that bad for you? We're all a collection of stacked up memories, aren't we? And not much else? My memory particles define me. They're not all good particles, either. But they're still me."

"Are they? I fight against that idea. Be here now, not then."

"Can you at least try? If there's anything more for us, I need some frame to understand who you are. Nobody could think that's unreasonable, especially after everything I saw and heard on Friday."

I knew I was coming across like a lovesick puppy, but what the hell? As Jennifer K. had pointed out, you're never too old for that. I moped on: "Even what you're saying now; can I trust that it's truth and nothing but?"

"Everything I've ever told you is true, Dixie. I don't see any other way."

"Then why doesn't it add up? I mean that sincerely; the math is easy. You said your mother had been reading Plato since she was a child. Then you said your father gave these books to her. How does that work?"

"Because my mother was eleven when my father made her pregnant."

"Oh, God..." I said, and I might have dredged no deeper.

But by then, he had started to speak. I watched as the smooth brown muscles of his cheek twitched, shifted, tightened and relaxed. And briefly, it seemed to me, in some transmutation to rival a magical pass of Don Juan, Julian became Julio.

I had a sense that he wanted to unburden himself and I let him slip the shackles. I really did want the truth, and it didn't seem to be the sort of story that was possible to tell in segments. He said, "My mother is from a different atmosphere, no question. But everyone from our *aldeia* is, and like all children of all mothers, her air was the one that bound us. It came from the forest and the river, and these were the forces that saturated us. Her world is filled with entities that, back then, seemed to have more interest in human affairs than I did."

He folded his hands on the picnic table, and I slipped from my side, moved over and sat beside him. I put my hand on his back and gently pinched at the fabric of his beautiful shirt.

"Until you've experienced it, you won't know, Dixie. Every plot of wilderness in the world is filled with fathomless things, things that exist just beyond what you can touch. In the wild, without infrastructure, without a support system, you have to be practical in all things or else you die. And even then, the process of recognizing what's true and what is emotion never bottoms out. The river, the trees, the sky, the birds, they connect you on a natural level. But the rest, the unnatural? The thing you found in your painting? That's the haunting."

'Haunting' was an ideal word for the phenomenon he was describing. I felt it too. I felt it everywhere, not just in the lake; I just hadn't found the breath to express it. He went on: "That's why I pay attention to detail. It's a lock on a reality away from the world my mother sees, where everything as a supernatural experience instead of opposite. And don't get me wrong, I don't doubt her for a minute. I don't doubt any of it. To me, the mission has been learning that there may be no difference between what's unnatural and what is real."

He told his story, and was so eloquent in the telling—even the horrors—and so flawed is my ability to recreate it verbatim, with all the nuance that his abstract symbols stirred and summoned, that I will have to summarize it:

Julian was the product of his mother's rape, no question. And his sister was as well. But sex—once the harmonious heart of that indigenous culture—had been perverted by poverty and debased by invaders, and in the face of epidemics and hunger, the *aldeia* had learned to overlook such trivialities. His mother, though a child, had given herself to the doctor in exchange for saving her life. She'd been penniless and beholden to the kindness of strangers. With that, I could empathize. Julian's father had another family in Sao Paulo, a wife and children, but to his arguable credit, he did not abandon his little preteen whore; he visited as often as was convenient and nurtured her, coddled her and doted on her as he ravished her. Again, there was no stigma attached; prostitution had become the village's most profitable industry, as it was in many of in these tiny, broken towns where the ancient methods of raising crops and trapping fish had been subsumed by a sickness of mind and body introduced to the forest by white men. Julian and his sister were not immune. Their Western coloring made them targets, and the from the age of nine, the family survived on the scant income the children earned from soldiers of the Borders Battalion scattered in garrisons about the Amazon, from vicious *garimpeiros* with their dredges, revolvers and mercury, and especially, from the mercenary *marreteiros* who traveled by boat and paid for sex with clothes and rum.

The surrounding forest had been violated as well of course, poisoned by outsiders, and to him, that made it kindred. To his young mind, the forest hovered at the periphery of everything, and it was, despite repeated assaults by loggers and narcotraffickers, much bigger and more formidable than the vermin that crept along its machete paths. It was tractless beyond such tracts, and these empty, humid places became his sanctuary. His emotional deliverance was there that his drive toward self-sufficiency along the shadowed arteries snaking beneath the leaves first found expression there. As a human being, he'd been maimed, and—I saw plainly, with personal embarrassment for having forced the confrontation— that if ever a boy was born who should be allowed to flee his memories, it was him.

I'd prodded, and he'd told me without equivocation that only place he'd ever felt whole and healthy was in the forest, without the white men. He'd once called his sister pious. That was, I presumed, her own version of deliverance. Now his voice was so charged with poignant poetry that I could scarcely contain myself as I listened. He shared visions of shattered and traumatized *gamines* fleeing into churning mists, his sister and he, losing themselves for prolonged periods amid the howls of and the clicks and the purr of jaguars, finding safety behind a stockade of green, the deeper and more invulnerable the better; deep enough to be engulfed in the spice and decay of earth itself, deep enough to encounter native tribes, their distant kin, with all their mysteries, music and spiritual cosms intact inside a place where history is not bound by time.

But, he said, this had ultimately run its course. When he was fourteen, his father died and left the three of them a substantial sum of money, enough for an entirely revised, reimagined existence. Whether or not it had been his intention all along, Julian couldn't say, but in the end if not from the beginning, his father had stumbled across the righteous course. The father had a cousin in Michigan, and before he died, he'd written her and she'd agreed to sponsor the family's transit there. The cousin spoke enough English to help with the house in Bloomfield Hills and invest in real estate. Specifically, the building on Ottawa Street. The neighborhood, at the time, had been better. Again, the math was easy. At the time, Julian's mother must have been younger than I was.

In Julian's description, the cousin turned out to be an unparalleled champion. Julian spoke of her with remote and quiet reverence: "She had Indian blood close to her surface, but even here, she managed to straddle both worlds without issue. She had no children of her own was eager to help us while my mother worked her enterprises. She eased our transition without allowing us to forget our source."

No children of her own. With a start, it occurred to me that the cousin must be Madrinha. She was the Godmother, the secret sharer, the heroine in a life thus far dominated by villains. But it also means that she had seduced him, a boy who had needed some seduction, but certainly not that kind. A cousin, too; it defined imagination; the nourisher becoming the seductress. Exploitation squared. But I suppose teenage boys will screw anything that comes on to them, and for all I knew, incest might be less freaky in that culture. The flow of the narrative was so mesmerizing that I didn't pursue it. I did interject, softly, to show I was following, "That's how Sophrosyne became your mother's business?"

"Her main one—rescuing stray animals doesn't pay. She did very well with it; she was born to it. The abstraction was pure enough, and it became ludicrously popular as a private club—*erastes-eromenos*, erotic attraction, the soul of free relationships, no shame. Illegal expression forbidden—at least, in theory. It was always underground and financed by aficionados. You know some of them. They're not my kind of people, but my mother was able to maintain order. She's no longer capable of maintaining order, as you saw, so I needed to remove her name from it, divest her entirely, and that opportunity presented itself. You already know that part of the story."

"I do," I whispered.

And I knew something else, too: I was a hot mess. It was vicarious trauma, maybe, but I was hemorrhaging for my boy and his story. For Serafin as well. And for my own unique, if greatly diminished tragedies. There were new urgencies fluttering in my womb, and although I didn't know it then, the hormones that had begun to squirt through me were affecting my emotions. I was in an edge state, and I wanted to hold Julian as tightly as a mother does a child.

But I needed space to work out the convolutions; that much, and absolutely nothing else, was obvious. What he'd told me made sense, and I wasn't comfortable with how much sense it made.

I said, "Pushing the club off on the lawyer? That sounds like justice. A solution. We agreed on it once before, remember? There is no justice with jail time, but there is with personal compensation. That's the soul of it. Handle it internally, the tribal way."

As his face relaxed and his expression became easier, I took the scope of his subterranean horror inside me as fervently as I had taken his body inside me. If that's where they needed to stay, and not emerge again, I was okay with it. Things that should have drained the poetry from him had nourished it instead. I was gentle. I stroked his arm; I fondled the gorgeous fabric. We sat for a long time like that beneath the bright buckeye flowers.

My pretty Julian; my sanctuary beneath the leaves—I absorbed him while I could. After a while, I said, "Did Madrinha make your shirt?"

"She did."

"It suits you, Julian. It's beautiful, like you. I can tell how much she means to you, whoever she is. Godmother, whatever. I respect that and I wouldn't interfere with those feelings. But with us, things can be different. Better. No impediments. We can be clean, wholesome people. If you want, no memories, not any more. No past. there's now. We can be here now."

He said, "Of course," and the supremacy of his serenity, having arisen from cycles of abuse beyond imagining, astonished me.

I replied, "You understand that I need time to line all this up, especially the stuff about Serafin. I feel like throwing up. I need my own forest without white men."

"That's fine," he answered.

"Not long," I added quickly. "I'm starting a new job tomorrow, but it's a temp thing. Let me work it out, and when I do, let's see If we feel the same about seeing each other."

"Always your own way, Dixie. That's the requirement."

"I love it when you say my name. Don't know why. It makes me turn red. If we see each other again, I have two conditions. Can I tell you what they are?"

"Of course," he answered.

"One is silly, I know. It's private. However lame as it sounds, would you write a poem for me? To *me,* Julian. Any meter, any style, any subject, any length. *To* me. How hard it might be to become Julio again, I don't know. Maybe too much, and that I'll understand. But the other one should be easy."

"What is it?" he said, and his face remained implacable.

"I want to talk to Gabriel. I want you to tell me how to get in touch with him, because I need to hear directly from him that Takosha got home safe to her sister's house that day. Drunk or whatever, it doesn't matter. I need to be convinced that she didn't get lost somewhere in August Lake park and run into Potter."

Julian agreed and that's where we left it. As it happened, by the time I discovered I was pregnant, he had made good on only one of those two promises.

22.

Molnar Manufacturing was about twenty minutes from my apartment, nearly all freeway miles. Still, I gave myself twenty minutes to get there plus an extra twenty, since there's nothing less professional than an employee who shows up late on her first day.

I almost made it too. The shot down M-59 was uneventful, but when I pulled off onto Mound Road, I joined a string of vehicles moving at a trickle through orange barrels. Road crews were tearing up the two left lanes, leaving a single artery clogged with commuters, each trying to outrun the traffic lights which appeared every couple hundred yards winking dumbly through clouds of fine white construction dust.

I was only three miles from Molnar, and I succumbed to the ludicrous optimism that initially overtakes everyone faced with traffic back-ups: *'This couldn't possibly last twenty minutes'*.

Fifteen stalled minutes later, I was in a full-blown panic; hair frazzled, brow glistening, heart palpitating and nails chewed to the quick. Outside the window, there didn't seem to be anybody actually working except for a hardhat on a lone excavator that looked like a yellow brontosaurus. I tried to call Molnar and the phone went to message. Duh; I was the new receptionist. I used my phone to find an alternate route through an adjacent subdivision called Spicewood, turning onto a street named Woodruff—the same exotic scent I'd picked up from Julian. Coincidence or mystic intervention, it didn't matter; these side roads were clear, and I wound among them, hanging a left at Tarragon and veering right at Allspice, passing through swaths of small, unkempt brick hovels, many with white statues of Mary in the yards—white virgins sitting in piles of bark, white virgins in upturned bathtubs, white virgins in wrought iron cages, a symbol of desolate purity. White seemed to be Sterling Heights' dominant motif. It was a land of bland white Speedway gas stations and chalky cemeteries and white-spired Lutheran churches. And white men—a forest full of them.

Molnar was also white. It was a cinderblock, one-story box painted entirely white with a white, crushed stone path leading to the entrance. It was so white that it hurt, like you'd just stepped out of a dark room into daylight. I pulled into the tiny parking lot at six minutes past eight.

Inside, the reception area was as stark as the neighborhood. There were three waiting-room chairs, a smatter of Parker awards on the wall, an American flag and a sign that said, *"Welcome to Molnar Manufacturing. Have a good day"* with 'Manufacturing' spelled *'Manufacuting.'*

The lobby was empty and the reception desk ran the length of a Plexiglas wall. In front of it was a bowling trophy and a telephone, which I thought was strange until I realized that without a someone at the front desk, people coming in just referenced the company directory and dialed the right extension. It made sense, and I was superfluous before I began.

Then the phone rang, and I stood there in the Navy blue rayon dress I'd picked up after Julian left, unable to decide whether or not I should answer it since my shift had already started. But, it stopped ringing and went to message and a moment later, a thickset woman with flaming red hair came through the door and introduced herself as Ivolya Ryvak, the owner of the company.

"Welcome," she said, smiling. "Next two weeks, you and me, without Giantess. To me will be vacation."

And that was the end of the awkwardness. My lateness wasn't mentioned, and my two weeks—and her vacation—began.

Ivolya had a sort of curdled Slavic accent where Ws were Vs and vice versa, so that it was *'velcome,' 'veeks'* and *'wacation'.* Beyond that, I quickly learned that she was a wonderful and tough cookie who'd come from some backwater dump in Belarus where people were still dying from Chernobyl fallout. She'd immigrated to Detroit as a lathe operator and banked her income so diligently that when Molnar had gone on the chopping block, she'd been able to buy it. For a successful businesswoman, she was proletarian to the gills and funny as hell, and everybody who worked for her was either a youngish woman or a man nearing retirement age. Other than me, all were immigrants from Belarus.

It turned out that the Stars 'n' Stripes was a ruse: Beyond the lobby, there were red and green Belarusian flags everywhere. Few of my co-workers were fluent in English, so I didn't get to know many of them well, but there was a warm, Eastern European hive-drive about the place. It was a village with everybody teasing each other, laughing and pulling together, and almost from the outset, I loved it. I didn't learn much about their personal lives, but I did learn a lot about their subculture—screw machine products. I learned words like multi-spindle turning and horizontal milling and CNC machining, and I learned that we could hold tolerances of five ten-thousandths of an inch. My predecessor at the reception desk had also been Belarussian, and everybody who mentioned her, even the customers, called her 'The Giantess' because she was over six feet tall. Somehow, doing something I never quite figured out, she'd fallen off the Molnar roof and ruptured her spleen, and was only taking two weeks off to recover: "Huge overflow testosterone hormone," Ivolya laughed.

I'd never done secretarial work before, and once I got over opening-bell jitters, I realized how mellow answering phones in a relatively laid-back office could be. Although I could make more money slinging designer meals at rich people, the stress factor here was minimal and at least I wasn't up to my areolas in kitchen grease. By the end of my shift on Friday, I had the job well in hand and I was riding easy in the saddle. This was the mental state that allowed me to think about painting again.

In particular, I thought about my painting of Gabriel. I wanted to show it to him. Actually, I wanted to give it to him. But given his situation, I thought perhaps I'd emphasized his pallor more than his strength. Too much chemo and not enough courage. On Thursday evening, breaking my rule about messing with a piece after it's done, I cranked up some Annie Lennox, pulled out my acrylics and rosied up his cheeks and added some softness to his angles.

And on Friday after work, dodging both Mound Road construction and hyper-Catholic neighborhoods, I drove out to visit him.

23.

Michael Ondaatje describes a certain style of handwriting as looking like it's written on ocean waves. That's how Julian's script looked to me on the back of the Kohl's receipt I'd exhumed from my purse, where he'd written, *'Gabriel Tobias, Room 2609, St. Luke.'*

St. Luke was Simon Mackie's hospital. It was also where Takosha's sister worked, so it had already imposed on my thought processes; it loomed over Pontiac's main drag, just beyond the downtown loop, a piece of abominable sixties modernism, once part of some imperial distain for the old school, now exhausted-looking to the point of silliness.

Inside was worse: Beyond the shuffling sick folks and skittering, scrub-clad medical folks, the lobby was a black hole of milktoast, hideous sculptures and a weird stainless steel Niagara Falls where the water fell in a square sheet.

On the second floor in the South Tower, in a secluded room at the end of a long hall, Gabriel lay as a tall, gaunt wisp on a gurney flanked by bleepgraphs and sterile cabinets. He looked like he'd lost twenty pounds, and I didn't think he'd had twenty pounds to lose. He gazed at me through heavy-lidded eyes. I hadn't called in advance to announce that I was coming, which was unspeakably rude and possibly even cruel, but I didn't want him to have time to consider what he'd say. Now, of course, I felt like a total dipshit.

Tom and Jerry was playing on the television. I'd brought the painting with me, but I hadn't brought it up; I wanted to find out where his head was first. Instead I was carrying some happy little daffodils from the gift shop in the lobby, the kind that Bob Ross would have painted outside a cottage in the springtime.

"Hi, Gabriel," I said tentatively, standing in the doorway. "I'm Dixie Pickett. You drove me out to August Lake Park a couple weeks ago?"

"I know who you are," he answered. His voice was thin and deep. "I remember."

I did a stage shrug, but my embarrassment was real. I stepped carefully into the room. "Here's some flowers. I was debating what to bring, because people do that, don't they? They bring stuff. I suppose flowers are sort of silly."

"*Tom and Jerry* isn't cutting it either but I can't reach the remote."

He had an intravenous needle in an arm that itself looked thin as a syringe. The remote had somehow gotten hooked on the bed railing then wedged beneath it and Gabriel was too weak to retrieve it. I laid the flowers on the folding food tray, squatted down, freed it and turned the television off.

Instantly, the silence was cloying. I didn't know what to say, and I realized suddenly that I'd rather just sit and watch cartoons with him, like a kid. Those were not bad days, as I recalled. But the show was off and I stammered, "Julian told me you were sick last week, but I didn't know you'd still be laid up."

"Well, they found something else. In my balls this time. They cut off my left nut. That's gonna keep me outta the Marines for sure."

Christ. I stammered, "I wanted to see how you're doing."

"That's why you're here?"

"No," I answered. "It's not."

Now I was glad I hadn't brought the painting. I had captured a demigod carved in calcite, an aloof and remote totem. A still life. In his dark glasses and cap, viewed through glass on a cloudy morning, he'd been that. But he wasn't that now, and in reality, he hadn't been that even then. The incorporeal mysteries that Julian believed I could see had failed me and the evidence of that was before me, prostate on snowy white sheets. Beneath the cap there was fragile human flesh and under the shades were youthful eyes that had already looked at life in the maw and seen all the way down to the asshole. Having your blood stream sabotaged was bad enough, but imagine a teenage boy lying there as his manhood was removed piecemeal. There were no words: This was clearly a kid who didn't have time for much, let alone pretense.

So I said it quickly, since it was the only dignified thing left to do: "I'm here about Takosha DeYoung. That one day, that Monday at the park, there was a girl with me. A black woman."

"Yeah; she found a booze bottle in the weeds and drank it. She was pretty wasted on the ride home."

"But there *was* a ride home? That's all I really want to know, Gabriel, then I can leave. Takosha's missing. She hasn't been seen by anybody since that day. You dropped her off at her sister's apartment?"

"I left her in the parking lot of some projects on Wide Track. Where she went from there, I have no clue."

"Well, thanks. That's positive information, anyway. Potter—that guy from the park with the tattoos? Well, you know Potter, obviously. He kept dropping hints that he knows her."

"He probably does know her. Every hustler in Pontiac knows every other hustler."

"Jesus, he's a prostitute? I knew something deviant was going on in that club, but I wouldn't have pegged *that* dude as gay."

"What does gay have to do with it? It's an income."

"But it's not like he doesn't already have an income, right? Didn't Julian give you all jobs to keep you *off* the street? All those guys I saw at Sophrosyne? I saw them in park uniforms too."

"How much do you think the park pays? Young twink can turn a hundred an hour at Sophrosyne just by letting a rich bear massage his feet—ten times that if he takes him upstairs. If he wants to, he can drive around in a park truck for the rest of his life like Stony. In a real world, where actual money exists, there's an expiration date on his ass."

There was such a fierce pragmatism in his responses that I realized that he was a spokesman for that life. It light of what I knew about his health, I didn't want to pursue it. If I did, I thought I might break down in tears. But I had to ask: "I know Julian has been a friend to you, Gabriel. Not sure if he told you, but I've been seeing him. Like, as in, seeing him. You don't need to rat if you don't want, but I need to know how he's involved in the club."

"He's not involved. I don't think he's ever been inside Sophrosyne, at least not as long as I've known him. His family used to own the building and I think his mother used to manage the club—she's a piece of work. But, that was a long time ago. I don't think Julian know how crazy it's gotten, but if even he does, so what? The family sold the place and they're done with it."

"Well, that's another relief, I gotta say."

From the window, you could see a second building, the North Wing. No sky, no trees, no birds. I stood there and gaped. I was overstaying and I knew it. I had said my piece and he'd said his, and now, I nothing else to offer. The painting I'd done now seemed like a perverse misinterpretation, and the rosied cheeks I'd added seemed like the same game the undertaker plays.

I felt briefly and thoroughly, helpless. I muttered: "Look, Gabriel, I am so sorry for disturbing you. My thoughts and prayers are with you, which is probably worth less than daffodils. But, thank you anyway—let me at least say that sincerely. You put my mind easier."

I smiled weakly and turned to leave. But I had a thought, and it was now or never, and even though it made me feel corrupt in some rather deep places, I turned back and disturbed him some more.

"Can I ask you one more thing, Gabriel? About the park, not about the club?"

"Go ahead," he said.

"Julian told me that Alan set up surveillance cameras, but Alan told me he didn't. He said Julian did it and he'd take them down if he could find them. Do you know anything about that?"

"I know why Alan wants them down: There's a video of him and Serafin Tercerio on the beach. I've seen it. It's pretty graphic. Why do you think he turned over the park to us? In case we went to the cops with it. After that, Alan's been good with sitting in the office all day. Now, if he comes up for air, it's to do something a long ways away from us."

So, that was it. Julian had lied to me about the cameras, and now I knew why: He wanted free reign in his forest, and he was merely adapting Alan's nature to an end. Now I did leave, and behind me, *Tom and Jerry* came on again.

It was the beginning of the holiday weekend, and, if I'd heard correctly, Memorial Day was the only time the park was busy. The weather promised to be spectacular, and I told myself that Julian would be legitimately tied up for the next few days. It was not the best time for a come-to-Jesus showdown. I told myself that I would be a distraction to him and the weekend crowd would be a distraction from me. In fact, I told it to myself over and over until I'd convinced myself. I wouldn't see him yet.

But that didn't stop me from obsessing over him in the meantime.

Although, I reckon that what I experienced wasn't OCD in the *Psychology Today* sense, because my thoughts were not intrusive, but rather, the opposite. Far from being an unwelcome foot in the door, this was me throwing the door wide open. I inhaled the steam beneath the bear skin until it became so sweet that I took off my clothes and lay in my bed and relived the night as I relieved myself. I didn't fight these thoughts; I embraced them, and in Julian's absence, I embraced myself. Not only that, but for me, for the time being, the steamy, dreamy boy was a better image that the distant man who worked at a park where kids were raped and had an apartment in Pontiac where the same thing happened.

I hoped that there was an explanation and I prayed that some hard-won, overarching street wisdom would allow me to winnow facts from façade. But that was a stretch, and I knew what I should do. After what had happened at Sophrosyne, I knew it instinctively, as every girl on every sticky seat in every darkened theater in the country knows, and I knew I should do it at full gallop:

I shouldn't go back in the basement.

So instead, on Sunday, I went to the zoo. I took a sketchbook and I wandered among caged beasts and trapped fish and penned reptiles, and I was even brave enough to enter the Free-Flight Aviary where the frantic fights were even creepier than the ones outside, because these birds were trapped, and maybe they've all been driven methodically insane in order to provide a photo op for Miss Crabtree's third grade class.

Technically, my animal sketches were not bad, but overall, they miscarried. I know precisely the quality I was after, and in the big cats especially. It was something that went beyond physiology: Some sense that behind the body language, in their docile gaze, within the atmosphere they displaced by their subtle movements, something sinister simmered. I believed this to be their incorporeal resonance— they were opportunists by nature and their low-key demeanor was a meticulously orchestrated ruse as they waited to devour the white men who'd ravaged their forest and carried them off.

That aura, if I could spot it, had survival implications, because I was the next one down in the food chain, being the daughter of Byron Mason Pickett, the whitest man I'd ever known.

24.

Self-preservation is a hallmark of life, because if the drive were otherwise, we'd have all succumbed early. My hunger grew and it was terrible and selfish, but even so, I should have stayed upstairs and locked the basement door, even as a sense duty. But I didn't.

My reasons for that, as complicated as they wound up being, coalesced in two words spoken by Ivolya Ryvak near the end of my shift on the following Friday. I'd continued to settle in at Molnar, growing accustomed to the groove. I'd memorized the strange names with their multiple Ys and sprawling consonants and on the phone, I'd figured out how to winnow the vendors from the customers.

On Friday I met my predecessor, The Giantess. She dropped in for a visit in the early afternoon, tooled along in a wheelchair by her long-suffering mother. Pushing the chair took effort since The Giantess was even gigantic sitting down. It was impossible not to wonder if she was the product of nuclear radiation. Anyway, the crew flocked around her, and I felt isolated until Ivolya approached me and asked me to stay another week.

"Too much chit-chat, too much iPhone. Now Giantess want one more week recover." *Veek.* "Wish very much I can keep you permanent, Dixie." *'Veesh wery.'*

"Me too," I admitted.

"But you leave anyway," she said with a flip of her wrist. "Become mother."

"What?" I snorted.

She shrugged and said her two words: "You pregnant."

"That's silly. I can't be pregnant—I have cysts on my ovaries. I don't ovulate."

"Don't know what you got, but you pregnant." She touched the side of my face gently with a hand that was bread-dough soft despite her career in machine shops. "I see here, in cheek. Anyway, I tell girl at Matrix you stay one week more."

And she left me to shake my head and scoff, sleepwalk through incoming calls and arrange paperclips at the my desk as a panic attack began to blow up inside me. I Googled the same medical sites as I had in the past, and for some reason, it seemed like my multiple previous readings had been selective. Wishful thinking? Hearing song lyrics wrong over and over? Getting pregnant with PCOS was difficult, but nowhere on *webmd* did it say that getting pregnant was impossible. It came down on me hard that if I'd been getting my advice from an actual doctor instead of a virtual OB/GYN on the internet, I might know more, but among everything I'd neglected beyond a buzz during my four lost years, health insurance was but a line item. Danny's Coney didn't offer an employee plan and the couple hundred a month that I would have had to pay at Alchemy for coverage had been a luxury beyond my means. Going forward, I vowed, that had to jockey for an upper berth on my expense account.

My periods had never been clockwork, but I would have expected one in the early part of the following week. I Googled the early warning symptoms of pregnancy, and—psychosomatic or otherwise—I felt the tips of my nipples tingle against my peach-colored Target blouse. I went to the rest room to check my underwear for signs of spotting. I examined my cheeks in the mirror to see if I could see what Ivolya saw, and I'll be damned if my Irish cream hadn't picked up a faint

Mediterranean bloom.

On the way home, I stopped at the CVS on Long Lake and Ryan and picked up a nine dollar First Response Gold kit; two tests in each box, custom-made for the diehard cynic. After I got home I procrastinated through a Lean Cuisine Chicken Masala, and halfway through, the texture of the meat began to nauseate me. After that, I sat on the toilet and for a long time, stared at a pair of plus symbols on my two-for-the-price-of-one, pee-soaked sticks.

25.

There's an indispensable tool in your survival kit: The knowledge the most dangerous people don't have the most dangerous faces. Thinking about that on Sunday night late, mulling over the weekend, I was reminded of a guy I once saw in the Lafayette Street bus terminal: Hoodie and a skull cap, brutal, skewed features and skin the color of the stained floor at Wolski's. He had one wonk eye and I thought he might have been the most dangerous looking man I'd ever seen. Ten minutes later, a young, frightened-looking teenager de-boarded an arriving bus and I watched as the dangerous man embraced him with all the compassion and love I'd ever before seen displayed between a father and son.

I thought about that day in particular: I was going to meet Corky in Chicago for the last leg of some ridiculous Comic Con he was attending. Why not? It was a splurge he was paying for, even the cab to the Greyhound station where I sat in the dingy terminal sipping an impromptu Bloody Mary, vodka poured into a V-8 bottle from the vending machine.

The bus was an hour late, and there I sat in the station, surveying the dangerous faces and the safe ones, intrigued with the notion that their secret lives likely didn't match. Outside the window, John King Books loomed in the cold grey Detroit morning. On the street below, a random seagull lit in the middle of the road while a safe-faced guy who looked like a vagrant from the neck down but exactly like Santa Claus from the waist up passed out free Bibles to passengers smoking cigarettes outside.

160

In the time before my bus arrived, a middle-aged black man approached me and winked, and not in a come-on way. He had a bottle of rye with him, and when you want somebody to drink with, you tend to scent each other out. You recognize each other as part of an alternate universe; I assume the men at Sophrosyne might have felt that way.

My drinking pal was also heading to Chicago, and we shared a seat. By the time we hit the Skyway, I was totally lit up, but not too much to notice that unlike Detroit, Chicago throbbed with life. Neighborhoods stretched west topped by church spires and smokestacks; soul and sweat, vertical commitment.

I fell asleep late on Sunday after I found out I was pregnant and around three in the morning, I woke up and wrote three words in my journal:

'Dark background love.'

It was a phenomenon I knew existed, but one that I'd never before confronted. My small troupe of lovers all had come from stable backgrounds; they'd been raised in rational affluence and by parents who'd tried to do right by them. Shades of darkness had been added by the shovelful, but after the fact and by the men themselves, often in defiance of reason. To my surface interpretation, Julian had taken the opposite path. He'd come up amid ultimate degradation and had found the light switch in the basement.

But, was that even possible? Were there backgrounds so dark that any light was only a patina over the pandemonium? This was a question that screamed inside my head and grew louder until, at dawn, I drove out to August Lake to find out.

I think by point, as far as I understood the term, I was in love with Julian Vaz. His influence had grown within me from the moment he'd stepped from the hallway shadows at the August Lake headquarters, and now, it was more than figure of speech. It was a cellular blitzkrieg inside my uterus; a living organism who, so far, seemed confident in its own agenda.

Not even an 'it', according to what I'd read that first night: Already a he or she from conception.

I'd never had to consider terminating a pregnancy before. The chance had not seemed within the realm of biological possibility. I wasn't morally opposed to the idea of taking an abortion pill, or even getting an early procedure done before any rudimentary awareness took hold, but I did believe that it was a decision that should at least be discussed by both parents. With Kyle, then with Jason and then with Corky, I hadn't wasted any time thinking about how we'd have reacted to a pregnancy, for reasons that had then seemed obvious. I probably should have, and to atone perhaps, I wasted a lot of time thinking about it now.

I believe implicitly that all three of my former lovers would have been relieved had I offered to abort, even—or perhaps, especially—über-Christian Jason Alton. He'd already decided he wasn't going to marry me the moment I broke my chastity pledge, and an out-of-wedlock child would have put the kibbutz on his OSU career path. Naw, old Jason—teen disciple at Christ Youth Ministries—would have driven me to the abortion clinic himself.

But I hadn't been in love with him or those other boys. Not even close. And I believed I was in love with Julian Vaz. Did it make a difference? I suppose it shouldn't have. Whatever was reddening my cheeks was, at this point, no more animate than the tube of Blick Cadmium Red I'd used to blush up Gabriel's face in the portrait. But, somehow, my love had reached a level where it made a monumental difference. I hadn't created my little plus sign as rage against the machine that killed my Daddy, nor as a display of wife-to-be obedience, nor as a commercial exchange of pussy for rent. I'd made love with Julian as aggressively and as sincerely as I knew how and I'd discovered some vital core of womanhood within me. Now, within me, that vital core had joined with Julian's core in a flicker of new life, defying all the odds that science could stack against it.

It was hard to downplay the power of that miracle, even if that tiny spark was snuffed out by me or by the course of nature. Miscarriage, I acknowledged, was as likely an outcome as any. My mother had suffered two of them before I came along and decided to hang in there.

Whatever happened, Julian deserved to be in the picture. Of that, I had no doubt. Whatever future we might have forged together I couldn't say, but the past was not forgotten. The past remained inviolate, unchanged, even if in the present everything had changed.

I drove out to August Lake as soon as it got light, fueled by coffee and adrenalin and, perhaps, a little latent prayer. But before I tracked my way to the cottage, I pulled off at a trail head and wandered into the damp sea of green and brown, intending to find some emotional equilibrium before I confronted Julian. The mental regeneration that's possible during a morning hike cannot be overstated.

I had a primary thought along those leafy trails: Did I feel like two people, as, now apparently, I was? Surprisingly, the further I walked, the less alone I felt. The presence within me was all the more compelling for being intangible. This was something to reconcile with any decision, of course. At what point does termination become, on some subconscious level, a form of self-loathing or contempt for your partner?

The trees towered over me, enlivening me like the church spires and smokestacks of Chicago, and in time, with my soul intact and my sweat flowing, I returned to my car and found the cottage.

Out front, a knot of boys were having a barbecue. A fire pit smoldered behind the pines and a stripped deer carcass hung from a branch of a massive oak tree. For a park without a lot to do, they seemed to hire a lot of kids not to do it. Serafin Tercerio was there along with half a dozen other kids, including some new ones: Among them was a handsome black boy in long dreadlocks and pretty Asian features and a teenager with a bowl haircut like Moe on the *Three Stooges*.

And Potter. He saw my car pull up and approached me carrying a plate loaded with food.

I prepared for a dust-up, but his face had changed entirely. His sneer had melted into a passable smile and his demeanor was almost subservient. I stepped out of the car and he handed me the plate of food. "Hungry?" he asked.

I looked at the pile of blood-red venison and almost barfed. "No. I'm looking for Julian."

"He's working out at the dam. Serafin can bring you out there in the Gator if you want. Your car won't make it. We have plenty of food back here if you change your mind. Julian started the fire pit last night, so it's all good."

It was the damnest thing. I might have felt a bit less animosity toward Potter now that I knew he wasn't involved in Takosha's disappearance, but I hardly wanted to be besties with him. Besides, the other boys were smiling too, and not in a smart-assy way. Suddenly, they seemed demure and ingratiating; even friendly. I was convinced that it was Jivarrão: The lot of them must have been partying with Indian tea all night. I shook my head as Serafin pulled up in a small green vehicle. His toothy smile had returned and he said, "Come on, *Guera;* I take you to see Julio."

I wanted to say something to him as we tumbled and jostled down a forest trail, rumbling over rocks and roots. I surveyed his smooth brown cheek and doubted that he even shaved yet. The last time I'd seen him he'd been dressed in a humiliating outfit surrounded by rapists, but today, he seemed unfazed. It was as peculiar as the changed expression on the park boy. Was there a chance that he'd forgotten that he'd seen me in the basement of that building? I wanted to know who he was. I wanted to ask him where he was from and why he'd come here. And how, in every sense of the word, he wore these strange and contradictory faces so fluently. I didn't know where to begin and his smile seemed oblivious and entirely bulletproof. His eyes were heavy and glittered when he glanced over at me. Despite what I knew of his history, he carried himself as a boy unscathed. I couldn't accept that in him, or, for that matter, in Julian. If anything, both were coping. But with Serafin Tercerio, my concern was peripheral and only vaguely Samaritan. It was not dark background love. I asked him how he was feeling. He said, "Very good!" and another mile passed in silence.

To my lasting shame, I allowed it to rest there. I did not pursue it. And suddenly that morning, it was too late: As we crested a leafy hilltop and through a grove of maple trees and scrub pine, I saw Julian.

Rather, let me be cheesy: I beheld him. At the base of the hill was a long, heavy mound of grass that formed a hummock between a dark inlet of August Lake and beyond it oozed a blackish creek where a series of stones were piled to armor an ancient dam. Off to one side, Julian's burnished figure was coppery in the sharp sunlight, writhing and heaving as he swung a two-headed axe with primeval, radical, inflexible fury.

The fury may have been inflexible, but he sure wasn't. I watched in steamy delight as serpentine muscles along his shoulders syncopated and expanded and the thwack of steel on fiber rang in the forest. I felt thrills I had not expected to feel and I squirmed softly on the vinyl Gator seat.

Forgive me if I carry the corniness a step further: An icon from archetypal mythology rose up in my mind's eye, a plate from a book I'd seen on Aztec art; the feathered serpent god of wind and learning. I leaned over and offered Serafin a quick peck on the cheek which made him redden and simper as I slid out of the vehicle and shooed him away.

I stood in forest mists and watch as Julian held the axe against his waist and turned an aurified face toward me. In that, I saw another archetype, one more personal than a page in an art book: I admired his physical being in a way that touched every facet of who I was, sexually, emotionally, socially and perhaps above all, symbolically. He seemed at that moment to embody the oasis sought by thirsty partners since the beginning of time: Bronzed in beauty, fearless in resolve, self-sufficient in the face of a natural world where every sling of outrageous fortune and every natural shock is aimed in our direction.

Not only that, but somehow—even from a hundred feet away—Julian knew I was pregnant. There may have been other reasons for that, but none at the time were more satisfying than the idea that the creature sleeping within me had fused our minds as well as our gametes. It seemed that he knew instinctively and the electricity of thinking that made my knees weak. And yet, every sensible fiber within me had come to finalize the thing, not prolong it.

Whether I had the child, flushed the child or strangled it with poison (when, in all its insensate biology, it was depending on me to do the opposite) I did not think that there was any force that would make me agree to become a permanent part of his world. Nor, as he stood there burnished in golden sweat and heaving pure air into pure air, did he seem the least inclined to become part of mine.

As in so many phases of this peculiar story, I was wrong.

He knew and he embraced me and when, mid-embrace, I sputtered out that amid our squish of lust we'd made a baby he said, as though there was no complexity in the situation at all: "The circle and the bridge."

Yet somehow, I couldn't get a read. I held him tighter and tasted pearls of sweat on his neck. I was hormonal, and of course it went deeper than desire, though I took off my blouse and pressed my chest into his. Any motive to push him away had morphed into a will to hold him tighter. His wet skin slid against my cool throat; my thin arms twisted around his taut tendons amid the sweet tang of body sweat and wood smoke. It was bizarre and primal coupling. But it was a clear submission to circumstance, and I needed better impetus to choose my next move.

"Are you upset? Happy? Indifferent?"

"Overjoyed," he said, and in his face I saw nothing but candor.

"But we don't even know each other, Julian. Not really. We made love once, *one* time, and I wasn't supposed to be able to pull an *oops* off even if I'd wanted to. And God, I hope you know I didn't want to. I didn't even think it was possible. I told you that first night I couldn't have children."

"You did. You told me a lot of things about yourself and you believed they all were true. But not everything you see clearly stays clear forever."

"Like Sophrosyne and you? Potter and Takosha? I feel awful about that, actually. I suppose I owe that racist little shit an apology too, but not today. Today is Dixie Pregnant Day."

"Then it's *his* day."

"His?"

"Your son." He placed a warm hand on my belly. "It's in your face; it's on your breath. I can taste it. You're carrying a boy."

"Oh, my fucking God, you can't possibly taste that, Julian. *Can you?* Why even say that?"

CHRIS KASSEL

And again, inexplicably, my eyes began to prickle and I started to cry. Again, it sluiced. "What would I do with a baby, boy or girl, Julian? I don't even like babies. And babies don't like me. They usually cry in my arms. I don't know how to comfort or talk to them..."

"Hasn't every new mother since the dawn of time said that?"

"I don't know, Julian. I guess. I remember just about everything you've said to me. It's nearly all poetry. *'Our lives are blinks, but the blinks go on for eternity.'*"

"We've made a start on our eternity, that's all."

In time, I pulled myself together. "So, then just make this easy on us. I need a simple answer, Julian; not some bizarre-Jivarrão Castaneda truth. Do you want me to keep this baby?"

"As opposed to what?"

Well, so I didn't want to say it. I knew, and obviously, he knew. I suppose the fact that he did not propose solutions, not behave in a way where he thought that the solution involved a set of options, but rather, was a single preordained, was the beginning of an exorable change of mind. Or, as I preferred to consider it, and as I truly believed it to be, a settling of mind.

He told me I could come and live with him at the cottage. He said he'd make it off-limits to anybody I objected to. That, he said, had been available to me all along. It was not what I wanted or needed or had come to ask for, but the fact that it was on the table meant a lot to me.

He said, "I have something for you at the cottage anyway; something I made for you. If you want, we can go there now, or we can go after I'm done here. An hour, at the most."

"We'll go after. Right now, I want to sit in the shade and watch you move. You're in your element, and I like that. I'm in love with that. I see things there that take twenty-eight years of frowning to the curb."

And I did exactly that. I watched him move. He was in process of dropping a stand of hardwood trees whose roots, I later learned later, were infiltrating the dam and gradually, resolutely, weakening the earthen infrastructure. In time, the century-old mound would have given way, collapsing and spilling the foul guts of August Lake over many surrounding acres.

Saving that dam thus became noble cause. Behind me, despite the heat and sunshine, the water appeared to be perpetual half-light; dead colors were scumbled with grey and purple and dissolved to chiaroscuro.

But opposite me was the portrait I had not dared to approach: Now, I wanted desperately to paint it. The archetype made flesh. I saw delicate gradations of pattering light and color, tint on tint, the harmony of warm opaque. I saw the framing woods in layered shadow, darkness within darkness, and in Julian's twisting form I saw ultimate strength, even if glazing it, I confess, I saw more brilliance than warmth.

In a life thus far caged by unnecessary angles, that day was soft to me, and afterward, the night was softer. At the cottage, which the boys had left to us, he did have something waiting. I'd hoped it was my poem, but it wasn't: He'd carved for me an exquisite dragonfly from finely-grained white oak. I didn't learn until later how rare this type of material was: It was almost extinct in northern woods.

My vision of him is forever the god of wind and learning. This dragonfly, he said, was his vision of me. I have it to this day, on my dresser, by my bed. *Libélula.*

We didn't make love, but we took off our clothes and touched each other over the course of many hours and it was even better. We did everything—not just kiss— with essence. He played the guitar and he was remarkable; he sang to me and it was superb. We hardly discussed the future at all, nor did I want to, but among the few things he referenced was his family. He'd mentioned that his sister was versed in *curandeira* medicine, and he wanted her to share with me the spiritual crux of pregnancy. I was entirely agreeable to that. I wanted to meet her, absolutely, along with their eccentric, disabled mother who lived in Bloomfield Hills, rescued stray animals and built gay Plato nightclubs.

But not yet. I an appointment on Monday evening to see an OB/GYN in Auburn Hills, and I needed some physical things about me confirmed. I wanted some risks fairly and professionally discussed. Not transpersonal shaman shit, although I hardly phrased it that way to Julian. I wanted to talk to someone who could tell me what my body was doing, what it would do if all went well, and how I'd managed to conceive through my PCOS, which, in honesty, had never been confirmed since first diagnosed when I was fourteen years old.

By the end of that night, I'd resolved to keep the baby. My child. Ours, although of course, above all, belonging to neither of us, but existing for himself and of himself as a thing of bright foreground love.

26.

At work the following morning, I tried to keep my news to myself; I was sure you were supposed to stay mum until a couple of months had safely passed, just in case—that way, there was no melodrama if things went south. But, midway through the day, I winked at Ivolya and placed my hand on my tummy in an open-fingered spread, whispering, "You were right."

Predictably, she wasn't surprised. "So, now you marry boy?"

"Naw, I don't think so. Well—he hasn't officially proposed. He did ask me to move in with him, but that's a pretty major step too. Maybe even more than being a single mom. We hardly know each other." I shrugged, "I guess we seem compatible enough."

"No worry—not everyone who make good love make good husband. Maybe you go back home to momma for a while and let her help."

"Oh, my mother is pretty churchy. She had some hardline expectations and I don't think she'll be too thrilled about wheeling my bastard baby around Cadence. Besides, she has a full-time job. She works for my dad." I corrected myself: "My stepdad. I haven't told her yet."

"Momma will be over moon," Ivolya scoffed, beaming with confidence.

"I dunno. Maybe *his* mom will be. She's nuts."

Ivolya hugged me; a big Slavic bear hug, and briefly, I felt a third mom enter the picture. Or, including me, perhaps a fourth.

I left Molar early, having been fortunate enough to have found a gynecologist with extended hours, and only twenty minutes away. Learning I was uninsured, the receptionist had nodded toward a sign indicating that all services needed to be paid at the time they were rendered. Like my Daddy used to say, they wanted cash on the barrel head. But Dr. Sz-Min saw me right after that. She took some blood, did a brusque pelvic exam and confirmed the pregnancy in a routine hCG, which was a pricier version of the First Response kit.

The doctor was chilly and perfunctory and tough to understand, but I was so jittery that at first, I didn't care. I said that my boyfriend—yeah, I used the 'bf' word—told me he thought that we were going to have a boy, on the ridiculous outside chance that as a Chinese woman, that might thaw her out. I heard somewhere that rural people in China stick girl babies out on rocks because they all want sons.

No dice. She said in a voice that was at once monotone and barky: "You have decided to keep it?"

"Why? Don't you think I should?"

Her expression didn't change. No wonder she worked the night shift, I thought; she had the bedside manner of an embalmer. She looked at my chart and said, "You are still relatively young; no insurance and no steady source of income. Having a child is difficult under best circumstances."

I got a little snippy. "I know, right? But I thought I couldn't get pregnant because of my ovaries so I wasn't taking precautions. This seems like a miracle."

"It does happen. We can run more tests, but nothing indicate PCOS yet—no signs. No excess weight, no acne. No hair on your body, unless you shave it?"

"No more than most women," I said, turning red.

"We'll run more tests. Termination is an option, nothing more. I tell you this to give you full information. At this stage, termination is no more invasive or risky than getting a tooth pulled."

I thought that the analogy was repulsive, but I was grateful for everything I learned. The exam covered a pap screening and a breast exam. Some results would be returned later, but as far as the doctor could determine, I was healthy, and barring the real chance of miscarriage, I'd probably be able to pull off this baby thing. I wanted to call Julian immediately and oddly—no doubt based on Ivolya's comment—I wanted to call my mother. I paid the clinic with cash, two hundred dollars I really couldn't spare, though if Julian wanted me to keep our little bridge to eternity, I was more than happy to ask him to pay a little of the toll money.

I stopped at CVS on the way home to fill my prescription for prenatal vitamins, and while I waited, I picked up a tub of Breyer's Cinnamon Roll Gelato. I assumed I was slipping with deceptive ease into a state that pregnant women have been embracing for generations: Sudden caloric liberation.

As it happened, the gelato thawed on my kitchen counter, unopened, untouched and unscarfed: On the landing to my building, stuffed into my little aluminum mailbox beside an electric bill and a bunch of coupons from Denice's Deals, was a thick envelope identical to the one I had picked up from Julian's lawyer at the gas station. On the outside was Julian's graceful, smoke-like script reading, 'For Our Seasons'.

Silly me; my heart went sappy with the thrill that he'd been here, countered only by twangs of regret that I hadn't been. I skittered inside my monastic digs, set the tub of Breyer's on the linoleum counter and tore open the envelope.

Inside, wads of cash were wrapped in mustard colored straps, and by the time I'd counted it all, the gelato was muck and I had a hundred thousand dollars spread out across my bed.

27.

I sat there, kneading my belly and hyperventilating. My phone rang. Serafin's name came up in the window, but when I answered, it wasn't Serafin; it was Julian. I couldn't find words. My ability to speak had been short-circuited. To devolve into Ohio patois, I'd wanted to hear from him, but now that I did, I was too poleaxed to

171

be juiced.

For starters, I'd never heard him on a phone before. Removed from his anatomy, his voice was ephemeral and rather monochrome, toned sepia with undercurrents of something smooth and soothing. A good voice for a father, I thought. He explained the money in the same way he'd explained the night club: He was divesting himself of things that were superfluous to him and of more worth to others. The money was available, and regardless of what I decided to do with my future, it was mine.

"This wasn't cash you had set aside for Serafin, right?"

"Of course not. And anyway, Serafin's gone."

"Gone? I saw him two days ago. Gone where?"

"Potter dropped him at the airport this morning. His money was wired ahead to a bank in Jalisco. He's gone home to his village to be an *agavero*."

"No way, Julian; seriously? That's excellent news, right?"

"He came here to earn money, and for what he wound up dealing with, he was compensated as far as he could be. He'll be a hero for what he brings back. He'll be revered as a saint. He'll be able to buy an agave farm and support generations. His family wouldn't understand the details if they heard them, but they won't hear them."

That much didn't ring true—even peasant people are smart enough to understand abuse. "I accept what happened, Julian. I don't agree with all of it," I answered. "But at least he's out of it. Away from the humiliation, off the street, far from Sophrosyne, beyond everything. That sweet, sweet kid. I hope he can hold on to sanity after the bullshit he's been through..."

Instantly, I realized my faux pas and was aghast, but Julian hushed me: "Transcending is a method. It's a process and he has the tools. He'll be a valuable guide someday, I'm sure of it. He'll be a preceptor."

"Like you?" I whispered. There was silence until I broke it. "I hope I can say it, Julian. You see yourself in Serafin."

"I see myself in the contradiction."

That needed digestion and I didn't want to say anything else stupid or insensitive. He'd once called himself the chaos, and now he called himself the contradiction, and I think, in that unique, disembodied bubble, he wanted to explain himself.

I think so because he called me by my name, and he rarely did that. He tried to do it in a series of soft, gentle words that were many years in sinking in. I'll try to replicate them as best I can, but, no doubt, it's an awkward translation of a poem composed in a language I didn't yet understand:

"I'm distancing myself from the madness, and the sharper it becomes, the further away I need to be. That's the physics. The rest is the philosophy. One way or the other, we're all trying to purge. It's our new solidarity. I'm the contradiction because I'm a mortal, and concern is only an affliction of mortals. A river doesn't care which way it flows. The wind doesn't care which way it blows. If I was able to ignore it, I could make it work right here, on these acres. It would simplify everything without oversimplifying it. But if it turns out that there's nothing but blackness between the stars, it becomes a misalignment. I've been thinking for a long time that there needs to be a natural, radical shift. Sooner, not later. I think the child sleeping inside you might be it. He might be the catalyst, Dixie."

How could an expectant mother not be blown away by such a declaration of commitment, even if she was not ready to accept it? I would take the money, for sure. I'd put it in an account for our son, and should he not survive gestation, I'd give it back *en toto*.

I had planned to call home that night, since my dear evangelizing mother deserved to know about my own radical shift. But then it grew too late: Julian and I talked until nearly midnight. Among the things we talked about was his family. Having gotten the requite medical endorsement from Dr. Sz-Min, I was now ready to visit his kooky mother and holistic sister in their Bloomfield Hills menagerie, and we agreed upon the following Sunday, a day to be spent with family in his culture and mine.

Beyond that, for the most part, Julian talked, and I listened. His narrative was sustaining and consistent with an undercurrent of humor that prevented it from coming off, on any level, as pontificating. The mosaic he shared was elaborate, and most of it went over my head, but he seemed to be as confident of it as he was in his ax stroke.

I was mesmerized by his words, but that was the least of it. I heard the lambent drone of his voice and the muscular scene that I held in the forefront of my imagination persisted above it. Race memory, perhaps? The paradigm? The belief that manhood requires the display of the ultimate invulnerability? A purist machismo not founded on personal insecurity but one besting the beasts, one by one, and living to tell the tale?

Like me, I think that most men would have viewed Julian Vaz as masculinity made manifest, but beyond that, they'd have had no ulterior motive. There was a different edge to my awe: I wanted to fuck him and make more of him. That's barnyard, but it's entirely accurate, and I believe that subconsciously, straight men look at awesome women like that as well. Beauty begets beauty, and inside me, tinting my cheeks and tickling the tips of breasts, perhaps I'd already succeeded.

In the meantime, I had my images. Art illuminates truth as much as it shrouds fact. That's irrevocable and I know that now. At best, my paintings were replicas of my sensations. In my mind, I saw Julian in his isolated forest, tracking deer and mowing down stands of maple trees, and in his pristine isolation, I sensed his desperate need of intimacy. Why? I reckon it's because human biology forges a need for love—survival depends on trust—and within Julian, I insisted on seeing love as the incorporeal that went deeper than vision, the nuclear constituent that was still working its way to the surface.

I was comfortable seeing that, but personally and emotionally, I still a smoking mess, neither adequate nor worthy of being its catalyst. I wondered, quite rationally, if that was too much of a burden to place on an embryo. That doesn't deflect from the fact that I was, in those early weeks, intellectually smitten, while basically and carnally, I felt the physically tug of him. He had touched me correctly, and no man had ever touched me correctly before. Or—as far as I could tell—had even tried. And because of that, no matter what else happened to me in my life, whoever I ended up with, nobody could ever duplicate the role he'd played in the awakening.

My awakening.

And far off in a nebulous future, perhaps that would be the title of a portrait I'd paint.

28.

Since Julian now had Serafin's cell phone and was suddenly amazingly and scrumptiously accessible, I had to fight the urge to exploit my newfound access as often as I'd have liked and I shuddered at my schoolgirl urge to close my eyes and will *him* to call *me.*

I did call my mother, though. The following day, at noon, when I told her quickly about the new job and how much I liked it, temporary though it was. Then, abruptly, I shot from the hip: "Oh, and I don't want to fight about it, Ma, but I also have something pretty life-changing to tell you."

"You're finally getting married?"

"Jeez. Close, but no cigar. Unless Paw-Pop wants to hand them out when the baby's born."

There followed a predictable pause wherein one could hear both a pin and a jaw drop. Then: "Oh, my God. Dixie. You're pregnant?"

"Yeah, Ma, that's pretty much where babies come from. *Pffft;* believe it or not, your little Dixie is up the duff. Isn't that what Aunt Rachel used to say?"

"I'm speechless, honey. I didn't even know you were seeing anyone. Don't tell me...?"

My mother did not know about the PCOS, of course, and now, I wasn't even sure I had it. I couldn't tell her at the time without also telling her how I found out, and after that, the condition had sort of faded into the general fogs of teenage denial, only exhumed when tactically necessary. If asked, I had intended to plead failed contraception, but I wasn't asked.

"It happened, mom; luck of the draw. It's still early days, but I'm going to keep the kid, so don't go there. I thought you should tell you this in person instead of in an email, so if you stroked out I could call 911..."

"Stroke out? Oh, don't be silly. You remember how old I am, right? Fifty-eight. It's high time I had grandchild. Crystal Graceson—remember her? Her daughter Rose? Well, those twins are in the first grade now."

I said, "Wow. Okay, well I must say I'm relieved at how well you're taking this. I'm at work, so I can't talk. I'll call you tonight and give you all the details, once your blood pressure returns to normal."

"Oh, nonsense, Dix—I'm over the moon as long as you are. And Paw-Pop will be too. I can't wait to hear more."

I'm not sure what I was expecting. Strike that; yes I was: Anger, confusion, hurt, name-calling, but not quotes from *Hey Diddle Diddle*. I had a few words of pre-prepared reassurance up my sleeve and that's where they remained. My mother's response had touched and heartened me from head to toe, right through to the little spectral presence in my belly.

Guess who had been right... again? I thought about asking Ivolya to be *my* Madrinha; she had some serious Slavic *savoir faire* behind that headband braid.

That evening, by the time I had microwaved a mundane trio of tamales from Del Pueblo and sat through a couple ancient episodes of *Seinfeld*, I felt that a non-sophomoric length of time had passed and I called Julian. It rang a few times, but ultimately, he picked up. He was back at the dam, he said, clearing timber and taking advantage of the lengthening daylight.

I talked about my day; my boss, my sensitive breasts, the fact that I'd called Matrix and they had nothing new lined up for me yet. He talked about insoluble spiritual wisdoms and the thin veneer of the 21st century, where everything is only a sunspot away from cultural implosion. He didn't avoid our reality; he called our child the prescription for peace and unity. It was heavier stuff than interested me, but the sound of his voice made me want to smell the scent of his breath and the sting of his perspiration, and I squirmed on my Salvation Army sofa until I'd worked up a head of steam.

Then, like an icy shower, the signal sizzled out, the steam dissipated, and in the intervening minutes, while I waited for him to reconnect, my mother called.

Talking to her mid-fidget was awkward, but Julian's cellphone fail wound up being as fortuitous as any technical glitch in my life, because my mother and me ended up sharing the warmest, most gratifying conversation we'd ever had. For the next two hours, I felt the phosphorescence of being the most important person in her life in a way I hadn't felt since I was a little girl.

Since I was unmarried, Christian propriety prevented her from pumping me for too much about my baby's father, so we got that out of the way early. I offered up few honest surface details about my beautiful, wealthy South American poet who could fell forests and poach trout. I actually felt a little guilty and didn't want to rub her nose in her own blue-collar, red-neck, Workaday Willie hubby who made dog chow for a living and hung drywall on weekends. I didn't dwell on Julian and she seemed relieved. She was more concerned with me, her only child carrying her only grandchild, and I told her what little I knew about the pregnancy. So far so good, I said. I felt fine and I was living healthy, less a few pints of Salted Caramel ice cream. Since I knew the day I got pregnant, my due date was in mid-February. The thought of a newborn made her giddy, and she launched into details about my own birth, sparing nothing—her pain, her joy, her instant love for me and my Daddy's inability to get his shit together and nearly having to be admitted to the hospital alongside her. Even I had to laugh at the poor old fellow, faced with a lot of paradigm shifts at fifty years of age. She told me things about my childhood that were impossibly sweet; heirloom details I didn't remember: Me pasting Christmas cards into a scrapbook, me critiquing Danielle Steel books by the age of nine, me doing fabulous chalk doodles on the sidewalk and bringing my first painted landscapes back from a birthday party when I was six.

Hearing these memories saturated in motherly pride was a treat so precious to me and my disoriented sense of self-worth that when Serafin Tercerio's name came up in my call waiting window, I actually put Julian off until the following day.

That day, and the three days that followed, were extraordinarily cozy. In context of how I felt, I think that's a sweet way to put it: The weather was balmy, my lover was attentive and my mother and I, for the first time in more than a decade, became friends again.

At work, word got around that I was pregnant, and henceforth I was handled with a deference that blew my mind, although I shortly discovered why: The Belarusian word for pregnant was *ciažarnaja*, which translated as 'burden'. These folks considered the burden of carrying new life to be an undertaking more heroic than going to war, so I was regarded with reverence and respect. When it came to sustaining the race, Belarusians didn't mess around: They worked until their due date and afterward, their maternity leave was three years long.

I was totally embarrassed and silly happy on Friday when, at the end of the day, the Molnar crew threw me a small baby shower, which doubled as a going-away party since it was my last day. We gathered in the break room and ate the stuffed dumplings that somebody had made, and afterward, Ivolya handed me two giftwrapped books, both the same one: *Motherhood: Belarusian Style.*

I was confused until she said, "One for you, one for *babulia*. Grandma. She will be help to you, and you allow her this, please."

Then, for a pre-ordained span of five minutes, a bottle of vodka came out, and so swept up was I in the moment that I actually accepted a small shot glass full, and I was going to drink it too, assuming that it wouldn't hurt, shouldn't hurt, couldn't hurt, that I'd earned it, and all the shit that Takosha probably told herself before her fall, but there was Ivolya again, gently taking the glass from my hand and flicking it into the break room sink and patting me on the head.

The last thing Ivolya offered was some old school advice about Julian: "Do what's best for baby, but for you yourself, be sure. Belarusian saying: 'Man never forgets woman he couldn't have, but woman never forgets man she could have'."

I had a soft spot for pithy old sayings. They got to be old because they're true. Likewise, the night before, talking to Julian well into the wee hours, he had left me with a couple of solid quotes of his own to consider.

My mother's reminiscing about important moments in our life together made me feel anxious to do the same with Julian, though we were still in blush of newborn romance. I reminded him of our afternoon on the cemetery hill, when all things in the cosmos had conspired in beauty: "I used to be creeped out by graveyards, but if there were ghosts with us that day, they were wise ones."

"You should see it at night with the moon painting the white angel. To me, that's proof that even death has limitations."

"What limitations?" I asked. "I'd like to know."

"Death can't prevent someone from having lived."

I saw the simple logic of it, and this was good. I was gestating a little wonder myself, both upstairs and down, and this was part of it. The relationship between goodness and logic was a neat revelation and I said so.

He answered, "That's the other comfort when your life seems illogical. The logic may be there, even if it's hidden. All natural events are logical. Evolution has bred out the illogic systematically."

This turned, inevitably, to his soft cynicism about my view of a universe devoid of deities, and what Julian said next has resonated through the intervening span and echoes in my theology to this day:

"God is the unbreakable unity in all things. When you regard everything as divine, the divinity of a specific God holds no particular significance."

The various conversations I had that week effectively offset many years of listening to routine *blah blah,* and I was left in awe. The intellectual union I felt with Julian and the homespun chats with my mom strung me delightfully between two worlds; one I didn't particularly understand and wanted to and another I understood too well and whose wholesome simplicity—the nesting drive, no doubt—I craved.

In my memory, that week isolates itself as the only the time in my life that those seemingly contradictory impulses and instincts, both of which shot straight from my soul, did not seem in conflict.

Emotionally, the week was pristine, and physically, it managed to go off without a hitch until the drive home on Friday evening when my fifteen-year-old Focus gave up the ghost along M-59 and I had to have it towed. In February, Perry Collision had replaced my brake discs or something and I had established with them a nominal trust that, at least, they wouldn't try to fleece me. Anyway, I didn't have a lot of options, even though the mechanic on duty said he couldn't get to it until Monday morning. So, I rode with the wrecker driver to the collision shop, then walked to my apartment complex a couple of blocks away.

At home, I called Julian. I should have called him from the road, he said, because he could fix the car, but by then, it was locked inside Perry Collision. Anyway, it was too new in our relationship to start playing damsel in distress. I didn't find that persona attractive and I didn't want to be anybody's domestic ballast: "I'd rather you were my lover than my mechanic," I said. "Too much trust involved in allowing someone to fix a car.

My humor sailed over the target again and I followed quickly with, "I just wanted to tell you that we'll have to make other arrangement to visit your family since I now have no transportation."

The plan had been for me meet him at the cottage and we'd head to his mother's house from there. It was no problem, he said. He'd pick me up at my apartment.

"How?" I asked. "In Serafin's Gator?"

"Oh, I'll bring my mother's car. She's beyond the need for it."

"Beyond the need? God, you need to feed me more here, Julian. Please. What am I getting myself into with this visit? I'm so nervous I have to pee every fifteen minutes. I don't even have any idea of what I should wear."

"Wear the dress you wore in the forest if you still have it."

"Still have it? The Madrinha dress? I treasure it. It's beautiful, I love it; of course I'll wear it. But you have to help me with the family dynamics here. The basics, at least..."

To some extent, I'd been walking on eggshells since Julian had first mentioned his mother and her issues, especially because he'd been so mysterious about them.

I'd avoided bringing it up, but now, I figured I was entitled to more detail. Love or no love, Julian and I remained virtual strangers operating on a strange seduction, and my un-estrangement from my own mom had revived in me how irreplaceable blood relatives were. I wanted to give him room and I didn't want to push it. I said, "At least tell me what to expect with her."

"Not much. I'm sorry. I told you once that my father treated her for a parasite she picked up from the water reeds we use as thatch, a river worm with bacteria living in its gut. It was controllable but not curable. It's one of the reasons he kept returning to our village—to treat her, and to have her. Even so, the parasite ultimately invades the brain and spinal cord. Knowing her now, in the state she's in—that's of no value to you..."

"I accept that and I'll be prepared for it."

"...But knowing my sister is."

"Okay," I said. "It's a tragedy about your mother, Julian. I'm so fucking sorry for everything you've dealt with. But there have been a lot of feminine influences in your life—that can't be a bad thing. Tell me about your sister, then."

"She maintains her tribal links. Once we came here, our cousin offered us a balanced dose of the practical and the spiritual. That's the symmetry that defines true culture. That's the unbroken unity."

"I think it's a beautiful way to view the world, Julian. I tell you honestly, I would have no problem with any child—our child—being raised with those ideals."

"We were able to live the balance in Taiambé, nature and supernature, the sensual and the celestial. We had to; we were integrated. Here, we aren't. We're disintegrated. We coped as best we could, and as it happened, I went one way and my sister went the other. I became a forester and she became a healer. I discovered how practical works. She understands how the alignment works, and in ways I never will. There's no shame in that—it's who I am and who she is; it defines us. The Luanhão word for pregnancy is *tse'a-quë*. It means 'purification' and it's considered an ablution. It's a rite; she feels this on a mystic level, which is what makes her such an effective *partiera*."

"What's a *partiera*?"

"A midwife. She's very good. Of course, I'd hope she could deliver our baby."

If I was nervous before, I was terrified now. I had to navigate delicately, though; I could see, more now than ever, that those waters were shallow in places and very deep in others.

"Julian?" I gasped. "That's a massive commitment. How can I agree to something like that?"

"You can't. Not yet. But you'll meet her. You'll see."

"Dude, you're hitting me up with too much at once here. I know I asked, but Jesus Christ; deliver the baby? This has to soak in—you understand that, I'm sure. Don't you? At least tell me your sister's name."

"Eloá," he said. "Her name is Eloá.

29.

If I was prone to making atrocious puns, I'd say that my lack of Focus was the spark that ignited the events of that bizarre, climactic weekend. According to the original plan, I was to spend Saturday with Julian, but now that I couldn't drive out to the park, I opted to spend the day making a gift for Julian's mother.

According to the protocol of my upbringing, when you visit a stranger's house, bringing a gift is the gracious thing to do. That led me to a triple conundrum: I had no idea what the woman's tastes were, I had no idea if she was lucid enough to remember what her tastes were and most of all, as far as I could understand the story, she'd once sold her children off to the highest bidder.

What sort of gift do you bring someone who pimped out her kids, even to put food on the table?

But what else was I going to do? I decided to paint her a picture.

That idea was rife with considerations of its own. How big a canvas was appropriate? What style might compliment pre-existing décor? For subject matter, should I be safe and good-bad, starving-artist schmaltzy, or did she have her son's appreciation for my incorporeal vision?

Did any of it matter? To me, it did. I could have called Julian to ask him his opinion, but I decided to wing it, and that winds up being another bad pun. I found a sketch I had done at the zoo the week before; a stunning hummingbird called the Crimson Topaz, named for its crimson plumage and metallic, orange-red breast. The drawing was animated and fun and I found some photographs of the same bird online. Such a splendid creature would lend itself to a color-rich study, and I figured that if anybody could appreciate a picture of a pretty bird, it was someone who rescued animals. The fact that the Crimson Topaz was native to Brazil was an added bonus.

By necessity it would be a small painting, because all I had available was 9" X 12"canvas. But that was fine. I could concentrate on a compact composition: The hummingbird with its wings extended, hovering opposite a red acanthus flower. I hauled my easel and paints out to the common area by the transformers and the buckeye, whose own red flowers were by then passing into history. I set up in the cool shade and went to work, attracting a few curious gawkers and a sweet kid of about five who watched me for twenty minutes, eyes wide. When I asked if he'd like me to give him an art lesson on drawing birds he blushed, and then I blushed when he said, "That ain't look like no bird."

The kid kept pestering me until I folded up my easel and moved inside. It looked like there was a storm brewing on the horizon anyway.

I finished the painting in my living room, and to ensure it would dry by morning, I set up my oscillating fan and trained it on the canvas. In the end, I really liked the piece. Despite the impromptu critique by my little ghetto urchin, it *did* look like a bird. It was theatrical and ecstatic and it displayed an uncanny intensity that I think was a product of my emotional state. It wasn't exactly Audubon , but it was sturdily in the Dixie style, and I was quite proud of it. It had symbolism and it had a nice roundness and relief to the golden-green breast and an echo of the long maroon tail in the sweep of the flower stem. Whether or not it would find a place in the recipient's home, I couldn't say, but I hoped that Julian would appreciate the time

I'd invested in it, the passion I'd shared and the insults I'd borne from a nappy-headed little shit who was way too old for the diaper he was wearing.

Whether or not his mother would hang it up on her walls remained to be seen. When I called him, he sighed: "You'll have to experience the walls. The house. You'll have to experience her."

I was a little short: "Okay, well, that's the idea, right? If she doesn't like it, she can put in a closet."

On a strange and inexplicable level, this amused him. "Oh, that would be a compliment. She loves her closet."

"This whole thing is going to be a major head trip for me, isn't it?"

"I'm afraid it is."

His mother was called Mãe. It was Portuguese and easy to pronounce, sounding like 'my'. Her birth name was Ya'kuana Xi , which was not easy to pronounce, and in their culture, mispronouncing someone's name was such grievous insults that if you asked people in his village what their name was, they'd say, "I don't know. Go ask somebody else," thus preventing them from being complicit in any future insults.

At that point, all I knew was that, all things being equal, no matter what she'd subjected her children to, there was a sort of sacred, newly-found bond between us mothers and I certainly didn't want to offend some poor soul withering away from parasites inside her Bloomfield Hills home by screwing up her name.

30.

It had all been an incongruity, right from the start, one thing after another; the club, the apartment, the stacks of hundred dollar bills I had secured in a safety deposit boxes at Genisys Credit Union. Even so, I shook my head, bemused and bewildered, when Julian pulled up to my apartment complex in an Audi A8.

"It's my mother's," Julian shrugged as I slid in beside him on a diamond-stitched leather seat. "Obviously, these are the sorts of things that are important to her."

"What about this kind of thing?" I asked, slipping the bird painting from its gift bag and holding it up.

Like he'd done with my portrait of August Lake, he examined it carefully for a long time, nodding and finally saying. "It's a Jivarrão vision, for sure. It lives. And it's you," he said.

"Forget me; it's for your mother. It's for Mãe. Will she like it?" I beamed. "Is it something she'd want to hang it on her wall like you did?"

Julian said, "There are quite a few things on her walls. You'll see."

Shortly after that, I hit on another bizarre incongruity. It was based on a simple enough question, too. Julian had asked that his midwife sister deliver our baby, and I asked for another detail about her. Only one: All I asked him is if she was older than him or younger and it turned out that he didn't know.

"Excuse me? Come on, Julian. I may be an only child, but that's totally insane. How can you not know?"

"Because I don't," he answered, as if it was the most obvious response in the world. "We were never told and we never cared. We don't care now. We existed as a unit then, and even if we're no longer that same unit, it still doesn't matter."

"I'm just not sure how that's possible. You said you've been in the United States since you were fourteen years old. How could anybody job the system like that? How did you handle enrolling in school and everything?"

"We didn't."

"You were home-schooled?"

"I suppose that's what you call it. We had a sponsor here. I said. My father's cousin. She taught us what we didn't know already and put into context the things we did."

"Madrinha," I said firmly. "I figured that out pretty easily, Julian—I'm sorry."

And then, before he had a chance to say anything else, something major occurred to me and I gasped audibly. "Oh for fuck's sake, Julian—are *you* even here legally? But, hang on. You gotta have documentation to work at the park, don't you? And besides, didn't you say you had papers listing your age? Are they forged or are they for real?"

"Record keeping was not a strong point in Taiambé, but for what they're intended for, they are real enough."

"Doesn't Eloá have her own papers?"

"Of course."

"Well, what do *they* say?"

"The same. The dates are the same."

"You're twins, then?"

"We might be twins. We aren't sure."

I threw up my hands. There was no way to reconcile this with any existing reality in my experience. "I'm totally at a loss, Julian, so maybe I should just drop it before I start freaking out. You understand, I'm trying to hold down the groove and work out my future, and any way you look at it, you and your family are part of it. That's why I'm here. I mean, if nothing else, I'm going to have to put something down on the birth certificate. You do realize that, right?"

"I do," he said easily, and then, nothing else.

So I slid into silence too, ears red, sucking Audi-flavored air, but it plagued the shit out of me and finally, I burst out, "At some point, for some reason, why wouldn't you just ask your mother? Out of curiosity, if nothing else—that's human; that's perfectly natural. And why wouldn't she tell you?"

"You'll see," he said again.

It was a simply and succinct response, and shortly and consummately, I did see.

In the meantime, at least the trip was sweet. I was used to the shocks of a shockless Ford, and now, my butt was buttressed by some high-priced mercy as Julian turned onto Opdyke and headed south toward Bloomfield Hills.

Bloomfield Hills. Bored and masochistically morbid, I'd driven through that tony community a couple of times simply to gawk at the privilege. Most of the houses sold for a million dollars, and some for considerably more. For the most part, it was the land of wrought iron gates, multi-acre lawns, backyard lakes, pyramid pines and mansions piled atop artificial hills. It was the zip code of moguls and superstars, and it was the home of Cranbrook Institute of Art, a vast compound of trails, gardens, fountains and sculptures, which—even though it was situated in the middle of the most affluent community in the state—was surrounded by a high wall to keep out the riff-raff.

The thing was, Julian made a left at Bristol and starting heading north, heading in the opposite direction. A few minutes later, he turned onto an unpaved side street and into a dark community of small, squalid hovels.

We had these kinds of houses on the outskirts of Cadence. In fact, amid the stench of stale aquarium water, I had lost my virginity in one of them. They were clapboard breadboxes with dirt driveways; we called them 'shotgun shacks' because you could fire a shotgun through the front door and none of the pellets would hit the walls before exiting the back door . Most were porchless and many were without house numbers except those painted awkwardly on shingle-siding. Lawns were un-mowed, weeds were un-pulled, and the shrubs that someone may have once planted with circumspection were now crazy and ridiculous looking. There were orange construction barrels stacked on one property, old appliances on another, mattresses and box springs on another, everything wallowing in foot-high grass.

Bloomfield Hills? Later, I accessed a map, and discovered that there was, in fact, a tiny tongue of the township that jutted out into Pontiac, perhaps as a hiccup in a cartographer's bad day from many years ago. In any case, at the end of that road was a grim, blackish house set back a couple hundred feet behind a chain-link barrier with an old sign that read *'No Trespassing'*.

And that was where we stopped.

Julian opened the gate and pulled the slick car onto a narrow strip of fenced property flanked by an overgrown lot on one side and groves of tired-looking trees on the other. The grass between was trampled and spackled with animal feces. He'd said his mother rescued strays, and indeed, stacked everywhere, between trees, against the fence, butting a small shed, were cages filled with desperate, sickly-looking animals. There were cats, raccoons, skunks, opossums and badgers while flocks of chickens and ducks ranged among them, scratching and pecking and fussing.

The yard was strange enough, but the house was far stranger. From the street, in the creeping shadows beneath the trees, it looked drab and nondescript, but as we pulled closer, I saw that it was entirely painted in elaborate and sophisticated designs, some so subtle that even from twenty feet away they seemed to slither off the walls and fuse with the backdrop. Across the front were a series of organic, earth-tone hieroglyphs—a wraparound, mural version of the sort of carving I'd seen in Julian's cottage. Naturally, I recognized the style. This was the work of Madrinha.

Suddenly, I felt conspicuous in my Madrinha dress. I couldn't think of anything else to say, so I asked Julian what the words meant.

He answered carefully: "I can tell you what they say: *'I went from God to God until they cried from within me: "O, Thou I"'* What they mean? That's a sad pilgrimage that ends right here."

The main entrance was covered only in loose fabric without a door, and I realized then that the sad road's end had dropped me at the fountainhead of incongruity.

An invalid shoved aside the fabric and crept out of the house. It was Mãe, and she was—for want of a gentler description—the most disturbing-looking woman I had ever seen.

I crunched the numbers. She was in her early forties, but from the distance at which I first saw her, she might have passed for twice that age. The parasites had not been kind. Gaunt as a stilt and hunched from the waist, she stepped into the filtered sunlight and peered out at us through green flames set deeply in a withered face. We left the car and as we approached, she seemed to flip though expressions like shuffling cards, alternating between a puzzled scowl, a savage smile and an insipid frown. She slinked forward to meet us on bare, bony feet. At the zoo the week before, I'd watched a puma move like that, but this one couldn't have weighed seventy pounds.

I felt dizzy and fragile. I said 'hello', and she responded instantly with a low and throaty chant; a song, I thought.

I looked at Julian helplessly. "Can't she speak English?"

"She can," he answered. "But she doesn't."

"What's she saying?"

"She says you're a phantom. An emissary spewed from the *muiraquitã*."

Now I was legitimately frightened and I wanted to get back in the car. "She knows I'm pregnant, right? With your baby?"

As if it was all some quiet joke, he said, "I'm not sure what she knows."

Julian's mother wore a dark, heavily embroidered hood and a long greenish skirt that clung to sharp hips. The dress had a limp scoop neck and her breasts sagged freely, bare and visible below her hunched spine. She was all acute, appalling angles, like the Crooked Man with his crooked stick. My stomach turned; I didn't want to get any closer to her. Her smell preceded her and it was atrocious. But on she came in a persistent creep, and to ward her off, I thrust out the painting. She snatched it and smacked her lips. Her nostrils flared. She put her face an inch from the canvas and I thought she was going to lick it. She blinked and the blue veins in her eyelids stood out like worms. Her lips drew back and her mouth contorted. Another trill slipped from between her teeth.

"What...?" I asked weakly.

"She recognizes the bird. She calls it Acúshi. She used to catch them in her garden and eat them."

I felt faint. The primeval stench seeping from the house was hers, only magnified, and there were flies beginning to gather at the doorway. I had no idea what to do next. "Can you help me here?"

"Sure," he said quietly. "Tell her what you thought of her car."

"It kicks ass. Tell her it rules. Tell her it beats the hell out of mine."

She understood me and she threw back her head and loosed a cry of righteous, ferocious glee that drove into my skull. The air was perfectly still, and no leaves moved in the trees, but I felt the weight of wind against me. I almost collapsed and Julian slipped his arm around my waist to hold me up.

"You're doing fine," he said in a soft tone. "We're almost done. There's not much else for us here."

"You *brought* me here," I sputtered back, almost bursting into tears.

"But not to see *her.*"

"Your sister? Then where is she?"

He turned my body toward his and briefly, locking eyes, I was quite surprised and ineffably moved to see the spasms of grief. I thought he might have been laughing as I flailed before his batty mother, but I saw the opposite: The ordeal was worse on him than it was for me, and it occurred to me in a download that the relationship between a mother and her offspring, with all its permutations and implosions and compounded sore feeling, is troubled enough under the best of circumstances, but here—with rape at its fountainhead and abuse as its continuum—it must be off the charts. He'd once said that his mother arose from a different atmosphere. My God, I smelled that atmosphere now. By the virtue of his DNA, his unbreakable umbilical cord, he must have breathed that same air from the beginning of his life.

But I was in love with him, and in that brief instant of communion, I shared some of his pain; if not the core of it, then the gist of it.

He told me I'd see, and I saw. All the while, the incessant, wobbling vocals continued. Mãe sounded urgent. I looked back at Julian and he said, pensively: "There's one thing more. My mother wants to show you her closet. We'll take a look, and then we'll find Eloá."

190

I nodded. If nothing else, Julian was steering me through this bizarre situation, so I allowed his mother to take my damp hand and drag me toward the painted bungalow to see her closet. My mood, barely holding together, imploded as soon as I stepped inside: As bad as the yard had been, the interior was an insane asylum.

The walls were completely covered in lifelike animal images, skillful frescoes done by someone with an eye for realism far more acute than mine. There were frogs and maned wolves, otters and lizards, a slithering black jaguar. The same artist had obviously done the murals inside Sophrosyne, and I had no doubt that it was Madrinha. There was no room for my painting here anyway—let Julian's ghastly mother eat it.

Madrinha's artwork only made the rest of the place seem more nightmarish: A few chairs made of wicker were tossed haphazardly about and a black onyx table identical to the one in the apartment above Sophrosyne was piled with fruit and candles around a green sculpted figure, a foot tall with hieroglyphics etched into the chest. It the only thing in the room that looked clean; the rest was filthy beyond description. Not hoarder filth, but animal filth; there were as many chickens inside as out, meandering and pecking and defecating.

There was little furniture, but there was an overabundance of books. Books were everywhere, and it might have been a saving grace except that they lay scattered in piles that suggested they hadn't been touched in years. I had little doubt that with a gas mask and a shovel, I could uncover some Plato. Like the floor, like the walls, like the yard, like Mãe herself, they were spattered with mud and dried blood and animal dung.

The smell was fiendish and it permeated everything. The shuffle of Mãe's bare, shit-encrusted feet and the clip played against the incessant voice and my head spun. I let go of her hand and she gaped at me. Her song rose to a shrill and dropped to a sigh. "What is she saying?" I cried.

"Nothing."

"Obviously it's something, Julian. *What?*"

"It's keening—it's what she does now. In her mind, she's inside a never-ending cycle and she's singing about it. The words mean, *"The gods became the saints, and the saints became the animals, and then the animals became the gods again."*

"I thought you sister was a healer, Julian?" I cried. "This isn't healed—this is broken into a million pieces."

He shook his head sadly. "It's impossible to explain it, I know. The parasites are in her spinal cord. She thinks the cosmos has crystallized right here and her goal is live in filth and not become contaminated."

By then, Mãe had stopped before her closet and was grinning and pointing. And yet, it wasn't a closet. It was the main bedroom of the bungalow. It was completely empty except for a chrome coat rack, on which hung a dozen fur coats.

I knew little about the worth of mink and ermine, but it seemed to me that these were top-of-the-line coats. And not only coats, but stoles and sheared jackets and tassel vests and multi-colored shawls and scarves and wraparounds, everything made the more bizarre because there were chickens roosting on top of them, fussing and shifting and flying about, and the coats were sheathed in inches of thick bird droppings.

The motherlode of incongruity. Julian shrugged. "These are the things that are important to her now."

I needed to leave. I needed to run; I needed to vomit. I could see a rear doorway and I burst through it, into a greener area behind the house and fell on my knees and threw up. I really heaved; purging waves of puke so severe that I thought I was probably endangering the pregnancy.

I went limp and then there were hands beneath my armpit; strong familiar hands, and I raised my head and saw Julian's strong familiar features. Then, with a visceral start, I saw that it wasn't Julian at all. I wondered if this whole thing had been a punk from the start, because the face had Julian's contours, his angles and curves, but it belonged to a woman.

"Eloá?" I whispered.

"Shhh," she answered and kissed the top of my head. I glanced back at the house.

192

Julian had not followed me out. In fact, I could see him leading his mother in the other direction, through the front doorway.

I was helped to my feet, supported, cradled, and with arms wrapped firmly about my waist, gently impelled through a small grove of vine-decked dogwood trees that formed an enclosed and living bower fifty feet from the house—inside, there was a woven hammock strung between twined branches and she helped me into it with movements that were steady and, I realized later, irresistible.

It was a remarkable sensation. I felt the same strength and tenderness in her hands as I had with Julian's, but here, there was no undertow of ambiguity. In my limited experience, every man touches a woman with a certain wariness—especially the first time—because he operates from private impulses and each partner he chooses, or who chooses him, may have a different response to them. Here, there was no vigilance, no sense of her being on guard, perhaps because she was my gender. Or perhaps because it was she was a skillful healer after all, and what was happening inside the house with her mother were made of darker energies than I could comprehend. In any case, she knew. I lay in the hammock and it swayed like a metronome beneath my weight. She knelt beside me, encircled my head, closed her eyes and slipped her long fingers down the front of my Madrinha dress to place her hand over my soft belly, massaging my hitching muscles. I didn't find it the slightest bit intrusive—I found it warming and somehow, vital. In fact, I felt an exquisite exchange between my body and her hand. It was erotic without lewdness. There was physical communion and in her, I felt that there was some ecstasy.

"Should Julian be here?" I asked quickly.

She crooked her arm to place a finger on my lips. I smelled Julian, or perhaps, that wild and special scent clung to them both. If Julian intended to leave me alone with her, I wasn't sure why, but even so, exactly and as inexplicably as I had inside his cottage, I felt suddenly complacent, sheltered and entirely safe.

When Eloá spoke, the cadence was instantly appealing: "Let Julio see to the woman. Mothers and sons are divine harmony. You know it already; you're carrying a boy."

I turned to her with the same wonder with which I had regarded Julian, and now that I could see her fully, it was obvious that she was really not her brother's clone. What I'd seen at first had been an illusion of sameness. In the sifted light of the bower, the impression she now gave was even more arresting: It was as if a lone subject had sat for two portraits interpreted by two different artists, each of whom saw different qualities in the single model. I stared at her until I could define it, and she didn't seem to mind.

She was in her element—that was obvious—and the elliptical leaves of the dogwood were mirrored in her oval eyes. Her skin had an olive cast that Julian's did not. There was a similar voluptuousness to their mouths, but her lips turned slightly upward, as with urgency; Julian's carried a benign sense of resignation. In him, this was understandable: It was his serial tragedy; he remained among the men who killed his jungle. But Eloá's expressed the wilderness undiluted. It showed in subtle ways and in surface ways. You had to study Julian to recognize his Indian roots, but in her, they gilded whatever white blood she had inherited.

Her dress had none of Madrinha's embellishments. She wore a simple brown poncho, warp-patterned, and a headpiece that wrapped around her head to hold back bronze-colored hair. A small beaded plate hung from her neck and fell halfway down her chest. I could see her breasts in firm contour beneath the fabric of her clothing and I noted with stab of wistfulness that they were much fuller than mine, although perhaps that was a condition that pregnancy would rectify.

In any artist's interpretation, Eloá was a savage beauty.

As Julian was, in his incarnation, a lovely and constrained demigod. My own demigod, in fact, but how I could work the mad mother into this hyperbole remained to be seen: Maybe when the tendons that bound a family's sanity were severed by circumstance and everything drops into the abyss beneath the lake, Mãe was the result.

Eloá stroked my hair and her hand cupped my belly. "In Luanhão, a pregnancy is *tse' a-quë*, a purification. For the pregnant woman herself, the word is not so pretty. When a Luanhão woman carries a child, she is renamed *Hiaaga*—it means 'Stomach'."

She smiled, and her smile was wonderful. The term clearly amused her. "And for the whole length of her pregnancy, she's nothing but a stomach. But that stomach encompasses many things—all things, really. The pregnant woman's stomach has become a symbol of creation, and the entire history of genesis is recreated within her. She is the creator god and as omnipotent as the one from the beginning of time, and she is treated with same awe and reverence. There are long, ancient sagas devoted to nothing else."

I felt her finger circle my navel and put slight pressure there, as if she was approaching the tiny thing within my womb. "This is where the Luanhão believes your soul sleeps. Here, in this cavity."

The sensation was amazing and I'd be lying if I didn't admit that I felt something far more delicious and intimate than I'd felt during Dr. Sz-Min's examination. If it was sexual on some level, it wasn't the itch to copulate, but the itch to trust someone implicitly, although again, I would be dishonest if I claimed I didn't tingle in places other than my belly. It seemed awful of me. She was a stranger, though not entirely. Her face, the voice... I now believed that she and Julian must in fact be twins.

She began a purring chant. Unlike her mother's off-kilter keening, Eloá's tone was clear and confident. It sounded blissful. The intonations were precise and the syllables had striking, unexpected syncopations that struck on off beats. The rhythms were loose and the meter was as mesmerizing as the drums outside Sophrosyne. It went on for fifteen minutes, and finally trailed away into a soft and unknown distance—another atmosphere.

"That is so beautiful," I said, tears rimming my eyes. "Can you tell me what the words mean?"

Eloá's cheeks was nearly against mine. I could feel her throat vibrate and I thought we were fusing in some female dimension far removed from my breeder trysts with Julian. She said, "It's the story of the origin of everything, something that happened many, many seasons ago in a white man's grasp of time, but now it is your eternal season, *Hiaaga*; the moons happen within you all at once. Within you and without you, chaos fights creation; that's how the Luanhão view the dark energy of miscarriage, and in the song, the chaos is depicted as a black jaguar that is prepared to defy and devour the creator god."

I lay still beneath the emerald dome. I was bathed in green; a glitter of blue appeared between braided branches and I had the sensation of having being transported from that squalid suburban backyard to some vast virgin jungle. She led me there: She explained how the fear of being eaten pervades every aspect of life within that jungle. Flesh-eaters are the perennial enemy and in Luanhão song cycles, evil always appears with teeth bared and claws unsheathed, generally as a caiman or a jaguar. For a pregnant woman, the loss of the child represents what in Western cosmology would equate to a catastrophe that ends the universe. There could be no cataclysm worse, except, perhaps, for one: The Luanhão believed that children with deformities were quasi-human and without souls, so ironically, they were thrown in the river or left in the jungle to be eaten by caimans or jaguars.

"Well, it's an intense way to think about childbirth, that's for sure. But I love the way it translates the pain into poetry. Your brother wrote some wonderful pieces. You know that, of course. It's what first attracted me to him—I found them online. His veiled creations..."

Her green eyes shone: "At first, the Luanhão didn't think that Julio was completely human. His attitudes were unique to any experience they'd ever had. They called him *Xam-Bioá*—'Sun-Youth'—and thought he was deformed from birth and had somehow survived the jaguars and the crocodiles. That made him a mystic; an intermediary—a man-spirit who had vanquished the flesh-eaters."

She smiled again. "And to be sure, he did."

"But what about you? You survived too. Weren't the two of together in the jungle?" I asked. "It's none of my business, I know..."

"We were together, of course. Always. In the jungle and in Taiambé with the decay and the maggots and the roaches, and we were together in the hotel room at the Eldorado in Sao Paolo. I knew how to slip into my tribes and become them. I was Á–Bioá—Moon-Youth—and I was one of them. He never was. He's always been an outlier. He considered himself an anarchist then and he thinks he's one now."

"He told me once that he was becoming the chaos," I said quietly.

There was, for the first time, an inflection of condescension in her response. "I've never known anybody less capable of becoming the chaos than Julio. He's trapped inside the chaos, that's all, like a bug in a jar. Chaos requires multiplicity and Intricacy, *Hiaaga*; he's no good at that. He's too simple. He thrives on being simple. Maybe we were ruined by birth, ruined from birth, but he was subdued by it where I was inflamed. Sweet irony. But here, he's maimed. The only place he can be whole and healthy is in the forest without white men. All he wants is his Jivarrão, his lover, his child and his solitude."

Did I trust this as truth unblemished? I certainly wanted to. I'd seen the state of the house. I'd recoiled from her mother, but Eloá's warm hand was pliant on my body and it felt reassuring. And reassurance, like Julian's solitude, was all I wanted.

"I'd follow him into the forest, Eloá. I hope he knows that. And I would have his children. Will we triumph over the jaguar? Julian and me? Our baby. This one?"

"Of course," she cooed. "You'll be fine, *Hiaaga*. You didn't see the table inside? That's a *moamo*; devotional sorcery."

"The shrine? I did see that," I said incredulously. "That's for me?

She smiled again. "It's for your father."

"My... *father?*"

"Yes, that's a greenstone *muiraquitã* with offerings for the warrior who created you; it will ensure that your son will be strong and healthy.

"My father's dead," I said softly.

"Of course," she answered. "I know it. Mine is too. There is divine harmony between fathers and daughters as well, and it grows more strident after death."

"I hope so. I hope you're right. I hope that my Daddy is a spirit and that he's paying attention to all this. I was fourteen when he died and I never got over it."

I lay there for a moment. I still felt easy, and I decided to risk saying it. "I know your father died, and I think we must have been about the same age, too. Mine, from cardiac arrest. If it's not too intrusive, can I ask how yours passed away?"

"Sure, if you like. I shot him in the forehead. And when he didn't die immediately, I cut off his head with a cane machete."

It was such an abrupt and unexpected response that I felt a wave of numbness run through my body. Absurdly, I stuttered, "Why would you do that?"

"What else was I going to do, *Hiaaga*? Let him live? That would have cost us *our* lives. We'd already forced him to empty his bank account—several of them, actually. He didn't think we were serious, but we were. He didn't think we were strong enough, and we were. He was very rich. Then, suddenly he wasn't anymore and *we* were. His legal wife ended up with nothing except his head inside a box."

My next comment was even more nonsensical. I see that now. "Does Julian know?"

"He knows he couldn't do it himself, that's what he knows. Fathers and sons have their own harmonies. But I could; our harmony existed in the divinity of justice. And after all, that's what we'd come all the way São Paulo to do. Don't look so horrified. My father was the flesh-eater and we triumphed."

I had no more vomit in me. Instead, I loosed a small wail.

"Hush, *Hiaaga*," she whispered, touching my lips again. "Say no more about it."

But I couldn't hush. I wanted to remove her hand from my dress, but somehow, I stopped as soon as I felt its outline beneath the muslin. I cupped it as it cupped my womb. I was chilled to my core, and I hesitated to remove the warmth that radiated there. As I hesitated, I remembered, and in remembering, suddenly, I got it:

A room with an evil man and a victim; a gun with a single shot. It's a crime against the family, not the state. It's tribal justice. It goes no farther; it's retaliation without consequence. One chance only. Eloá had taken it. And I suspected that I understood why they couldn't remain in Brazil.

"But what about your father's cousin?" I said, keeping my voice even. "The one who sponsored you when you came here? Did *she* know?"

"Graciela? That cretin? She had more parasites than my mother. She did what we paid her to do and she knew what we paid her know."

"I think Julian was very fond of her, right?"

"Probably. Young boys feel that way about the babysitter."

"Babysitter? Julian said she was his teacher."

Eloá had related horrors and now, she laughed easily: "Oh, did he? I taught Julio more in an hour than Graciela did in a decade. Trust me, out of their element, Indians are stupid beyond belief. In their forests, they're wise; in the forest of white men, namely civilization, they're drooling dogs waiting for the master to drop food. Graciela was the cleaning woman at the club. She was our janitor. Julio may have stayed with her in the chicken coop occasionally when my mother got to be too much."

I shouldn't have pressed, but I pressed: "He said he'd been intimate with her."

"God, I hope not. She only had about four teeth—she was sixty then; long dead now from the river worms she brought with her inside her spine. But, who knows what he might have done? He's removed in his intimacy, isn't he? You noticed that too, didn't you? That's removal, not presence. Only hatred can account for such removal."

"Julian doesn't hate anyone," I said and then I had a sudden and overpowering sense of clarity.

It settled into me slowly and irreconcilably. Eloá went on: "Of course he does. He hates me."

"He loves you—I know that. You must know it too."

The glitter in the sky was reflected in her smile. And for the first time, I recognized the mores of a primordial swamp:

"Ha," she said. "As we were owned and bred to a life, we've owned and bred. Julio crawls with lust for me; that's what I know. It's like lice. Like bedbugs on him—like parasites in the thatch. He's a volcano of lust—you've seen it, I know you have. Sure he loves me, and he hates that he loves me. And he hates me the more because I can't have his children."

"You can't have children?" I gasped as the final testament downloaded.

"It's no matter. What do I want his children for? I want my paintings; they're my children. Take him far away from me and give him his babies and leave me to my artwork."

I said it for my benefit, not hers, though I spoke her name: "Oh, God. Eloá. I fucked it up, didn't I? It's not the cousin, it's you. *You're* Madrinha."

"Shhh, little *Hiaaga*," she whispered. "I am not. *You* are."

And when she looked at me she saw me, and then she saw inside me, *O Thou I,* and then she saw things inside me that were in sunless corners, and then, her gaze drilled through me, into other atmospheres, and disappeared.

31.

I found Julian in the car. I was sobbing, and by design and deportment, inconsolable. I didn't want to confront him, I didn't want to cuddle him, I didn't want him to cup my belly. I didn't want to smell him; I didn't want his poetry and I certainly didn't want to get in a car with him. By then, I had already called a cab.

I didn't even want to talk to him. I was in my own atmosphere—one in which girls didn't shoot their fathers and boys didn't fuck their sisters. But I had to tell him something, if only to leave no doubt about my subsequent decisions: "I know who Madrinha is. I know who you're in love with, whose children you want, and I'll tell you for free, she's not the mystic you pretend she is. I know what happened to your father too, and I hope to God that it never comes back to haunt you."

As I sat on the curb and waited, he stood behind me, and to his credit, he didn't try to deny or explain anything and he didn't try to touch me. When my ride pulled up, the last thing I said to him was, "She's your mother, Julian-Julio, or whatever the fuck I should call you. That house is barbaric—it's an atrocity; somebody needs to call the health department or something. Maybe I will. You lied. You told me that Eloá is a healer. How could a healer let her own mother live like that?"

As I pulled the door of the cab shut, he said, "You missed the point, Dixie. My mother lets *her* live like that."

I didn't respond and I didn't look back. My mind was settled before I got to my apartment, and the tears evaporated from the simple relief of having made the decision.

I'd been briefly enthralled; perhaps it is the fate of an artist to wander the world with a lantern in search of an honest superlative. I'd perceived Julian as an ideal; an impossible masculine dream. Instantly and entirely, I'd recognized the same quality in Eloá: She was a paragon of our gender. And maybe, on some level, I still thought so. she was passionate, acquisitive, intriguing and, from what she'd told me, fundamentally ruthless. I couldn't deny that these were dynamics that I admired in women, and some—even those that went against my natural grain—I'd tried to emulate.

But in the end, I suppose I was more traditional than I was willing to let on. And although the dogma sounds old-school-Bible-thumper, I believed it anyway: Men could be passionate, they could be acquisitive, intriguing and fundamentally ruthless, but they couldn't carry children. That was our superpower, and it trumped all else in the world of paradigms. It tipped the balance. I'd spent too many years drowning in the irrational fear that as a woman I was incomplete, and although a radical feminist might have pilloried me for daring to think that way, I would have pilloried her right back for invalidating my private and legitimate angst. Not that I *had* to have children. But the fear that I couldn't. And now, abruptly, I was pregnant and Eloá could not be.

In the end, it didn't matter. My heart and my grit knew what was going to happen next. I just had to confirm some details. Practically, I was giving it until the end of the week since there were loose ends to sew up.

The decision to act it out immediately did not occur to me until following morning, inside Perry Collision, where I waited for the mechanic to put a bow on my new Focus alternator. There, to pass the time, amid the Valvoline posters and the acrid stench of grease, I exhumed a copy of *The Detroit News* from the stack of automotive trade journals on the waiting room table. It was dated the previous

Wednesday and the lead story in Metro section carried the headline, *'Mutilated Body Found behind Pontiac Landmark'*.

The story ran:

Pontiac police are looking for suspects after the decapitated and mutilated body of a teenage boy was found in an alley behind the former Masonic Temple Lodge 25 on the city's northeast side.

An anonymous tip to the police led to the discovery of the body of a young man with his head and genitalia cut off and his heart removed. Police spokesman Andrew Duran said that investigators believe the murder and mutilation happened at another location, saying "We're still trying to locate another scene."

Duran said police are withholding details about the cause of death, but the victim is believed to be Hispanic and between 12 and 16 years old.

Police are also looking into whether his body was mutilated before or after he died. "Law enforcement officials have searched local, state and national databases," Duran said in a news release Thursday, "However, there has been no positive identification made to date."

Duran also said that police are investigating connections between the body and a child trafficking incident reported earlier this year, but would not elaborate.

Anyone with information on the death is asked to call the sheriff's office at 248-670-7567

Eloá had said, "As we were owned and bred to a life, we've owned and bred."

I don't know how I knew that it was Serafin Tercerio in that alley, headless, heartless and sexless, but it was, and of that, I had no doubt.

I had no doubt about other things as well. Intrinsic things. Julian and Eloá's father was not my father; with Daddy, my relationship *had* been one of divine harmony. Although he was gone, the wisps of mist that circled his memory were still there, gathering in sweet places that I remembered and loved. And they were far away from here.

There was a standing offer of employment on the table, an old bedroom where my childhood remained preserved in the amber of nostalgia that only a stubborn, heartsick parent can muster up. I briefly considered calling the hotline at the bottom of the newspaper article, but I didn't, if for no other reason that it would have required me to stick around and fill out police reports. Instead, I blocked Serafin's number from my cell phone, then called my mother and told her I was coming home to Cadence have my baby.

She was delighted, but skeptical. She thought I might have fallen off the wagon.

"Not a chance, Ma," I answered. "I haven't been this sober since the morning you showed me my Daddy in his casket."

32.

Energized by resolve, a new five hundred dollar alternator and maybe some fundamental ruthlessness, I made two stops on the way home: One to Genisys Credit Union, where I transferred a hundred thousand dollars to my gym bag, and then to Del Pueblo market to pick up some empty boxes. I didn't have much to move—a paltry wardrobe and a few pieces of art—and I loaded the trunk and rear seat of the Focus with room to spare. I left a terse note for my landlord, clicked my ruby slippers together and transported myself up out of the basement and back toward my own backyard.

The trip was a trip, filled with sights and sensations I hadn't experienced since I was a kid. Unexpected memories reared like heat lighting and faded behind me like thunder. It began on the border, at Toledo.

For a little girl from a town where the tallest building was a grain silo and where ethnic dining was Peking Palace, Toledo had once held for me a sort of cachet of urbanity. In the fifth grade, I did a report on it and learned that Ohio had once gone to war with Michigan over Toledo and won. In exchange, the federal government had ceded Michigan the Upper Peninsula. When I was eleven, Toledo was cool and the tradeoff seemed fair, and it was only after I developed a passion for the sights and sounds of nature that I realized that we'd wound up with the shit end of the stick.

Twenty miles further down the freeway, removed from the hip-hop and heavy metal of city stations, Ohio tends to develop its own soundtrack. It kicks in suddenly and, if you happen to be taking I-75 to the end of the road in Florida, it dominates the airwaves the rest of the way down: White gospel music.

I'd grown up on the genre, and like my revelation about Toledo, I was an adult before I realized that Caucasians really can't produce gospel music to (forgive the pun) save their souls. White gospel has no funk, It slithers from the radio in a saccharine glissade. The recurring theme is *'Jesus, I am not worthy'* and *'Lord, I am undeserving,'* and at least musically, they're probably correct. Real-deal gospel—genuine, foot-stomping, audience-testifying stuff—doesn't come from white people on the Maumee River, it comes from people like Rosetta Tharpe on creeks called the Possum.

But that day, in that hour, I also heard the siren songs of childhood, so I turned on *Faith for Tomorrow* and all the way to my Cadence exit, I listened to the honky crooners and barbershop quartet holdovers who sounded like angel food cake frosted with Crème Anglaise and soaked in Milk of Magnesia.

The cliché cravings of pregnancy caught up to me on the freeway off-ramp and I stopped at my alma mater—the Love's Country Store where I used to work—and bought a Sara Lee Angel Food Cake with French Vanilla Glaze Icing. I didn't recognize anybody behind the counter, but the cheap toys stocking the shelves looked identical to the ones I remembered from my tenure and the cylinders of yuck spinning in the Roller Bites machine look like ones I'd left unsold five years earlier.

It wound up being a fitting metaphor for my homecoming, where everything had changed while everything remained the same.

I wanted to scarf the cake on the spot, but I kept it in its box as an oblation for my mother. According to the protocol of my upbringing, when you visit a stranger's house, you bring a gift.

I drove slowly down Scioto Street and it kicked out the same inflections it had during my stormy-sweet childhood; a conservative and shady bastion oozing middle class normalcy along with the aggressive patriotism of flyover states. Midway down the block, our old colonial had a wrought iron American eagle over the door, Old Glory in the flag holder and a pleated red, white and blue nylon bunting festooned from the porch rail. Then as now, I didn't understand who these feverish displays of nationalism were meant to impress. I mean, the town's demographics were almost exclusively built on natural born citizens and such bragging rights were pretty widely disseminated.

Anyway, my mother was waiting for me on the screened porch, drinking coffee with milk and listening to Sean Hannity. I saw that she'd aged in the four years since we'd been estranged, and I had that realization that people do after not seeing their parents for a while: They're mortal. As a kid, they always look the same, year after year, and it's a uniquely adult revelation that they're as human as anyone else.

We embraced tentatively and I could tell that she didn't entirely think I'd returned to her version of sanity, which, of course, I hadn't. But I was pregnant, and she was willing to offer me all benefits of parental doubt and we made the most of it. Along with her eye pouches and streaks of gray, she'd mellowed. We talked health, primarily. She'd had issues with hypertension and had given up coffee with caffeine. I showed her my prenatal Omega-3 soft-gels and she showed me her Zaroxolyn, and for a while we bonded over pharmaceuticals and Sanka.

Later, we bonded over her Swedish meatball recipe too. It was one of my childhood faves, and, as it happened, one of Paw-Pop Murphy's.

Since I'd been somewhat vague about my arrival time, she hadn't gone to the supermarket yet, so I went with her to the Great Scot on Route 180 to pick up meatball ingredients. There, I predicted, we'd run into a few familiar faces. "What should I say to them?" I asked, pointing to my belly. "How a big of a secret do you want to keep our little buddy?"

"Oh, heck, there's no shame or embarrassment about it anymore, honey. Half the girls who work at the market are single moms and not all the married ones had rings on their fingers in the maternity ward."

At five twenty precisely—as I presume he had on every workday since I'd blown

205

town—Paw-Pop Murphy came home from the dog chow factory, and by five thirty—again, as I presume had been the case on every workday since I'd left— dinner was on the table. Toby had undergone the same evolutionary ravages as Mom. He was balder and heavier and his tree-trunk arms had flabbed out. He looked like a well-fed old boar. Certainly, he had the demeanor of someone who was simply keeping his head down until retirement. He was as hard-boiled and simple as ever, but in the brief moment between the time my mother got up from the dinner table to wash the dishes and the time I got up to help her, he whispered to me that I'd made her very happy, and he appreciated that on a personal level. He said that he'd help me any way he could, and if the fifteen dollars an hour he'd pay me to look after the Murphy Construction Company books didn't cover my expenses, he'd willingly take care of the overdraw. It was an extravagant and affectionate offer, and I knew it. I should have been grateful. Instead, I wanted to fetch my gym bag and stack the dining room table with wads of hundred dollar bills bound in mustard-colored straps.

That night, I lay in my old Kid Kraft youth bed, awake for long, quiet hours, smelling potpourri and in the distance, meatball grease. True to her word, my bedroom existed in cryostasis, dusted and polished and Febrezed, but not upgraded since I was twelve. On one hand, it was sweet and poignant, but on the other it was rather creepy, since I'd never had a say in picking out any of the furniture. Everything in the room scratched the itch of my mother's tastes, not mine. I would have opted for a caliginous Victorian theme with a sanctuary bed, a mirrored vanity and a chandelier. Instead, I wound up with a home-assembled ensemble from Sears, where everything chalk-white with pink rosebuds, even the curtains, even the shelves that were otherwise filled with American Girl dolls.

The only thing in the room that was even vaguely 'me', or, at least, that I'd had a hand in approving, was the varnished Amish wardrobe that stood in front of the closet and contained the few prize dresses I owned. It wasn't exactly a Victorian armoire, but with its crown molding and tapered legs, it struck me as the kind of thing that would have appealed to Jane Austen. We'd found it at a garage sale when I was ten. I'd fallen in love with it, and my Daddy bought it for me, and although it clashed with the rest of the décor— more *Charlotte's Web* than Charlotte Bronte. I wouldn't let anybody mess with it, even after it began to fall apart. I propped it up with old phone books and rejected Paw-Pop's offer to repair it. The wardrobe was a link between me and my late father, and no usurper to the crown would come between us.

Even so, unavoidably, lying chilled beneath my old quilted comforter, I concluded that in my mother's queendom, the crown fit Toby Murphy's head better than it ever had my Daddy's. Byron Mason Pickett's subtle Southern charisma had been wasted on her; she'd never been the hoop-skirt belle to measure up. He'd been out of her charisma league. God love her, Ma was a pasty Buckeye to the bone, now quite settled in her boring middle-age. She'd traded brio for bro, and I couldn't deny that she seemed as comfortable and fulfilled as I'd ever seen her.

In accepting that, I had to at least give Toby Murphy his due. He'd entered the picture late, but with a sort of stodgy, Johnny Lunchbucket honor. In the real world, decent men and good providers married widows all the time. Hard to deny that he'd behaved better in the intervening years than I had, and at this late date, any festering resentment I harbored toward him was childish spite. The embarrassing truth was, I had always considered my family a class-notch above the rest of the town, and it was time to release that fantasy, to let it go like air from a balloon. It was time to sink back to earth. The Pickett-Murphys were, in every sense of the word, the living embodiment of Cadence, Ohio—no better and no worse—and Dixie was merely the prodigal daughter returned to the nest.

Besides, Paw-Pop was now my boss as well as my stepfather, so if ever there was time to find common ground and make peace, this was it.

With my mother too. She'd aged, for sure, but along the way, she seemed to have acquired some crucial growth rings. I caught her with an Oprah magazine and she seemed somewhat confused by my pleasant surprise. "Oh," she said, "Oprah is amazing—one of the good ones. She started out as a sharecropper or something and yanked herself right up by the bootstraps. I got a great recipe for skillet chicken from one of her magazines."

And the bastard kid simmering in my uterus? "Tish," she said. "We'll make do with that, honey, as long as you're both healthy. Lots of bedrock Christians in this town have been a little flimsy in practice over the years. Anybody dares throws stones, we'll throw 'em right back."

Over the next couple days, she helped me to re-establish myself in the prosaic, borderless nation-state known as Ordinary. We stopped at Pro-Medica where I set up an appointment with Dr. Sayle, an OB/GYN who was about my age and seemed sufficiently competent. Afterward, we had greasy grilled cheese sandwiches at the Thunderbird Café, and everybody remembered me, and by now—twenty-four hours into it—everybody knew my story.

Forty-eight hours into it, I was sufficiently decompressed to make a tough trip out to Pleasant Hill Cemetery where my Daddy was buried. The cemetery was neither pleasant nor on a hill; it was an acre of largely unkempt tombstones spiked by chestnut trees and surrounded by cornfields, vaguely peaceful in the summer when the pink phlox grew wild, but desperately forlorn in the winter, when he'd been put in the ground. At the time, I had not been consulted or else I'd have opted for the physical annihilation of cremation followed by a ceremony at the riverside where the current could have carried his ashes back toward his beloved birthplace in the South.

That morning, I was surprised when my mother wanted to accompany me to Pleasant Hill. In the past, these were pilgrimages I'd made alone. But she'd become more contemplative since I'd been gone, and as we wound together between the sad old markers, through the concrete geese and American flags, the plastic bouquets and overgrown yews, her sighs were audible behind the soft click of cicadas.

Daddy lay beneath a tall black marble obelisk, one of the more conspicuous tombstones in the cemetery, and after a quiet moment, she explained why she'd come along: "I felt I had to let you know about our final wishes, Dixie. You're the only child and nobody is getting younger. We bought plots here three years ago. This is my spot, right here next to Daddy. And over here," she said, pointing to a weedy patch next to hers overgrown with clover and violets , "...is where Paw-Pop will go. That's my honest desire, honey, with the grace of the Lord: To lie between them. If it's what you want, there's a spot here for you too."

I nodded. There didn't seem to be much space or reason to argue, or even to have an opinion. I stood there silently and the sound behind the summer bugs was a tractor growling and sputtering way off in the corn.

That afternoon, she explained Murphy Construction's finances to me. We went over her Quicken program, and as she'd said, it was ridiculously basic. But more significantly to me, there really wasn't anything much to do. The company only had four customers, and the work had already been billed. Obviously, this didn't represent a full time job, or even a part time one. Mom assured me that things would pick up as soon as Paw-Pop retired, but that made no sense; he was her age, and even an early buy-out was probably still years in the future. She deflected by showing off how talented he was, and what he could do in his spare time. In fact, throughout my childhood, the basement had been nothing but a spooky storage space filled with steamer trunks and boxes of off-season clothes, with everything valuable a foot off the ground in case of flooding. Now it was a fully habitable, waterproofed bonus room with plank flooring and a wet bar.

That night, after dinner, as a concession to the wacky turn of events, I approached Toby and asked him if he could take a look at my imploded Amish wardrobe. He brought his tape rule up to my room immediately and took measurements, and the following day, by the time I'd returned from my doctor's appointment, he'd fixed it. I found out later that he'd come back home during his lunch hour and done the work then, and, in fact, done it so skillfully that I could barely find the boards he'd used to reinforce it. To get at the innards, he'd had to remove my prom formal, my Harvest Homecoming dress and the knee-length white lace number I used to wear to church and they were laid carefully across my bed. By the time the varnish dried, I had already wrapped those dresses in cloth bags and stored them in the rear part of my closet, and the only garment I put in the wardrobe was my Madrinha dress. I hung it there delicately and with extraordinary tenderness, despite myself.

The week ran on, and without any real accounting to sink my teeth into, I did what I could to make myself useful to the so-called business. I swept out the work space in the extended garage and put all the half-inch ratchets in the half-inch slots and so on. On Thursday, I designed a Murphy Construction Company logo and sketched a little cartoon version of Toby holding a tape rule and a hammer that both he and my mother got a genuine kick out of. But by the end of that first week, I was already beginning to go little stir crazy, and I know my mother sensed it. As much as she cared and as much as she appeared to have expanded her worldview, she was still out of her depth in dealing with me and my achy preoccupations.

She suggested a Saturday trip to Cedar Point, a Sandusky landmark that exists on the excitement periphery of every kid in the Midwest. Cedar Point is a requisite summertime rite-of-passage for any Ohioan not a paraplegic or on life support, and probably for a few of them too. It's rides and junk food and animatronic dinosaurs and as such, it's a wet dream for anybody under twenty. The deal was, of course, that I was staring down the barrel at twenty-eight and the idea of the tallest rollercoaster on the planet didn't offer much allure to a pregnant woman afraid of heights. I wondered if this was some bizarre attempt to reinvent me as the little girl I wasn't any more; the twelve-year-old that all the Dippin' Dots on the planet couldn't make me again.

Cedar Point did, however, have a nice strip of glorious white sand that poked out into Lake Erie, and the weather forecast for the following day indicated that it would be double-plus beach-worthy. If I was going to put on a bathing suit, it might as well be now, while I could still fit into one. So, although the idea had some obvious emotional flaws, they were personal ones: The last time I'd been on a family outing to Cedar Point, my Daddy had been in the cockpit, and now, I was wary of my reaction to a replay with Daddy's understudy driving. In the end, that was my problem, not theirs, so I downloaded a map of the park, made reservations at a semi-decent steakhouse nearby and climbed pliantly, if not eagerly, into the rear seat of the family Honda Odyssey.

I realize now that the ride was probably even weirder for them than it was for me. Ten miles outside Cadence we ran out of clipped conversation and Toby cranked on the pabulum hit parade of AMEN FM. I sighed and looked out across the bounding Midwest main, grain fields and silos and red barns. Shortly, the station switched formats and some born-again Evangelist named Todd proceeded to walk us through his personal journey to Christ. Evidently, in his formative years he was addicted to *'the lies of Budweiser, the Playboy and the MTV'* and wound up killing his brother Kip in a drunk driving accident. Knowing my drinking history, the front-seat couple may have been embarrassed for me, but they needn't have worried: By then, I was resolved in sobriety and all the show did was make me wonder why so many Christian bluebloods name their kids Todd or Kip.

The beach was fine, too. I fell asleep and awoke to find that Paw-Pop had constructed an umbrella out of beach towels to keep me from getting sunburned. I knew they both meant well and that this was all a learning curve. At the restaurant, Paw-Pop ordered a well-done T-bone and Mom ordered a well-done filet, and I—who had become a bit of a food diva since my stint at Alchemy—went with the petite rib-eye, medium rare. I tried to right their culinary ship, but predictably, they were more amused than intrigued by the dishes I described, like kale guacamole and beef tartare with quail eggs.

By the time we pulled back into the driveway on Scioto, we'd all sort of withdrawn into individual microcosms, believing we were better off there, and as I drifted off to sleep in my Kid Kraft bed, I remembered that I still had to get through Sunday morning church with them.

I'd agreed earlier to attend services to please my mother. I think, at this late date, her goal was to show me off more than to convert me, and I thought it was a small enough accommodation to make. I could have worn my white lace fit-and-flare church dress, but for many complicated reasons, I chose to wear my Madrinha dress instead. On the brilliant, Kelly green lawn of the Church of Christ Redeemer, I received many puzzled and guarded compliments on the dress from people I'd known all my life, though in another life, but I'm sure they all rolled their eyes over it afterward.

Later that afternoon, I acknowledged to myself that I was already beginning to experience some North Korean-style suffocation and that if my Cadence rebirth was going to have any long-term chance of long-success, I'd have to find a path to independence after the baby was born. I remained ambivalent about how much of Julian's cash I should spend on myself. Clearly, I was within rights to spend money on health insurance, and I had already arranged a policy. But moving out of the Scioto house, where room and board were free, and finding myself an apartment? Using baby money for that seemed a little unethical when it wasn't entirely necessary. So, on Monday morning, as early as I could, I headed over to the Great Scot Community Market and filled out an application. Donna Hannon—a girl I remembered vaguely from AP English—was the store manager, and she asked me a few cursory questions amid the Price Slicer baby peas in aisle seven and hired me on the spot.

My first shift began on Wednesday afternoon at three, and after I'd slipped into my navy blue apron and mussed my new, short, blonde-tinted hair—on Tuesday, Dixie had gotten a pixie—I examined myself in the full length mirror and decided I could pass for every lonely, single, pregnant check-out girl in every small town in America.

When I pinned on my logoed name tag, which read *'I'm DIXIE: Expect GREAT Things from Me!'* I cried for fifteen minutes straight.

33.

The allure of color abides; it's what first compelled me coordinate my eye with my hand and create artwork. I'd loved my Crayola crayons as a child and the images my mind created from the names on those little wax ingots—Flamingo, Peach, Tumbleweed, Pacific Blue, some foreign, some familiar —each became a direct link between my small world and the giant one beyond.

Yet that year, in the weeks leading up to my birthday, I began to immerse myself in another world: The enchanted glory of greyness. It was a powerful grey, an omnipotent grey, a tincture of grey that sucked me into tunnels worming deeply into the Ohio countryside, down corridors without format, without anatomy and without color.

My Great Scot shifts ended at nine, and by the time I'd washed my face and arms in the employee john and hung my apron in my punk-ass locker, the midsummer sun had arced beneath the trees and monochrome of evening had swallowed the pigments of day and the hazy, receding blues and gushy reds of dusk. I was afraid that my bones might calcify if I returned to the smothering envelope of Scioto Street immediately, although I suppose that single people often feel this way, especially when the walls closing in are not even their own. I know many of my co-workers dealt with the same dread, and the pressure cock they favored was the Ten Pins Lounge.

For me, that option held no appeal, and instead, I would settle into my Focus and set out to wander the wild grey yonder.

It should have been desperately sad: Poor, poor pitiful Pickett again, emotionally isolated in the most generative season of her life. I expected as much and prepared for it. But I was wrong. The consuming greyness in the great dome of night and my compulsive and aimless drives became, to me, a persistent source of comfort, like Jonah finding a sense of peace in the belly of the whale.

Besides, inevitably, I was not alone. A small paunch had begun to swell my midriff. Dr. Sayle noted that it was mostly amniotic fluid and a growing placenta, but it was enough to make me forego jeans for a pair of leggings with a roll panel. Within me, my incubating treasure may have only been the size of a kidney bean, but he already had a heartbeat, fingers, toes and—if he was indeed a he—a penis. I could sing to him as I drove, and I often did, giving him an early indoctrination into Shawn Colvin and k.d. laing, my genre front-runners.

Although my routes were unplanned and intentionally arbitrary, I developed a certain pattern: As soon as I had cleared the Wash 'n' Shine on Route 180, I cranked down the window and let the wild smells of field and farm fill the car, and when I pulled off on an access shoulder to absorb the might and mystery of these odors— the perfume of the greyscale—I stopped singing and together, me and the kidney bean listened to the chorus of crickets and the snapping barks of distant, chained-up dogs.

I confess that there was also another presence in the car: Julian's wooden firefly. *Libélula.* I had called on Paw-Pop once again, this time to ask if he could install some Velcro on the bottom of the carving so I could mount it on the dashboard. The following morning, it was done. That it now occupied the spot where the in family Odyssey a plastic Jesus was affixed was an irony not lost on me, nor that the three of us in the car now made a sort of bizarre Trinity. Julian was my child's father, and despite anything and everything, I had no intention of ever downplaying it.

These rangy, remote and random drives would ultimately take me down every county road and unpaved tractor alley within fifty miles of Cadence. I lost myself in dark and splendid places, places where the greys were light and fleshy, especially when stars appeared overhead in a spackle of Dalmatian dots. I wound so far into the boonies that I should have been concerned that my old rusty Ford would die and stay dead and I'd have to call for help. But I wasn't; I believed I had a troubled deity looking out for me and the kidney bean from the instrument panel.

I poked into tiny villages with lone lights burning inside empty storefronts. I snickered at every adult bookstore, patronized (I guessed) by people so primitive they didn't have the internet. I found marvelous old train stations, some abandoned and some with old men in railroad uniforms standing out front copping a smoke. I sailed beneath an endless thicket of silos and grain elevators while juggernaut barns loomed and creepshow farmhouses reared. Billboards were an occasional landscape blight, but for the most part, it was an expanse of cornfield green turned twilight grey.

When the supermarket was slow, they'd sometimes boot me out a couple hours early, when there was still a lot of light left in the sky. It was on one of those trips, about fifteen miles from town, that I came across a small art gallery on a mostly-deserted stretch of Gilbert Horning Road, three blocks before it dead-ended at Cranberry Fork Creek.

To begin with, an art gallery plunked down the middle of nowhere was madly intriguing, even with a prominent *For Sale* sign in a boarded window, but something else about it fired neurons way back in my mind. I drove slowly to the turnaround at the creek, backtracked, and by the time I passed it again, I remembered: It was called Hedy's Art Park, and at one time, they'd offered art lessons. I exorcised fleeting images of myself as a child inside that boarded-up bungalow with my Daddy leaning over my shoulder, bubbling with pride. I remembered brilliant posters on the walls, and Hedy as an Earth mother type with dangly magenta scarves and a Sinead O'Connor crew cut. I recalled her as blunt, but pointedly instructive, showing me which direction on the color wheel my blends were skewing and I believe that my Daddy had been amused at how seriously I was taking her instructions.

Yet, when I asked my mother about it later, she presented me with a totally different version: "Oh, honey, that wasn't your father that took you out there; it was me. You were six—it was that birthday when Daddy had to be in Atlanta on a business trip."

"Are you sure?" I asked, miffed.

"Of course. The woman who owned the place was called Hattie, or Lettie, or something like that. You wanted to go for your birthday—she advertised a program for kids in the market and you saw the flyer before I did. I took you there on your sixth. I still have the paintings you did that day; they were very good. Remember, I was telling you about them that night we talked so much? Anyway, the woman was real eccentric, but she liked you. You impressed her."

"Then why didn't we ever go back?" I pouted.

"I don't know why," she frowned. "I guess because the woman seemed a little too hippie-dippie feminist for me. Back then, we had different values and we didn't appreciate that. She had psychedelic posters up, too. I think they had pictures of bare breasts and pot leaves on them."

I thought about it and realized that Ma was right, and I shuddered at my own invented memory: It had been *her* gazing over my shoulder, impressed with my art and gently amused at my earnestness. I nodded and she segued into asking me about my upcoming birthday. It fell on the first of August—a 'bookend', as my Daddy used to say—and would be the first one in years in which my mother and I would be together. She wanted to do something special, but I wasn't interested in a hullabaloo. The idea of 'celebrating' birthdays when you're beyond a certain age seemed almost comical to me, and even pregnant, with a lease on a future generation, I looked at the age of twenty-eight with something less than wonder, more as another fallen domino than as another ladder rung scaled. But I also understood that mothers see all birthdays as personal milestones, and the shock and awe reverberating from the day of my birth was probably worth commemorating to someone who remembered it. So, I caved and Googled some options, and came up with a cool and imaginative little restaurant in Findlay called the Northside Trattoria. It was only twenty-three minutes away, too, and I believed I could survive that interval in a car with the Murphy-Picketts. Not only that, but based on the menu, I thought I might be able to drag their palates into the 21st century.

Six days later, on my birthday, I slept until nine and lay in bed for another half hour before I came downstairs. There, I expected to find a sappy card from Mom and Paw-Pop and maybe some superfluous presents that I neither wanted nor asked for, because that's what sweet, somewhat clueless older folks do.

All that was there, of course, but in addition, sitting prominently in the middle of the kitchen table, was a vase filled with white Casa Blanca lilies—forty-seven of them. I later worked out that it represented one flower for every day since I'd left Michigan.

My mother swept in from the screened porch: "Happy birthday, Dixie, honey. Aren't those flowers lovely? They were just sitting outside when Paw-Pop left for work! We put them in water for you. They weren't from UPS or anything, just left by the mailbox. An admirer from the market? There's a package too."

There was; a thick envelope and a brand I recognized. On the front were words that looked as if they'd been written on an ocean wave: *'From our Forests, For our Seasons'*.

"I so love white lilies," my mother prattled on. "Don't you?"

I did. Desperately so. And all my greys coalesced and fused like the clouds that gather within the great vaults of sky before a summer storm. Inside the envelope were forty-seven poems—one for each day since I'd left Michigan.

That morning, I'd put on my Madrinha dress again. Was it significant? It was, if only in irony. My mother was now quietly and confidently quoting scripture:

"And why concern yourself with your clothes? Consider the lilies of the field, they neither toil nor spin, yet even Solomon in all his glory was not arrayed like this."

34.

Sunlight sleeps with tacit trust

In forest, fountain, field and fell;

An augmentation of the dust

Where all the gods together dwell.

Wisdom won who wanders wide,

And to divine decree is bowed.

Shroud lifts, eyes clear and ears abide

The promise ravens call full loud.

Xam-Bioá, Xam-Wã; youth and maiden

No wound endured cannot be healed

With whetted greed and bounty laden.

Thus, our pathway home revealed.

It's meant to counteract the plenum

Forged in fire and cooled in venom.

*

I am changed; condensed, expanded

You are changed, installed, unstranded

Forget the distance now existing; there's a focal spark subsisting,

Now expressing, coalescing; seed and soul at last have landed.

If the flesh-god we've created,

Braves the eaters and is fated

To conjoin us in seclusion, it becomes the chaste collusion:

Enfranchisement long awaited.

*

Dew is dropping in the dale; water trickles in the rill.

The new-formed Gilded Boy can hear: "Speak wisely or be still."

The forest wind, his breath of life, now whispers as his sage:

"To name the old-formed world is yours, for you have come of age."

The Gilded Boy has grown within a verdant sanctum here,

Far from men and basement bars; far from fawning fear.

But in a place bereft of names, and that's his void to fill.

So on this day, the wind has charged: "Speak wisely or be still."

"What name to call the flowing quick that runs across the land?

Bringing with it fish and fowl where banks of rushes stand?"

The Gilded Boy replied in turn, "I see this as a quiz:

"That flow brings death along with life; the Caiman-Road it is."

"Spoken wisely," whirred the wind, "And what to call the glow

That lately mocked you in the night where prowling jaguars go?"

"That glowing ball preserved my life; away the evil crawled.

She guided me through darkness and is Heaven's-Candle called."

"Wise indeed; now, Gilded Boy, what name to call the witch

Who feeds on corpses by the road and rotting in the ditch?"

"The raven is my kindred soul, a cleanser without shame.

As smart as men and twice as quick; the Blood-Swan is her name."

"And what of me?" the wind exclaimed, "Who cools your streaming brow?

Who gently fills once-dormant sails and hastens forth your scow?"

"I see the might behind your breath; the puffs are but a game.

You rage with fury at your whim; Tree-Breaker is your name."

"And of the man-wife in your home, what names will you give them?

Who gave you birth and raised you up as their unblemished gem?"

Gilded Boy was wisest now where stillness was his lot:

"They have given me my name, so I will name them not."

The wind then filled the mammoth maw with might and meek combined.

Like us below, my Gilded Girl, in love and intertwined.

Libélula, my dragonfly, who darts among the flowers.

This Gilded Boy belongs to us; the Gilded Boy is ours.

35.

It wasn't fair, nor was there any reason why it should have been fair since fairness is not the dynamic that makes these things percolate.

Like, how fair had it been for the artsy child to have been raised in a bedroom filled with heirloom figurines and crinoline curtains when she despised dolls and lace? And how fair was it that she reappeared as a lumbering pregnant woman pushing thirty and moved back into that same room, despising them still? Where was the fairness in my mother preferring a plebian wage-slave over a handsome and congenitally erudite Southern gentleman? Fair? Imagine me, standing there like a fool in my little blue apron, refusing Mrs. Spurlin's check for milk and ground beef because the last one bounced, when my mind was off somewhere under bearskins with a poet.

Maybe it was penance, but it wasn't fair.

I wanted to tuck my Julian away in another womb. By that point I was intending to raise his son (or daughter) in the spirit of his purity, but I couldn't find an unbroken chain of emotional cleanliness that went from our lone night in the forest to now. I'd wanted assurance that the nightmares of his youth had not stalked him into adulthood, and it seemed that I had confirmed the opposite. There was no high road to take where I could overlook what I knew let alone what I suspected, nor did I want the requisite confrontation where I might learn the rest.

I wanted my golden touching man again, history-free and sweating beneath animal fur with a litter of stars overhead. I wanted a single night repeated forever; a *Groundhog Day* of essence, and since that couldn't be, I was content to gestate the result of that night in the warmth of my juicy belly, where it was me and Kidney Bean, alone.

And then the poems showed up.

When I was a child, one of the highlights of Christmas was the complimentary Advent calendar they handed out at my Faithweaver Friends Bible class. For those not familiar with the pre-holiday compulsions of rural Christians, these gaudy wall-hangings contain only the forty days preceding Christmas. Each day has a flap of paper over a tiny box, and each morning us kids would open that day's flap; underneath would be a chunk of chocolate in a foil wrapper. I'd outgrown the calendars, but not the principal. Since, come February, I was anticipating my own nativity scene and was otherwise overwhelmed by the sheer volume of poetry within Julian's envelope, I hit on a plan: I'd read a single poem per day, out loud, and as many times as needed to convince myself that I understood it.

And on the evening of August 1, my own season of Advent began.

I remained true to my promise. As the days peeled away with the tabs on a calendar, I read the poems one by one and my awe of Julian's literary dexterity grew. I recognized the qualities of an epic cycle: The poems were presented in order and they were beautiful, each one precisely metered, peppered with true rhymes and intricate syllable patterns, everything anointed with graceful word pictures. There was an underlying rhythm, stressed and unstressed beats that were natural to speaking, making them both lyrical and delicious to recite.

Each one was different, but each was thematically pure: They were odes to the then-nonexistent concept of 'us'. Julian and I and our child, living in some alternate universe that— based on the imagery—contained only him, an untarnished forest and a lone white woman with their half-caste son.

Gradually, through those ticking summer days and into early autumn, the tenor of the poems changed and the cycle evolved. I realized with a growing and perplexed sense of certainty that Julian was not merely fantasizing about such a scenario, he was proposing it. He believed that we could make it work; that we could leave everything and disappear into the wilderness. That the three of us together as *'a triune soothed by sun and moon'* could forge an Eden so far from civilization than even the serpent on the Tree of Life couldn't find us.

I read pragmatism between facund lines: We had the time and the cash; he had the skill set and I had the son.

Well, he may have had the money and the survival chops and I may have had the baby, but I scoffed at the idea that he had a point. To abandon the world and simply vanish? Fat chance in this hyper-connected reality. But, at least I owed the bean in my tummy pouch the respect of hearing what his father was saying, especially when he was saying it so frigging eloquently. Lacking his torso, I reveled in his wordplay. I forewent my twilight treks into the Ohio countryside and instead, after work, I climbed into oversized sweats, situated myself inside my tight little-girly bedroom and read the poems to our unborn child over and over, and if I whispered about campfires and our little stone cottage in parts unknown, it was simply in the spirit of a bedtime story.

Story-telling was the compulsion in which I wanted my little bean indoctrinated, and by the time I had finished the forty-seventh poem, it was forty-seven days later and he was as big as the whole bean pod. He had fingerprints and vocal cords, and if by some chance he was not a he, she had enough eggs in her little ovaries to repopulate Toledo in the event of Armageddon.

I didn't try to contact Julian, nor did I actually think it was Julian who had left the flowers and the envelope, though I knew who probably had. He'd sent his peon gal Friday to do it: Potter, a dude I had thought capable of murdering Takosha, and now, perhaps, Serafin Tercerio as well. It was unsettling, no doubt, but it couldn't be helped, and that was the hyper-connection that made disappearing an impossibility.

So as not to concern my mother, I told her that my baby's father had hired a Uber driver to leave the flowers, and she seemed charmed and impressed at his romantic wherewithal. I had already invented a whole convoluted set of reasons why he was not the man for me, and I repeated them.

I believed at least half of them, too. But my breasts, which had not only swelled appreciably of late but had already begun to leak colostrum, were tender and needy. Dr. Sayle told me that the jolts of libido I'd begun to experience were normal and to be expected at around thirteen weeks. Since she knew I was single and not seeing anyone, she referred me to a Swedish company called Lalo that manufactured top-end vibrators. Their trademarked tagline was *'Clitorally Mind-blowing'*.

I already had toys, of course. It's not like these were new inventions. But I couldn't ask my SONA Cruise if it liked my new hairstyle. I couldn't ask plastic if it could figure out how to make oil paints from shit you find laying around the jungle, or barring that, if it could teach me to carve insects from wood. I couldn't ask a dildo you can see the stars from a rain forest.

Perhaps worse, I couldn't ask my SONA Cruise to simply cup my belly and sing to me softly in Luanhão while I squeezed my thighs together until I saw stars without the jungle.

These were honest thoughts. I didn't want to have them but I had them all the same, and more and more frequently as my gorgeous stack of poetry shrank, my love links dwindled and my belly grew. The images inside my head became Jivarrão vivid. They haunted me when I sat quietly at Church of Christ Redeemer listening to the pastor sermonize a link between being stuck at a railroad track on Monday morning and Genesis 29: 20. They swirled through ammonia smells when I was picking up Paw-Pop's Sunday shirts from *Cadence's Finest Dry-cleaners Since 1956*. And when Mrs. Mihalik insisted that the Price Slicer Special on Idahoan Steakhouse Soup Bowls was $2.49, not the $2.79 I'd just rung up, I was not standing at a check-out register in lane two, I was in a brushy blind waiting for my tom turkey to take one... final... step.

But I was here, not there. My future was Great Scot and downtown dry-cleaning and Church of Christ Redeemer, where my son would no doubt establish an indissoluble bond with God at his baptism.

And that, I thought, was what *really* wasn't fair.

36.

If Julian was waiting for me to thank him for the poems, he was disappointed and I heard no more from him. Relying on A.A. savvy, I expected my various cravings to subside, and to an extent, they did. It was for the best. I held the poems to my leaking breasts with the respect they were due. I read them all again to Bean Pod, but after that, I locked them inside a box in Huntington Bank on Liberty Street alongside boodles of cash. I forced them into my mind's own compartments, where they didn't fit quite as well. I worked my dreadful, anesthetizing job and I behaved myself at home and did whatever clerical bullshit Paw-Pop asked me to. I was punctual at my biweekly ProMedica checkups.

As September stuttered into October and the great pageant of autumn spread across the countryside, I took solace in walks through Van Buren Park, about twenty minutes down Township Road.

By early November, the final traces of summer had flitted away and it grew too wet to be outdoors much, so I took again to aimless driving, especially on my days off, when it was oppressive to sit for long inside Scioto Street sipping Sanka with Mom and watching Oprah interview LeBron James on TV.

These daytime trips were generally devoid of my nurturing greys, but with light, there were far more sights to blow the dust from ancient memories. One such memory cropped up a few weeks before Christmas outside an old spread on Fort Grange Road. My Daddy had called it a hobby farm. It was a few acres of flat land studded with a nineteenth century I-frame house that had gable ends and an outdoors woodburner. There was pasture in front of it, and every time Daddy and I had passed it on the way to Durhamville, we'd noticed a big swayback horse standing immobile against the frontage fence. He was a strange old beast with luminous brown eyes and mournful nickers, and he looked like he had huge notch cut out of his topline just behind the withers; Daddy said it was from too much riding. I fell in love with this stoic creature and named him 'Dobbin' after a horse in one of my kid books. I dug the idea that his years as a pack horse were over and that he'd spend the rest of his life standing in tall grass, never again to wear a saddle—an equine without white men.

Sometimes we'd pull over to the shoulder, get out and feed Dobbin ragweed or whatever was growing by the fence, but a few times, we stopped at Great Scot first and brought him bags of apples. One day, after many months, old Dobbin was no longer at his post and he never appeared again. I remember my Daddy's eyes tearing up along with mine. He spun it into an allegory as metaphorical, perhaps, as being stuck at a train track on a Monday morning.

This time, I wouldn't ask my mother about it. I wanted this memory of my father safeguarded. It would forever remain our treasured moment, our private allegory.

That day, I sat in front of the same farm on the same shoulder of Fort Grange and considered it in life-context. Dobbin was gone, my Daddy was gone and my childhood had vanished along with them. The I-frame had a hideous addition grafted to a gable end and the property now raised hops. Tall teepees spiked the pasture draped in dead vines like the skeletons of Jack's Beanstalk. Places like this are called touchstones, but try as you will, you can't really touch them; they're beyond reach. They're mirages that shimmer and sparkle on your horizon, but when you try to approach them, they always melt away into stagnant air.

Later, I found myself back on the snow-dusted dead-end road to Cranberry Fork Creek and this time, in the dirt driveway of Hedy's Art Park, there was an old puke-green liftback Prius that looked even more wasted than my Focus. The windows of the house were still boarded up and the *For Sale* sign was there, but smoke was trickling from the chimney.

Truth told, I'd actually inquired about the place. A realtor in Durhamville told me that the property had been on the market for a decade and I could probably pick it up for around thirty thousand dollars. It was, he pointed out, a textbook fixer-upper, and then the little troglodyte laughed at me and had the balls to say that he hoped I had a man around who was handy with tools.

Screw him, but at least it was an idea to toy with. I wouldn't even have to involve banks; I could pay cash. I certainly didn't want to raise my child on Scioto Street or in some stupid apartment complex that smelled like everybody else's dinner, and the idea of living on an ex-art farm appealed to me. Maybe Bean Pod and me could raise a Dobbin of our own. It was, however, way out in the sticks, and when I floated the idea by Mom and Paw-Pop, they brought up all sorts of practicalities like schools and access to pediatricians and the virtual lack of neighbors to call on in emergencies. Paw-Pop promised that if I was serious, he could find me a starter home closer to town and do the fixing-up himself.

Still, if kismet was a thing—and I still believed that kismet was a thing—this was the first time I'd driven by the place and seen signs of life. The liftback on the Prius was held down by bungee cords and the bumper was long gone. I pulled my car behind it and went and knocked, and knocked again. In a bit, a scratchy voice came from beyond the chained door: "Yeah?"

"I saw a car here. Is the house still for sale? I asked a guy from Van Rooyen Real Estate about it."

"Who'd you ask?"

"Some agent—a Russian name, like Leerskov. Bill Leerskov?"

"The Neanderthal?"

I laughed out loud: "That's exactly what I called him. He found out I wasn't married and said he hoped I had a boyfriend who knew how to use power tools."

Through the crack in the door, I could hear Joni Mitchell singing about a redneck on a Grecian isle. I smelled cigarette smoke and alcohol. The raspy voice said, "Performative masculinity—it encourages weak men to conform to narratives. Leerskov is a frat boy who couldn't change a roll of toilet paper, but the real estate listing is his, so love him or hate him, you gotta make an appointment with him if you're interested."

"To be honest, I'm really probably not. I just moved back to Cadence over the summer and I remembered the Art Farm. I used to take classes here with Hedy when I was a child."

There was some rattling with the door chain, and a strange old woman opened the door. Hedy couldn't have been more than forty on my sixth birthday, which would make her around my mother's age, and I hoped to God that this wasn't her, although a moment later, weird jolts from my subconscious assured me that it was. Where Mom and Paw-Pop had thickened, Hedy's body had gone the other route— she was shriveled and crooked as a crone from a fairy tale. Her hair—formerly punk-shorn—was downy white and done up in limp braids. The slate-steel eyes that had once squinted over my goofy farm scene bulged like hubcaps and made her look like a frantic owl. I guessed it was thyroid sleight-of-hand, but this was Hedy without question; she was wearing the same purple scarf that trailed down the same Summer of Love dress, like she was still breathing fumes from the '60s.

"I don't recall you, sorry. You'd think I would—I had few enough students over the years. Grover County is a black hole for creative phantoms."

CHRIS KASSEL

"It was only the once," I confessed. "I was six—my folks never brought me back, and that's too bad. I still remember your single art lesson, though. You have no idea how formative it was for me. In fact, I wound up going to art school and becoming an artist. A painter, really."

If I expected her to be charmed—even thrilled—I was mistaken. "Sorry to hear that," she croaked, throwing open the door the rest of the way. "Well, come on in before you drop that fidget on my front porch."

I remembered the interior too. There was a skylight carved into the far roof, and today it was obscured by snow, dousing the room in dismal light. There were paintings stacked against a wall, and from what I could see, they were wild abstracts filled with random shapes and colors. I wanted to flip through them, because although I know I should, I never quite saw the coherency in this genre. Maybe I'm an obdurate child of *The Saturday Evening Post*, but I'd be lying if I denied that my goal had always been to paint something people recognized and wanted to look at.

Inside, I experienced another memory bounce: The house smelled exactly like it had had twenty years earlier: Dry wood, stale Kool smoke, turpentine and patchouli. A paint-spattered table stood beneath the skylight, and it was the same one on which I'd created my fantasy farm all those years ago. Crowning it now was a box of donuts and a jug of Gallo Chablis.

"Have some wine," she said, fetching a Mason jar. "One glass won't hurt."

"I can't," I frowned. "I'm sorry."

"Have a donut, then," she answered, filling her own jar, downing it in a single draught and pouring another. "Enter here, you must trade the patriarchy for the pastryarchy—a vision of a better world."

She sat down on a hard wooden chair at the table and lit another Kool with the dregs of the first. The donuts looked ridiculously old and I refrained. In fact, the entire place felt dank and unhealthy and the cigarette smoke caught in my throat. At the same time, I was dealing with my own outsized delusion: That this silly, decaying ranch on a dead-end dirt road had been ground zero for all my artistic ambitions. So I introduced myself, sat down on the opposite side of table and pushed the donut box away from me.

"So why the fuck would somebody move *back* to Grover County, Dixie?" Hedy asked, coughing and trying to dislodge something from the back of her throat. "I've been trying to get shut of it since the day I was potty-trained. Well, you're leaving your lover, naturally—I suppose the question is rhetorical."

"Yeah," I said. "My baby's father had issues, so I moved back in with Ma and my stepdad until I can figure out something else."

"Well, you broke the first rule, Dixie. You put the car in reverse. Now you're breaking the second one: You're leaving the car in idle and waiting for the light to change."

She shook her head and sighed, and it sounded like the wind wheezing against a boarded window. "I forgive you that one, though. I was fixing to leave for good even before I started the Art Farm, and here I still sit, year after year, chain smoking and listening to the same goddamn tape loop as the day I put up the *For Sale* sign."

She held me inside her goggle-eyed gaze and I felt a peculiar, persistent pressure begin in the space around me. It wasn't unpleasant, but it was ominous, like the sparks of light that precede a migraine headache. Air constricted against my temples, resolute but nearly gentle. I thought of the clamps that Paw-Pop used to hold Julian's dragonfly still while he glued Velcro to the base.

"So, art school?" Hedy clucked. "What did *they* teach you to fuck up?"

"I don't know," I answered. "Truthfully, I only lasted a year. I was expecting sort of a super-magical bohemian place. Turned out to be a giant clique, not progressive at all. I suppose it taught me to remake my social space. "

Hedy, it developed, was entirely self-taught and put little stock in academic art. She drank her wine and lectured about the value of rejecting history and tradition and people who are empirically superior technicians, but only painted what they saw, not what they felt.

I knew what was coming, and for the next half hour I dreaded it. Finally she said,

CHRIS KASSEL

"You have a camera phone, I suppose. Everyone does. Let's see your work. Current stuff, please. That's the only spectrum that counts."

I nodded warily and unearthed my phone. I'd dicked around with a few paintings since I'd been back in Ohio, but I didn't have much of a portfolio to show for it. I did have some shots of the drawings I'd done at the zoo in May, but I wasn't sure if last May counted as recent. If so, I'd saved images of my portraits of Gabriel and Serafin too, and naturally, there was my painting of August Lake, which remained my *tour de force*, from design to craftsmanship to purity of form, even to influence since I'd lifted the composition from the Rackham watercolor. She might approve since I'd thought I'd been successful at capturing the sensory effect of the scene. Hedy's hands were calloused with red knobs that looked like a skin condition, but I handed her the phone anyway and hoped that whatever she had wasn't contagious.

She began flipping through the photos, coughing and snorting, sucking down more wine. Behind her, Joni was singing about Ray's Dad's Cadillac with notes reaching into the stratosphere. Back on earth, I sat in a nervous flutter listening to phlegm in Hedy's gullet until she finally burst out, "Too much realism, Dixie. It's something you'll outgrow, and the sooner the better."

I sniffed. "Well, sure, maybe. Maybe not. But for now, it's my style. I've had people tell me I'm pretty good."

Now she became slightly strident, and her Cheshire Cat eyes grew wider. "Who told you that? Your parents? Your girlfriends? *Reductio ad absurdum*—that's the black hole eating itself, Dixie. People around here think Margaret Keane is good. This place is toxic—Chernobyl for culture. It breeds diseased opinions. Not only will you never be able to expand yourself here, the opposite will happen. Your creative phantom will collapse down to critical mass. To find yourself, you have to push the car into overdrive, and not only will that not happen here, you'll lose yourself until there's nobody left inside to find. I can't believe you can't see that."

But I could. And of course, I did: As far as I could tell, Hedy was the embodiment of the concept and I was merely a mascot.

Now she wanted to show off her own stuff. She pulled five or six canvases from the stack, shoved aside the wine and the box of Darla Donuts and laid them out on

229

the table with a self-satisfied huff. "This is the direction you need to go," she said, tapping a corner of the first going with the confidence of the shit-faced. "I could take you there. Show you how to rethink your vision. Charge you nothing for it but your companionship, and that, I'd return with interest."

But I was appalled. The paintings were awful. I was no fan of abstract impressionism, but I could recognize immediately that these were mindlessly superficial works; they looked like pranks. I'd seen spatter by Pollock that said nothing to me no matter how hard I listened, but even to an untrained eye they were cohesive. I'd seen multiforms by Rothko that made no sense, but at least they offered interesting color contrasts. Hedy's colors blared and failed to mesh; her forms were either painted without texture or over-painted until they looked like slabs. Her brushstrokes were rough and unfinished. There was no personality in any of it. I assumed that she'd been inebriated when she did them, but then again, I had always assumed Pollock was too.

She went on as though they were otherwise, trying to define the various inspirations she'd channeled; women from Greek mythology, the Hindu goddess Durga, the Yoruba's Yemoja. She summed it up by saying, "Get the fuck out of Dodge and find your goddesses, Dixie. Soon as you can."

"Where to?" I chuckled. "I'm running out of deity bridges to burn."

"How's New Mexico sound?"

"Where?"

"New Mexico. To an art colony in a town called Madrid. Yeah, that's how they pronounce it, like 'putrid'. But it's not; it's marvelous, it's a bunch of brilliant creators cloven together. Everybody's into nostalgic funk and the whole town is about community, raising children as a village, that sort of thing. There are lots of kids in Madrid, all ages. They live off Victory Gardens and soul production. It's a massive art farm"

I envisioned a dirty hippie colony out in the middle of the desert where everybody was stuck in a time warp. It sounded more Charlie Manson than a viable escape plan. *"That's* where you want me to end up?" I asked, amused and bewildered.

Hedy rambled on: "Listen to me! I found an old school bus for sale that could be repurposed into a place to live. I mean, I found it a few years ago, but for what I'll get for the house and land, another old bus should be easy enough to come by. Or an Airstream fitted out as a house-studio with actual bedrooms, in case somebody had a baby or something. Somebody; anybody—a wife, a muse, a siren, a star..."

"Oh, my god..." I started.

"Why not?" Hedy said through dentures. "I could flip this place to Leerskov Flintstone and you could sell your car and we could leave in the Prius. Just like Thelma and Louise, only every scene could be the kiss at the end, minus the canyon floor. I can teach you how to paint, not illustrate, and finding lovers in the Bible Belt is tough—they subsist on denying the female appetite."

And that was her end game: She was coming on to me. Me, half her age and seven months pregnant, as delusional about me as she was about her cosmic space as a mandarin. She'd lost her ability to teach me anything. I didn't want to learn how to paint like she did. I wanted to learn how to avoid it.

The vice around my temples squeezed. I thought of Eloá and I saw the only spectrum that counts. These two—both talking about mystic realms and strange gods —were at opposite ends of the art crescent. They were antipodes: One filled me with an untapped crimson blush while the other made me want to spit up green pea soup.

But neither one was destiny, not on a bet. Even so, if I stuck my current game plan, I saw my future unfold before me with sudden, uncanny clarity. Me at the age of sixty, in some house just like this one—maybe closer to town—a stack of unsold paintings against a wall. Me, sixty years old, squatting at a paint-spattered table, back to jugs of Gallo which would be replaced with fifths of Five O'Clock by early afternoon. Because, why not? At sixty, my son would be nearly thirty, grown and gone, perhaps to find the forest without white men, searching for his father. Me, having been too sensible to have allowed him to be raised within his own legacy, but having nonetheless filled his childish head with poems about jaguars and caimans and lakes with sinkholes a hundred feet deep.

The yearning these words inspired in me was almost superhuman; imagine what they would do to a father's son. Julian was a fabulist, and the picture he painted of the new Eden out-mastered the masters.

Perhaps my son's life would be its own epic, worthy of a Luanhão song cycle. Doesn't *The Odyssey* begin with a youth in search of a long-lost father, a saga I'd intentionally written myself out of?

The wind then filled the mammoth maw with might and meek combined.

Like us below, my Gilded Girl, in love and intertwined.

Libélula, my dragonfly, who darts among the flowers.

This Gilded Boy belongs to us; the Gilded Boy is ours.

There were macro-considerations as always, but in the immediate, quite suddenly, I needed to leave Hedy's Art Farm and never come back.

37.

There was an expression we'd used privately in our groups at AA meetings, meant to temper some of the meltdown embarrassment we felt about our past behavior: *'The drunk man says what the sober man thinks.'*

It was actually a subtle way to forgive ourselves. When we were fucked up, without inhibitions, we didn't invent the truth so much as we flung ourselves prostrate before it. But when a sober woman tells her mother things intended to horrify her to the very pit of a hermetic existence, there is something more dastardly than booze at work.

That night, unable to sleep, I wandered downstairs and found my mother in the living room on the Colonial armchair Paw-Pop had built from scratch. She was draped in a quilt and reading a Danielle Steel novel. I made us some Sanka and some cinnamon-vanilla toast, and over the span of the next two hours, I told her some very heavy things about my childhood. I told her about losing my virginity at fourteen and my subsequent pregnancy scare. I told her about getting blotto before church and loading my mouth with Halls Mentho-Lyptus or overdoing perfume to mask the booze smell. I told her about hiding Southern Comfort in the neighbor's barbecue and I told her the real reason Jason Alton dumped me is because he was ashamed of me and my uncontrollable lust.

The information was of no value to her whatsoever. A detail that might have been, though—and one I didn't share—was that she'd been right to keep me away from wacky old Hedy and her art farm. But I wasn't interested in her feelings just then. I was abusing them for reasons of my own.

I told her, in excruciating detail, about my four missing years. I told her about doing cocaine off toilet seats in seedy nightclubs and getting so fucked up on LSD in Figure Drawing class that I thought the model's penis was on fire. I told her about getting involved with a jobless heroin addict and forcing myself to fuck him in order to cover the rent since I preferred to spend my paltry paychecks at Wolski's Tavern. I told her about going to jail, and I told her that my baby's father had come by his wealth by stealing it from his father. He topped up the kitty, I said, from the proceeds of a gay nightclub where young boys were bartered like Gucci knock-offs at a flea market.

I assumed my plot was better than Danielle Steel's, because my mother listened in rapt horror while tears poured down her face. Afterward, I left her to sputter and sob and returned to my bedroom to write a long, convoluted letter to Julian. I tried to articulate the whole mess I was in and explain my rational for having left without a goodbye. I wrote about my various awakenings since then and my emotional fusion with the child already sucking his thumb in utero, four inches from the hand with which I was writing.

It ended up being twelve perambulating pages of excoriation, concession, happiness, disgust, anger and incomparable, superlative ecstasy.

In the end, I tore it up and wrote another that said simply, *'If you still want us, be in contact after the first of the year,'* and addressed the envelope to Julian Vaz at August Lake State Park.

38.

I'd slashed a grievous rent in my mother's existence and our relationship suffered a permanent limp. Worse, I'd done it on purpose. My truth was uglier than anything she'd ever seen trotted out on her tabloid talk shows. She admitted as much in short, haunted clips the following day, the only time we ever addressed my upchuck evening. She'd seen the lives I'd described portrayed on *Jerry Springer* and *Jenny Jones*, and had assumed it was staged, played by actors as a ratings scam, which for the most part, it was. But she believed my stories implicitly, especially because I'd been so matter-of-fact about them. And it had occurred to her that if *my* dark world was real, then perhaps her own bright world of precious trappings—her collection of crystalline butterflies from Hamilton, her two books of wedding photographs, each kept in a separate corner of her closet, her Wedgwood Hibiscus tableware, her hardwood floors and raised-panel wainscoting—was not.

And perhaps it wasn't.

I asked her how she was processing things and her response was desperately sweet, if entirely deluded: "We're prayerful people. That's what we do, Dixie. I have confidence in approaching God to help me understand. I believe that anything I ask according to His will, He will hear."

Paw-Pop never weighed in and I assume she never told him. That was too bad, because he would have consoled her, and she needed that, although I suspected that she would always be, on some personal level, inconsolable. A lot of what I'd described had happened under her own roof, on her watch, before Toby was in the picture. She might forgive me for defiling my temple, but as a failed mother, she'd never forgive herself for missing the cues.

She geared up for Christmas just the same, because that's what prayerful people do. She burbled on about baby. She pulled out boxes of holiday gewgaws and Paw-Pop put up lights around the screened porch and a crèche scene on the lawn where all three Wise Men were Caucasian. We bought a nine-foot Christmas tree at the lot on Route 180 and set it up in the den, just as we had when I was a kid; we unearthed my favorite ornaments—a scowling Grinch, a felt snowman my Aunt Rachel had made, a hand-carved house with *'The Pickett Family'* engraved at the bottom.

On Sunday, we all drove into Tiffin where they'd set up a Victorian Village complete with Walmart mannequins dressed like characters from Dickens; Bob Cratchit, Tiny Tim, carolers, Father Christmas. The costumes were filled with moth holes and the faces were painted so crudely they looked ghoulish. My mother said, "I bet you could do better than that, honey. I *know* you could!"

She was tip-toeing around me gently, impossibly naïve, treating me as a victim, as though I'd unburdened my keel of a huge ballast and was now listing near the dock unmoored. I felt filthy and cruel about my current deception—allowing her to believe that I was home for the long haul. There was a nightmarish element to it, because if my proposal came to pass and I left Cadence forever, it would rock her foundations beyond repair.

But I couldn't divulge what I didn't know, and I hadn't yet heard anything back from Julian. I'd unblocked Serafin's number the day I'd mailed the letter, but no calls came through and mine went immediately to a *not in service* message. Each morning I peeked out my window each morning to see if there was anything waiting outside by the mailbox, and on Christmas Eve, after my Great Scot shift ended, I declined the invitation to a holiday party at the Ten Pins Lounge and drove home through a storybook snowstorm. The house on Scioto Street was bedazzled in icicles and twinkling lights and looked like a fantasy scene from Currier and Ives, but there was nothing against the mailbox but drifts. The next morning, like a ten year old, I ran to the door to check again, but there was so much snow that a plow could barely get through—there'd been no visit from the Great White North, Santa's workshop or the Department of Natural Resources.

The family bundled up, struggled to mass and sang lustily about merry gentlemen and poor little baby Jesus with no crib for his bed, that odd carol designed to make us feel sorry for God. Later, we drove to Fostoria to Cousin Sandy's house, and every distant relative with whom I became reacquainted was warm, slightly tanked and tickled pink that I had returned to the coven. Everyone wanted to touch the bloated belly wherein another Buckeye stirred. I ate hot ham and greasy green bean casserole with them. I shared non-spiked versions of their eggnog and showed them blurry ultrasound pictures. I sat and watched *Rudolph* with the kids and afterward, I curled my swollen legs under me on a Scotchgarded sofa and listened to stories about vacations and jobs and Ohio State football. They took for granted my interest in such matters. They wanted me within their closed ranks; they wanted me as a member of the Grover County dream team. They wanted me on the church rolls and they wanted to hold me a baby shower in the first week of January.

Me, I wanted to evanesce. I wanted to liquefy. I wanted to disintegrate into ash particles and let the Great Miami River currents take me and my baby away.

When there was no communication from Julian through the week that followed, I slipped into a mechanical depression, not at all uncommon in the post-Christmas Midwest, where the totality of winter's verve and allure orgasms on December 25 and after that, it's all shoveling driveways and dirty snow mountains in the Great Scot parking lot. My coworkers and customers were similarly lethargic and nobody noticed my mood, though by midweek, they'd begun to reload their spirits as they geared up for New Year's Eve. The hardcore gang at Wolski's used to joke that for amateur alcoholics, there were only two holidays of note: New Year's Eve and St. Patrick's Day. The day a budding drunk discovers that there are another 363 days in the year is one of both resignation and profound, self-annihilating euphoria.

That year, I was anticipating a dreadful evening of manufactured excitement with Times Square flashing across Mom and Paw-Pop's widescreen Samsung. There was already a bottle of Andre Champagne—$11 at Love's Country Store—chilling in the refrigerator. In delicate deference, Mom offered to forego the wine for sparkling cider, but I told her not to be silly. I wasn't even sure I could stay awake until midnight.

I barely did. At eleven, Paw-Pop found an old video of old Rod Stewart singing *Auld Lang Syne* inside a random old Scottish castle. I expected it to be painful parent music, but I found myself sniffling by the end of it and singing along. After that, I sat on the couch, shrouded in my upstairs comforter. My mother was settled in her handmade Colonial armchair, but Paw-Pop was restless. He messed with the fire in the hearth, paced in the kitchen, fiddled with an old radio he was refurbishing, and—I swore—peered at me through the corner of his eye as though he knew I was planning some hijinks. I refused to meet his gaze. I watched the crystal ball descend the flagpole into the waiting mayhem, then clambered off to bed amid a few perfunctory well-wishes.

I rose earlier than anyone else, and it was still dark outside when I padded downstairs in my maternity nightshirt and flannel robe and the fuzzy faux-shearling slippers that Mom had given me for Christmas. I heated up some milk in a saucepan and made a cup of Swiss Miss chocolate and proceeded to carry it into the television room.

There I smelled woodruff. I switched on the light and saliva caught in my throat: Eloá sat in my mother's handmade Colonial armchair dressed in a blizzard of white fur, smiling through pearlescent teeth.

"Feliz ano novo, Madrinha," she said easily. "How is little *Hiagga?"*

39.

I crumpled backward onto the couch and blurted out the first thing that occurred to me: "Please don't kill my family."

Eloá laughed and replied, "I have no claim on them."

"What are you here for then?"

"For you," she said, rising from my mother's chair, resplendent in snowy fur, intriguingly, fundamentally, and ruthlessly beautiful. She slid to her knees between my legs and ran her hands along my cold white thighs, over my ridiculous Labor of Love maternity briefs, up to my distended gut. "And him."

I was terrified, and equally, mesmerized. Everything around me was suddenly significant and I couldn't think of anything significant to say. My jaws were clenched in alarm and abandon. Finally, I sputtered, "How did you get in? Paw-Pop always double locks everything."

"I slit the screen in the porch, *Hiaaga.* I took off the window—the one with the sign that says *Pro-God, Pro-Life and Pro-Gun."*

237

I let her fingers stroke the contours of my belly. I let them trace the brown line that now trailed from my navel to my pubic bone. My breathing slowed and became shallow and I shut my eyes and said, "If Paw-Pop would have woken up he could have shot you," I said, and only later did the irony of the comment occur to me.

"They won't wake up," she whispered. "See the wine bottles by the television? They opened a second one and talked about you until it was almost morning. Now, everyone in the house is fast asleep... except us."

I wondered if she'd already been inside the house while they were in the great room drinking wine. I remained paralyzed with fear and fascination: "Did you hear what they said about me?"

"I did."

"And?"

"They want you happy, little *Hiaaga.* They want you fulfilled. The man saw goodbye in your eyes last night and was comforting the woman."

Her inflections were so similar to Julian's that I had to look at her directly in order to convince myself that it wasn't him. She met the scrutiny and returned it with a smirk I'd seen before, one that was entirely foreign to Julian. So I knew who it was, but then, she lowered her face to my belly, spread my robe open, lifted my nightshirt and puffed hot breath against my skin. I felt the tip of her tongue and the hard enamel of her teeth and I wondered if she would touch my breasts. My nipples stood against the rayon in peaks. Her hand made a starfish shape across my abdomen. My baby shifted and shimmied. I heard reedy wind in the attic vents. "What do you want me to do?" I asked, trembling, panting softly.

"I want you to go to Julio. Allow him to raise his son. There is no away, and there is no other way. The car is outside running."

"Is he inside it?"

She raised her head from my stomach, crooked her long neck and offered me her broad, nearly ravishing smile: "Of course not. He's back at the park."

"Why didn't he come for me himself? I wrote to him, not you."

"You wrote to support an alignment. Julio is arranging your *kutemë aypën*. Something to align you—your fastening. "

"What does that even mean?"

"In Luanhão custom, *kutemë aypën* is the man's gift for the woman with whom he has formed the understanding. There are no rituals, no ceremonies, no exchange of words; there is only the *kutemë aypën*. It simply means 'they are for each other restricted.'"

For reasons I can't entirely explain even today, I had a sudden, unrelated thought, and it wrenched me back to sense. "Is Potter in the car?"

Eloá responded with another imperious smile: "Of course not. I came alone. Those boys all move on in the wintertime when the park is closed. You should know that; you should know where they go, too. You should know their stories as well as your own: You are their godmother."

"Even Serafin Tercerio? Eloá, tell me the truth. Did he move on? Is that sweet kid in Mexico with his family or is he in the cold case files in Pontiac? And what about Gabriel, the young man with cancer? Did he survive?"

The hand that I thought might touch my nipples now made a circle across my lips to quiet me. "They've all moved on. Nothing more to be said about it. The only child in your charge today is burrowed and bundled within you. Feel the waves he makes as he turns in his sleep."

In fact, the child did exactly as she commanded. He heaved and kicked and changed position. But it was coincidence. It was my response to Eloá's touch. It was my hormones sending tendrils through my veins and into the baby, but it certainly wasn't hocus-pocus.

And it wasn't midwifery. Regardless of what came next, I couldn't let her deliver him. After what I'd seen of her filthy, emaciated mother, I wouldn't even consider it. I couldn't. And whatever I chose to do, I'd have to drop that bombshell on them sooner or later. I'd determined in advance that if Julian came to fetch me back,

I'd grin and bear the rest of the pregnancy, including the birth, with Dr. Sz-Min. I'd already contacted her, and she was agreeable to seeing me again as a patient, although predictably, she seemed as emotionally invested in the opportunity as if she was talking about a Focus alternator.

Meanwhile, maddeningly, I lay in delightful stasis as Eloá bewitched me and baby with her coos and tickles. Her chestnut hair was wrapped around her head in a snaky braid. The smell was clean and fierce and nearly overwhelming. I watched her scalp oscillate as she murmured to the restless creature inside me. And then, strangely, I felt our roles reverse as though Eloá was drawing energies from me. She rooted against my belly and licked me there, as if tasting for spectral emanations, as if annealing unity with the baby that Julian, by his DNA, had forged.

It made sense to me: It was her DNA as well, and she was barren. *Barren:* An odd word from a distant, sexist past. And yet, barren is precisely how I'd felt for all those years before my fecund gut started blowing up like a yoga ball.

Had I not felt that tug of empathy for Eloá that day, in those predawn moments, the rest of this story might have flowed differently. I might not have taken my next step in all its impetuous idiocy. I allowed her to take my arms and pull me to my feet. She peeled off her white fur coat; beneath it she was wearing a long, soft dress of cinnamon-colored fleece.

"You will see; I also offer you and my brother a fastening," she said as she swaddled me in the coat—now, apparently, my coat—pulled it closely around me and put her luminescent olive cheek close to my pale one, breathing, "I relinquish him to you formally, *Hiaaga*, just as a father might give away a daughter. *Ipútupo veyu kheoñe.* He's yours eternally. Take him from me irrevocably. Enter now the days of your life together and may they be long upon earth. *Ghasirü* tüküna-lâkâna aucéyre."

I stood and clutched at the fur. It was, by far, the most luxurious garment I'd ever tried on. I fondled its pristine and bestial suppleness. Eloá's warmth remained trapped inside it and radiated through my bare, brittle skin. There was no stirring yet from upstairs, but morning was breaking on the first dawn of the new year.

"Now, let's go," Eloá said. "There is nothing left for you here."

I stammered as I came back into that portion of myself still clinging to an iota of rationality: "But, I can't just leave. I have to gather up stuff; I have to pack. I have prescriptions from my doctor. I have a bank box on Liberty Street. I have a job I need to quit. I have to tell my parents *something*. I'll have to come up with a story…"

"Story time is over," Eloá said firmly and with some amusement. "You are *Xam-lina*, the Sun-Gilded Girl. You like to know the meaning of words? 'Luanhão' means 'People without Evil'. When you enter their world—their screeching forests, their churning currents, their thickets and thatch, their bogs and *cerrados*—you must do it as a virgin. In mind if not body."

No hedging. No excuses. I found her scenario hard to resist on multiple levels, but my acquiescence seemed irrelevant. The odd sequence of events unfolding around me was as irresistible as a cyclone. Any minute, obviously, Mom and Paw-Pop would be up asking about my new coat, asking about the slit in the screen on the porch, asking about this strange woman clad in vicuña fleece who'd been in our house all night eavesdropping.

I hyperventilated, ran to kitchen, fetched a pad of paper and scribbled a note:

"My baby's father came for me. I'm fine, promise, only things have changed. I know you want the best for me. Waking you up this morning would have been too awkward. I'm sorry. I will be in touch later today about my car and my things. And of course, about my baby. I'm really sorry."

I hesitated for a nanosecond and then added, *"Remember Matthew 19:5. I love you both."*

I left the note by the banana tree.

I was in a strange psychogenic state, a silly fugue, and undoubtedly I was not even responsible for what I was doing. I pulled the sumptuous coat tightly around my body went out the door and slid into the idling Audi. It was all too preposterous— too Harmony Korine. But I loved every un-Cadence minute of it. I loved that I was in a warm car facing outlandish adventures instead of counting a cash drawer for a third time to figure out why I was a dollar eighty short. Even briefly, I was insufflated in a different atmosphere and I experienced a tide of profound relief.

I shook my head in fearful joy and bit my lip so as not to burst out laughing. Outside, I watched as Eloá deftly replaced the window that said *Pro-God, Pro-Life and Pro-Gun*, then joined me in the Audi, slipping into the driver's seat. When it came to her own family, her divine harmonies may have been whackadoodle, but breaking into my house while Mom and Paw-Pot sat there in oblivion watching Ryan Seacrest on TV? That secured Eloá Vaz a place in the badass hall of fame.

40.

My Daddy's Christianity had not been the bombastic kind that bellows from AMEN Radio. It had been deep, introspective and abiding. Many Southern Protestants view Catholics as un-saved cultist, but Daddy had a quiet reverence for Papist pomp: I remember being twelve years old, feeling the first stabs of churchly doubt, and him resurrecting a picture of the Shroud of Turin from *Encyclopedia Britannica*. He explained that this image of the crucified Christ, which he trusted unreservedly, had only been truly appreciated after the invention of photography.

In fact, when you see the shroud as it truly looks, you see only smears of dark against pale fabric, and it's only in photographic negatives that the face of Christ appears. My Daddy had confidence in the authenticity of the Shroud without reservation, and that had been his empirical evidence of Jesus. He said, "Either you believe that photography is an ancient art that pre-dates Christ or you have faith that the image is genuine."

I had this thought as Eloá and I drove through the stark Ohio countryside because suddenly, I was living inside a photographic negative. When I'd taken the identical route in June, the land had been dark with vegetation. Now it was ghastly, ghostly white. The blue skies of midsummer had turned to the tangerine of daybreak. The compass was reversed; we were speeding north, not south, and instead of fleeing the chaos, I was barreling toward it. Fluttery snowflakes became meteors as they struck the windshield while muted cornfields showed a few lonely stalks standing stubbornly against the wind.

Eloá anticipated me: "You'll be fine. It's your transcendence. It's your immanence. If you love my brother, you'll love them both."

"I *do* love him, Eloá," and that sounded *Gone with the Wind* lame, so I asked her for a favor: I wanted her to fill the space that spread throughout the car like the dead land outside.

"I suppose you're due a favor for providing me my own transcendence," she laughed. "Liberation from the *Xam-Bioá*."

"Would you sing another Luanhão chant?"

"Of course," she said, and the fierceness seemed to fallen away from her—she sounded mellow and content. "But there are many cycles; there are love songs, hunting songs, death songs and victory songs..."

"Are there any white-chick-from-Ohio-hoping-she-doesn't-regret-her-decision songs?"

"Perhaps your lover will write you one."

"Sing any one of them. It won't matter what it's about. I won't understand the words anyway."

"But you will. They're composed in such a way that you can tell what they're about by the tone; by the inflection and the cadence. But, actually, there is one cycle that combines them all, so perhaps I'll sing that one. It's a parable. It's the story of the Sun Youth and the Moon Youth, one as bright as the blinding sun, the other as dark as the water in the Uguõdo river. They were found in the forest by men with spears and arrows and they came to the village with packs on their backs. At first, the people thought they were the spirits of tapirs. They'd been lost for a week and by then, they were mud-slicked and covered in sores and bites—they had survived on nothing but handfuls of nuts. But the village elders saw the thing inside them that was still more corrupt than their flesh—they'd had evil done to them and they'd done evil in return, and they would surely have been turned away if the chief hadn't recognized their Luanhão blood and taken them in. They were fostered by these people; they were fed piranhas and rice and these people tried to cleanse

243

them of their toxins, like the poisons they boiled from manioc. In time, these youths were swallowed up by the great forests again, but they returned, over and over, each time more sovereign of spirit, more potent, more Luanhão. They became emissaries from Terra Incognita with nothing to teach the village, but only to learn from it, because these were the People without Evil—people who had divested themselves of evil with the leaves of Jivarrão and had no inclination to learn it again."

I placed my hands on my ungainly gut, now mantled in snowy fur, and I shut my eyes and drifted as her voice moved: Like the morning in the bower, she found strange rises and sudden falls; she trailed over jarring and dissonant notes. Her song was clear and sonorous, but sprinkled with strikingly inharmonic passages. Hearing them was like eating something sweet and tasting bitter bits.

I knew the story she was telling because she'd laid it out for me beforehand, but I saw the images in my head just the same. I saw brown people with red streaks painted on naked bodies; I saw them with seven-foot bows and six-foot arrows. I watched cobras and armadillos bury themselves in holes when sun burned the region. I saw bogs and islands and vast fields of mud. I saw bursts of rain and rickety, wooden-slatted bridges over the raging black Uguõdo. I saw the jungle and through the fronds I saw blue-tinged mountains where two children straggled through the dissipating mists. This was another photographic negative: A Grimm's fairy tale with a brother and sister lost in the woods. In the original, the parents were trying to kill the kids while in this one, the kids were the parent-killers, and when they found a hut in the forest, the witch was them.

Eloá sang, and through her breathy stops, something carnal rose up in her. When she was finished, it was briefly sated in her, if not in me. "Is that the place where Julian wants to take me?" I asked in a hushed voice. "To raise our child? Is that the forest without white men?"

"I wouldn't know. But he thinks there's a forest like that somewhere, for sure. Maybe south, or maybe north where he trapped for those years. Perhaps overseas. Maybe anywhere and maybe nowhere. But it's been his fantasy since we left Brazil."

"What has your fantasy been, Eloá?"

"A forest without men at all," she laughed. "A forest with white paint. That's my fantasy, little *Hiaaga;* orange from *achiote,* brown from *cumaca,* pink from *huacamayo caspi,* purple from *mishkipanga* flowers. A life of art is my fantasy, life in a place where there's no man who wants me. "

"I like being wanted by a man," I pouted. "The right one, anyway."

She looked across the seat at me. Instantly, her amusement had twisted into a sharp scowl of disgust. Her alabaster teeth now seemed like the teeth of a carnivore. She said, *"They cried from within me: "O, Thou I.* You know what my mother and I—and not only us, but your Sun-Youth too—withstood at the hands of men who wanted us? Better to fall beneath the demons than give in to the wants of men."

It was true; I'd forgotten that. I was embarrassed at myself, chagrinned at my insensitivity, but I was still seven months pregnant and it had to be said, and this was as good a time as any to say it, when we were at odds, so I burst out with it: "I can't have you as my midwife, Eloá. I need the birth to happen in a hospital, with a staff—with equipment available in case things go haywire. I can't have you deliver my baby."

Just as quickly, her patina of menace faded. Her laughter returned, and she looked at me in puzzlement: "Why would I want to deliver your baby?"

"Julian said it was the expectation."

"Whose? *His?* Hardly mine. He's not *my* salvation, *Hiaaga*—he's yours. And you are his; I'm not. You're Madrinha now. My charge was to pick you up and leave you off at the place where he has arranged your *kutemë aypën.* There, may you begin a new life, and from that point, I hope never to see you again."

We crossed into Michigan without another word. The silence suited as it had to suit; my questions were now for Julian. In another hour, we would be back at August Lake.

I watched the languid empty places outside the window and a couplet came back

245

to me from many years ago. It was from Sappho; I'd written it on the cover of my Staples composition notebook in English Lit:

In dewy damps my limbs were chilled,

My blood with gentle horrors thrilled.

41.

Julian had written *'For our Seasons'* on my pack of poems, and as Eloá channeled the roads that skirted the park's North Unit, pushing through three new inches of soft new snow, it struck me that I had now known Julian through all four seasons.

I had an indelible image of him in the springtime, sitting placidly on the cemetery hill, his profile already deeply tanned in mid-May and his hair like the hair in the Shroud of Turin would have been had color photography been an ancient art. I had a summer vision of him with a savage sun igniting his sinews as he whacked at oak flesh less tough than his own, swinging without abandon, but with abiding, ferocious dignity. Although he owed me an autumn image, and hopefully many of them, his winter image was there, quite unexpectedly, at a snowy trail head near the path we'd taken on the day of our first luscious coupling.

August Lake was closed and the barrier we approached was chained and padlocked. Julian was just beyond it with a rust-colored worsted cap pulled low on his brow and a hood from a long buckskin coat draped over the top. His shins were crossed with each moccasined foot slipped beneath the opposite knee. Behind him, visible through a screen of denuded forest, the sky was laced with strawflower clouds and dewy blue.

He was a bizarre anachronism, for sure, but to me, somehow, it was ineffably charming. He looked like a Frederic Remington study. I vowed to paint the scene one day; all these season scenes, in fact, in my own Luanhão story cycle.

His eyes were closed and he didn't open them. He said nothing to his sister, nor she to him. Nor did she speak at all. But I did. I'd been trying to think of something significant to say to her since Toledo, and around Monroe, I recalled a quote from the book on Rumi I'd been reading the morning I sat outside Julian's cottage waiting to ask him about Sophrosyne:

"Thank you, Eloá," I said as I opened the car door. I hoped I wasn't mangling it: *"Fly toward secret skies, cause a hundred veils to fall each moment—take steps without feet."*

She winced, smiled, sniffed and shook her head at the absurdity of me trying to pass along poetic advice to her rather than the other way around. She remained inside her own world, where me reciting poetry to her was the photographic negative.

And then she did speak. She said, *"Huitillo."*

"What does that mean?"

"It's the color of August Lake."

She drove off and left me to Julian, and a moment later, our forms were locked with my white fur parted and my big belly compressed against his waist. Rayon rubbed fringed leather. My arms snaked around his back and looped his belt as I clutched him again and breathed the smoky musk of maleness. "Are we strangers? Or are we together again," I asked, "irrevocably?"

"Apart is not away," he said, and I took that as a sufficient affirmative and we didn't say anything else for a long time.

He led me carefully along the wet trail, up a hill to the place we'd first been intimate, a clearing a few hundred yards from the rental cabin where Kevorkian had dispatched his dying people and Girl Scouts made S'mores and Takosha's crystal necklace had sparkled in the sunshine.

Near the spot where he'd built the original campfire, where we'd lain beneath the big bear fur and in turn beneath the sequin stars, there was now a tiny hutch built of sapling poles buried in the ground, bent into an igloo shape and covered with bark and skins. Inside was a pit with a log fire burning and our bearskin spread across a platform raised above it, and that's where we went. He pulled a flap closed and I peeled off my fur and my nightgown, and then, his leather garments, and for

247

the second time, we made genuine love, ponderously pregnant though I may have been. We found a way; we found positions, and in the moment, it didn't seem the least bit indecorous or crass. It felt steamy and erotic. My mind was there with him and inside him, and although he was inside me and inches from our child, it all seemed appropriate. I assumed that things like this happened between pregnant couples since the beginning of time.

Feeling that way, even in the throes of passion, it occurred to me that there might have been time when he and Eloá lying together might also have been appropriate. Sex between siblings may have also happened since the dawn of everything, and although it wasn't a mental image I wanted, it was a revelation even so. I'd been righteously repulsed by the idea that he'd slept with his sister, and now, having felt tugs of her myself, I wondered how much of my implanted Cadence prudery would have to be unlearned in adulthood. Not the prohibitions about incest particularly; maybe that taboo is in place to prevent pandemonium. Maybe siblings routinely lusted after each other. I'd never had a brother to lust after, so I didn't know. In any case, the notion of sex while radically pregnant had always seemed kind of ugly to me, but it turned out that it was better than good. And although there were moments when I felt that Eloa's long fingers were cirrus threads curling up my thighs, like gentle vines snaking down my spine as softly as eyelashes, an idea came to me despite myself: Hansel had tasted Gretel and there was a mystery even more compelling at the root of it: Julian and Eloá might be twins more identical than most, and I wondered if making love to each other had been like making love to themselves.

For me, what happened on that first morning of the first day of the new year was a beautiful communion. I felt wonderful about myself and my body and its thrums of desire. I was inside a benign bubble and it went on for the rest of the morning, and when it was finally satisfied, we curled together again under the bear skin, bones knit, as outside, through the smoke hole, the weather was schizophrenic, blowing huge gusts that rattled the skins as the sky cleared, then clouded again to a charcoal overcast.

At some point, Julian mentioned the *kutemë aypën* and in total surprise I said, "Isn't this it? The wigwam, the fire, the bearskin, our morning together?"

248

"No, no, of course not. It's inside the cabin, where it wouldn't get snowed on."

"Oh my!" I said. "Will you go up there with me?"

He shook his head, and his face contained elements of seriousness and the self-deprecating candor that formed a core of him that I dug: "It's your Luanhão experience, Dixie. It's the fastening; cognitive orientation. The decision of how to incorporate the *kutemë aypën* into her future belongs to the woman alone."

I laughed and pulled him closer. "Well, now I guess you have me totally intrigued. But really; I don't want a *kutemë* whatever from you—I want what I have, the gift of us, for us and about us, and right now, he's kicking up a motherfucking storm."

I moved his hand to my gut and we spent the next few minutes feeling the child shimmy and roll within me. It seemed like a good time to broach hospital care and my insistence thereof, and while we were at it—as touched as I was with the wigwam—the reality that I also needed a warm and clean place to see out my two remaining months of bearing his child. It all registered with Julian. Apparently, it now went without saying. The park was closed for the season and in anticipation of me he'd divested the stone cottage of all traces of the crew. It was our home exclusively for as long as I wanted it. I loved that cottage, and for the moment, this promise was good enough. The questions I had about everything else—the club, the boys, the future, the newspaper article I'd seen in the greasy waiting room at Perry Collision—would be asked in their own time, and when they were, I trusted that he'd tell me truth.

I was satisfied because I wanted to be. I wanted to feel the supremacy of new beginnings. I was surrounded by smoke and love, anticipation and hope, and outside, the breeze, the bluster and the brightness were all shifting in rapid fire.

In time, though, I grew sheepish with curiosity, and he helped me pulled on my fur coat and fur boots and watched me trundle off toward the cabin where I expected to come upon a large wooden carving, or a stack of new poems, or a mountain girl wardrobe, or tickets to white-men-free forests.

But that's not what I found.

By then, I'd teased out many disturbing details from Julian's life and I suspected many more, but I believed, with a conviction like religious dogma, that he'd risen above them. There was an urgent integrity behind everything he said, and now—after the fact—I realize that he trusted implicitly that with me, it was the same. Was it? I had actually thought so; that was my goal in most things. But the things we say in heated moments may have bottomless consequences far off on our horizons, and in the quick analysis of the scene I encountered when I threw open the cabin door, I realized that Julian didn't really understand how I thought at all.

Just as clearly, I had missed some crux in his thinking. What the room contained was not an example of how a human being thinks, but of how an animal thinks. It was like the mangled mouse a cat leaves as a bonding offering on a front porch without a clue of how demented the recipient would find it.

Handcuffed to the metal frame of the bed was a naked black teenager. His knees were splayed and the thread of his penis looped obscenely between his legs, shriveled against the hard mattress. He'd worked his gag free, but in that instant, he was too frightened to make a sound. It was not one the park crew boys I'd seen before, nor anybody I remembered from Sophrosyne. This was a strange boy filled with hollows, from the pathetic concave of his stomach to his gap-toothed mouth to the emptiness in his bewildered eyes.

Eloá's voice reverberated in my skull: *"They cried from within me: "O, Thou I..."*

But that's not what the boy screamed. When I pulled back my hood, the boy made a long, drawn and hopeless squeal and cried out my name.

42.

My initial impulse was to help this terrified, blubbering boy. The cabin was Kevorkian cold and I had no idea how long he had been here. Fear came off him in waves and filled the room with the caustic smell of his sweat, flowing despite the cold. He'd pissed and his urine was glittering frozen on the wooden floor. I tore off my fur coat to throw over him, and as I did, I looked more closely at the features behind the crude, compelling face and with a jolt of recognition, I realized that

250

I knew who he was. He was Tivon Grimes, the kid from my old neighborhood in Woltown; one of the little crackhead thugs who used to take up space in the tiny lobby of Danny's Coney Island.

Giddy foreboding flooded through me like it had in the Sophrosyne basement. I was seeing familiar faces where they shouldn't be. I thought I might collapse again, and for the same reason—these incongruous juxtapositions tend to happen primarily when you're sleeping and, so my brain was telling me, I should be lying down. This time I stayed on my feet as Tivon began to burble: "I'm sorry, I'm sorry, Dixie; it ain't like that. I was tripping—I just wanted to fuck wid him a little, take his money and if he had weight, that too. It ain't coofee but..."

In consummate confusion I asked, *"Who?"*

"White boy. Dope fiend. Corky."

Honesty is especially keen among those with something at stake. And it made sense in light of the thin cord between us: Tivon had known me, known where I worked and drank, where I lived, who I lived with, and probably he'd probably known that Corky slung a little Grey Ice, though more to keep an in with folks who dealt the quality shit than to make money. My God, I thought. The little shit had broken into our home to steal and wound up beating Corky to death with his own baseball bat.

I saw the dystopia and cynicism of the street reflected in Tivon's expression. He'd already assumed his life had drained away, maybe years before he wound up here, but there was also a ferociousness in clinging to it. It was equally street: The optimism hard-wired into the young. I put my fur coat back on and left him to shiver.

Tivon was sputtering, "Real and raw be running together that day, Dixie, life and booshit mixed up. He had a fat mouth, but I ain't got to have gone and done like that, no call to flat nobody head—had that hail smoke flowin' in my veins. Back then I pledge allegiance to the pipe, but now I go to school, got my momma, my auntie, my sis..."

I stepped back, fascinated, and in a minute, my own terror melted away like frozen lather on a window sill. My heart stop skidding around my chest and my stomach stopped churning. Tivon was helpless, exactly how Corky had been in his final moments, and as I assumed Julian's father had been in his. I was in no immediate danger. The poor kid before me clearly recognized that he was in considerable danger, and poignantly, desperately, was unable to stop running his mouth. The rant was so rabid that I couldn't follow it, but by then, I didn't need to.

"Thought I was in a movie or a dream that day," he cried. "Swear to God. Feel like that right now, feel me?"

Well, I did, and although I hadn't yet begun to speculate on the details of how he'd ended up here, the reason he was here was obvious: On the pine storage chest to my right lay a handgun, and if I checked it, I was pretty sure that the chamber contained a single bullet.

Real and raw did indeed run together. Life and bullshit was mixed up. "I be in a daze all that week," Tivon gabbled on. "Keepin it one hundred now—my momma, you know my momma, LaDonna Grimes, she be missing me right now; don't shoot me, Dixie..."

I inhaled his fear. I puzzled over his expression, his burps of agony. I knelt down in front of him and told him to shut up, because I didn't want him spitting saliva on me. He did shut up, and for a bit, I examined him closely and insolently, like I had studied those caged carnivores at the zoo. Like them, he was restrained, and like them, if released and given free space, I knew he had the capacity to tear me into pieces and leave my brains on the floor.

But he was handcuffed to the bedframe, and in that minute, I marveled over the idiosyncrasies of his naked visage, jet-black but still emanating pallor. I sucked in the technicalities. He had a high forehead, beautiful facial bones and skin with the sheen of licorice. His eyes blazed. Oily tears made streaks on his face like slug trails. His mouth was oversized, like a Warner Brother's pigmy, and against his inner tube lips, his teeth were so white it was arresting—they looked like porcelain Chiclets. His animal panting came in pristine white plumes with red bubbles forming at his nostrils.

"What did Corky say to you with his fat mouth?" I asked, tilting my head, genuinely curious: "Did he call you a nigger?"

252

"Naw. Wouldn't have kilt nobody over that."

"Then what?"

"Called me a pussy."

It actually made me laugh. "You killed him that? For calling you a girl?"

He nodded uselessly, wretchedly. He blew dead air.

Tivon had his circuits primed for submission. He probably always had. Corky, it turns out, hadn't. I was glad of that if nothing else. But suddenly, of course, it wasn't about Tivon Grimes or Corky Geshke. It was about me. Perhaps, if I reconsidered it, Julian was behaving with a certain prudence here. Perhaps he wasn't clueless after all. Maybe this was my brutal baptism, saturated in the reek of perspiration; blood bonding as a ritual. He'd said that the thing in the cabin was mine to incorporate into my future, and an obvious option was to put a bullet through the head of the person who'd murdered my common-law husband.

Or not. I remembered the conversation plainly, sharp broadheads among the bluebells, bubbles on the silvery brook: *"Blood for blood, without legal ramification. When it was over, the matter would be over too."*

"See, that seems like justice to me" had been my answer, and at the time, without question, that's what I'd believed. I still do, to this day. Now the time had come to walk the walk, and I wondered what was expected of me. Not by Julian or Tivon Grimes, or even Eloá, but by me, of me, although above all, for us—me, Julian and our child, the triune. I wasn't even sure I knew what to do. Point the barrel and pull the trigger? Weren't there safety locks and stuff? I'd never shot a gun in my life. What if I missed? What if I winged him like I had the turkey? What then? Was I supposed to wring his neck or slit his throat or beat his brains out with the barrel of the gun? Crunch time came quickly for the animal or the woman or the outraged next-of-kin to take the reins, and I believe that Julian knew exactly what I'd do.

I asked the bound boy, "Do you know where your clothes are?"

"They in that box," he said, a glimmer of hope appearing like a lodestar in a black sky.

I picked up the gun and looked inside the chest. Indeed, they were.

"Do you know where the handcuff key is?"

He shook his head and profusion of agonized sobbing burst forth, as though that might be the balance on which his life teetered. I wondered what expression he'd worn while laying open Corky's skull. When I pictured the scene, I imagined he'd been crying then as well. Corky had called him a pussy, and for the most part, Corky hadn't had a whole lot of use for pussies, not even mine. It's too bad it cost him his life, since Tivon was not a pussy at all. He was a flaky, impulsive man-child, Y-chromosome to the marrow, and the coke comedown probably hadn't helped.

None of it mattered now. What mattered was this isolated moment in the cabin. I tried to meld minds with Julian and I had a spark of insight. I turned to the window behind Tivon and dangling exactly where Takosha's crystal necklace had been was a tiny key on a long string.

Of course. And the resolution was obvious. Corky wasn't my kin, except in some convoluted, peripheral sense. I hadn't even particularly liked him. I still didn't know what his middle name was because I'd been in jail when *The Detroit News* printed the story. If the bullet in the gun belonged to anyone, it belonged to that sad old couple down in Naples, Florida, and of course, given the chance, they'd never use it. They weren't made of that sort of stuff. They trusted the state to serve them justice like a Grand Slam breakfast at Denny's, and the state intended to leave them hungry.

But I wouldn't get stuck in their kitchen. I couldn't dole out justice for them, so there was no reason to prolong the thing except for one, and it terrified me all over again: In my brief span of complete control in the face of total subordination, I'd found a new sense of exultation. Cognitive orientation. Within me, my baby hung suspended in identical subordination. The ease with which I could have handled his dispatch—a pill, an aspiration tube, and injection of potassium chloride to the heart or whatever method these clinical dispatchers use with no ramifications to anyone but the baby—was mind-blowing, and it scared the shit out of me.

I was flooded with the complexity of emotion and *that*, not the boy, was my *kutemë aypën*. I was sure of it.

Well, I wasn't going to shoot Tivon Grimes, but I also wasn't going to get shot by him in some dumbass miscue, so in the end, I unlocked the cuffs while holding him at gunpoint—a feat of some dexterity, I must say—then watched his feverish tugs and sprawls on the piss-soaked cabin floor, floundering, pulling on filthy jeans, a black hoodie, a Green Supreme t-shit, flashy Jordans, crying and spluttering gratitude until I told him to shut up again since he'd missed the point. He continued to miss the point all the way to the door, where he took off stumbling into the wet winter afternoon.

"That's how a pussy behaves," I called out after him proudly, and I knew it must be true because I had one and he didn't.

I let him go because I had no claim on his life, and that alone, I believed, had been the test. Had circumstances been otherwise, I would have pulled the trigger without hesitation.

Like Eloá had.

Obviously, Tivon didn't see Julian by the oak tree. But I saw him. The air around him glowed with the rising fog. It another portrait for the bucket-of-paint list: Julian, stock still in his Fenimore Cooper duds, hand-crafted bow and homemade arrow poised, exuding a sort of lurid radiance.

43.

To love someone unconditionally is invasive on a titanic scale. It first requires a complete dissection of your subject down to the capillaries and then it requires you to cut the capillaries open and kiss the gore. You must knead the filth in the colon and accept it. You don't have to approve of it, but you have to cradle it.

That afternoon on the first day of the new year, Julian didn't let the arrow loose because he had no greater claim on Tivon Grimes' life than I did. But Julian watched him go, eyes narrowed, sight honed and sharp. As I watched him watch, Tivon's unimpeded escape began to worry me, and despite my coat and the warming day, I began to shake.

I shook savagely and Julian stepped up to me and led me tenderly to our camp area, where a blast-furnace blaze now roared in the stone pit. Julian was as soft and solicitous as he'd ever been, and for the next hour, with the bow close at hand, we did not talk about what happened inside the cabin. He knew what had happened, of course. Instead, he whispered explanations that went as far as I needed them to go. His crew had creepers extending into the crevices of many fractured neighborhoods, and finding information on the street was an easy proposition with cash and threats. I suspected Potter, but who knows? I didn't ask. It was beyond my need or desire to know. Nor did I ask if Tivon Grimes would go to the police. He wouldn't of course. He'd murdered Corky Geshke and had only, by chance, escaped today with his own life intact. I'd extended him a courtesy that neither he'd had no right to expect, probably due in part to the sanctity of the life within my own viscera.

I wasn't worried about police, but I was worried that the he might get lost and freeze to death, thus negating the mercy I'd shown him. Or worse, that he might double back and do us harm. I clung to Julian as he explained someone was waiting by the road to fetch him back to his own private shithole. It was unlikely that he knew where he'd been taken, nor was he—at fifteen—a player with enough street clout to retaliate.

I didn't ask who was waiting for him. I didn't ask if that same person would have cleaned up the cabin had things gone down otherwise. I didn't want to know, and I wanted that even less when Julian followed with the rest of his original quote: "There's room for compassion, Dixie—that's justice as well. And that's an end to it."

I wanted an end to it. I wanted our trajectory to be nothing but forward. I looked closely at Julian; at the branching lines that crept from the crease of his beautiful eyes, celery-green above the golden glow of his cheeks. His skin was limber and light, even in the shade. I imagined him stately and rugged at sixty, the age I'd imagined myself inside Hedy's Art Farm, and I now, I envisioned better things. My spirit was stabilized. I sucked in the pungent tang of soot and skin. I nestled and nuzzled against leather and I listened intently as he filled in some blanks. It was now or never, because like the scene in the cabin, I wanted this to be the only time I'd have to mention them.

He told me sad news: Gabriel Tobias had passed away in September, but he'd been at his bedside and said that the death had been easy enough as such standards go. The boy was buried in a pretty cemetery in rural Gonega and Julian would take me there if I wanted to see how peaceful it was. Then he told me happy news: Serafin Tercerio was alive and a landowner in Jalisco, and along with his parents, he now raised agave for the tequila industry; he'd show me the letter received, written in floral, free-flowing Spanish . Such closures fit my mood, and were orchestrated to do exactly that, and it was fine. That's what I wanted. I clutched his arm and let him help me find a way beneath the shadows of the dark firs, where the boughs were upholstered with pads of snow, making them ponderous and unwieldy, like me and my gut. *'Grávida'*, he told me, was Portuguese for both.

He offered to run and fetch me a snowmobile, but I was fine. I felt energetic and emotionally settled, unwilling to kick off my wild future as a wimp who couldn't manage a winter trail without a Ski-Doo. Of course I could, so long as I had him to support me. As we walked, he collected edibles along the paths. Unique and marvelous resources were everywhere. Rosehips abutted trails, freshwater clams stippled the creeks; there were cattail stalks and chickweed bunches and burdock roots that, he said, tasted like roasted carrots. He pointed out animal tracks and identified them. I'd learn, he promised—coyote showed nails, bobcats did not; turkey prints were three toed and deer hoofs were cloven and looked like little hearts.

In the forest, winter air smells so clean it almost takes your breath away. What's more, stripped of their skin of leaves, trees don't look dead, but like an exposed nervous system, vital and eerie and rippling with life. Scuds scuttled overhead, the sky cleared and beneath it, frozen mire spread in a glistening sea. We plodded though the wildflower pasture where I'd shot the turkey; stiff milkweed stalks now punched through a coat of snow and patches of exposed dirt made the field look like gingerbread with white icing.

In an hour, we were back at the stone cottage, deep and still within the dell, and with the background sky bathed dusk-orange, I took a photograph of my picturesque new home and sent it to my mother, saying, *'Don't you think this suits me better than Molly dolls and Great Scot aprons?'*, and in case it sounded too spiteful, quickly added, *'More later; I can't thank you enough for what you and Paw*

Pop did for me.'

In further conciliation, once inside I took pictures of Julian's hand-hewn canoe, his hand-made bow and his hand-crafted guitar and sent them to Paw-Pop with the note, *'Julian made these from scratch—I think you two would get along.'*

I knew there were flaws in my approach. I was excited to be here, and I wanted Mom to know that, but I'd told her some pretty awful things about Julian, and I doubted she'd forgotten them. Above all, I wanted her to believe that Julian felt proportionate excitement about me being here, but I wasn't entirely sure. I could have asked, but I was afraid to: He had a way of speaking that invited speculation to the contrary and despite my joy and relief, I remained antsy about the inscrutable distance at the bottom of many of his responses. He spoke with an air of elsewhere. His mysterious smile and infinite calm were beautiful to me, but they concealed complexities beyond my ability to grasp and behind a lock I couldn't pick. Were his expressions reflexive or entirely genuine? Could such a relationship evolve with a baby in the mix, and would that x-factor cultivate it to perfection? Such was my theory, and in the weeks that followed, it was the hope I polished.

Besides, when Julian was silent, I could imagine that Eloá remained part of the fusion of our spirits and I was certain that there had been synchronicity when she stroked the trembling skin of my torso. I suppose it was borderline awful to admit it, but my memory of those moments remained close to my surface.

We didn't speak of Eloá at all, but that night, wonderful aromas threaded through the cottage as Julian taught me how to roast pheasants and make bread made from black walnuts, which we slathered in crabapple jam from our cupboard. When we were done, he capped my contentment with a series of photographs he spread across the oak table. They showed vistas of old-growth hardwoods beneath enormous skies and evergreen armies climbing up rugged hillsides; they showed swooping cliffs and summery meadows dusted with purple rue.

"My god, that's beautiful," I exclaimed.

"Look at this," he said, showing me a photograph of a sapphire lake so broad that it rippled all the way to the horizon, the other side too far away to be visible.

"I don't understand," I said at last, and he told me that he'd purchased a thousand acres of virgin timberland in Baraga County in Michigan's Upper Peninsula, and not only did it contain a quarter mile of Lake Superior shoreline, it was adjacent to the Vieux Terre Indian Reservation, which had a few of life's amenities available should they became necessary. They even had an accredited school our child could attend if we agreed it was best.

And that was his proposal. Not Mosquitopia in some malarial rainforest in the Amazon basin, not some Russian steppe where you could still find people who didn't know World War II was over, but a sanctuary within driving distance of our odd and strangely precious families. He showed me the place he wanted to build our house: A bluff that overlooked Longfellow's shining Big Sea Water.

"That's our forest, Dixie. That's our lake."

He knew the land, he said. It's where he'd trapped. To a lesser extent, I knew it too: In the sixth grade, the year after my report on Toledo, I'd done a research paper on the Upper Peninsula, Michigan's consolation prize in the Border War of 1835. At the time, I been intrigued by the idea that Michigan was the only state with the good sense to carry a spare state around on its back in case of an emergency, and as far as I was concerned, with the emergency swelling my torso, that time had arrived.

That night Julian and I lay together in the carved bed that I'd slept in that first day in May, warm beneath the quilts, and I flipped again through the photographs. This idea seemed workable to me—this was not a winding filament of pretty words or dreamy concepts, this was an arrangement. I could see raising a child adjacent to these rolling hills and glistening waves, as far from Cadence as you could get without having to build a boat.

Within me, beneath my thin membranes, our baby gyred. I felt the down of Julian's cheek against my belly, the plushness of his lips and a thumb near my navel, too callused to belong to anyone but him.

The weeks that followed were as close an idyll as anything I have experienced in my life. January was both demure and devilish, sending northern blasts howling through the park, then warming through bouts of rain. Stark sunny days were followed by heavy snowfalls where flakes as thick as cotton clots and big as June bugs gathered into pillowcases laid across a world gone zealously dormant. A soft swallowing comfort permeated me as our cottage slipped beneath gentle engulfing dunes.

I had what I needed, within and without. There was a wardrobe provided for me; soft woolen ruanas that were floppy to contain my aggravated pregnancy. By then, I looked like someone had opened an umbrella in my torso. There were dresses lined with rabbit fur and long alpaca socks that bound my swollen ankles, everything doused in scents that were now to me as natural and real and delightfully personal as my own.

I also had couriers to take me to doctor appointments and trips for other things while Julian was busy in the park, winning daily bread. The park boys were still around, though it was a new set and no one I recognized. None of them ever spent the night at the cottage or even stayed for a meal, although, toward the end I began to ask them to. They always declined. Still, they showed up at appointed time in pre-warmed SUVs. They were young, handsome boys who spoke in measured monotones and wore vacuum expressions and deferred to me so entirely that they almost seemed like wraiths. There were three of them, and they alternated trips; they told me nothing about themselves but their names—Kurt, David and Savva— and as many times as I told them my name was Dixie, they never called me anything but Madrinha.

Ultimately I didn't object, and when they were shy about their private lives, I didn't pressure them. I didn't pry and I didn't ask if they did awful things outside our encounters. I saw them as part of this spectral season, bound to me, and I was to them as their Madrinha, only by a temporary tether.

They took me to buy the girly stuff I needed, especially pregnant girly stuff, voluminous underwear and vitamins. They took me to buy a set of art supplies so I could paint, and they sat in the lobby when Dr. Sz-Min did my checkups. Those visits with my OB/GYN, however intimate, remained charmless, but I wasn't looking for charm; I was after efficiency and professional reassurance. Sz-Min checked my urine to see if there was signs of preeclampsia because of my bloated ankles. She took measurements and fluid levels like a grease jockey at a ten-minute oil change. There remained something fundamentally insensitive about the way she touched me—it was un-Éloá-like, I guess—but in the end, it didn't matter since everything was progressing well and that's all I wanted seen to, along with a 3D ultrasound that showed a beautiful, doughy, handsome, gnome-faced boy.

After these excursions, I sometimes spoke briefly to my mother, mostly to offer pregnancy updates and caption the photos I'd been emailing her. She behaved a little like a jilted lover, petulant but ever-hopeful and I really didn't blame her. I knew that Kurt or David or Savva would have driven me to Ohio to visit her if I'd wanted them too—Julian had promised as much. In response, I felt strained and embarrassed. I recognized plainly that my Cadence months had been spent compacting my gut into a hard ball of denial, and now, the lump in my throat was even bigger because going back to explain myself in person was the last thing I wanted to do.

In the evenings, when Julian returned from the park, we pored over our pictures and timed our move. We were good in the cottage for as long as we wanted to be there he assured me; the delicate dance he'd been doing with the supervisor made our lease here rock-solid. Adam Loya had arrived at his professional summit years before and the park itself was so irrelevant in the state's system that as long as there were no complaints, there'd be no interference. I also remembered what Gabriel had said about the video tapes Julian had of Adam and Serafin Tercerio, but there was no reason to bring it up since Gabriel was dead, Serafin Tercerio was an agave farmer and Adam was nodding into a brown paper bag in a shuttered building at the outskirts of a closed park.

So we focused on our future, and we agreed that it seemed prudent to remain in the cottage until our son had crested his first and most precarious year of life, then to make our way north in the early summer. As a plan, not only did it suit me, it filled me with such a sizzling rush of excitement that I felt as if I might detonate. A healthy pregnancy and the total devotion of the baby's father? No expectant mother could ask for more. We talked about what he'd look like beyond the squished-up sock face that appeared in the ultrasound—our sweet, putty alien— and of course, we talked about names. Julian had rich, beautiful tribal ideas in mind, and today I no longer remember them because I had, by then, pretty much converged upon a single shimmering word; one of his own, actually: On the outside of the sheaf of poetry he'd given me on my birthday, ratifying something within me that was raw and righteous, he'd written, *'From our Forests, For our Seasons'.*

So, the boy would be called 'Seasons'. It was an outrageously left-field name, entirely personal, and my mother would never approve of it. Along with Paw-Pop, she'd have held out for a Biblical name. I intended to quote from the cryptically touching Ecclesiastes 3—*'to everything, there is a season'*—and hoped that explanation took. But Julian thought it was a lovely name and it was settled. Seasons was who he would be from that moment forward and through the infinitude of seasons we hoped would follow him and swallow him throughout a long and prosperous life.

I never felt closer to Julian than during those cozy interludes within the cottage, and certainly, I was never closer to Seasons than when he was drawing sustenance from my pulse. As I offered him my womb, the cottage became my own womb—a warm and nurturing vesicle—and I felt exactly as my baby must have felt. We had purchase on one another, on our home and on our seasons.

It was vital, I thought, to keep active, even in the press of winter. I assumed that the park was a dress rehearsal for a genuine northern winter. From what I'd found out online, this is the sort of weather Baraga County saw in October. I was *grávida* but I wasn't an invalid and if I was beyond jumping jacks and push-ups, I could certainly walk, and I did so eagerly: I took to daily forages down the old logging roads, along glorified deer trails and across clear cut areas where the pastoral winter ruled, where I could listen to nature's muted conversations as Seasons went through his final refinements within me.

Sometimes, the crow that Serafin had named after himself flew down and landed on a nearby bough with brutal grace. He'd hop on the ground in front of me or hang on a branch like a gargoyle. After a day or two, I could get him to take food from my hand. I was enchanted and unnerved by the ghostly blueish orbs set in the bird's obsidian face, brighter than any set of human eyes in history. I took to speaking to him as if he actually was Serafin Tercerio, or could carry messages to him as his emissary. I told him I was glad that he wasn't dead in an alley without genitals, and that if somehow, something in Julian's story didn't pan out, that he was finding his new life in feathered form to be transcendently liberating.

I thought I'd come a respectable distance from the girl who'd begun the game vaguely and persistently spooked by birds, and I liked this version of myself; it was much more aligned with the hum of the forest life to which I'd pledged my fate. I was finding deep connections, weaning myself from electronic devices and demands. Julian showed me how to read a topographical map and use a compass, neither of which required batteries.

In the end, however—as to fate and as to everything else—I held a little glow of Heartland gumption close to my heart, and I reckoned that Julian knew it. An escape hatch hovered on my horizon if ever, for any reason, I thought I needed one: It sat locked inside a safety deposit box on Liberty Street wrapped in mustard-colored bands.

One day, near the end of the month, I took a hike out to August Lake. My *piece de resistance* painting still hung above the hearth in the cottage, and although I loved it for the time and place and person it represented, I had not forgotten Julian's more evolved perception of that eerie body of water, wherein he saw beauty inherent in its truth while I—regardless of what he believed about my inner vision—saw only *huitillo*.

It turned out that Eloá had identified the lake's odd, ugly color with perfect accuracy. *Huitillo* was a fabric dye extracted from an Amazon shrub. I'd found photos of the plant's blue-green-grey leaves online. My hyphen-words were not satisfying, but the lone Portuguese word *'huitillo'* was, in part because, like many Latin words, it was poetic on an abstract level: *Huitillo* roots produce a chemical that kills off neighboring plants, creating a monoculture grove that—according to the Wiki entry—is called *Jardin da Curupira*, 'The Devil's Playground'.

In any case, I wanted to see the lake in winter, and I thought that a conciliatory gesture might be to do another portrait, when the water was imbued with a different mood. I wanted to capture a profile that was less malignant and her hues less dead. Like the leafless trees that lined the trails—naked titans whose vitality stood raw and exposed in the winter—I thought that August Lake might likewise display a face that lay hidden in May. I wanted another posture for myself as well. Not submission, not placation, not deference, but at least, a measure of cooperation.

Over that weekend, a blizzard had cossetted the park with a great, ermine-gloved hand, but the morning I set out, the sky was blue as a healing crystal. The air, unfiltered and sharp, was taintless. I bundled up extravagantly and walked out about an hour after Julian had left to do the maintenance still required in the park's off-season. I was dressed in wool and fur from top to bottom, with my phone charged, just in case. I was not being careless or flippant in my late pregnancy, I was being hearty. I thought of Ivolya Ryvak and her Belarusian horse sense, and I thought she'd commend me for approaching my burden with heroism.

I should never have gone out, of course, but those are my pointless afterthoughts. Those are bouts of self-flagellating that serve no purpose but to reinforce my guilt; a feather in the cap for theists, perhaps but in me, something more diabolical. I crossed over a mangle of deadfalls and ditches and approached August Lake from the rear, coming upon her suddenly, seeing her through a palisade of trees spreading like a dull grey lozenge beneath the empty sky.

At the time, I remember being a little relieved to find that in her winter garb, August Lake had become uninspiring. I could see the little beach on the far side where people swam in the summer, the one that Adam loved to rake. Behind it the concrete prow of the changing rooms was half-buried in drifts. But August Lake seemed to have lost all her trenchant menace. Even in my most charitable, most painterly read, she appeared uninteresting and non-compelling; nothing more than an astral void.

But the sky overhead did not. When I left the cottage it had been clear, but now, quite suddenly, a front began to move in. A frothy welter expanded from the north and swallowed the sun in the quickest onslaught of any storm I'd ever witnessed. By the time I'd found the path that led back to the cottage, sheets of slicking sleet were falling. I felt rebellion in my belly and pains racking my forehead, and when I finally made it back to the cottage, I was soaking wet and approaching hyperthermia. Gratefully, by then Julian was already home and he instantly built a fire in the stove big enough to test its limits. He peeled off my clothes and wrapped me in dry blankets and gave me one of his herbal tea concoctions; I swallowed it in low, delicious drafts and allowed the heat to course through me in tongues. I owned up to the silliness of the expedition, but there was no censure beyond my own. Julian laid me tenderly on the bed and pressed me into his leather and light.

He kissed me as the strength leached from my bones and he stroked my brow as I dropped off an edge and into dreams of lapping lakes with gleaming beaches, of quiet rooms where I was warm and blameless. He held me until I seized awake in the middle of the night and went into labor.

44.

For a brief phase when I was fifteen or so, true crime books were my private rage. They could be had for a dollar at Dog Eared Books on Liberty Street. In one of them, a bunch of small town girls lit one of their classmates on fire. I remember keenly the words of the detective with the awful job of investigating: *"Try as I did, the final piece of the puzzle just wouldn't fit."*

That phrase haunted me even more than the cheerleader bonfire; it stank of consummate and metaphorical hopelessness, of coming to the tall end of an arduous journey, nearly reaching the finish line, then being prevented from crossing it by some stupid and probably foreseeable circumstance.

A jigsaw puzzle with one piece missing is worse than useless. It becomes an obscenity. The gap invalidates every other puzzle piece. However small, the piece that refuses to fit into a predetermined slot becomes everything. In the case of the true crime girls, who were all Pentecostal Christians, the misfit piece was the source of their unaccountable sadism. But in any story, when a final piece refuses to cooperated, you're left to re-consider the other billion parts you've already pressed into place. Maybe you've wedged them all in wrong, one by one, forced them into slots where they didn't go, only it hadn't become obvious until the end.

My groin woke me, and not in a good way. Through my sleep, purling waves on a pristine beach became a raging, relentless surf against coastal cliffs. Julian was beside me, his long arm draped across my belly, and it felt like the vice in Paw-Pop's wood shop. I slipped from under him, and after a foggy moment, I came fully back into myself with the assumption that these were the Braxton Hicks contractions that Dr. Sz Min had prepared me for; a non-crisis that would pass. I fetched my phone to check the time and the screen was a dead-eye; it had survived the sleet storm in which I got drenched, but some latent demons must have taken it.

That was bad, no matter what Seasons decided to do. I went to the window and outside, the wind was wailing and the trees were braced against the onslaught, not huddled, but pleading, as if with arms raised. There were icicles dangling from the gutters like frozen spittle; the pane itself was rimed with frost and juddered in the wind. Beneath, the snow was heavy and set and a crisp crust spread from the cottage to the stand of pines where morels grew in the spring.

A second wave crashed against a great seawall, and it felt like my uterus was becoming petrified, turning into one of the boulders than lined the trail to the cemetery ridge. I'd set some water on to make tea, and the hiss of kettle became a scream. Julian was up, instantly, stoking the fire, fetching packets from the chest in the corner. "What time do you think it is?" I asked.

"Around midnight," he answered.

"I think this might be it, Julian. Show-time. What in the fuck are we going to do? My phone is dead. We're trapped."

"Hardly," he answered, cupping his own face at the window and peering through beads of condensation. "If you're in labor, we have two options: I can make a sprint to the park trucks in about half an hour, be back in ten more. I can take you to the hospital and make it there quicker than if I call for an ambulance from headquarters."

"What's the other?"

"I can deliver the baby."

If I had been more than thirty-six weeks along, I might have said yes. I really believe we could have pulled it off—woman have been delivering into the arms of partners for ten thousand generations. But weeks premature was something I needed a professional to deal with; there wasn't a smidgen of doubt about that. I realized then, with a silly start, that all my fantasies involved non-contingencies, and that's the flaw in dreamland.

I contracted again and panicked. Julian was entirely calm, perhaps more than the situation called for, but I was grateful for his measure of taking charge. He passed me dark green leaves and told me to chew them: "They'll help."

"What do they do?"

"*Corondcillo*, for pain—it's stronger than aspirin, but not much."

I was familiar with Julian's assortment of pharmacons. He kept them inside a pine chest that matched the one in the Kevorkian cabin and consisted of spicy-smelling bundles and paper bags filled with fronds and petals and Mason jars with phonic names written on them. Some you applied to the skin, some you boiled and drank and some you burned and inhaled. There were pungent powders, withered vines like mummified snakes, brown leaves that crumbled like pages from an old book; there were sweet berries dried into little mouse turds, herbs braided into green rosaries; there was fungus and moss, and one special packet that contained opalescent flakes that Julian told me had come from the back of a bullfrog. On my bucket list was the vow to learn everything I could about them and classify them, just as I had done with the Rolodex cards at Molnar Manufacturing and with Paw-Pop's ratchets, my contribution to a common cause. Initially, I'd been wary of ingesting them, but I was in a place where I needed to establish unbreakable trust, so I'd begun to relent, and so far, with positive effects. They fixed the sniffles and eased the backaches. Now I chewed *corondcillo* leaves and felt a delightful tingling numbness begin in my lips and course through my body. Julian was efficient; he pulled out other things from other bags and stirred them into a pot of water and the smell that wafted through the cottage was aromatic, comforting and sweet: "Natural antibiotics; *Gëshpiu, Shirampari, borũca* root..."

The pot simmered, the wind howled and the trees supplicated. We moved back to the bed where Julian stroked my hair and nuzzled me. The contractions lessened and the next two, though coming at regular intervals, were little more than period cramps. We thought that was a good sign. Maybe the in their muted guise these contractions were false labor after all. Perhaps we could wait until the storm passed; maybe until morning. Going out now would be like Eliza crossing the Ohio River. In a bit, I drifted off In Julian's arms and thought I heard the boomeranging axe crack as he lopped down trees above the dam that held back the sullen *huitillo* waters. It was a hazy, gorgeous memory, standing under a white summer sun with his bronze-limned arms girdling me, enshrouding me, twining me, while beneath

267

our feet, the funky rural dam wobbled and danced as if alive.

But then, without warning, the dam broke, and it was like pissing, only with a bladder the size of a weather balloon.

So that was it. Fickle fate had decided it. In a whoosh, my water had broken, and I needed to be in a hospital. I knew the risks; I knew the timeframe: Julian needed half an hour to make the headquarters, ten to get back to the cottage in the state vehicle, and then, it was maybe another twenty to St. Luke's, likely longer if the highway was covered in black ice. There was no equivocating, except for the tea. I didn't want any, but Julian insisted. Natural antibiotics, he said. I knew that Seasons was huddled inside my body on his launching pad and poised for take-off, but now without a natural barrier between him and all the microbes and that white men had coughed into these forests over many centuries.

I had at least an hour in which I still needed to protect him. I'd either go with the tribal wisdoms or I'd wing it with luck. So far, luck had not been with me, but the wisdoms had. *For our Seasons.* Our *Seasons*—so I swallowed the savory sips, one after the other, tasting the family confectionary, the feral flavors I'd come to associate with both Julian and his sister, absorbing them, feeling them sluice through every branching channel in my body.

But now he *had* to leave. That was unavoidable. There was whirring in my ears and a fog in my skull. The wind chorus outside grew to a polar roar. Trees thrashed and my womb thrashed back mightily, bashing against the shore, twisting and stabbing me, unsure if it wanted to rupture my abdomen or contract to an infinitesimal point beyond return. In those final moments, while Julian's face remained near mine, he was a floating vision as beautiful as anything I'd ever seen. To me, he was luminous and holy, and I wondered if the men and women in Canaan, or in Galilee, or in Nain, watching the Master whispering syllables, inhaling and exhaling love, touching them with magic fingertips, had considered Salvation to be as kissable. But that was insane. I was thinking about sucking face when I should have been thinking about the epidural lady in the maternity ward.

Within me, the tea surged and coruscated. "You have to hurry," is all that I could get out, and gently, without the urgency the plea required. I didn't want to shed the moment. His face was filled with abstruse and abiding affection, and as always, his intangible sadness—the infinite melancholy that drove down deeper than the hole at the bottom of August Lake. It was the void that our son was intended to fill.

He pulled furs over buckskin and as he did, he began to sing. He'd put music to my poems. This was the first time I'd ever heard tunes behind the words and they sounded like hymns. They swam through me, seeping inward into clefts and crannies. With the echo of his voice reverberating and the shifting weight of our impatient son inside me, I felt anything but alone, even after the door opened and closed and he pounded away. The blast of arctic air fused with the hot stove exhalations, and I was a part of the flow, a component of the effusion.

Another contraction came, and this time, it was different. The intensity was my personal creation, my inner romance, a cleansing storm on a private sea, pain and pleasure bound. I was instantly and mysteriously inside Seasons as much as he was inside me. I felt his urges keenly, and it was the great trans-world passage. This was him being flung from our vessel into the waiting arms of a nurturing shore.

I understood that there must have been Jivarrão in what I drank, but it was too late to do anything but puke it up, and when that was over, there were trails of light when I jerked my head, lines of color above ordinary vision. The bag of iridescent flakes on the oaken table throbbed and seemed to change back in a rainforest bullfrog. I sat on the edge of the bed and looked around. The cottage was my womb and the walls contracted in tandem with me. The eaves quaked with something celestial. The flake bag undulated. My painting of August Lake looked angular and abstract, like something by Chagall, but I could see an overlay of cryptic glyphs that I must have painted there as a welcome from my subconscious. Somehow, in the moment, I found that deeply satisfying, and the next contraction was another whitecapped wave that hove me closer to my Seasons.

I lay back in the bed, onto the gigantic fur that Julian had spread above my fluid leak. The ceiling pinwheeled. I didn't fall asleep so much as arose to sleep, like a vehicle wafted upward. Shortly, I awoke to another full-body crunch and I bore it well, legs spread, crooked at the knee, shrieking in ecstasy. I slept again, only with my circuitry rewired—my dreams were not my own, but Seasons' dreams, swaddled in an organic glow of elemental wisdom and security, filled with energies without limit. I was with him in his formless void—as it was in the beginning, and was now, in every rational sense, his beginning.

I had some sense of passing time, protracted through many more contractions, and I felt that I might ultimately have to deliver my son myself, right here on the bear fur in the cottage in the dell. And I was up for it. Seasons and I might live this epic together, traveling as companions, just him and I without a physical need for Julian, or the epidural nurse, or Dr. Sz-Min.

Or Eloá. But there she was on one of my surface journeys, scrunched between my legs, one hand on my vulva and the other massaging warm scented oil into my belly. Her palm was flat and firm; her fingers were spread and silky soft. She made clockwise circles towards the right side my stomach as I quivered in the muffled colors of drifting candlelight. My head swelled and my eyes blurred—I swam through harmony and perfection and, I believed, hallucination. I didn't think she was real. I thought she was an extension of some dream wisp, the immaculate symbol, a primordial goddess sent to urge me safely through the perpetual adventure of re-creation.

Whatever she was, ghost or Gaia, she was tender and she was tenacious. She eased me into new positions; at first laterally, on my side, a posture I held until it became too uncomfortable. She helped me to my knees and it was better with my ass pushed forward and my torso crushing a wad of animal fur. She reached between my legs and palpated my belly, feeling the contours of my uterus, finding the being within the being.

"The baby's head is down," she said. "He's descending. He's early, but he's fine."

At last I asked, "Where did you come from?"

"The park building."

 "Where's Julian? "

"Back there, trying to get the truck started. It's a cataclysm, this storm. I came on the snow sled."

"Can't he call for paramedics?"

"The power is out. Now, hush. Breathe and don't push, not yet."

"I have to get to the hospital," I said, groaning.

"It's too late, the baby is coming now. Push when I tell you. Short breaths; it's almost done."

My limbs were numb and I contracted again. I vaulted over a crest, and then tumbled down a valley. Eloá's splayed hand rotated on my gut, across my pelvis and down my lower back where she extinguished flaring fires. She mopped moisture from my face. She lightly raked my arms with her fingernails and soothed me. I roared. I brayed like a mule. I whinnied like old swaybacked Dobbin had when he saw me with a bag of Great Scot apples. The surf pulled back and I relaxed and fell briefly out of it, drifting beneath percolating inks. I believed that this ferocious tribal midwife, genuine or illusion, had now joined with my life force; she had become part of me, a part of Seasons. She was radiating inside me, inside us and we were spreading out inside her.

"Don't sleep now," she urged in a guttering whisper. "Carry through to the finish. Be *Hiaaga* no more. Be Dixie again. Be here now. We're nearly there. Afterward, you can sleep, and when Julio comes, he'll see to you both."

That was good; that was fine. I heaved forward, the intensity redoubled, but she was kissing me, bracing me, working me, and I sailed into it, fronting it and bursting through it. The anvil crunch subsided, and during that those final contractions, I submitted. I saw no other option, and it was just as well since I had no longer wished for another option. Somehow, it had all become a mosaic of bliss. Eloá was here with me, not that steel-cold Chinese bitch. Real or fantasy, I gave myself to her willingly:

"Eloá? It's the tea, I know. But it isn't, is it? It's more— it's you. You're remarkable. Can I say that? You're part of me right now. Part of us. You are entirely in the moment. Is this what a Luanhão midwife does? Even one who's never been pregnant...?"

She paced her voice to my panting. "Silly *Hiaaga*. Of course I've been pregnant. Many times—as a child, I was fantastically fertile; incomprehensibly so. You know my occupation in *Taiambé;* it was a hazard. My mother took care of the pregnancies—*borũca* root; and when I was fourteen, enough was enough. My father was a surgeon. He sterilized me."

This, I couldn't absorb. Not just now—there was no time. My womb began to launch its final spasms—the grand finale—even as thickets of revulsion sprang up in me. My vision reeled and the tenor changed. The cottage contracted until I felt so claustrophobic I thought my brains would burst from my head. I needed to be pushed out, ejected from the image of a father sterilizing his daughter, but there were imperatives more massive than the horror at the core of Eloá's revelation. Had I known her story, I would have never said a word, obviously. But it was irrelevant; I hadn't known it, I hadn't asked, and now Seasons' moment came with all its heady portent. I exhaled in short, gasping punctuations, pushing as I would have the cottage push.

The wind outside was an ethereal drone. I was on all fours, and Eloá murmured reassurance until Seasons exploded from me in a bloody backfire, a squalling tussock of puckered pink flesh—my flesh, his flesh, Julian's flesh. Eloá was a smudge above me. She placed the baby on my naked chest and slipped frozen flakes between my lips—chips of ice, a common thing to feed an exhausted woman who has just given birth I thought; they were as bitter and fresh as the arctic world outside the window.

My tiny cherub was alive and he was healthy. My breasts were swollen for him. I couldn't stop smiling. I hugged him to me and I gurgled at his sleepy perfection, and in those brief moments, I forgot about Eloá and Julian entirely. Any mother would. And mustn't she be forgiven that? The storm wheeled and screamed and a dripping sound came from outside. In the flickering candlelight, as I lay still with my Seasons on the hand-hewn bed, it seemed to drip into my veins and fill me with a slow, paralyzing hush, a comprehensive pall. It devoured me and funneled me into a soundless abyss, and I dropped into emptiness as complete as anything I had ever known, as acute as the missing burr of my father's voice and as deep as the frozen lake on the distant end of the park.

It was the ice chips, probably. Something had been frozen inside them. Some opiate, maybe frog flakes. I never learned for certain. As my consciousness was spirited away, so was my Seasons. I woke up twice. The first time, it was to a remarkable, arresting vision, a Biblical icon: Eloá as the Madonna in the manger, an eternal mother sitting in a sea of warm wool, hair as a lush, nut-brown cascade, her left breast suckling Seasons who twitched and drew from her in kinetic contentment. And I wanted to cry out—I wanted to thank her and venerate her and call her *Madrinha*. The God-mother. Imagine that.

But into this scene stepped Julian, and as I watched—helpless, immobile, drooling onto my own barren, freckled chest—he draped his arm around his sister and regarded her with an expression of such essence, such omniscient love that I could not find my voice. But he could: He sang softly to her—*Veiled Creation*—and I realized that all vestiges of melancholy had been extinguished from his mint-colored eyes.

When I awoke the second time, it was midday and I was alone.

45.

I knew it was midday. In fact, the time was precisely 2:20 PM. I knew it to the minute because my cellphone sat on Julian's hand-hewn oaken table, working again and blinking blankly. I found it when I dragged myself from beneath the Kodiak fur that now engulfed the bed. Somehow, I'd been washed and combed and dressed again in clean nightclothes, the same maternity nightshirt and flannel robe I'd been wearing in Cadence the morning that Eloá showed up in the television room of Scioto Street. In the cottage, the candles had dwindled to nubs, the stove had been stoked and the room was a dry vacuum.

I was still drowsy, leaky in my private places and infinitely sore, but there was blood roaring in my ears and I scrambled about, finding no baby, no note, no carving and no poem, but only the fuzzy faux-shearling slippers that Mom had given me for Christmas. Outside, the light looked sterile; a dull burnish filtered from a sky like pale chalk. My mouth contorted and air burst from my lungs. I screamed a trio of names again and again, then I screamed nothing at nothingness, and then I called 911.

When Star Ambulance arrived with sirens shrieking and two deputies from the Fuller County Sheriff's Department close behind, I was in front of the cottage, on all fours crawling, looking for tracks in the snow.

I'd gargled out a hysterical story to the dispatcher, and as the pair of deputies prodded me with laser questions, I tried to get out a more cohesive version. They had problems with every detail, and naturally so: The situation sounded no less preposterous to me and I was living it. Describing what I remembered was hard enough; explaining it was impossible.

A big, bald brown-shirted deputy called Kilkoyne took the lead, and behind his skepticism and professional monotone was a scintilla of honest horror: "You say there were two other people here? The baby's father and his sister, who was your midwife? If a baby was kidnapped—and so you understand the law, it's not actually legally possible for a father to kidnap his own child unless there's a court order—but, let's say that's what happened. Is it possible that the brother and sister were not the ones who did it? That they were also abducted?"

Someone else involved? I had no rational response beyond my overwhelming, fundamental doubts. It was beginning to dawn on me what had really happened—and what had been happening over these many months under my nose—but I had nothing concrete to back it up. I had only hazy memories of the night before, seams of logic and a growing, unfathomably sick suspicion that my labor had been induced by something from Julian's pine chest. Eloá's word shreds: "My mother took care of the pregnancies—*borũca* root." Hadn't Julian put *borũca* in the tea he coerced me into drinking?

Confirmation could come later; for now, I was giddy with fright about the immediate.

The bald man's partner was a lanky veteran with a coarse, puckered mouth and a white-flecked caterpillar mustache. He assured me, "We're treating it as an abduction, of course. State Police are already involved; there's an Amber Alert. We'll have a canine unit here in twenty minutes to canvas the area, as wide a parameter as we need to. We'll bring in helicopters with thermal cameras. The priority is the missing child. If your baby is in these woods, we'll find him. "

"Seasons," I said warily, weepily. "I named him Seasons."

The bald cop squinted at me, and his voice remained as impassive as a tree stump: "I've been on the job eleven years, Ms. Pickett, and I've never seen anything even remotely like this. Some of these questions are tough, I know, but we have to ask them. You said you believe you were drugged—the hospital will run a tox screen, for sure. But is there any possible way that, in that altered state, you got mixed up yourself? You were outside the house when we pulled up. Could you have lost the baby yourself? Left him outside somewhere? There's a lot of emotional trauma associated with a birth."

My eternal Cadence naïveté: Here I was again, back to Go as a suspect in a crime where I was the victim. Spinning madly, the nightmare began to plummet and unravel. No, it wasn't possible, I said. *'From our Forests, For our Seasons'*. My Seasons. Julian and Eloá took my baby because they couldn't have children of their own.

"I thought you said they were brother and sister," Kilkoyne frowned.

Overhead, the staccato lights of the ambulance squinched. I was hustled onto a gurney and briefly, the detectives deferred. A tiny, efficient female paramedic introduced herself as a life support specialist, had me sign a release, asked about my medical history, then did a superficial examination. Afterward, I heard her low murmurs: "Cervix parous, colostrum; recent birth is totally indicated, how long ago, the hospital can say better than me. Within 24 hours, certainly."

An investigation unit arrived along with a truck filled with dogs. There was a bevy of barks and a hive of swarming voices pushing at my skull; an orchestration of proficiency and suspicion. A freckly youth with a cowlick and Gold's Gym biceps tied a blue ribbon around my own translucent arm and started a slow intravenous drip while the mustached deputy relayed information about Julian Vaz back to their lieutenant at the station: *Possible suspect. Be on the lookout.* Last known addresses? Julian lived here, in the stone cottage, I said. I couldn't remember the address of the mother where Eloá lived, but I might be able to find it on Google Earth. We'd get to that, he promised. Preservation of life came first. No, I had no pictures of Julian other than the ones I had in my head, unpainted.

The caterpillar-faced detective rode with me in the EMS truck to St. Luke, continuing to question me as we swung through the park and onto the interstate . "Is there anybody you'd like me to reach out to at this point, Ms. Pickett? Family?"

I thought of the three people I'd like to reach out to: Seasons first, then Julian and Eloá. The authentic triune soothed by sun and moon. Beyond that, I knew who I had to contact, obviously, and though I dreaded it, my guilt and embarrassment was tempered by my grief. I almost had him call Ivolya Ryvak—that was a gallon of wisdom and strength I wanted to mainline, frankly—but with the sirens blaring, in the midst of my thickening despair, he got me through to my mother.

46.

The following two days at St. Luke were a distillate of the two weeks of horror I'd spent at Building 500. All the deranged personal implosions were there lacing through heavy hours of helplessness and the shit-dipped dread that the next instant might bring life-altering news, and equally, that it wouldn't. Worse, they had me in the postnatal section of the Birthing Center where I had to listen to newborns crying and new mothers purring, a punishment more cruel and inhumane than administrative segregation or waterboarding.

Dr. Sz-Min provided my initial examination and it felt like she was frisking my uterus, patting me down, searching for contraband, like my baby might still be in there somewhere. Her questions were so cold-blooded that I finally had to ask her if she'd heard what had happened to me, even though she must have. The expression she threw back was one of supercilious bafflement, as though she'd known all along that nothing was going to end well for this pregnancy and I had no excuse for not knowing it myself. It was all I could do to avoid slapping her across the jaw.

My mother and Paw-Pop showed up an hour later and at least got me into a private room at the far end of the ward. Like everyone, they were haunted by the details they knew and more by the ones they were imagining, and they pestered the sheriff's department until they were convinced that all due diligence was being done. It was breaking news, and shortly, there were many requests for interviews, and my mother thought I should do one of those weepy pleas for information from my hospital bed. The truth was, suspicious cops were bad enough and the last thing I wanted just then was public scrutiny. I lay in a sinkhole of my own creation, and began to flesh out an elaborate, insane fairy tale with an ending to-be-determined—a song cycle about my Seasons, a surrogate mother and a genuine father vanishing into a misty forest so remote that even the serpent on the Tree of Life couldn't find it.

I didn't want to go on television, and to his infinite credit, Paw-Pop sided with me. In doing so, he found his role within the hellscape: He ran interference for me in media inquiries. My mother held me with one hand while wringing the other, but good old Virginia-Ham-armed Toby Murphy, who I suppose might have been a cop in a life without Purina, braced himself near the hospital entrance and shooed away the press flies.

Throughout that first night, we had regular updates from the sheriff's department, but they were mostly neutral; obligatory, earnest, and without much substance. The area search had turned up nothing. The storm had blanked out a lot of the tracks, but the forensic team found snowmobile tracks between the park headquarters and the stone cottage; since a snowmobile was how Eloá claimed to have gotten there, that part of my story checked out. But beyond my bizarre suspicions, there was no evidence that pointed to an abduction. Besides, my toxicology screening had come up negative, as it naturally would: Whatever had been surging through my veins—*Corondcillo, Gëshpiu, Shirampari, borúca*—was not from Hamilton's Pharmacopeia.

By mid-morning they'd found Mãe's dark house on a palsied peninsula of Bloomfield Hills. According to the detective who called me, it had been in foreclosure for three months and when they got there, there was an eviction notice on the door and the place was empty except for a rack of dung-polluted furs and wandering chickens. A property record search showed the owner as Graciela Rey, now deceased, but the name that appeared on outstanding tax bills dating back years.

As for Julian himself—or, for that matter, Eloá and their mother—there were no hits in any database the detectives could access. No fingerprint records, no rap sheets, no warrants and nothing from Homeland Security or the Department of Motor Vehicles. How could anyone pull this off? Simply vanish? Live, work, drive, run a business, all without leaving a trail? The detective shook his head, then shrugged. He'd heard that courts could disappear public records, and by my description of the family, they were off the information grid from the beginning. It was a nutty system and anything was possible, he said, segueing into a political rant: The United States was on its way out as a world power. We couldn't control our borders and ten million undocumented aliens had the country by the short hairs.

Poor Adam Loya was trying to cooperate through his blear of fumes because he knew his private jig was up. Julian had never been on any official payroll, and I later learned that according to the DNR, Julian's weeklong trip to the northern wilds in May—the one that had first drawn me into his world outside the park—had never happened. Who knew where he'd been in that critical week, or, when I thought back on the specifics, if he'd even been gone at all?

If it had all been a hustle from the beginning, the things that were churning and thrilling within me were not. I had an involuting womb that had produced a tactile being; I'd held him mewling against my breast. Seasons was the fusion of genuine gametes from genuine intimates. I'd cuddled a baby, not a wisp of smoke. I may have been in love with a trope, a phantom concept, but the man himself had been flesh, and the poems he wrote were tangible things, works of art that I had stored in a steel vault on Liberty Street along with a boatload of cash.

Ah, the money. I hadn't breathed a whisper about it to the detectives or the Murphy-Picketts. It was mine, and as far as I was concerned, it had been a gift without strings. I didn't want it taken as evidence, and since I was pretty sure it hadn't come from legitimate sources, seizure went without saying. Once it had been sequestered in some dusty locker in the Fuller County Sheriff's Department, I knew I'd never see it again.

There were plenty of other things I hadn't mentioned either: Tivon Grimes in the Kevorkian cabin, the pedo club in Pontiac or the disappearance of Takosha DeYoung. From the outset, I'd fastened my soul to the most outrageous hope that there somehow existed a satisfactory explanation for what had happened on that stormy night inside the stone cottage, and my cooperation with the police was predicated only on the chance that I'd get my baby back. If Seasons was returned with Julian attached, maybe that was fine. Without a court order, a man can't kidnap his own child—that's what Deputy Kilkoyne had said. I wasn't looking for anybody to be brought down; not Adam Loya, not Potter the prostitute, not Dr. Mackie, not even the lawyer in the powder-blue Lexus. All I wanted was my Seasons snuffling against my tumid chest again, and I filtered the information I was willing to offer to serve that end, not to some esoteric sense of justice.

As for the money, which I would shortly need, I now had means to go get it. Mom and Paw-Pop had driven to Michigan separately. She'd come up in the family Odyssey and he came in my tuned-up, refurbished Focus. Over the month I'd been gone, he'd replaced the ball joints and the steering linkage and even patched up the rust spots with Bondo and sheet metal. For that, my gratitude abides. After two days, when I was discharged from St. Luke, he used his VISA card to install me a Holiday Inn about a mile from the Fuller County Sheriff's mini-station, then returned to his job in Cadence, promising he'd be back up on Friday after work.

Mom stayed with me, of course. She took an adjacent room at the Holiday Inn and we spent many anxious hours awaiting updates from the detective. These became increasingly discouraging as one by one, leads evaporated. For me, perhaps the saddest news came from the sheriff of Baraga County, who said that the thousand acres adjacent to the Vieux Terre Indian Reservation—including the shoreline—was actually owned by Blackwood Resources, a forest management group who had been harvesting the timber there the since the '80s.

Although they wouldn't let on just yet, I could tell that the detectives were losing hope as the case grew inexorably colder, like something on a coroner's slab. They had protocol, and my situation didn't fit any of it and this left them flummoxed. But on Thursday night at around midnight, long after my mother had thrown in the daily towel and gone to bed, everything changed: I got a text from someone named Grace Tobias.

It read, *"Gabriel Tobias is my brother. He's here and he asked me to send you a message. He says to tell you that he has some of the answers you need."*

Below the message was an address in Gonega, the town where Julian said my alabaster angel had been buried.

I was leery, obviously. I'd been the victim of a huge betrayal and an avalanche of bullshit and I sent a single text back saying as much: If Gabriel was actually alive, I asked the sister to provide some evidence.

Ten minutes later another message arrived; it said simply, *'Daffodils and Tom and Jerry.'*

47.

Across the intervening years, I've come to see life's process as a colander suspended above the void. It accepts and filters an endless mudslide of memories, your personal floodplain of occasions and accidents, exploits and endeavors, daily triumphs and nightly forfeits. As you go along, for reasons not entirely explainable, most of what you experience washes through, so that in the end, at the bottom, all that remains is a small collection of hard and precious gems, pebbles that somehow caught in the sieve while a billion other events wash through and are gone.

These nuggets are not always in proportion to their significance, and yet, they're made of gold just the same: The wiry resistance in an old nag's mane, the smell of roasting cashews inside a department store, a paper-thin rabbit shape on an urban side street, the brief, impossibly sweet feel of newborn skin against your own, boiling with life.

I would have left for Gonega immediately, in the middle of the night, but I couldn't disappear on my mother again, so I sat up and binge-watched some old favorite films from the hotel's surprisingly decent playlist. No horror; just the laid-back stuff; *Babette's Feast, The Graduate, Ida.* As soon as it was light, I woke her up and explained that I'd heard from one of Julian's friends who might have some information, and I told her that I had to go alone and she had to stay there to field any calls from the investigators. I told her not to worry; I'd be fine and I'd be back in the afternoon.

I set out in my spiffy good-bad, new-old Focus and took a series of highways north through the frozen spectacle of rural mid-winter. Undulant ropes of clouds ringed the far horizon; above, the sky was clarion clear and below the fields were splayed in dormant deserts of white, as flat as if they'd been ironed. I'd always appreciated the emptiness in this time of year, where nature blots the canvas clean in preparation for rebirth. As I drove, I felt pumped and hopeful, with my spirits as high as they'd been since my baby disappeared.

Gonega was a small town about halfway up the state. I saw at once that it was Cadence transplanted to a point that was almost cellular. Instead of a Purina Dog Chow silo, the dominant skyscraper was an Archer Daniels Midland grain dryer, but beyond that, the municipal aura was cloned, with the same VFW hall, the same gun shop, the same fading storefronts, the same irrelevant intersections, the same frozen ice cream emporium with a sign that read *'See you in the spring!'*

Grace Tobias lived a couple miles on the far side of Gonega's insignificant downtown, down a long dirt road and in a tiny frame house surrounded by swamps and underbrush. It was podunk poverty, no question, but at this time of the year, a lot of it had been swallowed up. Snow covered the woodpile, the corrugated steel storage shed that was collapsing into itself, the rusting backhoe out back and the several old cars on blocks in front. The miniscule porch had been shoveled. It was a wooden deck ringed with pine boards with cut-out heart-shapes. Alongside it, from a shepherd's hook planter, a basket of plastic flowers dangled.

Grace Tobias met me at the door along with two children in diapers. They looked to be about three or four years old. She was tall like Gabriel, sharp-boned and statuesque. She was as shy and taciturn as he was, too—that was plain as she shook my hand stiffly without a word. But suddenly, her pale eyes became the color of a blue gas flame and she said, "I'm sorry about your loss, ma'am. God's truth. But my brother has been through a lot. We only just recently mended things and we're family again. Please don't get him into trouble over this."

The walls of the house were bare. The furniture was second-hand and nearing the end of that reincarnation, but everything was clean and tidy and there was laundry folded on the coffee table. Grace extended a mayfly arm to usher me in while the pretty children beneath her whimpered softly and hid behind spindly, jean-clad legs.

Gabriel was in a room at the end of a short hallway, supine on a cheap platform bed . I saw at once that this had been a child's room, and like mine on Scioto Street, was mostly held in suspended animation. There were splashy, kiddie graphics on the wall—a Marines propaganda poster featuring a beefcake dude with face camouflage holding a black, savage-looking weapon was the only adult accoutrement. One shelf held toys from fast food kid's meals and one was lined with multiple trophies from high school sports, and on the desk, beside a computer, was framed photograph of a young blonde boy in hunting gear holding up the head of a glassy-eyed bear with a bloody nose; a blonde man hunched over him, beaming.

"Your dad?" I asked.

He nodded. "Mark. Never called him dad, always only called him Mark."

"Where is he?" I asked.

"Anchorage, I think." He cranked a thumb at the photograph. "That's was the last time I saw him, that hunt. My first bear—nearly three hundred pounds and a twenty-inch skull, a trophy."

"Your dad looks proud," I said, then cleared my throat. "Julian said you were dead."

"I guess I almost was," Gabriel shrugged. "They're saying partial remission. It's a break from treatment anyway. We'll see."

"Why would Julian have said that about you?"

'Obviously, he wouldn't have wanted you finding me. I know too much about him and the park crew."

"Do you know where my baby is, Gabriel?" I asked quickly, holding my breath.

"Not for sure," he answered. "But I'm sorry—I think he might be gone."

"Gone where?" I said slowly, as tears began an oblique streak across my face.

"To the same place as the black girl is, the one who came to the park with you."

"Oh, God," I gasped, letting the air out in a hiss and falling back on the swivel chair in front of his computer desk.

"Well, I'm not totally sure," he repeated. "But I want to show you something. I have to show you; it's the right thing, regardless of what Julian did for me. Decide for yourself and you can take it to the cops if you want to. I'll deny where it came from, but you can have it anyway."

My pulse was drumming insanely and my mouth was paper-dry: "What is it?"

"It's surveillance video from the park. We had a camera at the beach. Julian knew he was leaving and he told Potter to take them all down and destroy them. But Potter's Potter, right? He waited. He didn't do it right away, then the storm hit, and when he went to do it afterward, he found this..."

Gabriel had shifted his thin frame to the edge of the kid's bed and now he reached a long arm out and hit the mouse on the computer. I watched as the screen reassembled into a monochrome image of August Lake. From the visible vantage you could see a bit of the snow-covered shoreline in the foreground and I guessed that the camera must have been wedged somewhere in the crevices of the concrete building where people changed and showered and shat. The time signature said 7:47 and the date was the same as the morning I'd given birth. At that point, the storm was petering out, but bare winds blew eddies of snow across the frozen lake, lying beneath in septic tension.

"I paused it here," Gabriel said softly. "Right before. Watch."

I watched. Shortly, a hooded individual entered the frame and walked across the ice toward the center of the lake. From the distance, it looked like a monk or a revenant, but he was lithe and he moved with kinesics that I recognized. "That's Julian," I said, immediately.

"Oh, it is," Gabriel answered, nodding. "No question. Look."

The figure stopped near the center of the lake, partially obscured by blowing snow. His movements became exaggerated. I'd seen these dynamics before, at the dam, when Julian's hard shoulders and coiling back worked an axe against an oak trunk.

On that morning I'd regarded him with a mixture of prurience and fascination. Now, I recoiled as he began to chop a hole in the ice.

Gabriel said, "This goes on for ten minutes; it's frozen solid this time of year. I can fast forward if you want."

"No," I said. "Please. Leave it on."

It was grisly, but I couldn't look away. At the dam, he'd been tinseled in sunshine, plated with gold, and my silly heart had gone ragdoll, soft as a biscuit in warm milk. Now and for many minutes I watched him through colorless swirls, framed as a silhouette against the snow, and he looked very black.

Finally, he managed to hack open his hole and raised the axe overhead. But not in triumph: As a signal. A moment later, a snowmobile ripped across the frozen water, and on the back, dark hair and feathery white fur streaming, was Eloá.

"My Madrinha," Gabriel answered, shaking his head and gritting his teeth. "At the park, at the club, on the street. She was godmother to all of us, from the moment I met the family up until a couple weeks before you showed up. Something happened."

On the computer screen, I watched as the pair embraced, and the physical language they expressed was palpable from across the lake, across the beach, through the fogs of static, through the glass of the camera lens, infecting the pixels.

My voice was shaking: "I left them, Gabriel. I went back home; I never needed to see either one of them again. I had my future mapped out. It wasn't the best, for fuck's sake, it was better than this."

"I think they had an idea, though." he said, "After you left. About you. And your baby."

"I couldn't know that, Gabriel. Could I?"

He paused the video: "Nope. And I didn't either, I swear. But the pieces fit. I knew Madrinha better than anyone but Julian; she was incredibly close to me when I first got sick. She was convinced she could heal me and frustrated when she couldn't. Their mother was dying and that frustrated her too. At the end, she hated everything about her life here. She wanted to take Julian back to where they'd been as kids and she was tired of waiting for him. But he was fused. He couldn't tear himself away from the park. The crew. Then, you and the pregnancy. I think she threatened to leave without him, and that was something he couldn't face either. The idea to take your baby with them was probably hers, not his. Not that it's consolation anyway."

"Knowing when you've become the chaos? I don't know if it's consolation, but it's lucid."

Gabriel said, "You don't have to watch the next part if you don't want to."

But I wanted to. The video started again, and the pair worked a bundle loose from the back of the snow machine—it was wrapped in something, maybe skins, maybe cloth, maybe woven fabric with embroidered designs snaking across it. It was on the far side of the machine, but what they did was still obvious: They slipped the bundle into the water and stood there together as it sank beneath the surface of the lake.

"Is that the place where the sinkhole is?" I asked in a tone that was nearly reverential.

"Yeah," he answered. "I'm sorry."

On the screen, Julian and Eloá mounted the snowmobile together and Gabriel hit the mouse as soon as they left the frame. A potent silence descended between us. In the far room, I could hear the diaper kids puling.

"It was their mother," I said at last. "That bundle was too big to be my baby."

"I wish that was it. But I don't see it. There must have been weights inside there too. Or other evidence. But I knew Mãe before she got really bad. We all did. She was the dominant one when I first met the family, two or three years gone. In the day, she was a force bigger either of them. The club was hers, and so was the hustle we were working at the park. She was the most terrifying person I've ever met. It's only over the last year that she fell apart. They were afraid of her; really fucking

285

terrified. They believed in ghosts and the crazier she got, the more they believed she commanded them."

He was talking himself into a lather. To him, the idea that they'd put Mãe into the lake was unthinkable. He had his own ghosts to believe in and he almost exploded: "A baby is one thing. I'm not saying it's cool, but... she was their *mother.* Julian would never have agreed to that."

The divine harmony. Right? I wondered if Gabriel knew what they'd done to their father. But I didn't ask him because suddenly, strangely, my queasiness passed like a bout of hiccups and a runnel of calmness trickled through me. It unknotted my guts and tapped dry the tears on my face. All I said was, "But why go through the trouble of delivering my baby and then drowning him in August Lake? Why does that explanation make any more sense?"

"It doesn't. So it's possible the baby died? I'm sorry, Dixie, but to me, that's what's most likely. Wasn't it premature? Madrinha wasn't the healer she thought she was—I know that first hand. But I knew the family. I think wherever they went, Mãe went too. But you're right: I don't have any answers, only the video."

He sounded sincerely mystified, and suddenly, I didn't want to push him about Seasons any more. There was to nowhere to push him to anyway; he'd seen the same thing I saw, and he had come to a conclusion that worked for him.

And so would I.

He ejected the memory card and left it in front of me on the desk, saying, "Potter brought it to me and wanted me to give it to you. And that's what I'm doing, so now it's yours; you can do what you want with it. It's all crazy, I know. I'd have to deny where you got it from—Potter and me have been through a lot together. But, I'm going to tell you something: I was gonna go into underwater tactics with the Marines, be a combat diver, and I've been reading up. There's gear that can search lake bottoms, high-frequency GPR, side-scan sonar, all sorts of things. They can find out what went in the water. But you'd have to do it now, because by spring, there won't be anything left."

I nodded. In fact, there wasn't much left right now; not for me, not inside this room. I had a couple more questions and before I got up, I asked, "Why did you say that my baby and Takosha are in the same place? Is Takosha in the sinkhole at the bottom of the lake?"

"Well. Yeah. You must have worked out what the crew in the park was up do, right? Not park work, that's for sure."

I had worked it out, after having fought against it. But I still wanted it spelled out, so I put on a blank face and played art school credulous and Cadence naïve.

He said, "Johns would come to the park because it was secluded and empty and nobody ever patrolled. It was perfect for them; safer than a rest stop or some random alley in Pontiac. Your friend Takosha worked out the game immediately because she recognized everybody, even Julian. I told you, every hustler in Pontiac knows every other hustler. Potter couldn't just let her leave. It wasn't worth the risk."

I deflated and nodded stoically, but I was angry. "I asked you in the hospital, Gabriel. You told me you dropped Takosha off at her sister's house."

"I lied. I lied because Potter and me have been through a world of hell together, since we were thirteen, fourteen on the streets. I'm sorry about that now. Sorry about a few things, actually."

"Did Julian know what happened Takosha? That day?"

"Of course. It was survival shit, Dixie. Something that needed to be done. She was dangerous, a predator at the edge of our camp."

Like a jaguar or a caiman? At last, it made abominable sense. I had a final question: "Serafin?"

He shook his head and his voice cracked. "That wasn't us. No way. I loved that kid. That was between him and Kevin Winters, the dude who bought the club. I never learned what happened; I was in the hospital, and by then, I'd pretty much stopped giving a shit about anybody but me. And maybe Grace. She had it rough as a kid too, but she took the high road. She's only beginning to forgive half of what I did, but she's willing to work on the rest."

"Well," I said, slipping the disc into a pocket in my purse and rising up out of the swivel chair. "That's what family does when it isn't killing each other off."

I said my goodbyes and my thank yous and retraced my path slowly through the wintery landscape. I realized that something inside myself had been dislodged in that frame house in Gonega, and that I'd left a big dollop of Dixie behind. It was toxic stuff, stuff I was needed be rid of before it metastasized. I hoped that Gabriel would recognize it for what it was: Survival shit. What I'd cast overboard was nothing for him to take inside himself.

I drove in the hum of introspection, and by the time I got to my Holiday Inn exit, I'd pretty much decided what I was going to do with the video. Or, to the point, what I wasn't going to do with it. My rationale has grown sharper through the intervening years, but on that day, on that trip, all I knew is that the decision left me with an eerie, unbridled sense of elation. Nearly ecstasy. Uncertainty is inoperable, and it occurred to me along the way that maybe I had an opportunity—perhaps my only one—to trade a life of festering worry for a single wound that that, however catastrophic, could heal.

I'd also resolved not to take my exit. Instead, I drove two more hours to Cadence, where I found the spare house key behind the neck of the wrought iron eagle over the porch, let myself inside and removed a trio of items from my bedroom. I took my painting of Gabriel, my old gym bag and my key to the safety deposit box in Huntington Bank on Liberty; there, I removed my wads of ill-gotten, hard-won cash and replaced it with the memory card from the park. Maybe I'd turn it over in the spring, when there was nothing left to find. Maybe I wouldn't. I left Julian's poems where they were.

For the present, I used the time to mourn. On the way down, once free of Toledo's sprawl, I pulled over and howled for Seasons until I thought I'd rupture something; I loosed a tidal wave so loud that I had to roll down the window to let it escape and disappear into the floury, ice-clad day. And heading back, after business was seen to in my hometown, I mourned for everything I was leaving behind again, and this time permanently: My armoire, my backyard buckeye, my reading spot by the Great

Miami River, my Daddy's shimmering obelisk in Pleasant Hill Cemetery. I had made these things forfeit the first time I left, and this time—the last time—I confirmed it.

I wrung myself out until I was dry. Now I was heading north to my son's memorial; a focal point for all this grief, my new epicenter, and in order to incorporate it into the place where I needed it most—within the hollow of womanhood that Seasons had once filled—I had to believe that he was not living in perpetual danger in an unknown forest with a man and woman who had adapted me to their end, but sleeping in silence beneath *huitillo* waters.

48.

By the time I got back to the Holiday Inn, the sky had turned pale shades of strawberry, like sherbet melting into the horizon. Earlier, I'd called my mother, telling her I needed these hours to reflect, and she assured me that the detectives had no new information to report. I told her that Julian's friend hadn't offered anything of substance either, but that he had turned over a sum of cash that he'd owed to Julian and in light of the circumstances, now figured should be mine. I didn't mention my trip to Cadence, and I certainly didn't mention the SanDisc that held the last bit of information I needed from anyone.

Paw-Pop showed up at around seven, and we had dinner at a grill chain across the street. Over Philly Burgers and limeade, I told them that I'd reached the end of my tolerance for Holiday Inn mattresses and stomach cramps every time the phone rang. I told them that I refused to become the chaos. I explained to them that on Monday morning I was going to find a permanent settlement in the area where I could remain in touch with the cops but begin to move forward into some semblance of productivity, and I assured them that whereas I loved them both, I really, really needed them to go back to Cadence and be themselves again.

In the twelve years that have gone by since that bleak, cathartic January afternoon, I have never been back to Cadence to see them, not even once. On some abstract level they understand my reasons for that, and they've been up to see me more times than I can count.

The following week I leased a beautiful townhouse in Royal Oak, and right after I bubble-wrapped the portrait of Gabriel and sent it to him and his sister in Gonega along with five thousand dollars in cash, I contacted Ivolya Ryvak.

She was delighted to hear from me under any circumstances. Apparently, the Giantess had figured out that she was entitled to disability benefits and decided she preferred a life of daytime television to answering phones, so remarkably, I was able to take my seat again behind the long reception desk behind the bowling trophies and Plexiglas, and that was exactly what I needed.

Over the following weeks, all leads regarding Julian Vaz and whoever might be with him withered on the vine and the detectives began to lose any semblance of professional interest. I don't think they entirely believed my story anyway. In that period of time, Ivolya became my strength and my salvation; she became my *Chrosnaja*—Belarusian for Godmother—and remains so to this day.

Also, she's now my sister-in-law.

Not long after I returned to work at Molnar, she introduced me to a wry, presentably handsome electrical engineer with long nose, a ready laugh and a persistent five o'clock shadow; her brother Maxim. After a length of time that seemed appropriate to Slavic sensibilities, he asked me out, and we went on several dates that, one by one, grew less tentative. He proposed in December, and as a wedding gift, Ivolya offered him a partnership in the business. By default, Molnar has become my own business, and it has thrived remarkably.

As the years slipped by, I painted more and more, and I have occasional exhibits in galleries around town. Recently, in front of a full length mirror, I did the aged-forty physical inventory that I'd sniffed at contemptuously at twenty-eight and back then, dreaded through my snickers. And guess what? I fucking liked what I saw.

I can say without equivocation and without artifice that I love Maxim Ryvak dearly and desperately. He has coddled me and respected my voids and although there haven't been children, that suits both of us in some airy, sweet, and possibly selfish space. But I'd once been adapted to an end, and now, I felt entitled to use the experience for my own end: Peace, in some measure, for the rest of my days.

I keep my memories about Julian to myself, not because I am afraid of them, but because they have no business intruding on the places where I now exist. I think of Julian as an intriguing canvas that a frustrated artist simply couldn't figure out how to finish. I never did his portrait after all, because if I had, I knew I wouldn't have preserved the effort; I'd have thrown turpentine all over it simply to watch the colors bleed.

That's our lives and our myriad trials and triumphs, and ultimately, we have nothing else.

I have become serene about it. It's the only way. I'd floated on a sea of Julian, admiring the panorama of sea and sky, bobbing on a surface where it was always calm and spectacular, oblivious to a sinkhole beneath that grew deeper all the time. Julian had once told me I could see the incorporeal and, like a ghost than haunts places it has been in life and tries eternally to right wrongs and is eternally unable to do so, how much better off we are in learning to incorporate those wrongs with grace.

Maxim has heard this story, as he has heard all my stories, and since he knows how they define me, he gives me wide and gentle berth. He doesn't object when on hot days in the summer I take solitary trips to the park and wade in the shallows of August Lake to feel the clammy water lap my legs, to feel the mud between my toes, to revere it and to revel in what it is made of.

He knows that my final wish is not to be interred in Pleasant Hill Cemetery but to have my ashes scattered here, to have them filter down to become part of the silt and the sludge and sanctity, to be reunited with my son at the bottom of August Lake, where all the tones are natural and all the laws are real.

Made in the USA
Middletown, DE
11 September 2019